ZAN

Big Booty

Dear Reader:

All that I can say is that Cairo is definitely "The Man." He has outdone himself with this novel, *Big Booty*, and he is the only person who could ever outdo him. He is in a league of his own so he has no competition. Big Booty is something else. One of the most interesting, diabolical characters that I have personally ever read. Trust me, that is saying something. I was on the edge of my seat the entire time, wondering what she could possibly get into next...or who would get into her.

Now Big Booty is not the type of woman that most women would ever aspire to be with—she has a personal football team full of kids by a gaggle of trifling men—but there is something very empowered about her. Some people drown in their fate and others embrace it and learn to deal with it. That is what she does. She realizes that she has made some mistakes, that she has her flaws, but she is determined to live her life instead of sinking into depression over her self-inflicted circumstances.

I do not want to give away the book, but it is nothing short of amazing and I guarantee that you will be thinking about this book long after the last page has been turned. Cairo is something else and he has a long, marvelous future ahead of him. The sky is truly the limit when it comes to his talent.

As always, thanks for supporting Cairo and the authors that I publish under Strebor Books. We appreciate the love and we strive to bring you the best, most prolific authors who write outside of the traditional publishing box. You can contact me directly at zane@eroticanoir.com and find me on Twitter @ planetzane and on Facebook at www.facebook.comAuthorZane.

Blessings,

Zane

Publisher
Strebor Books International
www.simonandschuster.com

Also by Cairo

Retribution

Slippery When Wet

Man Swappers

Kitty-Kitty, Bang-Bang

Deep Throat Diva

Daddy Long Stroke

The Man Handler

The Kat Trap

ZANE PRESENTS

Big Booty

A NOVEL BY

CAIRO

SBI
STREBOR BOOKS
NEW YORK LONDON TORONTO SYDNEY

SBI
Strebor Books
P.O. Box 6505
Largo, MD 20792
http://www.streborbooks.com

This book is a work of fiction. Names, characters, places and incidents are products of the author's imagination or are used fictitiously. Any resemblance to actual events or locales or persons, living or dead, is entirely coincidental.

ISBN 978-1-59309-434-8
ISBN 978-1-4516-7842-0 (e-book)
LCCN 2012951352

First Strebor Books trade paperback edition March 2013

Cover design: www.mariondesigns.com
Cover photograph: © Keith Saunders/Keith Saunders Photos

10 9 8 7 6 5 4 3 2 1

Manufactured in the United States of America

THIS BOOK IS DEDICATED TO
all the *Big Booty* lovers who rode it out with me
from beginning to the hot, juicy end.
Let's make it bounce. Make it clap.
Make it pop-pop, goddammit!

Acknowledgements

Aiight, I'ma keep it quick 'n' sticky this time. Seven books in and I'm still bringin' the heat!

To the sexually liberated and open-minded: Thanks for continuin' to wave ya freak flags, ridin' this hot, *nassy* wave with me, and gettin' down with the juice. Let's keep it wet, keep it sticky, and always keep it ready! The Cairo Movement is here to stay!

To all the Facebook beauties 'n' cuties and cool bruhs who make this journey mad fun: Real rap. Y'all my mutha-effen peeps! Thanks for vibin' with ya boy! Mad luv, much respect, for real for real.

To my peeps, the ATL/Augusta freak master himself, Shamar: Yo, playboy, keep slingin' the wood, bringin' the honeys to their knees 'n' beatin' that thing up, my dude! You already know what it is!

A special shout-out to Johnathan Royal and his alter-ego Jayce: Yo real talk, you one of the coolest, realest, funniest dudes I've met in a minute. Keep bein' you, bruh. Thanks for always pumpin' ya boy's joints up on ya FB wall, for the reviews, and for the mad luv!

To Allison Hobbs: Whew, sexy ma-ma… You already

know what it is with you and me! You're my partner in crime, my peeps, my damn heart! Real talk, thanks for bein' so special!

To Zane, Charmaine, Yona and the rest of the Strebor/Simon & Schuster team: I hope you all know how much ya boy appreciates the never-ending luv!

To the members of *Cairo's World:* Y'all already know how it goes down. Let's keep it on the low. 'Cause what's said on the other side, stays on the other side. ☺ I know I've been neglectin' y'all like crazy. But I promise I'ma make it up to y'all soon, real talk!

And, to the naysayers: It's because of you that I keep it raw, hot 'n' oh-so *nassy!* Keep juicin' the haterade, my peeps. It keeps me horny and keeps me strokin' out that hotness! Lick them fingers or keep it movin'. Either way, I ain't goin' anywhere!

One luv—
Cairo

One

Shit. Everyone knows I like *most* of my men tatted up and on parole. Love my dicks thick, dark, and in Magnums. Love my pussy beat down to the seams. And this fat, juicy ass eaten with a buncha whipped cream and a whole lotta spit. Yes, lawd! The mofo better know how to heat this hole up right if he expects to get a taste of all this dark chocolate goodness. Flick, lick, tease the rim, and you'll be guaranteed a night of some hot, freaky sex. Big Booty, baby…mmph, thought you knew!

Ain't no shame in my game, sugah-boo. Bend me over, finger it, eat it, toy it, fuck it…do whatever you want with it as long as it's filled. Yes, baby, this ass's so good. It'll have a niggah nuttin' up in less than ten minutes; in less than five if I start talkin' all nasty 'n shit to 'im. Please, most of these lame niggahs can't hang with all this golden-brown goody-goody. Once I bounce this juiciness all up on 'em, they get all strung out on it, then wanna fall in love 'n shit.

Knees on the edge of a bed, back arched, ass high up

in the air, I'm a horny bitch always eager to feed a niggah this booty, lettin' him spread open my cheeks, then lean in and bury his face in. His thick nose breathin' in the heat and steam from both my ass and pussy—both, hot and horny for a good fuckin'. Yes, baby! Do me right, goddammit! Give me a niggah who kisses my sweet hole, runs his tongue over and around it, then along the seam of my crack as he squeezes a chunk of asscheeks in his big hands and gobbles up this booty; his tongue lappin' my tight, hot spot, slowly wedgin' its way in. Oooh, my pussy's gettin' wet just thinkin' about it.

Yes, Lawd! I live for wigglin' my ass up on a dick. And I love poppin' a niggah upside the head with each booty cheek as he indulges in sloppily eatin' it out. Big Booty, baby, likes to be ate out right, *okay?*And I have a whole lot of it to gobble up. Always have; always will. And not one of them nastyasses with a buncha stretch marks or crater dips in it either. Oh no, sugah boo, this ass is smooth, sweetness wrapped around twenty-pounds of hot goodness. And any niggah who gets his tongue up in this knows he better eat it up like sweet potato pie, or get his face clapped the fuck up.

And if he wants to run his dick up in it, then he definitely better bring his tongue game correct. And his dick stroke better be legit. Bitch, *what?* Fuck what you heard, baby. Big Booty don't play! I love, love, love it in the ass! Love bein' fucked deep in it. I know, I know... many tricks and hoes and niggahs think ass-fuckin' is dirty. That it's downright nasty. But, baaaaaby, don't get it twisted. Takin' it in the ass is eroticism at its best. Whew, yes Lawd! Some of my best orgasms have been from anal, boo. Mmmph, you better ask somebody. This asshole sucks in a cock like a Hoover vacuum. *Sluuu-uuuurp!* And you best believe. I bring a niggah to his knees and shut him down every time. Big Booty don't play, *okay?!*

Oooh, wait, sugah-boo…just so you know. My birth name is Cassandra Beulah-Ann Simms. But don't tell nobody that shit. Beulah is my old evil-ass grandmother's first name. Ann is the name of the junkie who gave birth to me; my grandmother's daughter. And since the sperm donor's name was Cassidy, she called herself namin' me after his triflin' ass. Then tossin' in everyone else's fuckin' names. Personally, I think the bitch was high when she did that shit. Why the fuck else would you scar your child for life with some goddamn middle name like *Beulah-Ann?*

But whatever! The damage's already done. So movin' right along. Anyway, the bitches and hoes closest to me call me Cassie. But, everyone in the streets knows me as *Big Booty.* A name I was given in sixth grade 'cause I had more ass than all of them lil' young-ass hoes put together. At first the shit bothered me. A buncha lil' niggahs callin' me some goddamn *Big Booty* and always sniffin' 'round me like lil' dogs in heat, always wantin' to feel it and grind up on it. Mmmph! But, baaaaaaaaby, once I learned exactly what this big juicy ass was worth to them lil' horny bastards, I embraced it with pride and started poppin' 'n bouncin' these hips and collectin' their lunch money as payment. Climbin' up on this bootilicious badonkadonk wasn't gonna be no free ride. And it still ain't. Oh, no, baby, *Big Booty* gets paid and stays laced, okay. Hair did, nails did, and everything else did; I'ma real fancy bitch. Shit, I'm thirty-six and got the niggahs thinkin' I'm twenty-six 'cause I'm hot like that. And I've been turnin' heads and stoppin' traffic since I was eleven years old.

See. Unlike these trick-ass hoodrat bitches 'round here, I don't give out free pussy and I ain't gobblin' down dicks for peanuts. Oh sure. When I was young and dizzy and sizzlin' in the drawers, and didn't know any better, a few times I slipped and let a niggah run up in me—sometimes raw, most times wrapped—and didn't collect them dollars, but that wasn't no regular-type shit with me. And it ain't now. A niggah wanna dick me down or want some of this throat work, then you best believe he's diggin' in them pockets, *deep*. Shit, I got kids to feed.

Okay, okay. Hold up, boo. I'm real with my shit. So, yes, even now...every now and then my pussy does the talkin' and thinkin' for me and I gotta jump down on some cock and give out a little sampler-pussy or do some charity-dick suckin' when the need arises. Hell, sometimes givin' out a lil' free pussy goes a long way. You never know when you might have to cash in on a favor and do some things to get somethin' handled, if you know what I mean.

Still, I ain't dumb with it. I stay tryna school these young hoes 'bout fuckin' a niggah up off'a his paper. But, they ain't tryna hear me. Here's my motto: If you can't feed, fuck, and finance me...and I do mean all three...then Big Booty ain't got shit for ya.

Shit, even my homegirl, Dickalina, don't get it. Look, don't even ask. I already know what you thinkin'? What the fuck kinda name is that? Baaaby, puhleeeze. I'm not one of them gossipy-type bitches who runs her mouth and tells everything. But, boo-boo, listen up...her momma, Lina May—God rest her raggedy soul, used to do a buncha dope and spent a lot of time on her knees suckin' a buncha dick. And there you have it! Anyway, Dickalina lives in buildin' three over in my old buildin'. And for years I've been tryna get her ass to upgrade her niggah picks.

But, *noooooooo!* That dumb bitch ridin' the short bus on four flats. She'd rather ho-it out with them bum-ass niggahs who can't even pass a driver's test to get their L's. Like that niggah, Knutz, she's fuckin' with. Mmmph. She's been fuckin' that niggah off and on—although it's more off than on 'cause he can't keep his no-good ass outta jail—for almost four years. And when he is out all he wanna do is fuck, drink, and control her ass. Sorry-ass niggah don't even wanna work. His thievin' ass would rather go out and knock a niggah in the head and snatch his shit, instead of goin' out there and slingin' a few packs to get his paper up. No, he'd rather stomp in a niggah's head and run his shit. What kinda bullshit is that? You don't wanna sell drugs, but you'd rob a niggah. Coon, *boom!* If you ask me, that's one dumb, backward-ass niggah! But, he ain't my headache, so movin' on.

I pick up my ringin' cell. *Mmmph, speaking of the dumb bitch now.* "Hey, sugah-boo," I say, slippin' outta my panties, then bendin' over and pullin' out my butt plug, wishin' it was bein' replaced with fingers, a tongue, then a hard, thick dingaling. My asshole is relaxed and opened, ready, for a good fuckin'. Oh, how I would love a nice, fat dick deep inside it right about now. Had I not answered this phone, I'd be ridin' down on one of my dildos. Oh well…

"Bitch, why you ain't tell me Cleotus' son June-bug was arrested for fuckin' that invalid down at the nursin' home he was workin' at? You know that's some nasty shit, fuckin' that old-ass lady like that. She was like eighty-nine…"

I roll my eyes. "She was ninety-five, Miss Nosey. And I'm not the cock patrol out here monitorin' what the fuck some niggah does with his damn dick. I don't give a damn about him runnin' his dick up in some old, dusty pussy. So I know you're not callin' me with this dumb shit."

She huffs in my ear. "Well, excuse the hell out of me, Miss High Almighty. No need to get all testy. Anyway, all this pussy out here and that freak-nasty niggah had to go and fuck some decrepit bitch. Now his dumb ass is goin' to prison. And he done lost a good damn payin' job behind that shit. That niggah was makin' nine-dollars an hour and he fucks that up for some old, rotted pussy. Mmmph. Niggahs are so fuckin' stupid these days."

And so are bitches like you, thinkin' nine-dollars an hour in Jersey is a good damn job.

"Lina, look, sugah-boo. You're wastin' my time with this shit. I got things to do. Call me later when you have somethin' more interestin' or important to talk about."

"Are *you* serious, bitch? Fuck you, Cass; you a real funny-style bitch. Go do you."

The line goes dead.

Dickalina is a lil' off, but that's still my damn girl.

So, anyway...My guilty pleasures—besides what I've already told you—are designer handbags, stilettos, jewels—and not that costume shit, either, good smoke, dark liquor, and young boys huggin' the block. Yes, you heard what I said. I also love fuckin' the young boys who get that paper. Shit, them get-money niggahs know how to get this pussy cracklin'. And as long as they eighteen and I ain't gotta worry 'bout DYFS comin' up in here tryna lock a bitch up for underage fuckin', then we good. There's nothin' like a super-sized order of some young, hard dick on the side. They can't ever be my men. But they can always pop a cork in this ass and chow down on this pussy.

Shit, fuck what you heard. I don't make no excuses and I don't live with regrets. That young dangalang can handle an all night-long, good fuckin'. I don't need 'em to pay these bills. That's what four of my baby daddies do with them child support checks I collect every month from 'em. Although, now that I'm standin' here thinkin' 'bout it. All seven, I mean eight, of them no-good, big-dicked muthafuckas should be payin' child support. Yes, you heard me correct. I have eight baby daddies. And ten kids. My two oldest sons—Darius, 23, and Jah'Mel, 21—have the same no-count niggah for a fahver. And my eight-year-old twins—Fuquan and Tyquan—have the same fahver as well. Then, of course, my other six kids have different fahvers.

But, uh, be clear. I had my kids when I was real hot in the ass and very young—when I didn't really know any better. And I was poppin'babies outta me back to back, like nobody's damn business. But, trust. I shut shit down and stopped lettin' niggahs knock me up when I was twenty-eight, okay. Shit, after havin' all them kids—and they all got pushed outta this pussy, I know I gotta big juicy coochie. That's why I only fucks when them big-dick-type niggahs. 'Cause any other type of niggah swears they be beatin' somethin' up. They be just a sweatin' 'n choo-chooin' it up. Swish-swishin' all 'round this pussy, like lil'-ass guppies tryna fuck a beached whale, okay. All they fuckin' is a buncha air. Shit, my pussy eats the dick like it's a snack, okay. So a little-dick niggah can't do shit for me, except eat my ass—and, *maybe*, fuck me in it. That's if I'm feelin' generous. And *after* he's dug in his pockets and sponsored me.

My phone rings again. I grin. Speakin' of sponsors, it's one of them now. Mmmph. Gawd may not come when you call Him, but He's always right on time. 'Cause Lawd knows I been down on my knees prayin' for a new handbag and now it looks like my prayer is bein' answered. I'ma fuck the skin off this niggah, and get me that new bag.

"Heeeeeeeey, sexy niggah," I coo into the phone as the muscles in my asshole spasm.

"Yo, wassup. You free?"

"Ooh, you must know I wanna be fucked."

He laughs. "Yo, you stay tryna fuck; that's why I fucks wit' you."

I laugh with him. "Niggah, you fucks with me 'cause I know how to handle that dick right. And you love how it feels stuffed in my ass, with your big-dicked, nasty self."

He keeps laughin'. "Yo, you shot out, for real."

"Whatever, niggah. What you want pussy, ass, throat?"

"You already know what time it is. I want all three."

I grin. "Huh-uh; just what I thought. You got some paper for me? Momma wants a new handbag I done seen."

"What you need?" I tell him two grand. "No, doubt; I got you. But, damn, I'm sayin'...when you gonna let me start hittin' that shit for free?"

"Never, niggah. So scratch that shit from your head." I tell him I'm goin' down to the salon to get my hair done, then can meet him afterwards. He thinks that shit's a waste of time and money since all he's gonna do is sweat it out. I let the niggah know, stayin' sexy and fly is never a waste of my time or money, especially when it's his money I'ma be spendin'.

"Yeah, aiight. Whatever. What time you gonna be done?" I tell him I should be finished by noon. That I need to be done fuckin' him by two, so I can get home to my kids.

"Aiight, cool. All I need is an hour wit' ya sexy-ass, anyway. I've been thinkin' 'bout fuckin you all up in that fat ass for the last few days. On some real shit, yo, I'ma beat that asshole up for you poppin' so much shit all the time."

"Uh-huh, promises, promises. That's what ya mouth says, niggah. Now let's see what the dick does."

Before he can open his cheatin'-ass mouth to say anything else, I disconnect the call. Not tryin' to hear shit else he has to say. Show me, niggah! Anyway, niggahs like him ain't shit any-damn-way. And they're only good for two things: givin' me the dick and givin' me the dollars. Nothin' more, nothin' less!

Two

"Hey, Cassandra," Felecia says, smilin' at me as soon as I walk through the glass door of Nappy No More hair salon to get my hair and nails done up right. I've been comin' to Nappy No More for years and can't a bitch on the East Coast fuck with my girl Pasha when it comes to servin' up the hair, hands, and feet. "Wasssup, girl? Long time no see, boo. You haven't been here in ages. What'chu been up to?"

"Heeeeeey, Miss FeFe," I say, pullin' my Chanels up over my eyes and restin' them on top of my head. "Yes, girl. It's been a while. But I'm here now, sugah-boo. You know how I do it; ready to get this wig did, boo."

Shit, the last time I saw Felecia was at Pasha's weddin' over the summer. And, oh, what a spectacular event it was! A real five-star, red-carpet affair with loads of dollars, dick, diamonds, drinks, and hot drama! Whew! It was everything a girl could ask for. And I served 'em like no other in a white silk dress that wrapped around this body like gauze, leaving nothin' to the imagination. If I have nothin' else, body is it! I gave 'em ass, titties, and a tiny waist! Yes, boo, if you gonna do it, do it right! Steal the goddamn show! Serve 'em heat! And keep 'em all talkin'. Big Booty, baby!

Mmmph. Anyway, I had 'em all doing double-takes and snappin' necks to get a look, okay? But the real show-stopper was the drama that kicked up with her cousins—these three hoes, identical triplets—no less, who share the same dick. Baby, I'm all for sharin' another ho's man. Shit, I do it all the time. But, those hoes took dick sharin' to a whole other level. And one of 'em was real scandalous with it. Pretendin' to be one of her sisters, then fuckin' her sister's secret sidepiece like it wasn't nothin'. From what I heard that night, Miss Messy almost got away with it. But the niggah she was fuckin' behind her other sister's back was in the weddin' party and is related to Jasper, Pasha's husband. Baaaaaaby, do I need to say more? Explosive! Whew! And I saw firsthand, along with Felecia, all the messy fireworks. *Boom!* That bitch was scandalous!

"I know that's right," she says, pullin' out her BlackBerry. She scrolls through it, responds to somethin' and then slips it back inside her front pocket.

I glance around the shop. There are only about eight or nine chicks waitin' and four sittin' under dryers. There are four new stylists here that I am not familiar with. Usually on Thursdays it's practically wall-to-wall hoes tryna get it right for the upcomin' weekend.

"Mmph, it's real quiet up in here this mornin', boo. I see Miss Pasha got some new workers up in here, too."

She flips through the appointment book. "Yeah, girl. She had to. After that shit that popped off with Alicia's man comin' up in here beatin' her ass…"

"Oooh, Miss FeFee. And I'm still pissed I missed that tall, dark-chocolate niggah beatin' her down. I already know watchin' that big, strappin' niggah whoopin' that ho's ass woulda had me all juicy. I woulda had to change my drawz on the spot. And somethin' told me to bring my ass down here that day, too."

She laughs. "Girrrl, you're too much. But, chile, he wore that ass out right up in Pasha's office. That crazy niggah had us all shook. They carried Alicia's ass up outta here on a damn stretcher, and him out in handcuffs."

"Ooh, and I bet that niggah looked sexy as hell bein' dragged out all sweaty and whatnot."

She cracks up. "Girl, I can't with you."

"Uh-huh. I know you can't. That bitch didn't deserve a big, thick niggah like Chauncey any-damn-way. Stupid ho."

"Girl, all over her suckin' some other niggah's dick at some party. A mess. And then that shit with Shuwanda."

"What about that ho?"

"Girl, she was talkin' all kinds of shit about Pasha behind her back."

"What? What was that bitch sayin' about Miss Pasha, girl?"

She looks around the shop, then over toward the door, leanin' in. She lowers her voice, "Well, remember all that crazy shit that was happenin' around here with the front window bein' smashed out, then the day that crazy niggah came up in here callin' Pasha out like that..."

I tilt my head. "Callin' Pasha out like what, boo?" I already know what she's talkin' about, but I wanna hear the two-faced bitch say it. And this ho's supposed to be Pasha's family. Mmmph. This messy bitch makes me sick!

"Girl, you remember when that niggah came in here and said one of his boys told him that she had sucked his dick and he wanted his sucked, too. I think he called it a deep throat special or some crazy shit like that."

"Mmmph. I don't remember all that," I lie, runnin' a hand through my weave.

"Girl, I don't know how not. You were sittin' right there in her chair. Then you said you wanted to hunt him down to find out who he was, remember?"

"Oh, that niggah. Girl, I had forgotten all about that crazy-ass shit."

"Well, I didn't. And, didn't you think it was kinda strange that Pasha didn't even wanna know who the hell he was? I mean, who does that?"

I raise a brow. "Umm, boo-boo, why you care? Maybe she ain't wanna deal with the shit. But, anyway, what did Shuwanda's phony ass have to say about her? You know I can't stand her ass any-damn-way."

"Yeah, I guess. But, still. She didn't even want Jasper to know, which I thought was kinda strange."

"Bitch, it's really not ya business. You do know that,

right? So why is you standin' here tryna be messy? Now tell me what the hell that dirty-bitch Shuwanda said about her?"

"Oh, whatever. I'm not bein' messy. Anyway, girl, that ho was goin' around sayin' she thought the shit about Pasha was true. That Pasha was nothin' but an undercover cum freak. She told one of her clients this, and the girl went back and told someone else who told Pasha about it."

"Mmmph. Miss Pasha shoulda beat that bitch's ass. I'm glad the bitch is gone. I realized she was a hatin'-ass whore the minute I peeped her; broke-ass bitch."

She laughs. "Girl, you a mess. You know Pasha is always a lady with hers. She isn't goin' to be out here fightin' and whatnot."

"Well, that's why she shoulda called me. She knows I love a good damn fight; especially with a bitch I don't like. And Miss Pasha is my damn boo. You fuck with her, you fuck with me, goddammit."

I toss my weave for emphasis. Not that I need one. Bitches stay thinkin' I'm bald-headed, but my real shit hangs to my shoulders, boo. Don't fuckin' get it twisted.

Miss FeFe pushes up from the counter. "I know that's right. Anyway, it's so much calmer up in here now that those two heifers are gone. They kept a bunch of shit stirred up in here. They were a mess."

Mmmph. Like you!

"Yeah. Hot, shitty ones." I glance up at the clock. I've had enough of this bitch. "Where's Miss Pasha?"

"Oh, I almost forgot. I was so busy runnin' my mouth. She told me to let you know she's runnin' about fifteen minutes behind. She should be here shortly."

"Well, then I guess that gives us time to get caught up, huh, boo?"

"And you know it, girl." I ask her how Pasha's baby's doin. "Girl, he's gettin' big. And as cute as ever. He's teethin', which is why she's runnin' late. She was up all night with him."

I shake my head. "I remember those days. Better her than me. If I had to go through that all over again, I'd blow my fuckin' brains out."

She laughs. "And you did it with nine, wait, *ten* kids."

"Ugh, don't remind me."

"So, tell me. What's been goin' on with you? You haven't been here in a few weeks."

"Uh-huh. It's been a minute. You know how it is. All these damn kids I have keep me extra busy. I had to get 'em ready for school. Then Labor Day Weekend I took their bad-asses to Disney World. And them little mother-fuckas turned it out."

"Oh, no!" she says, placin' a hand up over her chest. I can't stand an overdramatic ho. "What did they do?"

"Chile, the question is. What didn't they do? The twins wanted to go to the Haunted Mansion over at Magic Kingdom, then they get up in there and start yellin' and screamin', scarin' all them white folks. Then the next day they started in on Minnie Mouse at the parade..."

"Girl, nooo," she says, soundin' amused. "What did they do to poor Minnie?"

"Baaaaby, they started talkin' shit to Miss Minnie, callin' her all kinda ugly, big-foot bitches." Felecia is hysterical laughin'. "And you know I didn't wanna have to go ghetto-momma on 'em in front of all them white folks, especially down there. But, baby...I had to bring it to their asses. Then Isaiah and Elijah got to fightin' on one of the damn rides over who was goin' to sit where. And when the ride attendant stopped the ride and told them they had to get off, they jumped on his ass."

She's cracking up. "Girl, I can't."

"And Day'Asia's crazy-ass threw some knotty-head girl into the pool, then jumped in and fought her over some little boy they both were eyein'. Both of them—wild, hot pussy—fightin' over some rusty-ass niggah who was gonna forget about their asses the minute he took his tail back to wherever he came from. It was a mess. I swear, I can't take their asses no-goddamn-where without somethin' poppin' off."

She's in tears from laughin' so hard. "Ohmygod, your kids are a mess."

"No, they're fuckin' crazy; that's what they are. I don't know where the hell they got that shit from, but it definitely didn't come from me. And they all have some filthy-ass mouths. It makes no damn sense. Word of advice: don't let a niggah nut up in you unless you've done a thorough background check. And a full damn psychiatric assessment on just how fucked up his family is. 'Cause, baby, if I woulda knew then what I know now about some of my baby daddies, I damn sure wouldn't have had all these damn kids. Plan A woulda been just suckin' and swallowing and fuckin' me in the ass. And Plan B woulda been the Morning After Pill. And I woulda been poppin' them things like breath mints."

She keeps laughin', shakin' her head. "Girl, you're a mess. I can't with you. Not this morning."

"Chile, please. I have ten more years until the twins are eighteen, and I'm counting down. As soon as it hits midnight, I'm tossin' them out. Then I'm packin' up my shit and I'm doing a disappearin' act on all their asses."

"Cassandra, please. You know you're not throwin' your babies out."

"Mmmph, watch me. I've already told 'em. 'The minute you turn eighteen your motherfuckin' asses are outta here.' And I mean that shit."

She laughs. "Girl, I'll believe that when I see it."

"Sweetie, well, believe it. Even a blind ho will see I ain't playin'. Anyway, girl…how them three messy cousins of yours doing?"

She rests her arms up on the counter. "Who, the triplets?"

"Yes, honey, those scandalous divas."

"Girl, from what I hear they're doing well. Paris, the one that was pregnant, had a little boy and she's still with the father, you know, the one Persia was fuckin' behind her back. You remember Persia, the one who got cursed out in the bathroom?"

"Ooooh, yes. Miss Messy Bessy."

She laughs. "Yeah, her. Anyway, so Paris is happy as ever from what I've heard. And Porsha is gettin' married to this...whew, fine-ass chocolate drop the three of them used to fuck, girl."

"What? Girl, shut your mouth. She's marryin' one of the niggahs they all used to fuck?"

She bats her lashes. "Boo, you heard what I said. All I know, it couldn't be me. But, whatever! Different strokes for different folks. You know I ain't one to gossip."

I give her my "bitch, puhleeze" look, smirkin'. Of course it goes right over the gossip whore's head. "And Persia... well, chile, let me tell you. She done snatched herself up some fine, young Caribbean boy-toy—whose parents own a bunch of restaurants. And from what I heard, they've been goin' at it real hot and heavy. She has turned his ass out."

"Allllllriiiiight now. You know how I feel about that young ding-dong, girlfriend. There's nothin' like that Everready, Energizer cock to jumpstart the day and night. Mmmph."

I set my oversize Balenciaga bag up on the counter.

"Oooh, girl, that bag is sharp. I noticed it when you walked through the door. Is it real?"

I see this bitch wants me to punch her in her throat! I raise my brow. "Miss Girl, don't do me, sugah boo. You gonna have me reach around and slice you. You know better."

She laughs. But I don't see shit funny. "You know I'm only messing with you. I know how you do it, girl. All I can say is, for someone who doesn't work, you always stay fly."

"What you mean, I don't work? I work. Shit, I'm still raisin' seven kids. Trust me. That's a job-in-a-half, boo."

"You're definitely right about that. Still, I always wonder how you maintain your lifestyle." She leans in, looks around, then lowers her voice to almost a whisper. "You still doing those credit cards?"

See. Now this bitch's crossin' the line. Let me tell you about Miss Messy, she's a silent hater. Always has been, always will be. But the bitch covers it up with fake smiles and sugary compliments, then tries to slip in some kind of slick remark like I don't peep the shit. So do you really think I'd tell this nosey ho if I was or wasn't? No. The only things she and I can ever talk about are shoes, handbags, and dick sizes. Oh, and salon gossip. That's it.

I glance up at the clock. It's 10:54 a.m. My appointment was at ten-thirty. *Pasha should be walkin' in any minute.*

Felecia leans up on the counter. "Ooooh, wait. I knew there was somethin' I wanted to ask you. Chiiiiiiiiiiile, have you been up on Facebook lately?"

I blink. I don't mean no harm here. I like Miss Felecia. I really, really do. But this bitch is too goddamn gossipy and nosey. She loves runnin' those big, dick-suckin' lips of hers. And those kinda bitches you have to watch with both eyes open, at all times. Still, we cool! Bottom line, she knows if I ever catch her wrong, I'll beat her ass right.

"Miss FeFe, I haven't been up on that shit in weeks. Why?"

"Chile, more Alicia and Shuwanda drama. Alicia been fuckin' her man behind her back..."

I frown. "Wait. Not that niggah, Melvin, with them big, ashy-ass lips?"

She nods. "Girl, the one and only."

"Mmmph, these bitches have no standards; just fuck any ole niggah."

"Girl, tell me about it. And they say he has one of them big, long, ashy dicks with all that extra skin hangin' from it."

I twist my face up. "Ugh!"

"Tell me about it. And now the two of them done got into it. It's all up on Facebook. Honeeeey, they slinging mud at each other like it's nobody's business."

"Well," I say, pullin' out my cell as it vibrates, "I've never featured them hoes any way. Both of 'em fuckin' triflin' if you ask me. By the end of next week, them bitches will be right back drinkin' and sluttin' around together."

I glance at the screen, rollin' my eyes. It's a text from Marcellus, one of my thick-dicked baby fahvers. This niggah's Baby Daddy Number Three. And fahver to my seventeen-year-old son, Marquelle. More about this six-foot-five, two-hundred-forty pound niggah some other time. I open the message. IM GONNA P/U QUELL FROM SKOOL 2MORROW

"Mmmph, you're probably right. When I heard they had a threesome I knew it was gonna eventually be a problem. It always is."

I text back. IS HE STAYN DA NITE?

I look up from my phone, shakin' my head. "Them bitches deserve each other."

"Cass, girl, you haven't even heard the best part. Chile, they've been lickin' each other's pussies on the low."

"Nothin' those bitches do surprise me."

She frowns. "Still, that's some nasty shit."

"How you know it's nasty? Have you tried it?"

"Hell, no. I don't get down with that."

I shrug. "Well, Boo, different strokes for different folks. They grown ass women so if that's what they do, then that's what they do. Why you care?"

YEAH. ILL BRING HIM HOME SUN NITE

"Girl, the shit's funny; that's all."

U STAYN DA NITE?

"Wait," she says, keepin' her voice low. "You've tried it?"

YEAH. BUT I AIN'T BEAT 4 NO BULLSHIT CASS. I WANNA FUCK, NOT BEEF WIT YA AZZ

I tilt my head, quickly glancin' up at her, then back down to my phone as I continue typin'.

WHATEVER NIGGAH. I WANT MY PUSSY N ASS ATE 2

"Tried what?"

U SUKN THIS DICK?

"You know, eating pussy?"

I roll my eyes up in my head. IF DA SHIT STAYZ HARD, MAYBE.

This niggah has almost eleven inches of dingaling and the shit don't always stay rock-hard. I mean, it'll be hard, but not brick-solid, like I like it. And I need me a dick harder than a damn diamond to satisfy me. I told his ass the last time we fucked to invest in some of them blue pills, but the niggah said he don't need 'em. I told his ass he was delusional to think he didn't. But whatever! I don't gotta fuck him on the regular, so what I care. As long as his black ass pays his four-hundred dollars a month in child support on time, I'll toss him some occasional pussy. Besides, he'll eat my pussy for most of the night, before he slides his ding-aling in. I let him fuck me from the back and the niggah'll cum in ten minutes. His ass ain't ever been able to handle this pussy heat doggy-style. Pop, pop, pop!

"See, Miss FeFe," I say, droppin' my phone back into my bag as Pasha hurriedly races through the door. She's lookin' fierce as ever. She's let her hair grow out and has it pulled back in a sleek ponytail with her signature bang sweepin' over her left eye. Ears and wrist blingin' with ice, girlfriend looks like she's dipped and paid out the ass. And she should be, considerin' the kinda paper Jasper's dirty-ass is pullin' in. "There ya nosey ass go tryna be all up on mine."

She laughs.

"Girl," Pasha says, shiftin' her oversized Louie from one hand to the other; practically outta breath. "I'm so sorry for having you wait like this. Jaylen had me up all night."

I wave her on. "No worries, Miss Pasha, girl. Miss FeFe has been keepin' me very entertained."

She smiles, shakin' her head. "Oh, I bet she has. And bringing you up-to-date with all the street news while she's at it, I'm sure."

We laugh.

"Oh, whatever," Felecia says, wavin' her on. "I like to stay informed and keep my finger on the pulse of what's goin' on; that's all. Don't hate."

Pasha looks over at me, then back at Felecia, shakin' her head. "Yeah, yeah, yeah. I love you dearly, cuz. But let's face it. You can't keep your nose out of other people's business. You've always been like that. Any calls for me?"

She sucks her teeth. "Oh, whatever. Call it what you want. I'm inquisitive; that's all."

Pasha laughs. "Yeah, code for nosey."

Miss FeFe sucks her teeth. "Anyway, your three o'clock cancelled, but she's in for tomorrow. And Mona called. She said she couldn't reach you on your cell. Call her when you get a moment."

She hands Miss Pasha a stack of mail. Pasha tells me to follow her back to her station.

"Oh, and Cassandra," Felecia calls out to me. "I'll be waitin' when you get done to answer the question, inquirin' minds still wanna know."

I look back at her. "I suck dingaling, boo. I get my pussy ate. And, with the lights out, a wet tongue is a wet tongue, no matter who's eatin' it. Get horny enough and you'll know what I mean."

She cracks up laughin' as several customers glance at me. "Girl, I can't with you; not today."

Bitch, you sure can't. Not today; not ever!

Three

"Girl, what's been goin' on with you?" Pasha asks as she snaps the cape around my neck. "I haven't seen you since the wedding."

"Miss Pasha, ain't shit new, boo. I'm doin' me. Ridin' down on a nice hard dick every chance I get and collectin' them child support checks. And, of course, I'm always in search of new sponsors."

Pasha laughs. "Girl, you and your sponsors. But I ain't mad at you."

"Girlfiend, puhleeze. These trick-ass hoes better get with the program. Ain't no sense in fuckin' for free when you can get paid for it. Although if I was a niggah, I wouldn't pay for shit. I'd have hoes payin' me for a ride on my dick. And hopefully I'd be one of those niggahs blessed with a big, ole long, black, veiny dingdong."

She laughs.

"I'm serious, Pasha, girl. Shit, think I ain't."

"Girl, I already know."

"Mmhmm. If I'm gonna wet a dick, then I need to get paid to wet it. Shit. I have kids to feed."

As I'm lookin' in the mirror, I see some rusty, dusty bitch sittin' in the chair across from me, makin' a face, but I put her on ignore real quick since I'm not sure if she's makin' that ugly face because of what I said or if her stylist's pussy stinks since she has it practically all pressed up on the bitch's neck as she braids her hair. Now, you know, I like to try and keep it classy before I turn on the ghetto switch and hooker-bop a bitch in the mouth, which is why I decide to dismiss it.

But in my mind, I'm thinkin', "Strike one, bitch!"

Pasha cracks up laughin'. "Ain't nothin' wrong with that, girl. Do you."

"Always, Miss Pasha Girl. If I don't do me, who else will? That's what's wrong with a lotta these hoes out here today, they don't know how to do them. They too busy hatin' on the next bitch and stressin' over the dumb shit. And no-count niggahs. My motto is: hump 'em 'n dump 'em. A niggah can't act right, move onto the next. How you think I ended up with eight baby daddies? Besides the fact I love the dingdong."

Rusty Crusty frowns again. *Strike two, bitch!*

Pasha spins me around in the chair again. Now I'm facin' the bitch across from me. She shifts her eyes. I stare her down. "Speaking of your kids, how are they?"

I grunt. "Bad as ever. Hell, the only ones who don't give me any problems are DaQuan and Marquelle. They are both doin' great. DaQuan's still at Howard. And my baby Marquelle is in his last year of high school." She wants to know if Marquelle's still playin' basketball. "Girl, what else is that six-foot-five niggah gonna do, but play ball? I will fuck him up real good if he even thinks about messin' up gettin' me floor seats at all the NBA games. Honeeeey, LeBron James' momma aint' gonna have shit on me, okay. I'ma be runnin' all through them games, doin' it up, boo."

She laughs as she starts cuttin' out my sew-in. "Girl, you're a mess. I heard that. And is he goin' away to college in the fall?"

"He better be if he knows what's good for him. Or get fucked up, okay. I might be many things, but a mother of some bum-ass niggahs ain't one of 'em."

"I know that's right," one of Pasha's newest stylists says, smoothin' a relaxer through her client's hair. I ask her who she is. She says her name is Rhodeshia, then asks, "How many sons you have?"

"Nine," I say, eyein' her. "I have nine boys, and one girl."

She gasps. "Ohmygod, you have *ten* kids?"

"Yes, boo." I tell her their ages.

"Girl, get. Out. And your body *still* looks like *that?* Shoot, I had one baby and it practically tore my body up. I had to have some lipo work done to suck out all the extra fat that wouldn't go away on its own."

"Ooooh, poor thing," I say. "Bless your lil' chunky heart. Body is one thing I've always had."

"Yeah, that's true," Miss FeFe's nosey-ass says as she comes through with a broom sweepin' hair up around some of the stations. The only reason the bitch pushes a broom back here is so she can hear what the fuck everyone's sayin' 'cause there ain't shit happenin' up front. "This traffic-stopper makes me sick wth all that body and booty."

I catch Rusty Crusty curlin' her lips. But I don't strike her ass out since I'm really thinkin' her stylist must have a rotted cock stuck up in her cooch. So I keep pressin'. "Oh, Miss FeFe, hush. All these niggahs see is this big, juicy ass. They could give a damn about the rest of my body."

"Girl, please," Pasha says, wavin' me on as she removes the last track of weave. "Those long, sexy legs and small waist...mmmph. Folks are still talking about you and that dress you wore at my wedding." She laughs. "I think you got more attention than I did that night. And it was *my* wedding."

"Sorry, Miss Pasha Girl, I didn't mean to snatch your shine. But hon, you know how I do it. If I'm comin', then I'm comin' to steal the show, damnit. I don't play no games, okay?"

She laughs. "I heard that. And girrrl, before I forget, I'm lovin' the bag. One word: fierce!"

I toot my lips up. "Uh-huh; like me—*fierce*, sugah-boo. You know how I do. Had one of my young boos sponsor this bag."

Pasha chuckles. "I know that's right. Booty, you're a mess. Oops, I didn't mean to call you that. You know I always forget your real name, girl."

"Miss Pasha, girl, you know you cool with me, boo. So it's all good. You know the niggahs love them some Big Booty, baby."

She chuckles. "Yes, I know they do. Anyway, back to you and them young boys. You stay messing with them. That sounds like too much drama."

"Chile, you know there ain't no shame in my game. Honey, I love 'em young. Ain't nothin' like gettin' you a dose of some young tender cock every now and again. Shit, why shouldn't I? I look damn good for my age and they stay thinkin' I'm still in my twenties, so hell yes, I'ma wear them dingalings out. And let me tell you, sugah-boo. Them niggahs can bust off a round back to back to back and still have enough energy to go out and make that money after an all-night fuckfest. Yes, boo, I love that young dingdong. And trust me. After I put it on 'em, they hustle up all their paper to get back up in these hips. And, no...they don't come with any more drama than some of these no-count older niggahs. You simply have to know how to handle 'em. And know when to dismiss 'em."

She laughs, shakin' her head. "I heard that. And I know you don't mind runnin' their pockets, either; that's for sure."

"Nope, never have; never will. But, shit. I don't discriminate. I like 'em young and old. Well, not too old. The last time I had me some senior citizen dick I was fifteen tryna get my rent money up. And they didn't have Viagra back then. So you know his old ass was servin' me nothin' but prune-dick; shriveled down to the damn gristle."

Everyone in the shop laughs.

"Anyway, as long as a niggah's dick can get hard and *stay* hard, then we good. Shit, I gotta keep that big-ass gas guzzler I have outside filled up. And my shoe and handbag collection up..."

JT's big-dicked self pops into my head. No good-niggah-bitch! Crazy niggahs like him, you gotta fuck in small doses. Give him tiny rations of pussy and ass and throat to keep him from gettin' all nutty on you. Married or not, I think the niggah has a damn screw loose. No, scratch that shit. I *know* he does, which is why I keep a can of mace and a gun cocked and ready in case his ass ever tries to bring it to me.

"And I already got my eye on my next victim. A young, tasty niggah who I heard is reppin' for the Mandingaling tribe."

Pasha and the Rhodeshia chick laugh.

"*Mandingaling?* Girl, I can't," Pasha says, shakin' her head. "I've done heard it all."

"Miss Pasha Girl, what can I say? I likes 'em tree trunk big."

Rhodeshia chimes in. "Oooh, yes. A woman after my own heart. That's exactly how I like 'em, too."

I wave her on. "Oooh, what you say? Yes, honey-boo. Anything under eight inches is a bore."

"But what if he's extra thick, but short on length?" the

chick sittin' on the left of me asks as her stylist—I think her name's Keisha or Kendra or some shit like that—finishes up her microbraids.

I grunt, pursin' my lips. "Sweetness, all that is for me is a butt plug. Give me length and width. I wanna be stretched, stroked, and stabbed. I need to be gutted, boo."

She and the two other stylists laugh.

Rusty Crusty is ear-hustlin' real hard. I catch her eyein' me on the low.

Yeah, bitch. I see you hatin' on me.

When Pasha finally finishes removin' the rest of my weave, she leans my head back in the sink, then washes and conditions my hair. "Girl, I can't get over how long your hair is. I don't know why you mess with all these weaves when you have a head full of beautiful hair."

"Miss Pasha, girl. Give me body, boo. I like it long and full. Long hair and long nails to go along with long dingdong. Besides, I like lettin' these hatin' hoes think I'm baldheaded. And honey, the only thing bald on me is my pussy."

Everyone laughs.

When Miss Pasha's done she blots my hair dry with a white, fluffy towel, sittin' me up in the chair. She wants to know what I want done. I tell her I want another sew-in; that I want her to turn me into a chocolate Pocahantas with the bangs and all.

"Do me right, boo. Don't do me like Miss Beyoncé, though. And I love me some Miss Bee. But that shit she wears always looks tore up. Mmmph. All that goddamn money and you can't wear you a decent damn weave. Shit, even my girl Dickalina would lay her out right."

Pasha laughs, then asks how Lina's doin'. "Her ass's still retarded as ever. But whatchu gonna do? Still gotta love her. Anyway, back to my damn weave. I don't want no games, Miss Pasha. I'm goin' down to the CrackHouse tonight for a few drinks and hopefully some cock, so I need you to do me right, sugah-boo."

She keeps laughin'. Tells me she has the perfect look for me. Then has Miss FeFe go to the back of the shop to the supply room and bring her out a bundle of 18-inch Indian Natural Wave.

"Girl, you will love this hair. It's L-10 hair and it will give you just the look you want. She starts ramblin' about how it's virgin hair that can be colored and flat-ironed with ease. She blow-dries my hair out, then starts partin' my hair for cornrows.

"Oooh, yes...do it, sugah boo. Give it to me good. That's what I'm talkin' about. So, Miss Pasha Girl, I've been meanin' to ask you. You ever have you some young dingaling?"

She drops her comb, laughin' and chokin'. "Chile, I'm a married woman. I'll leave all that for you."

"Mmmhmm," I laugh, eyein' her. "But you ain't always been married."

"True. Let's simply say I've had my share of experiences."

I laugh. "Uh-huh, I'm sure you have. Welcome to the club, boo. We all have a story to tell."

I catch her as she shifts her eyes. "Yes, we do."

Again, Rusty Crusty is lookin' at me. She shifts her eyes.

Here's my thing, if you gonna fuckin' stare, then speak, goddammit. Don't keep eyeballin' me like you wanna get knocked in your fuckin' sockets. "Boo, do I know you?" I finally ask, tiltin' my head. I lean up in my seat in case I gotta leap up on her ass.

She acts like she doesn't know I'm talkin' to her. So I ask her again.

"Excuse me?" she finally says.

"No, bitch, excuse you," I hear myself startin' off, but I catch myself. I take a deep breath. "Chick, I asked you if I knew you. Everytime I say somethin', you sittin' over there rollin' your goddamn eyes up in your head and makin' all kinda ugly-ass Cookie Monster faces—that you don't even need to be makin' with ya ugly ass self—and I wanna know are you makin' them at *me* or does your stylist's pussy stink?"

The Rhodeshia chick frowns. "Girl, wrong answer. I keeps the kitty fresh."

"Then I guess this bitch is doin' me then, huh?"

"*Bitch?*" Rusty Crusty screeches. "You don't know me—"

"And, bitch, you don't know me to be eyeballin' me like you wanna put some work in. So either you want some of this fat pussy or wanna get your ass beat, which is it? 'Cause I know I didn't fuck your man. Or did I? And if

I did, remind me who he is so I can go back and ride his face tonight, then send him back home to you with my pussy juice stained on his tongue."

"Oh, no. Not today, girl," Pasha warns, watchin' me through the mirror. "Please, not today."

I glance up at her. "Not to worry, Miss Pasha. I'm gonna stay classy with it. You know how I do."

"Yeah, I do," she says, narrowin'her eyes and spinnin' me around in the chair, facin' her. "And I'm not having you tear my shop up," she hisses. "So don't."

I laugh. "Miss Pasha, I wouldn't do you like that, boo. But you right. I'ma let it go. But tell that ugly bitch to stop starin' at me, like she wanna eat my ass out or somethin'. She's makin' my asshole ache."

"Trick, the only ugly bitch in here is you."

I laugh, decidin' to fuck with her ass. "Bitch, you on crack. You see all this fabulousness over here, so don't even front. Call me a ho, boo. Call me a slut. Don't ever call me ugly, bitch. 'Cause you and I know it's all lies. I know you like what you see, hatin'-ass trick. So, what you wanna do, fuck or fight? I bet you gotta big-ass dick, too. What you want, some of this pussy, boo? Oh, and I love it in the ass, too." I pull up the cape and spread my legs. "I don't have on any drawers, either."

I make the bitch uncomfortable. Everyone in the shop gasps.

"Booty! I mean, Cassandra!" Pasha screeches through clenched teeth. "I will burn the shit out of you with this hot iron if you don't stop. I told you I don't want no shit up in here today, or any other day."

I am crackin' up. "Oh, Miss Pasha, relax, boo. I'm only fuckin' with her ass. She's lucky I'm in a good mood, though. Othewise you know it woulda turned messy up in here." I crane my neck, lookin' over at Rusty Crusty, flappin' my tongue at her. I make the ho nervous. But she keeps her goddamn eyes off of me for the rest of the time I'm sittin' here. Bitch, tryna eyeball me. Puhleeze.

Ten minutes later, Pasha has finished installin' my lustrious weave. And as always, it's flawless! It's silky and flowin' down to my asscrack. And I feel like a sexy-ass chocolate Barbie. Miss Pasha knows she can do the hell outta some hair.

I pay my bill, walk back over to Pasha's station and slide her a hundred-dollar tip, then sling my new hair over my shoulder and strut out the door. With all eyes on me!

Four

"Spread your legs, baby," JT says as he slaps me on the ass. I arch my back, jiggle and bounce it for him. He's a dark chocolate, get-money street niggah who I've been creeping with for the last ten months. The niggah loves the streets. Even after doing two bids in prison, he still can't stay away from the fast life, the fast cash, and all the fast ass that comes along with it—includin' mine, which is exactly why I'm bent over slap-jackin' my ass for him.

But his indiscretions or weakness for a good fuck isn't my concern. I've known the niggah for at least ten years. Hell, he did his first bid with one of my baby fahvers. And even though I always caught him eye-fuckin' me, knew he secretly wanted to run his dick up in me, I still played it off. I always kept my distance. Never, ever, crossed the line with him—after all, I also know his wife. But ten months ago somethin' changed. The niggah kept pressin' me hard. And once he flashed me a stack of paper, the fact that I know his wife no longer mattered to me. Gettin' in this dirty niggah's pockets did. He wanted this ass. I wanted his paper. And now we have a special kind of arrangement goin' on. He buys me nice shit, like the Range Rover I drive—among many other things—and keeps them Benjamins in my purse. And I give him access to all the ass and pussy his horny tongue and cock can handle. Not a bad tradeoff, if you ask me. Shit. I love to fuck any-damn-way. So we both get what we want. Then he gets to go back to his lil' white picket-fenced life with the beautiful wife and kid, well-fucked. And I get to go back to my life a few thousand dollars richer.

He grunts. "Damn...big, juicy fat ass. I'ma tear this shit up. I see you got that shit already ready for me, too." He slaps me on the ass. "You knew Daddy was gonna call for this good ass, didn't you? Got that shit stretched all wide for this big-ass dick."

"Lick it, fucker," I say, glancin' at him over my shoulder. He flicks his tongue over it, then dips it in. My pussy moistens. This niggah's so damn fine and no damn good and I shouldn't be fuckin' with him, but heeeey...a bitch like me loves livin' on the edge of danger. And this niggah right here is dangerous! And fuckin' crazy! Still, I love fuckin' his cock. I love his tongue. Love the way both feel deep in my holes. Love the way his dick stretches open my ass and causes my nut to burst outta my pussy. Mmmph.

I eye him, lickin' my lips. His hard, chiseled body is positioned in back of me, dripping with sweat. His scrumptiously thick nine-inch, veiny dick stabs at the center of my pussy, teasin'ly. He pulls back, pulls open my asscheeks, then buries his face in. The nasty niggah shamelessly shovels his tongue deep into my asshole.

"Yeah, you nasty motherfucka, that's right. Eat it up, niggah. Lick that sweet asshole. Hmmmhmmm, make love to it with that nice wet tongue..."

Two hard smacks sting my ass, causin' my pussy to clench. "Oooh, yes, Daddy...smack that ass, you nasty motherfucka." He smacks it again, then dips his face back in between my cheeks and laps my hole all over again. He digs his strong fingers deep into my chocolatey cakes, flickin', lickin', slurpin', and slappin' my ass up while I play with my clit; bury a finger into my pussy. My pussy is sooo wet, wetter than ever. "Mmmm...mmmmm...give me the dick, niggah...let me feel that big-ass dick in my asshole..."

JT has a nice thick, ass-fuckin' cock. The kind of cock that makes your asshole burn in delicious heat when it's being stretched open. I love that feelin' of being stuffed, deep and full. And I love it when a niggah moans when he pushes past the resistance and snugness and I squeeze him, milk him, with my trained muscles. Love it when he pushes in, slowly works one inch in at a time, allowing me to fuck myself on his dick until I have him buried in me balls deep.

JT groans, strokin' his rock-hard cock in his hand.

I coax him to put a finger in my ass. He jabs his middle finger in. Slowly fingers me, readyin' my steamy hole for a good, long, deep fuckin'. I tell him to pull his finger out. To slide it into my mouth; feed me my ass. He does. I suck his finger clean, then tell him to slide it back in. He does, again.

"You a fuckin' freak, yo. You know that, right?"

"Yeah, I know it, niggah. And you love it. That's why your nasty ass stay tryna sneak out to fuck me on the low every chance you get."

"Yeah, aiiight. You got that." He slaps my ass again.

No good motherfucka!

"Yeah, I know I do, niggah. Now put another finger in my ass. And shut up all this goddamn talkin'. I ain't here for all this extra chitchat."

Whap!

My ass bounces.

"Yeah, aiight. That's what ya mouth says. Freak-ass, nasty bitch. I'ma fuck the shit outta this phat ass, yo..."

In goes his index finger. He gives me a nice, slow, two-finger fuck. I wind my hips and moan. "Mmmmhm..."

"Damn, you have a beautiful ass," he says. He kisses and licks it, his warm tongue leaving wet streaks of desire all over my skin as he fingers me. He bites each cheek. "Nice and big and fuckin' juicy, yo. I can't wait to feel my dick all up in it."

I reach under me and finger my slippery clit, flickin' and pinching it every so often as I push backward onto his fingers. "Take your fingers out and put your tongue back in."

This time he sucks his own fingers. I grin as he buries

his face back between my cheeks, teasin' my asshole with his tongue, swirling it over and around it. "You like that, ma?" he asks, takin' his tongue out long enough to ask the question before divin' back in, tongue deep in my ass.

What you think, niggah?

I moan; strummin' my clit. It is swollen and sensitive and aching. "Oh, yes, you ass eating motherfucka...eat Momma's ass up...oooh, yes...Big Booty, baby...do that shit, boo..."

"Oh, now I'm ya boo. A few minutes ago I was e'ery kinda muhfucka." He draws the tip of his tongue in lil' circles around my hole, then burrows back in.

I moan again. "You still are, bitch. Mmmm...eat that ass, niggah..."

He moans, then grunts.

Neither of us not caring who hears us.

After all the fuckin' and suckin' and sneakin' we've been doing, JT is finally learnin' the rhythm of my body. Finally knows how to give it to me how I want it, the way I need it. He services my asshole the way a mechanic fine tunes a car—with precision and purpose. The end result being perfect performance.

A nut is swirlin'.

He licks faster. He is aware that I am about to come. He wants me to nut with his tongue in my asshole. I push back, booty-clap my ass up on his face, forcin' my hole onto his tongue. "Ohfuck ohfuckohfuck...yes, yes, yesssssss...tongue my ass, you nasty motherfucka!"

I arch my back, tell him I am gettin' ready to nut, then bite into the pillow and let out a loud moan as he slips his mouth over my pussy and waits with it open until I squirt streams of sweet, sticky pussy juice into it.

He knows that once I shoot my first nut that my asshole is ready to be fed his cock. He leans over my shoulder and shares his tongue with me; the scent of my pussy and ass lingering all over it. The niggah kisses me and I'm surprised at myself for kissing him back. I try to figure out when this became part of the script.

Yeah, this niggah's fallin'!

I smile.

Big Booty, baby...does it to a niggah e'ery time!

"You ready for this dick?"

"I stay ready, fucker," I say, windin' my hips, then jigglin' my ass for him. He slaps it. It is hungry and horny and ready to be fucked. I tell him this. Tell him to mount me and give it to me deep. "I want it fast, hard, and dirty. Now let's hope you can deliver."

"Oh, yeah, aiight...you already know what it is. I'll show you a fucker." He reaches for the Eros Body Glide— my lube of choice for his thick dick, then squirts a glob out into my asshole. My hole is well-trained to take a dick. Still, I like it extra slippery and wet; like it to feel like a gushy pussy as it slurps in the dick. He slips one finger in, then two, then three. He finger fucks me in a delicious rhythm; my ass gulpin' him in knuckles deep.

I toss my head back. "Stop teasin' me, motherfucka.

Give me the dick, niggah. Feed my bubblicious ass that cock....Mmmph...oooh, I want the dick...let me nut all over that big-ass dick..."

His knuckles rim my hole. I clench, then relax. I am soooo mothefuckin' ready to be fucked. My ass is on fire! With one hand busy with its fingers in my ass, he reaches for a condom, rips it open with his teeth. I buck and roll my hips. Slurp his fingers in. "Yeah, that's wasssup, ma...you got my shit hard as a muhfucka, too."

I glance back and watch as he rolls the condom on. He reaches for the lube again, pulls out his fingers, then squirts another glob into my hole. He knows I am open and ready but wants to keep fuckin' around back there, teasin' me; tauntin' me.

"Motherfucka, will you put your goddamn dick in me and stop playin' around. I wanna be fucked! Now!"

He laughs, slappin' me on the ass, then rammin' his dick in. I yelp. "Is this what you want, ma?" He grabs my hips and pulls me onto his dick. My pussy explodes into tiny fuckin' slippery pieces, cum spurtin' out everywhere. He holds onto my hips, and rides me hard, thrustin' from his knees, gruntin' and pantin'.

"Oh fuck...yeah, yeah, yeah...ooooh, shit...this mutha-fuckin' ass is dangerous...aaaah, shit..."

He yanks me by the back of my Bohyme Remy hair and starts speed fuckin' his nine inches into me as if he's riding a horse. My asshole starts to smoke from the rapid friction. The dick is feelin' sooo goddamn good. But the motherfucka is yankin' my hair back, like he's tryna snatch my scalp off. And I'm not diggin' that shit.

"Motherfucka!" I snap, swingin' my arm back and hittin' his arm. "Will you get off my goddamn weave like that. Shit. This hair ain't cheap, niggah."

"Yo, go 'head with that dumb shit." He lets go, slappin' my ass. "I'll buy ya ass some more hair, shit. Now shut the fuck up and take this dick."

I lie flat on my stomach and he locks his arms up underneath my armpits and fucks me faster and deeper. The mattress beneath me bounces. He bites my shoulder, kisses my neck, nibbles on my earlobe, and whispers, "Oh shit, this ass feels so gooood, baby...you gonna fuck around and have me buyin' ya ass a house next if you keep givin' up this ass like this..."

I grin. *Niggah, that's not all you gonna end up givin' up.* I match my movements to his as my ass opens to his width. My asslips suckling the length of his dick. He is, as with every other niggah I fuck, amazed at how easily my hole handles his cock. He is fascinated by how hot it gets. Enthralled at how his dick gets swallowed up inside of it, asscheeks clappin' up, down, around it.

"Yeah, motherfucka...aaah, yeah, niggah...oooooh... dick is good...c'mon...that's all you got, niggah...bang that dick up in me...beat that asshole up...yeah, yeah, yeah...mmmmph..."

I lift up on my knees again. He is squatting—one hand balancing him with my shoulder while the other slaps my ass with each deep thrust. It doesn't take long before my pussy comes again. Ooooh, he is fillin' me up. Feedin' my ass the dick in deep, delicious strokes. I am on the brink of comin' again; my pussy and ass convulsin'. The two of us our in perfect sync. His hand has snaked its way up under me, playin' with my clit and pussy. I gush all over his fingers.

"Damn, you know how to take some dick...Mmm-mmm, fuck...you got some good ass, baby...oh, shit..."

JT pushes in and outta me slowly. My ass openin' with every thrust. My pussy tightening as a nut builds up inside of me. "Oh, yessss...fuck meeeee," I whimper, bucking my hips. "Give me that big-ass dick, niggah. Oh, yessss...you like how my fat ass gobbles up that dick, huh, daddy?"

"Aaaah, shit...oh fuuuuuck...yeah, ma...Ass is so fuckin' good... Damn, you got my knees shakin'..."

I smirk, knowingly.

He grunts and moans and groans. My toes curl. And ten minutes later, I feel him shakin' behind me. I look over my shoulder. His eyes are closed. He is about to nut. I clench my ass and bounce back on his dick. "Uh, uh, uh, uh...aaaah, aaaah, aaaaaaaaah...mmmph... ohhhhhh, shiiiiit..." He clings to me, shuddering. "Oh, fuuuuuck. Goddaaaaamn...you the fuckin' truth, word is bond..." His body jerks again. "Aaah, shit..."

I pause, shut my eyes, bite my bottom lip and swallow back a low groan.

It takes him a few minutes more to get himself together before he slowly pulls out and collapses. He is sweaty and breathing heavy. I pull the sticky condom off, then put it up to my lips, hold my head back, and squeeze out his nut into my mouth. I swallow, then lay on my back beside him.

"Damn, girl," he says, grinnin', "you gonna fuck around and have me fall for ya ass, real shit, yo."

I turn my head toward him and stare at him. "Oh, yeah? And what about your wife?"

He lifts up on his forearms, raisin' his thick brows. "What about her? I'm good. I'm not leavin' her, if that's what you askin'."

I roll my eyes. "Niggah, that's *not* what I'm askin'. Don't get it fucked up. I don't want you. So no worries, boo-boo. You can keep your happy, cheatin' ass right where you at. The only thing you good for is dick and dollars. And a buncha drama."

He laughs. "Oh, word? That's all a muhfucka's good for?"

"That's all you'll ever be good for."

He reaches over and grabs another condom, tearin' it open with his teeth, then rollin' it down on his dick. He climbs on top of me, pushin' my legs open with his. "Then a muhfucka better get his money's worth."

I hoist my legs up over his waist, givin' him full access to my wet, sticky pussy. "Yeah, niggah, you better. 'Cause after tonight, the fees are goin' up."

He laughs. "As much paper I'm kickin' out, I need to put ya ass on lock, real shit. I don't want no other niggahs hittin' this shit."

I frown. "Niggah, you don't own me. And you don't tell me what the fuck to do with my pussy, ass, or throat. I suck and fuck and do what, and who, the hell I want. You can talk that dumb shit to your wife, but I'm not the one."

"Yeah, aiiight. You talk a lotta shit."

"That's right, motherfucka, I do. Now shut the fuck up, and fuck me."

He pushes the head of his dick in. "Is this what you want?"

"Uh...mmm...yeah, niggah. Make my pussy nut."

He reaches up underneath me, cups my ass and drills my pussy, then slips his tongue back into my mouth. He fucks me non-stop for another thirty-five minutes, then quickly hops up and heads for the shower after he's nutted again. I shower after him. Twenty minutes later, we're both dressed and racin' out the hotel's door—him to pick his son up from daycare and me to get home before the twins get out of school.

"Yo, who else knows about us?" he asks in a hushed tone as we walk toward the bank of elevators.

I frown, stoppin' in the middle of the hallway. "Niggah, when have you ever known me to kiss and tell?"

He eyes me. "Yo, lower ya voice."

"Bitch, you lower yours," I snap, flippin' on the ghetto

switch. I'm classy ghetto, but will go straight hood-ghetto when a niggah takes me there, like now. "Fuck outta here, comin' at me like I don't know how to stay on script. I should be askin' ya sneaky-ass that shit, niggah."

His jaw tightens. "Yo, who you talkin' to like that?"

I look around, yankin' open my bag. "Niggah, I'm talkin' to you. And what you gonna do about it? Break my jaw? Stomp me out? I wanna see you try it." I pull out my gun. "I ain't ya wife, bitch. And I do know how to use this."

"Yo, go 'head, Cass, talkin' all that crazy shit. And put that shit away, yo; for real for real. For you end up gettin' fucked up. I only asked you a fuckin' question. All that extra shit ain't necessary. You stay wildin', yo."

"And you stay talkin' dumb shit, niggah. Like I said, I don't kiss and tell. You make sure you keep your motherfuckin' lips shut. Now where's my money, niggah?"

He shakes his head. "Yeah, aiight, yo. Just makin' sure." He hands me a knot of money.

I snatch the roll and drop it in my bag, then snap it shut. "Niggah, you just make sure you keep a hard dick and my purse full. And we good."

"Yeah, aiight. I'm dead-ass, yo. Keep ya mouth shut about this."

I tilt my head. "Niggah, I don't know who you think you're talkin' to. But I done told you I'm not your motherfuckin' wife. And I ain't ya jump-off or one of ya mistresses. I'ma bitch runnin' your pockets and wettin' up your dick; that's it."

His thick index finger presses the button for the elevator. His jaw clenches. He pulls in his bottom lip, then blows out a buncha air. "Yo, your mouth is real fuckin' slick, you know that, right?"

"And my pussy's real juicy. And this ass is real deep. So what the fuck you sayin'?"

The doors open, and I step in. *This motherfucka got me confused. But he'll learn.* I turn to face him.

He shakes his head. "You gotta lotta shit wit' you, yo. You lucky you ain't my wife; I'd beat the shit outta you."

I laugh in his face. "And you'd be one dead niggah. Thanks for the dick, bitch." I say as the doors close in his face. He'll wait for a few minutes, then take the next elevator and slide outta the hotel, like always. I step outta the elevator into the lobby, pullin' out my cell and makin' a call. "That niggah ain't shit," I say, walkin' toward the revolvin' glass doors.

"I know," the voice on the other end says. We disconnect.

Not to worry, though. We about to do his ass real lovely. One by one, all of them slimy motherfuckas gonna catch it… startin' with him!

Five

My cell rings. I glance at the screen and roll my eyes. It's JT. *O-M-muthafuckin'-G, wasn't I fuckin' this niggah like five hours ago?* I'm really startin' to think that this niggah is an escapee from the cuckoo farm. He's fuckin' crazy! It's six o'clock in the goddamn evenin' and this niggah's already ringin' my shit off the hook and textin' me like we haven't seen each other in weeks. I swear this niggah's retarded. And he's gettin' on my last goddamn nerve! "Niggah, what? Why the fuck is you blowin' my phone up like you my man?"

"Take all that tone down, Cass; for real for real 'fore you have me snatch ya ass up. And I ain't 'preciate that shit you pulled out in the hallway, either."

"Get over it."

"Don't have me fuck you up, yo."

"Yeah, right, niggah. You ain't stupid. Try it if you want."

"Yo, let me stop fuckin' wit' you. So what's good?"

I twist my lips up. "Niggah-boo, don't play. This pussy and ass is what's good. You already know. That's why you keep callin' me like you a damn fiend. I know Big Booty got you hooked on all this goodness. Now what the hell do you want?"

He laughs. "Yo, whatever. I'm sayin', though. Why the fuck you ain't answerin' ya phone when I hit you up?"

"Niggah-bitch, don't get it fucked up. I don't answer to you."

"Yo, what I tell you about talkin' to me all reckless and shit? I ain't ya muhfuckin' bitch, yo. So watch how you talk."

"Niggah, fuck you. And I keep tellin' you to save that shit for ya wife. Speakin' of her, where is she?"

He sighs. "Yo, Cass, real shit, stop wit' the bullshit. You pop a lotta shit, ma; for real for real. But she's out wit' my lil' man, shoppin' or some shit. Why?"

I suck my teeth. "Uh, why the fuck you keep callin' me like you crazy?"

"Yo, I done told you to fuck all that dumb shit. You already know what it is. I want some more pussy. Why the fuck else you think I'ma be hittin' you up. Did you count the stack I hit you wit'?"

I roll my eyes. "Yeah, niggah, I counted it."

"Well, aiight, then. That three grand's ya retainer to be on-call. I don't want you fuckin' no other niggahs, yo. I want that shit all to myself; for real for real."

I laugh. "Niggah, boom! Not gonna happen. You paid for three grand worth of pussy, ass 'n throat earlier. You want more, you pay more, niggah. I'm not ever gonna be on-call for you or no other niggah, so good luck with that."

"Yo, real shit, Cass. We both already know what it is wit' us. You know I fuckin' dig you, yo. And you know my situation. I ain't leavin' my home, yo. But I wanna wife you on da side, yo. So when I call, that's what it is. I wanna fuck. I can slip out later tonight. So wasssup?"

Yup...it's official. The niggah's a nut! "Look. Ain't shit up unless you got more—"

"Mommmmmmmy!" Elijah yells at the top of his lungs, burstin' into my room. "Joshua won't help me with my homework."

"Tell him I said to help you with that work. And don't come in here with all that damn noise again."

I hear him yell as he closes my door, "Joshua! Mommy said she's gonna fuck you up if you don't get your black ass in here and help me with my homework."

I shake my head.

"Yo, sounds like you need a dick break. Let me fuck you down real good again wit' this dick tonight."

"I—"

This time Joshua bursts into my room. "Yo, Ma, why I always gotta help Elijah with his homework? Why can't Day'Asia or Marquelle help him sometimes?"

"'Cause I told you too, that's why. Now don't come in here askin' me no dumb shit. Get yo' ass in there and make sure Elijah does his homework right."

"But, he doesn't wanna listen."

"Joshua, I'm on the goddamn phone! Get in there and

help your brother and get outta my motherfuckin' room."

"Okay, now what were you—"

"I'm sick of this shit," Joshua snaps, slammin' my door. "He shouldn't be so fuckin' stupid. I can't wait to get outta this muthafuckin' house!"

"Look, I got more important shit to handle than you at the moment, so call me later," I say, jumpin' up off my bed. "I'ma 'bout to tear this house up."

"Yeah, aiight—"

I disconnect on his ass, swingin' open my bedroom door. "Joshua!" No answer. I storm down the hallway. "Joshua! Who the fuck is you talkin' to?!"

No response.

"Joshua!"

"He went outside," Elijah says, sittin' at the dinin' room table, tryna act like his ass is so into tryna get his homework done. But I ain't fallin' for the okey-doke. Not today.

"Outside where?"

"Some girl was at the door for him and he went out with her."

"Oh, this lil'niggah is really feelin' himself. He must be fuckin' or gettin' his cock sucked down real good for his black ass to storm up outta here poppin' shit." I swing open the front door and spot his ass standin' at the curb talkin' to three hot-in-the-ass lil' hoes. I step outside, hand on hip. "Joshua! Get ya black ass back in this motherfuckin' house before I embarrass you in front of ya lil' friends."

"I'll be there in a minute."

"No, niggah, now! Don't have me act a fool out here 'cause you know I will turn it up on ya ass real quick. Now get the fuck in this house! And help your brother with his damn homework!"

He takes his slow, sweet time. And, the whole time I'm watchin' him, I see myself chargin' over there and bustin' him upside his head, but I don't feel like chasin' him down. And I really don't wanna make a scene when it's still light out. So I stand and wait. "Joshua, now!"

He sucks his teeth. "Dang. I said aiight. I heard you the first time. Get off my back."

I blink. *So this niggah wanna show off in front of these lil' bitches, I see.*

"Bye, Joshuaaaa," one of the lil' bitches coos, like he done got her pussy all wet or some shit. "You better hurry up before you get beat."

"Yeah, right," I hear him say. And he has the nerve to be goddamn smirking.

I musta blacked out and grew a pair of wings. I don't know when or how I moved, but the next thing I know I have him by the back of his shirt swingin' his disrespectful ass down to the ground. Fuck daylight, fuck who sees. I hook off on his ass. He tries to block my slaps and punches. But he musta forgot that I'ma strong, solid, biscuit-eating bitch who fights like a man. I press my forearm down into his neck. *I'ma crush his goddamn neck!* "Niggah, I will. Kill. You."

"Aaah, ma…I. Can't. Breathe…"

"Oh no, too bad, bitch. Don't 'aaah ma' me, now. You wanna raise up on me, niggah. I'm goin' to jail tonight and your black ass is goin' to the morgue." I slap his face up with my free hand. "You came outta my pussy, niggah. I suffered givin' birth to ya ass. And if you think you're gonna talk shit to me when I'm the one who makes sure you have a roof over ya goddamn head, you got another thing comin'. I will bury you before I ever let you think you can talk shit to me and get away with it." I slap his face again. "I'm not one of them lil' bitches out here on the streets. I will fuck you up, niggah. And you know this."

I smack him again. "If you ever raise your voice to me, or slam a goddamn door in my face again, or even look like you wanna bring it, I'ma punch ya motherfuckin' eye sockets in! Do you understand me?"

"Yesssssss."

I slap him again. "Yes, what?"

"Yes, ma."

I lift my arm from off his throat, then slap him one last time before gettin' up off of him. He starts coughing. "Now get ya black ass in the house and help your brother with his goddamn homework before I really go off on ya ass." I walk back toward the house. "Talkin' shit to me like I'm some bitch you been fuckin'. Niggah, you done lost your motherfuckin' mind. Matter of fact, let me find out you stickin' your dick in anything other than your damn hand and I'ma kick you in your goddamn balls.

You really crossed the line, niggah. Talkin' slick and greasy to me. You know I don't play that shit."

I glance over my shoulder across the street and see the lil' bitches have their phones out, recordin' and snappin' pictures like I give a fuck. "And make sure you send a copy to DYFS," I say, turnin' to face them with a hand up on my hip. "'Cause the next time that lil'niggah tries it, I'ma punch him in his goddamn throat. And the name's Cassandra Simms. Be clear."

"Who the fuck cares, you crazy bitch?" one of the lil' bitches says. "You lucky I don't fuck you up myself, conceited bitch."

The two other hoes start laughin'.

"Well, bring it on, you lil'baldheaded bitch. Ugly, trick-ass ho! And I'll give you the ass beatin' ya stank-ass mammy shoulda gave ya disrespectful ass, you fuckin' hoodrat. Fuckin' roach-ass ho."

I sprint out the yard and they take off runnin'. "Crazy bitch," the one with the big titties shouts out.

"I'll show you crazy, ho!" I yell back. "Bring ya fresh ass back here and let me show you how crazy does it! Fuckin' disrespectful hoes." I walk back into the yard, then into house. "Crazy bitches comin' around here talkin' shit."

Joshua has his ass at the dinin' room table. I walk by and he ducks his head down, but I slap him upside his head anyway. "I wanna fight yo' black ass, niggah, tryna show out in front of them lil' dusty-ass bitches. You fuckin' them hoes?"

Elijah laughs.

"Boy, ain't shit funny. If you don't get that homework right, yo' ass is gonna be next. You been home all damn day, this shit shoulda been finished by now. What the fuck was you doin' all goddamn day, huh?"

He stares at me like I'm crazy.

"Oh, you not laughin' now are you, huh? What the fuck you sittin' there starin' at me for? I asked you a question. Why you ain't do your homework when you got home from school?"

"I tried. But it's too hard."

I eye him, twistin' my lips. "Mmmhmm. I bet you did. Hurry up and get that homework done, and get yo' musty ass in the shower."

He sniffs under his arms.

"Ya stink-ass," I hear Joshua mumble under his breath.

"I am not. You stink," Elijah shoots back.

"Listen, both of ya asses stink. So shut the fuck up and get that homework finished. And, Joshua, I know you don't want me to get back on that ass, again. You still ain't answer my question. I asked you if you fuckin' them bitches you tried to show out in front of." He says no. "Mmmph. Who were them lil' fresh asses, anyway?"

"Some girls," he says.

I ball my fist. "See, now you tryna be funny. Niggah, do I look stupid to you? I know they're girls. You must really want your goddamn eye punched out, don't you? I wanna know their names."

"Why? They ain't do nuthin'."

I blink. Take a deep breath. "Joshua. I don't wanna go to jail today 'cause I'm tryna go out and have me a few drinks tonight. But you are really, really pressin' your luck. Now, I'ma ask you one more time before I take it to your head. Who. Were. Them. Lil' bitches you were outside showin' off for?" As soon as I start walkin' up on him he tells me their names: Pinky, Talitha, and Chasity. I ask him which one was the dark-skinned girl with the big lips and titties since she's the one who got slick at the mouth. He tells me Pinky. Ain't shit pink about that lil' ho. I roll my eyes. "And where does this Pinky bitch live?"

"Why you wanna know all that?"

I take a long, deep breath. Count to twenty in my head, then backwards. I walk down the hall, go into my bedroom, then come back out with an aluminum bat. I've have had enough of his shit for one day. And if I have to go outta here in handcuffs I want it to be for somethin' good. Like smashin' his goddamn jaw and knockin' all of his motherfuckin' teeth out. I walk back out to the dinin' room calm as ever. I have one hand on my hip, and the other holdin' the bat.

"Niggah, I'ma ask you one mo' gin before I break ya face up in here. Where does that lil' fresh-mouth bitch live? And before you roll your eyes or suck your teeth or tell me you don't know, you had better think long and hard."

Elijah eases up from out his seat and gets out of my way as Joshua hops up. "Okay, okay. She lives over on Frelinghuysen. They used to live over in Seth Boyden."

I grunt. Seth Boyden was one of the worst projects around before they shut 'em down. "Oh, I shoulda known she was some lil' gutter-rat hood bitch. No manners. Who's she related to? Her mammy's probably some crackwhore." He tells me he doesn't know. But I know his ass is lyin' so I decide to let it go 'cause I'ma find out any-damn-way. And then I'ma ring her doorbell. "Boy, help Elijah get that homework done, then get out of my damn sight. I still wanna fuck you up for tryna do me. And you gonna pay to get my goddamn nails done. I'm takin' it outta ya allowance."

I stare him down. He shifts his eyes and starts helpin' his brother with his school work. I walk into the kitchen and go off. "Day'Asia!" There's shit everywhere. The stove is dirty, the floor isn't swept, and the goddamn dishes are piled up in the sink. "Day'Asia!" I scream, headin' toward her bedroom.

"She went up the street," Fuquan yells from upstairs.

"Up the street where? I told her I wanted this goddamn kitchen cleaned. I'm gettin' sick of her black ass thinkin' she can do what the fuck she want around here."

"I think she's at that girl Crispy Cream's house," Elijah happily offers. He'll tell on anyone to keep himself outta trouble.

"Who the fuck is *Crispy Cream*?" He tells me she's one

of the girls who used to come around here for Marquelle; that her name is Cremola. *Cremola? What the fuck?* I shake my head. "Well, why you callin' her Crispy Cream?"

"That's what everyone calls her because she got burned in a fire."

I frown. *These damn kids today say some really cruel shit.* "Not that girl with them big-ass teeth and black gums?"

"No, not that one," Elijah says. "The one with the three chins."

"Yo, I think Marquelle hit that, too," Joshua says, laughin'.

"Ill, he's nasty for that," Elijah says as Marquelle walks through the door. "Marquelle, Josh said you did it to Crispy Cream. Did you?"

He sucks his teeth. "Yo, shut up with that. No, I ain't do it to that ugly-ass girl. She wanted me to. But, hell no. she wasn't gettin' none'a this sausage."

I eye him. At six-five, his milk-chocolate ass keeps a buncha horny young hoes followin' behind him. And I know he's been servin' them that long, black dick just like his no-good fahver, Marcellus, used to before his dinga-ling started malfunctionin'. But before that, whew! That niggah used to beat my pussy up right.

Mmmph. Anyway, I keep a tight rein on Marquelle's horny ass. Basketball is his life. This is his last year in high school and he's been offered scholarships to play at eight different colleges. And the last thing I wanna see is him fuck it up behind some hot-in-the-ass ho. DaQuan's in college doin' good. And now I gotta make sure he gets his ass in college, too. Knockin' some ho up is not an option.

I raise a brow. "Marquelle, ya ass better not be out there servin' a sausage or any-other kinda goddamn meat to any of them hot-pussy bitches unless you wrappin' that shit up. And I mean it. Better yet, you better double-wrap that shit."

"Yo, chill, Ma," he says, bouncin' his ball up in his big hand. "You wildin' for real. I ain't servin' up no raw meat."

I narrow my eyes. "Mmmph. You shouldn't be out there servin' up no kinda meat, boy. But I know you hot in the balls like your damn fahver. So I know you fuckin'. But I'ma tell you this. You get some ho pregnant and I'ma slice ya meat clean off. So if you don't have a condom to use, you had better use some Saran Wrap and seal them juices in; otherwise I'ma fuck you up."

"Yeah, yeah, yeah," he says, walkin' up on me, then leanin' down and kissin' me on the cheek. "I know, Ma."

"And she's gonna fry it up in a pan," Elijah says, laughin'.

"Boy, don't 'I know, Ma'. I mean it, Marquelle. And, Elijah, stop fuckin' around and get that homework done. And shut your fresh mouth up. Now, where you been, Marquelle?"

"Playin' ball," he says, walkin' into the kitchen. I eye him as he opens the stove, then the microwave, then the refrigerator. "Yo, Ma, you ain't cook? I'm hungry."

"Boy, you better wash ya damn hands. And no, I didn't

cook. You shoulda ate wherever you came from. Text your sister and tell her to get her black ass home and get this kitchen cleaned up."

He shakes his head. "Asia stays on that dumb shit, for real. She's fuckin' dumb as hell."

"Marquelle, what I tell you 'bout cussin' up in my face? You know I don't play that shit. I don't know where the hell y'all get them filthy-ass mouths from, but I'm not gonna goddamn have it up in here. Now do what I asked you, please. And tell Day'Asia she has fifteen minutes to get her black ass home."

I take a deep breath as I walk to my room, then shut down. *I'ma need more than a blunt to keep from goin' off tonight.* I smile when I check my cell and see a text from Born Wise—one of my sexy boy-toys wantin' to meet up for some pussy. He's twenty-three, six one, and tatted up. He's also been in and outta jail since he was fourteen. He's also a Five-Percenter—a way of life he picked up when he was in prison. But that makes me no never mind. I'm not interested in buildin' with him. His teachin's and him bein' a God-body have nothin' to do with him rockin' my body and makin' this pussy skeet, which is exactly what I need to unwind. The only thing I wanna do is elevate up on his long, thick dick, then ride him down into the mattress until I roll over on my stomach and inch up on all fours for him to do me right.

Yeah, I know I fucked JT earlier; so what? I'm tryna get this paper, boo. And I love fuckin', so why not do both. I'll wait 'til I know the kids are knocked out, then dip out for a dose of dingaling. I text him and tell him I want my asshole eaten, then beatdown to the seams. Less than a minute later, he texts back: I GOT U!

We go back and forth for a few minutes before decidin' to meet at the Courtyard on Route…'cause ain't no niggahs comin' up in here unless you one of my baby daddies.

I tell him about the new thirty-six-hundred-dollar Louie bag I have my eyes on. I let him know I want it. And although the lil' niggah says he can probably give me half of the money to buy it, I already know that after I finish lettin' him face-fuck, pussy-fuck, and ass-fuck me tonight, he'll be doin' an extra shift on the block to get that paper up.

Six

I moan as Born swirls his tongue around my clit, then down and over my thick, juicy cunt lips. He slithers it into my wet hole. Ooh, fuck, my pussy's so wet thanks to this niggah's masterful tongue work. He gobbles my hot pussy like it's coated with honey. Yes, goddammit! Do me right!

I thrust my hips up, pump my pussy in his face as I pinch my nipples. He grunts as he feasts on my coochie, suckin' on my pussy lips, lickin' my clit, then pullin' it between his teeth...ooh, yes. This boy is young, but he knows how to eat the hell outta this pussy. But he ain't know shit 'bout eatin' pussy or ass-fuckin' 'til I taught him how Big Booty likes it. Now the niggah's a pussy-eatin', ass-fuckin' pro.

"Ooh, niggah, that's it! That's it! Eat that shit, lil' niggah...oooh, yes...do me right,goddammit..."

I shut my eyes and rock my hips against his tongue thrust. "Yeah, yeah, yeah....mmmph...make my pussy skeet..."

He grunts, then stops lickin'. He comes up from between my thighs with his face glazed and sticky like a donut. His fingers are still stuffed deep in my pussy, massagin' my spot. I hump and grind on his hand.

"You wanna see me skeet, niggah, huh?"

"Yeah, ma, nut on my fingers for me so I can lick that shit up."

"Oooh, that's right. Get that shit, motherfucka. Ooooh, I'm gettin' ready to cream, niggah…mmm. Put your mouth back on that pussy and let me shoot my pussy juice in ya mouth." He wraps his mouth around my pussy and gobbles me up, his tongue greedily flappin' 'n lappin' all over the place. "Yeah, get that shit…"

My hips buck up off the bed as my cum gushes out, coatin' his mouth, lips, and tongue. He swallows, then laps around my pussy and over my clit to get all of my drippings.

He sucks his fingers clean of my pussy cream, then licks his glistenin' lips, rollin' over on his back and grabbin' at his hard dingdong. "Shiiiiit, that was good. You got my dick harder than a muhfucka. Now what you got for me, ma?"

I shift my body so that my face is directly in front of his hairy dick. I kiss the head. "For starters, head." I kiss his dick again. "Then some pussy." I kiss it again. "Then some of this deep, hot black ass."

He grins. "Yeah, you mad freaky, ma. That's why I love fuckin' you."

I smirk. *And I love spendin' ya money. And I'ma love it*

even more when I get my hands on that handbag. I lick up and down the sides of his dick. His medium-size balls are smoothly shaven. I flick my tongue over the head of his dick like a snake, slitherin' around it, flickin' his piss slit while massagin' his balls. I jack him off in slow strokes as I lap at his balls, then take them into my mouth. I wet them up real good. I want that handbag so he will get the dick suck of his life. I wrap my fingers around the base of his shaft and take him into my mouth until I am swallowin' him down. I make sure to give him all throat and tongue action as I hum and coax his swellin' balls. He grunts and groans as I suck him harder and faster. He fingers my pussy as he thrusts his hips upward. I make all nine inches of his cock disappear.

Seconds later, his body is twitchin' as I suck a new Louie bag outta him, swallowin' and swallowin' him down to the gristle. His dick gets harder and harder in my throat, the head swellin' and sealin' my airway. He slaps my ass.

"Aaaaah, fuck...aaaah, shit...suck that dick..." I pull him from outta my neck, then look up at him. "Aye, yo...why you stop? That shit was feelin' mad good. Get back on that dick, ma."

"I want you to face-fuck me, niggah, and smack my pussy up," I say, shiftin'my body around so that my head is hangin' off the bed. He quickly hops up off the bed. His hard dick bounces excitedly. I lick my lips. "Feed me that dick, lil'niggah."

I open my mouth as he positions himself over me. He

eases his dick into my mouth, slowly. Slides it in deep, then pulls back out. He teases my throat. My pussy, my ass, my entire body is on goddamn fire. I want that motherfuckin' handbag!

He lowers his balls into my mouth. "Suck them muthafuckin' balls, baby." I suck one in, then the other. With a mouthful of balls I make garglin' sounds, then moan as he leans forward and slaps my pussy. He slaps it again, makin' my clit swell. He pinches my clit, and I come, grindin' my ass down into the mattress.A few minutes more and his balls are replaced with his cock. I reach up and grab his smooth ass, pulling him deeper into my throat.

"Aaah, shit, aah shit, aah shit...I'm gettin' ready to bust...aah, fuck..."

I keep suckin' him, rapidly, tuggin' at his balls until he spurts out a long, thick, creamy load of bitter cum that coats my tongue as it slides all the way down into my throat. Ugh!

As nasty as his nut is, I still gobble him up, then shift my body. "Niggah, you better buckle up. The party's just gettin' started," I say over my shoulder as I hoist my ass up in the air. "Now go get a condom. And fuck me deep in my ass."

He grins. "Yeah, ma...I've been waitin' for some more of that."

I know you have, niggah.

Anal sex, whew...I can't get enough of it, boo. And Born

can't either. He loves havin' his dingaling slurped up in this ass. Mmmph. But I know some niggahs who think assfucking is nasty. And there are some closed-minded bitches who think it's nasty, too. They even feel if a niggah wants to fuck her in the ass that he's probably on the down low, but, boo, them some real stupid bitches if you ask me. Ain't shit downlow about a niggah wantin' to feel a woman's tight, hot ass wrapped around his dingdong from time to time. Now, if ass is all he wants, then, um, sugah-boo...you might have a potential problem on ya hands and you might wanna have a chat real soon, then monitor him closely. I'm just sayin'...

But a niggah who enjoys ridin' up in some ass to please his chick is always a delicious treat. And a bitch like me prefers bein' fucked deep in my ass over givin' up the pussy any day. Honeeeeey, with the right sized dick attached to a niggah who knows what he's doin', mmmph... he'll hit spots you never knew existed. But the niggah must...repeat, *must*...know what he's doin'. If he wants that ass, he needs to work his way to it. It's his business to get you relaxed and ready. He needs to have you beggin' him to fuck you in it. If he's too rough or too eager, you need to toss his ass off of you 'cause the mofo ain't ready for none of that tight, hot chocolate goodness.

Unless you have a well-primed asshole like mine, the last thing you need is to have some careless niggah rammin' his dingaling up in you, tearin' ya seams up. That will make for a horrible experience. And trust. There's nothin' horrible about it. That's not to say everyone who tries it is gonna enjoy it, or wanna do it again. And that's their right.

Bottom line, sugah-boo, ass-fuckin' ain't for everyone. And it ain't somethin' every niggah is worthy of. Oh, nooo, sugah, unless—again, you're like me and prefer it in the ass over all other sex, you need to be picky about who you givin' the ass up to. It's all about trustin' him to do you right, goddammit! And it's somethin' you have to want to try. You have to be open to it. You have to be comfortable with experiencin' new things. Otherwise, if you an uptight bitch, you will not enjoy it. Mmmph. But get you a niggah who knows how to stroke that hole just so, and you'll be in heaven, boo.

Born walks over to his jeans that are crumpled up in the middle of the floor and pulls out a condom. I eye his sexy ass as he tears it open with his teeth, then rolls the rubber down over his hard dick. In no time, he is back between my legs, his dingaling ready to drill all up in this bootyhole.

Ooooh, yes...the anticipation, the achin' excitement, of bein' deliciously stuffed with dick is causin' my pussy to clench. JT did me right this afternoon. And now Born's gonna do me right. And with the eighteen-hundred I collected from Born and the knot I got from JT's crazy ass earlier, I'ma be able to snatch me up some heels, a handbag, a belt, and some new damn shades to match. And I might even have a few dollars left over to hit up

Walmart to pick up a new thirty-inch flatscreen for Elijah and Joshua's room, since one of them bad-asses cracked the screen on the other TV they had. My goddamn kids don't take care of shit!

Anyway, although I love fuckin' and the smell of sex thick in the air, there's nothin' I love more than the smell of tax-free dollars, boo. And with the child support checks I get every month, along with the line-up of sponsors I have, I rake in a good five to six grand a month. And all I gotta do is keep it sexy; keep it wet, and always keep it ready!

I try to school these dumb bitches. You wanna run a niggah's pockets, you wanna niggah to put a ring up on it, learn how to keep his ass on his toes. Fuck his ass silly. Keep that niggah hungry for more. And don't ever, ever, not keep his dingaling wet. You do, and you'll make room for another bitch to jump up and down on it. Or have another ho collectin' that paper. And I'm not havin' it. I'm tryna fuck and spend up a niggah's cheddar-bake, boo. Thought you knew!

As I wait for my lil' stud daddy to stretch up this ass, I play with my clit. My fingers slip and slide over it. My pussy, still gushy from his tongue-fuckin', skeets again as I think about the ass-poundin' he's gonna put on me with that hard, thick eight-incher. Born has a pretty-ass dingaling. It's a thick cocoa-brown slab of man meat that curves slightly to the left and has a mouthwaterin' mushroom-shaped head attached. Oooh, I'ma wet, juicy mess.

"Pull open that fat ass for me," he says, inchin' in back of me. I reach back and pull it open for him, givin' him a full view of my ripe, puckered hole. I clench and unclench it. He slaps it, then buries his face up in it, stabbin' it up with his tongue, then a finger. The niggah already knows I'm ready. Shit, I've been ready!

And the key for beginners is to get ready. Rinse, relax, and lube it up, boo. Yes, hon, flush that ass out good, boo. Ya room shouldn't smell like you rollin' in a bucket of chitterlin's, okay. So wash, rinse, flush, and wash again. No niggah wants shit all up on his dingdong. So don't ever offer up no shitty ass. Well, not unless the nasty niggah is requestin' a load of shit on his stick. Mmmph.

A good ass fucka will do whatever he needs to in order to get you in the mood. Lots and lots of lickin' 'n kissin' 'n fingerin'. Yes, goddammit. He should be slappin' ya booty up real good before he dips his face between your cheeks and laps your hole with his tongue. Mmmm, yes… his strong fingers should dig into those humps as he licks and flicks, slurps and slaps, grabs and gropes. Ya ass should be his playground, boo. His hands, fingers, mouth, lips, and tongue should be all over you. Ya ass, ya pussy, ya clit, nothin' goes untouched.

And there should be tons of dirty talk and loads of lube, boo. And not that ghetto lube, like Crisco, margarine, or lotion. Oh, no, boo. That's a no-no. And definitely not a wad of spit unless you wanna get it in real gutter then, yes, let the jailhouse games begin and let the niggah split ya asshole down the seams, goddammit! Mmmm, on second thought...the idea makes my pussy purr. Yes, goddammit, I like it rough 'n dirty—rapid rabbit strokes or fast, long, deep thrusts. Feed this booty that dingaling, goddamn you! Make my pussy skeet, yessss!

Mmmph. But I also like it gentle 'n slow, boo. Yes, slow stroke this booty. Tip drill it. Slam in, slowly pull out. Slam in, slowly pull out. Oooh, yes, do me right! But no matter how I want it in this juicy ass, there must, must, must, be plenty of lube. Wet, Astroglide, Maximus, KY; it doesn't matter. Whatever helps the dingaling glide 'n slide in this hole is all that matters. Personally, I use Platinum Wet or Eros Body Glide 'cause they're high quality, long-lastin', and ooooh so good. Yes, boo, the more slippery it is, the better; especially if ya asshole isn't broken in right. And trust. I stay with a tube of lube and a butt plug in my bag. Always wet, always ready, sugah. Oooh, yes, goddammit!

Born slips two fingers into my pussy as he licks my asshole. I moan. Yes, hon, bein' relaxed is a must. I shake my hips from side to side, clappin' his face up. That's his cue to serve me the dingaling. He pulls his fingers outta me, sucks 'em, then presses his dick in between my cheeks, squeezin' them shut around his dick and glidin' it back 'n forth across my hole. Oooh, the dirty fucka is teasin' me.

"Put it in me now, goddammit!"

He slaps my ass, causin' it to sting.

"Fuck me in my ass! Give me the dingaling, niggah!"

A good ass fucka will take his time with you, boo. He's

gonna want you to enjoy it as much as he does. Yes, boo… he wants to get all up in that ass puddin' and pump his load deep inside you while ya pussy's skeetin' out that sweet, sticky cream. Yes, goddamn, you ain't had an orgasm 'til you experience havin' one outta ya ass 'n pussy at the same damn time.

I wind my hips. "Oooh, fuck me, daddy-boo."

Born pulls open my cheeks, pushes the head in; pokes my hole up with just the tip. Real slow at first, then he speed drills it. All head. Pop, pop, pop!

"Yessss, goddammit!"

In and out!

In and out!

Oooh, yes!

My hole opens wider with every thrust. Once you get used to the sensation of havin' a dick completely inside of you, you'll welcome it, like I do.

"Is this what you want, ma?"

I gyrate my hips, then push back on that dick. I want it all in me.

Finally he grabs me by the waist and rams his dick deep into my ass. Sparks shoot through me. "Is this how you want it?" He bangs it into me. "You like it…rough, bitch?" He grunts and groans with each thrust. "Aaah, shit yeah… take…all…this big…mmmph…dick."

I snap my neck, glancin' at him over my shoulder. "Niggah, puhleeze…mmmph…I can't even feel that lil'-ass…ooooh…dick… aaah…"

He slams in harder, slappin' my asscheeks up. "Yeah,

aiight, lyin'-ass slut...you know you feel this big-ass dick...up...aaah, shit...in them...mmmph...guts."

"Give it to me, lil' niggah...oooh, yes..." He gives it to me harder, practically liftin' me up off the bed with each thrust. "Is that all you got, lil'-dick niggah? Uhhh... mmmph...you better go back and find the rest of ya dick..." I squeeze my ass muscles, grippin' his cock as he moves in and out. He loves it when I call him all kinda lil'-dick niggahs. He knows and I know ain't shit little about his dingaling, but it makes him wanna fuck harder hearin' it, even if it is a buncha lies.

He grabs my titties. "Oh, shiiiiit...aaah, aaaah, aaaa aaah...ass is so fuckin'...mmmph...hot..."

"Yeah, niggah...you like that booty, don't you?"

"Mmmm, fuck yeah, ma...uhhh..."

He pinches my nipples as I pinch my clit. Pussy juice splashes outta me. He snakes his right hand under me and slips his fingers into my wetness. "Oh, shit, ma...ya pussy's so gushy. Yeah, mmm-hmm...cum all over my hand, ma...ooooh, shiiiiit..."

He long strokes my hole. Pulls his dingaling all the way out, then rams it back in. I keep squirtin'. Oooh, he's guttin' me good, goddammit.

"Get it, Daddy...that's it. Do me right! Just like that... fuck my shithole...ooooh, yes, goddammit...make it sizzle, lil' niggah..."

"I wanna nut in yo' ass, baby...you gonna let Daddy nut up in this ass?"

I laugh inside every time one of these lil' young niggahs

calls himself *Daddy*. I know it's all about strokin' a niggah's ego, so what do I care? I am a master at strokin' big dicks and even bigger egos, boo.

"Give it to me, Daddy…bust all all that hot cream deep in this booty, boo…oooh, ya dick is sooo good, Daddy…I love it when you fuck me in my ass…thick, black dick all up in these guts, niggah…aaah, yes…"

"Mmm, fuck…" He's ridin' this big, juicy caboose like it's on fire. "I wanna get my nut all up in this hot ass… uhhh…""

"Bust in my ass, Daddy…come on. Come on…give me that nut, boo." I hoist my ass up higher.

His body jerks. "Ohhhh shiiiiiit," he moans. "I'm cummin'. I'm cummin'." I squeeze my ass around his cock, clampin' down tight, releasin', clampin' down tight, releasin' again. I milk his dick real good, gettin' more turned on by the sound of the slush, slush, slurp of my asshole as he rams in and outta me. There's lots of squishin' 'n squelchin' 'n skin-slappin' 'n moanin' goin' on. It doesn't take much longer before this ass heat gets the best of Born and has him nuttin' deep in my ass, fillin' the condom up with thick, gooey cream. His body jerks again, then shakes. "Ohhh, fuck!"

He keeps grindin' and thrustin' inside of me as I wind my hips. I am creamin' again, outta my ass and pussy, all over his dinga-ling and fingers. He kisses the back of my neck and shoulders. His dick stays lodged in my ass 'til it softens and I squeeze it out.

Born collapses beside me, pullin' me into his arms. I glance over at the digital clock on the nightstand. It reads: 2:40 a.m. It'll be time to get my kids ready for school in fours hours.

I glance over at Born. His eyes are closed. He has his bottom lip pulled in. The niggah is still breathless. I grin. "You like that ass, lil' niggah?"

He slowly opens his eyes, lookin' dazed. "Whew... you...the...truth, ma," he says in between gasps of air. He takes a deep breath, then slowly blows it out. "Yo, real shit, ma. Ya sex game is sick. I need you on my team on da regular."

I smirk. *Of course you do. They all want Big Booty, boo.*

"Umm, Born?"

"Yeah, what's good?"

"I need that handbag, boo."

I grab his dick and start strokin' it. It slowly starts to thicken. I lean over and cover his dingaling with my mouth, suckin' hard, while teasin' his swollen head with my tongue.

Born gasps, "Ohhhh, shiiiiit...uh...I got you, ma. Goddamn..." He rotates his hips, fillin' my throat with his entire dick. I increase the pace, frantically bobbin' my neck back 'n forth. "I'ma hit you...mmmm...wit' da rest... uh...shit...later tonight..."

I'ma suck this niggah outta a pair of heels, too.

Juices start to seep from my pussy as I sniff in the lingerin' scent of my pussy 'n ass in his cock hairs. I cup his smooth balls, then slowly lick 'em before takin' his dick back into my mouth. I massage his balls while throatin' the niggah down to the gristle. I suck his ding-aling so good he grips the sheets, openin' and closin' his toes. He moans, "Ohhhh, fuuuuck…uhhh…"

I know the niggah's on the verge of crackin' his nuts, and I plan on suckin' down every goddamn creamy drop. "Give me that nut, lil' niggah," I say in between sucks. I shift my body so that he can play in my ass. "Stick ya finger in my ass, boo."

I make slurpin' 'n poppin' sounds with my mouth as he slips two fingers into my hole. He's knuckles deep in my ass. And I'm lovin' it! "Oooooh, yes…bust this big dick down in my slutty throat, niggah." I wiggle my ass. Clap it around his hand. "Give me that nut, boo."

"Yeah, uh, uh, uh…mmmm…I'm gettin' ready to nut, ma…aaaah, shiiiiit…"

"You gonna get me that handbag, boo?"

"Uhhh, shiiiit, yeah…I got…you, ma…"

Seven

Eleven A.M., I'm poppin' my hips outta Gucci with two shoppin' bags in tow. Like he said he would, the niggah Born came through—well, actually I met him downtown—with the rest of the thirty-six hundred dollars he promised me. So with that money and the money I got from JT's ass, I treated myself to a fifty-six-hundred-dollar brown ostrich shoulder bag. Yeah, it's a bit pricey. But, oh well. You only live once. And I live for handbags, heels, and a hard goddamn dingaling! So I bought it, along with a sexy-ass pair of six-inch Gucci heels that were on sale for four hundred bucks. I dropped six grand in less than twenty minutes, and still have another two grand that I'm gonna blow in Macy's buyin' my kids shit.

See. Most of these gold-diggin' bitches they don't know how'ta save. But I do. Yeah, I spend thousands of dollars on me and my kids, but I also know how'ta stash them stacks, too. And, although—on record, a bitch only got three hundred dollars in checkin' and another forty-six dollars in savin's—I have over forty-five grand stashed that I don't touch for nothin'. And, yeah, it's not a lot. But, guess what? For a bitch like me who came from nothin', it's more than what most have. I know what it's like to be broke and hungry and not know where the fuck you gonna lay ya head at night. Or whether or not some grimy, snake-ass niggah is gonna try 'n rape you or molest one of ya babies.

Thankfully, ain't no one ever try 'n steal my pussy or do no nasty shit to any of my kids. But a bitch still fell on hard times, and I had to do what I had to do to come up on top. Now, I do what I gotta do to stay there. And I don't give a fuck who don't like it. Big Booty's hood fabulous, sugah-boo. Thought you knew. And I'm always lookin' for a way to get me and my kids to the next level of hoodliciousness. So anyone who gotta problem with that can eat my ass out and choke.

I catch my reflection in the huge window of the Louis Vuitton store as I strut by on my way toward the escalators and smile. I'm a sexy bitch. Always have been, always will be. When I was a young girl workin' the yard, I had the lil'niggahs on the playground handin' over that snack money. When I was a teen workin' the poles, I had the niggahs droppin' the dollars, makin' it rain twenties, fifties, and Ben Frankies up on me. And now here I am still got the niggahs gazin' 'n dazin', tryna get them dicks and tongues glazed with this pussy and ass, while peelin' back them stacks. That's what bad bitches do, boo. Fuck a niggah so good that he's willin' to give you almost anything you want.

Yeah, this pussy's been all ran through, but guess what? It's still good 'n juicy and I know how'ta work the hell outta these muscles. And I'm lucky or blessed—or both, that my shit's not hangin' inside out from all the miles of dick I've rode down on over the last twenty-four years. And, hopefully, I can get another twenty, thirty, years more of mileage outta it before it starts to break-down and need to go in for repairs.

Okay, shit. I'ma confess somethin' to y'all's asses. I did go in and have my pussy rejuvenated three years ago. I sure did, boo. Had them tuck in these lips and tighten these walls. And I had one of my sponsors foot the ten-thousand-dollar bill, then let him be the first to slice his dingaling up in it once the doctor cleared me for fuckin'. Shit, it was the least I could do to let the niggah test drive his investment.

Anyway, I had me a real Grand Canyon-sized pussy before my surgery, but now...mmmph. This snapback pussy can bring a niggah to tears.

I open my Prada tote and pull out my ringin' cell. It's Day'Asia's fahver, Mustafa—Baby Daddy Number Four—with his six-four, size fourteen-foot self, and six-inch dingaling. And it's skinny. Fuckin' sinful! Why I ever let this lil' twig-dick niggah nut in my pussy is still a terrifyin' mystery to me. But he always kept a pocketful of money and the dick did feel good in my ass. So he was good for somethin'. But the niggah ain't good for shit now, except maybe eatin' pussy 'cause the limp-dick niggah-bitch's crazy-ass girl tossed lighter fluid up on it four summers ago while he was drunk and naked, then struck a match to his shit. Niggah's dingaling and balls went up in flames, and his ass ain't been right since. Yeah, her ass spent two years up in Clinton, the state prison for women. And his dumb ass was retarded enough to wanna ride it out with her when the dickless niggah should been tryna be a fahver to his daughter. Sorry-ass niggahs make me sick.

"Yeah?"

"Wassup, Cass? How you?"

I blink, walkin' through Bloomingdale's. "What you mean, 'how you'? Niggah, I'm broke. And I ain't seen no child support money from you for your daughter—you do know who that is, right?—in almost two goddamn years."

He sucks his teeth. "Here you go wit' this shit. Yeah, I know who my daughter is."

"Well, ain't that special," I say, stoppin' at the perfume counter. "'Cause she sure as hell"—I take a whiff of Jimmy Choo, turnin' my nose up—"don't know who the fuck you is." I pick up a bottle of Signorina by Ferrragamo. "She hasn't heard from you or seen you in almost three years, niggah. She's sixteen now, niggah-bitch, with big-ass titties bustin' outta the seams"—I spritz a lil' on my wrist and sniff—"and a hot-ass pussy that needs constant supervison." *Oooh, this is nice.*The bitch behind the counter with the pressed powder caked up on her face shoots me a look. I shoot her one back. "Can I help you, Casper?"

She shifts her eyes away. "Then stay outta my goddamn mouth..."

"What? I'm not in your mouth. Well, unless you want me to be."

"Niggah, puhleeze. I wasn't talkin' to you. And that lil' burnt-up dick of yours will never feel the inside of my mouth. So don't even do me, niggah. So why is you callin' me?"

"I know I fucked up, Cass. Shit's been hectic. I've been all cased up and I ain't makin' money like I used to. But I have a few dollars put up for you. I wanna do right by you and DaNaqueesha."

I pick up a bottle of Viva La Juicy by Juicy Couture. I sniff. Miss Juicy has always been one of my signature scents, along with Clinique Happy, Dior Me, Dior Me Not, and Gucci Envy. *Oooh, this is cute.* I decide to buy a bottle of it for Day'Asia.

"Niggah, who the fuck is a DaNaqueeta? The daughter you have with me is Day'Asia. Stupid bitch, how you not gonna know ya own daughter's name?"

"Damn, I meant Day'Asia. DaNaqueesha—not DaNaqueeta, is my other daughter. I got 'em mixed up. You know I know who my daughter is wit' you."

Shit, I ain't even know the niggah had other kids. Then again, I didn't give a damn if he did or not, which is why I never asked. Shit, I was only with his ass for two months before I found out I was pregnant. And it was over between us by the time Day'Asia was three weeks old.

"Mmmhmm. And how old is this lil' chick?" He tells me she's thirteen. That she lives in Paterson with her mother. "Mmmph. So you was raw pumpin' that lil'-ass dick every which way, huh?"

I peep Miss Powder Puff lingerin' around the counter so she can get an earful. I decide to entertain her nosey ass. "I wish that lil' piggy-dick of yours wasn't all burnt up. I'd let you run it in my ass like old times." I glance over at Miss Powder Puff. "Remember how it used to feel gobbled up inside my asshole?"

Miss Powder Puff blushes.

His voice dips low. "Daaaamn, we used to have some good sex. I still think about all the nasty shit we used to do. Cass, I really shoulda stayed wit' ya freaky ass."

When I was with this niggah it was all good for the first four months, then his ass started gettin' too caught up in the streets, grindin' 'n hustlin' and tryna sling that lil'-ass dingaling all around Jersey. Ain't no way a bitch like me was puttin' up with that shit. I don't care how much paper you puttin' out, I'm not gonna lay around waitin' for you to bring me home no disease. Oh no. That niggah had to go; especially when he had bitches bangin' on my door tryna bring it to me. Puhleeze. What the fuck I look like, fightin' over some niggah with a pencil dick? Them hoes had the wrong one. If I'ma fight some bitch over a niggah, trust, it's gonna be over one with a horse dick. And even then I still might tell the ho she can have him. Big Booty don't sweat no niggah, boo. Never have, never will.

I laugh. "Niggah, puhleeze. No, you shouldn't have. I'm glad ya cheatin' ass dipped. But I'm not gonna lie, niggah. You did feel good in my ass. But that's it. I couldn't suck the dick and I couldn't feel it in my pussy. Sorry, boo, that lil' dick of yours bored the shit outta me. I woulda never stayed faithful to ya ass, niggah. So it was best you ran off and fucked that barracuda bitch with them big-ass teeth."

"Damn, that's cold."

"Oh, well," I say, tellin' Miss Powder Puff to give me a bottle of Juicy and two bottles of Signorina. "So why is you callin' me?"

"I wanna see you and Day'Asia."

"Niggah, you can see Day'Asia if she's beat for you, but I ain't on the menu. The only thing I wanna see is some goddamn child support money. Where you stayin' now, anyway?" He tells me in Philly with some bitch he met on Facebook. This niggah's pathetic. "Mmmph, what happened to Barracuda?"

He sighs. "I don't wanna talk about that shit. It ain't work out."

I crack up, handin' Powder Puff two hundred dollars. "See, niggah. I already know what popped off. You let the bitch jail off you for them two years, then when she got out she traded ya ass in for some prison pussy. Some butch-dagger ho with a dick bigger than yours turned her ass out. Oooh, I know that musta tore ya spirits down. A bitch leavin' you for a ho with a clit bigger than ya dick. Mmmph. A mess, boo."

I can tell I done got the niggah hot. Oh well. Fuck him! He sucks his teeth. "I see some shit ain't ever gonna change. You still a bitch."

"I sure am..." I pause, blinkin' when Miss Powder Puff places my change down on the counter instead of in my hand. "Look, I gotta go. If you wanna see your daughter call me later tonight, and I'll let the two of you work it out."

"Aiight. I'll—"

I end the call and go off on Casper. "Ho, I handed you two hundred goddamn dollars, you pasty face bitch. And you shoulda put my motherfuckin' change in my hand. You don't toss no motherfuckin' money at me, like I'm ghetto trash."

She quickly apologizes. "I-I-I didn't mean to offend you. It was clearly not intentional."

"Bitch, I *am* offended. And it'll be intentional when I snatch that goddamn blonde wig off ya head and beat your face up for tossin' my money down on the counter. I want my motherfuckin' change put in my goddamn hand." By now we have an audience, and I don't give a fuck. "Bitch, I wanna see a manager, *now!* You white bitches stay tryna fuck our men, then wanna act like you better than us. I ain't ya slave or ya housekeeper, ho. And if I was, bitch, I'd be fuckin' ya goddamn husband and runnin' his pockets."

Oh, now this ho's shook. I got the bitch practically in tears. And. I. Don't.Give. A. Fuck! This bitch done cranked on the ghetto switch. And I'm ready to light it up.

When the store manager comes over, she eyes me and I eye her back. She's Cover Girl ready. Face beat to the seams. Hair pressed and parted in a sleek snatchback. Huge diamond studs in her lobes, icy rock on her hand. Oh, she's done up right. "Ma'am, what seems to be the problem here?"

"Boo, the problem here is this Casper bitch, tossin' my change down on the counter, like I'm trash. I've dropped six grand up in this motherfuckin' mall today, okay. Ain't shit trashy about me and I don't appreciate her tryna do me." I slam my tote up on the counter. "I feel like smashin' these goddamn perfume bottles in her face."

"Ma'am, please. Lower your voice. There's no need to make a scene, or make threats of violence."

"Bitch, I ain't bein' violent. And I ain't makin' threats. I'm tellin' you what I feel like doin' to that ho. I came up in here in good goddamn spirits until this bitch tried to do me." Miss Manager apologizes and sends Pasty Face on. I eye her as she scurries from around the counter like a damn roach.

I should chase that bitch down and stomp her out. I decide to keep it classy.

Six security officers make their way over to the counter. I eye them. And they eye me back. "What the fuck y'all lookin' at?"

"Ma'am," one of them says to me, "we're gonna need to ask you to leave the store."

"Bitch, I ain't leavin' to go no-goddamn-where." I hold out my hand. "I want my goddamn money in my hand.

And I want service with a motherfuckin' smile or you Robocops better call in for back up 'cause I'ma turn motherfuckin' Bloomingdale's out today."

Miss Manager quickly gathers up my change, then counts it out in my hand. I pull open my bag, then toss the money in. "See, all that bitch had to do was do me right, goddammit, and I woulda been on my merry way."

I gather my shoppin' bags, then get escorted outta the store by security. As soon as I get to the mall entrance, I tell 'em all to eat the inside of my ass. And I slap it for emphasis. See. They better be glad I'm not tryna get charged with lewdness today. Otherwise, I would drop these jeans, peel down this red thong I have on, then bend over and pull open these fluffy asscheeks for 'em.

I strut through the mall, ass bouncin', titties poppin', finally makin' my way to Macy's when I spot this tall, sexy, dark chocolate niggah pushin' a stroller with one hand and holdin' two shoppin' bags with his other. He stops in front of Bare Escentuals—a high-end skincare store, obviously waitin' for someone.

I blink when I realize who it is.

"Hey, boo," I say when I walk up on him. "Weren't you in Jasper's weddin'?"

He eyes me. "Yeah," he says in his deep, panty-wettin' voice. "I was his best man."

"I knew you looked familiar to me. I was there wrapped in a white dress, stealin' the show from Miss Pasha."

He laughs. "Oh, right, right. I remember you now."

Of course you do, niggah. I ask him his name. He tells me Dez. I take every inch of his dark-chocolately self in, wonderin' what that dingaling looks like naked and how it would feel stuffed in my ass.

I open my mouth to say somethin' else when the chick he's waitin' for comes outta the store with a bag in her hand. I ain't gonna front on boo-thang. The bitch is fly. Hair did, nails did. Footwear, handbag, and jewels on point. "Baby...." She pauses as she looks over at me.

Sexy Chocolate reaches for the bag in her hand. "Babe, she was at Pasha and Jasper's wedding."

She eyes me and smiles. "Oh, hi."

"Oooh, Miss Sugah-boo, your ears musta been ringin' 'cause me and Miss FeFe...I mean Felicia, were just talkin' about you and ya sisters last week when I went into the salon."

She blinks. "Oh?"

"Chile, I asked her how her messy cousins were doin' from the weddin'. And Miss FeFe gave me the filth on y'all."

She blinks again.

"And who do I run into, but you. It's a small damn world for sure. Oooh, I'm so glad you got your man back, boo." I eye him again, then peek down into the carriage at the lil' chocolate baby all dressed in blue. "Y'all look damn good together. And the baby is just as cute as he wanna be. And, girrrrl, judgin' by that rock on your hand somebody is keepin' her man very happy. But, I hope you keepin' ya eyes on that messy sister of yours, and keepin' her scandalous ass away from him 'cause Big Daddy is sexy, boo. And she done already had her hot pussy smeared all up on him."

I peep the niggah tryin' not to grin as she reaches for his hand. "Thanks. Well, you take care," she says, tryna hurry up away from me like I done said somethin' to hurt her feelin's.

"You, too, boo. And remember what I said. Keep that messy ho away from ya man. She fucked him once, she'll fuck him again." The bitch dips without sayin' another word. *Mmmph, what the fuck is her problem?* I think, headin' toward Macy's to do the rest of my shoppin'. *I can't stand a sensitive bitch.*

Two hours later, I'm finally walkin' up outta the mall, loaded down with bags. My cell rings. I stop and fish it outta my tote, then glance at the screen. It's Dickalina. "Yes," I answer, walkin' toward the parkin' garage.

"Bitch, turn the stank off in ya throat and let's go down to the Crack House tonight for a few drinks. Knutz ain't probably gonna be home until late. And I'm tired of sittin' up in this house waitin' on his black ass. So, let's make it pop-pop before that crazy niggah decides to come home and wreck my nerves for the night."

I disarm my alarm, then open the door and slide behind the wheel. I'm really not in the mood to be out with this ho tonight and I tell her so. She sucks her teeth. "See, bitch. You stay dissin' me, ho, and I'm not likin' it one damn bit. You act like you can't even go out wit' ya girl for a few goddamn drinks. Damn, Cass. Every since you got ya lil' truck you been actin' like a real stuck-up bitch."

I roll my eyes. This bitch is always tryna make someone feel guilty. "Trick, I'll be there at six. Have your ugly ass downstairs." I end the call pullin' outta the mall's parkin' lot. I ain't been out since last week so hittin' The Crack House and tossin' back some yak ain't a bad thing. *Mmmph. And I can serve it up in my new heels.*

Eight

Baaaaaby, tonight is *not* one of those nights where I'm in the mood for some crusty-ass niggah to be all up in my goddamn face. Everything about this niggah-bitch standin' here in my face is wrong. Dead wrong! From the half-moon fade up on his head—like, really, if you're balding, shave that shit off! There's nothin' sexy about a niggah's hairline startin' where his ears are. Not it! Not for Big Booty, baby! Then his I-Can't-Believe-It's-Not-Butter teeth are enough to make me wanna throw up. Oh, no. A niggah with yellow corn kernels can't get anywhere near this coochie 'n ass. What the hell I want with a mofo who has teeth that look like mini chicken McNuggets tryna gnaw up my pussy? I think not! Then this fool has the nerve to have two of his nuggets trimmed in gold.

I frown.

"So, I'm sayin', baby," he says, lickin' his big, juicy lips. "When you gonna stop playin' games and let Big Daddy chill with you?"

I blink. Tilt my head. Look around the bar for my girl,

Dickalina's dumb ass. I don't know why I even let her talk me into comin' down here tonight. She knows ain't shit poppin' off in this dump on a damn Wednesday night. It doesn't get live up in here until Friday and Saturday nights, then it's packed wall-to-wall with them thorough, get-money, hood-type niggahs. Otherwise, you're sittin', or in my case, standin' here looking in the face of rejects, like this busted-ass niggah gawkin' at me, hopin' to score some pussy.

I bring my attention back to him. "What was the question, again?"

"Yo, stop frontin', baby. You standin' here lookin' and smellin' all good, got me wantin' to take you home and do some thangs to you. When can I spend some time with you?"

I slowly lick the crushed peppermint and sugar from around the rim of my glass. I do it deliberately to fuck with his ass. Tonight I'm drinkin' a Gut Twister, one of the Crack House specialty drinks. And somethin' he'll never get to do. Not with me anyway.

"Easy, boo," I say, slidin' my lips over the tip of my straw, takin' a sip of my drink. He keeps his eyes locked on my lips. And the whole time I'm lookin' at him all I keep thinkin' about is him tryna gnaw my pussy 'n clit up like it's calamari. I cringe. "When you invest in a new set of teeth and let me run your pockets down into the ground, then I might consider it."

"Oh, damn. It's like that? Why you gotta go in on my teeth?"

"No, the question is why haven't you taken your black ass into a damn dentist office?" I walk off, shakin' my ass real hard and nasty-like. I sashay around the bar until I find Dickalina.

I hope this ho's ready to roll.

I spot her over by the pool table, laughin' it up with Buddha—this tall skinny, sexy-ass, light-skinned niggah from around the way I've had my eye on ever since he was sixteen, patiently waiting for his ass to turn legal. And now that he is, mmmph…I wanna fuck the shit out of him. He's with some other niggah who looks like someone I've seen somewhere before. And the closer I get to them, the more certain I am that I have. I may be bad with names. But there are two things I don't *ever* forget. The face of a niggah I've fucked and the face of one who's a snake. And since I know I ain't ever fuck his ass that leaves only one other option. He did some shady shit somewhere around me and his ass can't be trusted!

I eye him for a hot minute, then shift my eyes over at Dickalina. She's shooting a game of pool with Buddha. Mmmph. I heard he had a big-ass dick. And I'm ready to find out up close and personal. *I'm about to reel his ass in nice and slow.*

"Hey, girl," Dickalina says, lookin' up from the table. "You ready to blow this joint?"

"Ho, I've been ready," I say, walkin' up on them. "But now that I see Buddha's fine ass up in here, I might wanna hang around a little longer."

He grins. "Hey, Miss Simms. How you, ma?"

I smile back. "I'm good. But, I'd be even better if I was ridin' down on somethin' thick and hard."

He laughs.

Dickalina shakes her head. "Girl, you're a damn mess."

"No, I'm horny. And ain't a damn thing messy about that." Buddha eyes me, pullin' in his bottom lip. I imagine them pretty lips nibblin' on my clit, kissin' up and down my pussy lips. "Buddha, what you been up to, lil' niggah?"

"Shit. Chillin'. Tryna stay outta the heat. Shit's been kinda hot lately."

"I heard that. Yeah, your fine ass don't need to be gettin' clanked up."

He smiles. "Nah, I ain't beat."

"Where's your ole nappy-headed sister at?"

He laughs. "Locked up."

"Mmmph. What her dumb ass do now?"

"She violated a restrainin' order."

"Again?"

He nods. "Yeah."

I roll my eyes. This is like the third time her dumb ass has been locked up for violating a restrainin' order. Her ass is crazy! "Anyway…boy, how old are you now?"

"I'll be twenty-two in two weeks."

"Oh, really? I didn't know you were *that* old. Damn time flies. We gonna have to celebrate."

"Oh, aiight. That's wassup."

"You lookin' real fine, daddy. Where you been hidin' at, Buddha? I ain't seen you around in a minute."

He grins. "Yeah, I know. I was stayin' up top for a minute. I have peeps in Brooklyn so I was out there tryna lay low for a while."

I lick my lips. "You shoulda had me lyin' with you. I woulda dropped down real low for you."

He laughs.

"Damn, son," his boy says, laughin'. "She's ridin' you real hard."

I shoot him a "mind-your-motherfuckin'-business" look.

Dickalina eyes me.

"*Whaaat*, ho? Why you lookin' at me like that?"

She shakes her head. "Oh, nothin', boo."

"Oh, I ain't think so." I turn my back to her, blockin' her view. "So, anyway, Buddha. You out here gettin' a buncha pussy?"

Sneaky-Ass laughs, again. "Yo, son. Ya peeps wildin' for real."

I cut my eyes at him, again. *Oooh, this thug niggah's kinda fine, too, with his sneaky-looking self.* He has dreads and big, round brown eyes. And he reminds me of...damn, I can't think of the name of that little sexy mofo who plays on *CSI: NY.* Damn it!

"I do me," Buddha says, slicin' into my thoughts. I don't mind though 'cause I want the niggah slicin' into this ass, too. "Nothin' serious. But I gotta few *friends*."

"Mmmph. I bet you do. But I bet them young bitches can't handle no real dick, though. What you need is a woman who can fuck your lights out."

He and Sneaky-Ass laugh.

Where the fuck have I seen him? He looks at me. *He probably got one of them short, stumpy-type dicks with the big balls.*

I should walk over there and grab his damn crotch real good to see what he's workin' with. I shake the thought of yankin' his boxers down to see how the niggah's hangin'. "Lina, what's the name of that real-tiny, sexy niggah who plays on *CSI* and has those books out?"

"Oooh, Hill Harper, girl. Why?"

I walk over to the Hill Harper look alike. If he wasn't so short, he'd be fuckable, too. But short men don't do it for me. But there's always an exception to every rule if the price is right and if he has an exceptionally big dick. *Now where the fuck I know him from?* "Who are you?"

"AJ," he says, lookin' me up and down. *Damn, I've heard that voice somewhere before.* "Why? You see somethin' you like?" He licks his lips.

"Niggah, *you* the one eye-fuckin' me. So maybe you like somethin' *you* see."

He shakes his head, smilin'. "Maybe I do."

I laugh. "Boy, you wouldn't know what to do with all of this right here." I turn around and slap my ass, glancin' at him over my shoulder. I see the lust buildin' in his eyes. "If I sat all this ass up on your face you'd nut before you got your tongue in it."

"I'ma grown-ass man, ma; real shit. I handles mine. Believe that."

I step up in his face. Lick my lips. "That still doesn't mean you can handle *me*."

"Try me."

"You like your dick sucked?"

"All day."

I raise a brow. "Pull your dick out and let me see what you're workin' with then." When he doesn't budge, I roll my eyes. "I didn't think so, lil' niggah. You ain't ready for none of this."

Dickalina misses the pocket she called out. "Damn you, Cassie! You done made me miss my damn, shot fuckin' with your crazy ass."

The Hill Harper lookalike laughs. "Yo, ma. You wild."

"And I'm thirsty, too. How 'bout you make ya'self useful and buy me another drink. Then come back and let me tell you how wild I am."

He eyes me, suspiciously, then looks over at Buddha. "Yo, she's your peeps?" he asks.

He nods. "No doubt. Miss Simms good people."

"Aiight, ma. I got you, then. Whatchu drinkin'?"

"I *was* drinkin' a *Gut Twister*. But now I think I want me a *Blow Job*. Yeah, that's what I'll have. And tell him I want it wet and sloppy."

"Damn, it's like that?"

"It would be if I were talkin' about suckin' your dick. But it's not. That's how I want my drink, niggah. Sloppy and wet; that's no ice with an extra shot of Patrón."

He smirks. "Oh, right-right." I wait for him to walk off toward the bar, then turn to Buddha. "Where's that niggah from?"

He raises his brow. "Who, AJ?" I suck my teeth, rollin'

my eyes. He chuckles. "Oh, he's from Irvington. Why, you diggin' him or sumthin'?"

"No. I'm diggin' *you*, but you act like you all scared 'n shit. I know you ain't scared of pussy, lil' niggah. Anyway, that niggah seems real sneaky."

He takes a sip of his Heineken. "Nah, he's cool peeps. But, nah. I'm not scared, ma. And I'm def not scared of pussy. It's just that, you know. Jah and me used to be mad cool. And you his Moms and all. I'm not beat for no beef, feel me?"

I nod, knowin'ly. Jah, well Jah'mel—my twenty-one-year-old son, would be ready to whoop his ass if he even thought I was lettin' him hit this. But, shit. Who says he has to ever know?

"I won't tell if you won't," I say as I lightly rake my nails along his forearm. I glance over at Dickalina as she pulls out her phone and starts textin'. I roll my eyes. "Besides Jah's ass is still sittin' in the county."

"Oh, word? Damn. What he get popped for?"

"Child support and drivin' with a suspended license; what else. You know my baby ain't tryna do no real time. That boy loves pussy too much. He'd lose his damn mind if he had to do a state bid somewhere."

He laughs. "Right-right."

"Fuck!" Dickalina snaps, still textin'. "A bitch can't even go out and have a few drinks without Knutz's dumb-ass nuttin' up 'n shit. I'm so sick of this motherfucka."

I roll my eyes, iggin' her dumbness, keepin' my attention

on Buddha. "Anyway, so what you got good on you? I want some get right tonight."

He eyes me, puttin' the bottle to his lips, then tossin' his head back. I watch as his Adam's apple moves and down his throat as he guzzles the rest of his beer down. He burps. "Oh, shit. I didn't know you get on. But, nah, I don't hold no weight on me, ma. What you want, though?"

"Niggah, I ain't no fiend. I roll and smoke and get lifted, but you know I only do that with Darius and Jah'mel. So I'm not talkin' about that."

"Oh, damn. My bad, ma. Then what kinda *get right* you talkin' about?"

I lean in toward him, whisper in his ear, "I'm talkin' 'bout this"—I grab at his crotch—"I want some dick, lil' niggah." I squeeze it for emphasis.

"Damn."

I step off when Tupac's "Wonder Why They Call You Bitch" starts playin' from the jukebox. "Aaaah, shit. They takin' me way back with this right here," I drop down, then pop it back up. "This used to be my shit." I throw up deuces. "Rest in Peace, Tupac, baby!"

I jump up and down, stepping back up in Buddha's face, singing. "You wonder why they call me bitch?"—I pull him by the arms—"'Cause I take it in the ass, bring a niggah to his knees. Give him head. Suck that nut out and swallow. Fuck him in another bitch's bed..."

He starts laughin'. "You funny as hell."

"Yo, here you go, ma," Sneaky-Ass says, finally walkin'

back over and handin' me my drink. I tell him thanks.

Dickalina snatches her bag off one of the nearby empty tables. "Girl, Knutz is talkin' a buncha shit. Let's get outta here before he comes up in here tryna set shit off."

I suck my teeth. "Bitch, fuck him! We're out having a few drinks. Make that niggah wait. I keep tellin' your retarded-ass to get rid of him. You know that niggah's not playin' with a full deck. I told you I think they took half of his brain out at birth as part of an experiment. But you don't wanna believe me."

Buddha laughs.

Dickalina shakes her head. "Now why in the fuck would they do some stupid shit like that? Ain't nothin' wrong with my baby."

"Bitch, how the fuck I know? He was probably a part of some botched brain study to cure retardation."

"Whatever. I'm ready to go. I don't feel like arguin' with his ass all fuckin' night, so let's roll."

I raised a brow. "Girl, you better hop a ride on a dick, or walk. I'm not ready to go."

She huffs. "Oh, so now you not ready to go. Mmmph, ain't that somethin'. Just a few minutes ago you said you were ready to bounce. Now all of a sudden you done changed ya mind."

"Yeah, ho, I *was*. That's until I knew Buddha was up in here and *before* I knew Knutz was spazzin' out, poppin' a buncha shit. Now I wanna stay. Knutz's ass is already pissed, so let him stay pissed until we finish gettin' our drinks on."

"Well, yeah. You gotta point there. Fuck him then." When the music stops playin', she yells over to the bartender. "Hey, Leroy, let me get a Bloody Tampon; extra bloody."

Girlfriend knows she's gonna need that extra shot of yak 'cause the minute she stumbles through the door, Knutz's crazy-ass is gonna whoop the shit outta her.

I grin. "That's what I'm talkin' 'bout, girl. Show that crazy niggah who's boss."

Nine

"Girl…I'm so glad…that we…stayed," Dickalina says, leanin' over toward the passenger window. She has the window down so the air can hit her in the face. She's real twisted. Mmmph. There's nothin' worse than seein' a bitch that can't hold her liquor. "I had a nice…time…"

"Yeah, and a little too damn much to drink."

She turns to face me to say somethin', but starts coughin' and gaggin' and dry-heaving.

"Bitch, if you throw up in my damn truck, I'm gonna push your ass out and leave you on the damn curb for the garbage truck."

She glances over her shoulder at me. "Oh, fuck you, Stank Booty. Ain't nobody gonna throw up in yo' shit. I'm feelin' nice. I ain't fucked up. You always somewhere talkin' shit. That's why I can't stand ya ugly ass."

"Ho, shut the fuck up with your dumb, drunk, ghetto-ass. You the ugly one with that stank-ass name of yours. Dickalina." I laugh. "Who the fuck names their child *Dickalina?* Don't even get me started on your Rent-to-Own ass, boo-boo."

She leans her head back on the headrest. "Eat my ass."

I laugh. "Yeah, right. Save that shit-stained cavern for that buck-tooth niggah of yours. He seems to like his teeth brown any-damn-way."

She playfully swats me on the arm, chuckling. "Oooh, fuck you. You wrong for that. Leave my man's teeth alone. He can't help it if his triflin'-ass mammy didn't do anything about gettin' his teeth fixed when he was younger."

I frown, stoppin' at a light. "Ho, that six-foot-five, two-hundred-and-somethin'-pound niggah is a grown-ass man."

"Yeah, but he ain't got no dental insurance," she says, soundin' all pitiful.

I cut my eyes over at her. "That niggah stays robbin' niggahs. He should be takin' some of that money he gets for sellin' that stolen shit and invest it in shavin' down them damn horse teeth instead of trickin' it up on drinks and smoke."

"He don't be trickin' all of it up. He buys groceries and pays the cable bill too, ho. Don't get it twisted."

So this is what it's all come down to. Having a niggah to buy your groceries and pay your cable bill. And a bitch is cool with just that. I sigh. Shit, I know I'm ghetto. But at least I'm classy-ghetto with mine. But this ho right here, she's straight gutter-trash with hers. And you damn sure can't take her ass anywhere outside of the damn hood unless you wanna get embarrassed. And that's exactly why I only hang with her ass down at the

Crack House. She could never roll with me up to any exclusive-type shit.

I reach over and pat her hand. "Girl, what can I say? You definitely snagged the door prize."

"I know, girl. I mean, don't get me wrong. Knutz does some fucked up thangs sometimes. But y'all don't know him like I know him. I wish you'd get to know him a little better and you'd see. He's really a good man, Cassie."

Yeah, and he beats your ass. And is in and outta jail. Oh, and he robs niggahs. Yup, that niggah's real special. I yawn. "Okay, boo-boo. If you say so."

"Ohmygod, it feels like the truck's spinnin'. Can you slow the hell down?"

"Bitch, I'm at a light. That's your head spinnin'. Your ass is fucked up, ho."

She hangs her head all the way out of the window and throws up. When the light changes, I pull over to the side of the road and let her get herself together. "Bitch, you better not have gotten any of that nasty shit on the side of my damn truck or I'ma bang you in your motherfuckin' head. I told your dumb ass to not suck down all those Bloody Tampons."

She sucks her teeth. "Ho, shut up. I ain't get nothin' on your precious truck."

"Better not. That's what your drunk-ass gets for being so damn hard-headed. I told your ass them things were gonna sneak up on you. That's why I don't drink 'em."

She groans. "I can't wait to get in the house. Everything's goin' around and around. I feel like I'm on a merry-go-round. I need to lie down. Ohmygod…I'ma have'ta give Knutz some pussy; otherwise he's gonna think I've been out somewhere fuckin'. I hope I don't throw up while he's on top of me."

Ain't no one tryna hear that dumb shit. I roll my eyes up in my head, turning the music up.

"Ohmygod, can you turn that fuckin' music down? My head is poundin'."

"Uh-huh. That's not the only thing that's gonna be poundin' when you walk through that door. Knutz is gonna punch your ass into a wall."

I glance at the digital clock up on the dashboard. 9:10 p.m. *It's still early as hell. I shoulda put this ho in a taxi and stayed down at the bar a little longer.* I was startin' to have a good damn time talkin' shit to Buddha's fine ass. And after I tossed back my second *Blow Job* I was even poppin' shit to that niggah AJ, who I'm even more sure I've seen him somewhere before. It's gonna bother the shit outta me until I figure out how and where I know him. Anyway, I'm glad I slid Buddha my number on my way out the door. I told him he needed to call me before Jah got out of the county, then whispered in his ear, "I wanna fuck you." I stepped off with his eyes glued to my ass, and him grinnin'.

I pull up in front of Dickalina's buildin'. "Give me your phone so I can call one of your daughters to come down here and help you upstairs. I don't want your ass breakin' your neck tryna get up in the house."

Her phone starts ringin'. She fumbles around in her bag for it. "Hello?"

"Yo, where da fuck you at?" It's Knutz spazzin' out like a damn maniac.

"I'm downstairs, Knutz. Damn."

"Why da fuck you ain't been pickin' up your muthafuckin' phone, huh? You was 'posed to have ya sneaky ass home two hours ago. You stay on that dumb shit, Lina. Then you wonder why I be wildin' 'n shit. You gonna fuck around and lose a good man behind ya dumb shit."

I shake my head. "Ho, you need to stop lettin' that niggah talk to you any ole kinda way."

She covers the mouthpiece, the shoots me a look. "Bitch, mind your business. And stay up outta mine."

"Well, you can get the fuck up out my car with all that dumb shit y'all talkin'."

"Yo, who da fuck is that in the background?" I can hear him ask. "How da fuck you gonna be talkin' to someone else when I'm tryna have a civilized conversation with you, Lina?"

Civilized? Mmmph. Ain't nothin' civilized 'bout that coon.

"I know, baby," she says, lowerin' her voice. "I'm sorry. Let's talk about this when I get upstairs. Can you come down and get me? I'm tore up, Knutz, baby. I need you to help me walk into the buildin'."

The next thing I hear before the line goes silent is, "Hell no! You must be outta ya rabbit-ass head. I told you to bring ya black ass home two hours ago, and you said fuck me. So, fuck you and ya drunk ass. Crawl ya dumb ass up to da muthafuckin' buildin'."

She stares at the phone. "Hello? Hello?" She grunts. "I'm so fuckin' sick of his black ass. I'm good to that niggah, you know what I'm sayin'?

"No, bitch, I don't."

"Every time his ass gets locked up, I'm the one runnin up and down on gawtdamn stinkin'-ass buses and trains 'n shit to see his ass. And I ask him to do me one gawtdamn thing and he can't even do that. I'm done with his ass. I'm putting him out."

Okay, I've heard this before. "Uh-huh," I say, diggin' in my handbag for a stick of gum. "Keep playin' the violin. I've heard this tune before."

"I'm serious, Cassie. I'ma put his sorry, black ass out tonight."

"Mmmhmm. Let me know how you make out with that."

She sucks her teeth. "I know you don't believe me, girl. But watch."

"Yeah, whatever. Do you."

"Don't judge me. I—"

I cut her ass off before she starts tryna explain her craziness. "Look, I would love to sit out here and play Love Doctor, boo. But I need to get my ass home. Call one of your daughters and get one of their lazy asses to come down here and help you up."

"They're not home. They're at the movies."

"On a school night?" I ask, looking at her like she's

half-crazy. Then again, she is. Any ho who'd name her daughters Candylicious and Clitina is a fuckin' nut. Candylicious is eighteen, still in the tenth grade. And Clitina is fifteen, still in the eighth grade and fuckin' everything that's not nailed down. Them hoes ain't have half a chance from the start with a mother named Dickalina.

Shit, you can say what you want about me. I might drink and smoke with my two oldest sons. And, yes, I've even tossed a bar up alongside 'em and gotten locked up with 'em. Hell, I've even fucked a few of their friends. And, yeah, I have a buncha damn kids and baby daddies, *and?*

Every last one of my kids is taken care of. I'm not sittin' on my ass collecting a welfare check, so there you have it. But I do get my food stamps every month. Shit, that EBT card comes in handy. Ain't no shame in my game; these kids gotta eat. And, yeah, I've had to do some extra things in the past to make sure my kids were provided for, like fuckin' and suckin 'niggahs for money when I wasn't beat to fuck with 'em; like carryin' drugs for a niggah, or two, across state lines, and into prisons. Like boostin' shit—although, I only did that shit for three years. And I had my reasons for doin' them. I needed to survive; period, point blank.

Beulah, with her ol' crusty old ass, had thrown me out on the streets at fifteen because she said she was tired of lookin' at me and my two babies. She didn't give a fuck where I went. Said she couldn't keep takin' care of some hot-in-the-ass little girl who used her pussy more than she used her own. So what the hell was I supposed to do? My babies needed milk and Pampers. And we needed a roof over our heads. I had to do what I had to do to survive. So boosting shit is how I did it. And, yeah, okay, fuckin' older niggahs—not too old, though, because I was scared into believin' old men gave you worms. So, I never fucked anyone over forty. Well, one time...okay, okay, like six times, I sucked a fifty-seven-year-old man's dick for a hundred dollars while he fingered my pussy. That lasted for four minutes and thirty-seven seconds. It was always the fastest hundred I'd ever made in my life.

Then I started fuckin' with them stolen credit cards for about four years until about two years ago. Shit started gettin' too hot. And after my connect got his dumb ass popped and sentenced to fifteen years for identity-theft, fraud, and a buncha other crazy shit, I had to drop that scheme real quick. I don't mind doing a little county time when I have to, but a bitch with a state number ain't it. Them horny bitches in there would be tryna ride my ass with a broomstick. Oh, no thank you! That's not how I do mine. Shit, I still have seven more kids to raise. So, I knew when to pull out. Still, that niggah had some good dick, too! Dumb fuck!

And yeah, growin' up, I mighta spent more time on my back, or in the backseat of some horny niggah's car, then I did in school, but the one thing a bitch can't ever say about me is that my kids are ever dirty, raggedy, disrespectful, or dumb as fuck.I mighta dropped out of school when I was fifteen. But my three oldest boys graduated. And because of them, I took my ass back and got my GED two years ago.

So, yeah, I'ma hot mess. But, guess what? I don't give a fuck. I'm real with mine. But this drunk-ass bitch right here—love her dearly—is all over the damn place and lets her kids do whatever the hell they want. I wish the hell Day'Asia would; I'd beat the snot outta her ass.

Dickalina presses her cell up to her ear. "I'm callin' that niggah back and tellin him to stop dickin' around and get his ass down here now."

"Yeah, you do that and hurry up about it. I wanna get home."

"I'ma tell him to get his ass down here now, or he can pack his shit and bounce."

I roll my eyes up in my head. *Yeah, picture that.* "Way to go, girl."

"Knutz, are you comin' down here or what?...I'm not fuckin' crawlin' nowhere, niggah. Stop playin', niggah..." She must have lowered the volume this time. I can't hear what he's sayin'. "...was not...I was out with Cassie...I know I was 'posed to braid your hair and trim your cock hairs and the crack of your ass..."

I frown. Oh, this bitch has gone too far. Now she's shavin' the niggah's asshole. What's next, her fuckin' him in it?

"...but you weren't home," she continues, "...was not

out braidin' no other niggah's head. And I wasn't out fuckin'..." She huffs, openin' the truck door. "...Are you comin' down here or not?...Knutz, stop, damn...I told you. We were down at The Crack House...no, there wasn't. I—"

I count to ten, then snatch the phone from her. "Knutz, stop the shit, niggah. Get ya retarded ass down here and get this drunk bitch outta my fuckin' car so I can get home to my damn kids. Shit, you can argue with her ass upstairs."

"Ohmygod, Cassie, don't do that shit." She tries to reach for her phone. I slap her hands away. "Give me my phone."

"Nah, fuck that," he says. "She was 'posed to been had her ass home to braid my hair and handle some other thangs. And she out trickin'."

I blink. "Oh, you got the wrong party favors on the table, niggah. She was out having a few drinks, period. And so what if she was out tricking? Good for her. As much dirt as your grimy-ass does, you have no room to be talkin'."

"Yo, c'mon, Booty. Chill wit' all that shit you talkin'."

"Niggah, you don't know me like that. Have we fucked? It's *Big Booty.* Somethin' your woman wishes she had. Not no motherfuckin' *Booty.* Don't get it twisted..."

"Wait a minute, bitch," Dickalina snaps. "What you tryna say? That my ass is flat? Well, my man loves my ass just the way it is. Thank you very much."

I ignore her. "Let me tell you somethin', Knutz—you

ain't shit, niggah, okay. Lina is the only ho dumb enough to put up with your triflin' ass and you walk around here givin' her your shitty drawz to eat..."

"I ain't dumb," she says, suckin' her teeth. "Stop callin' me that."

"You are too dumb, ho, for lettin' this motherfucka keep shittin' on you. He can't even bring his sorry ass down here to help your drunk ass up in the motherfuckin' buildin'. Fuck this niggah. He done pissed me off now."

"Damn, Cassie," he says, soundin' offended. "You don't have'ta go in on me like that. I don't want no problems wit' you."

"I know you don't, niggah. So get your black ass down here and come get your woman before I run up on you with a hammer and knock them big-ass fronts out your raggedy-ass mouth."

He laughs it off. But I'm fuckin' serious. And he knows it. I can't stand him. And I've been lookin' for a reason to set it off on his ass. He might beat up on Dicklina's dizzy ass, but I'm not the one. "Aiight-aiight. I got you. Give me a sec to put some drawers on. I'll be right down."

Ugh! I disconnect, handin' back her phone. "He'll be down in a minute."

"Ohmygod, girl, why'd you do that? You're always startin' shit. Now I'ma have'ta hear his mouth all fuckin' night."

I glance at the time. I can't believe I've been out here with this ho for almost fifteen damn minutes. "Bitch, I got his ass to come down to get your drunk ass. So don't pop shit to me. Next time handle your damn liquor and we won't have to go through all this dumb shit."

My cell vibrates.

"Here comes Knutz's dumb ass now," she says, stumblin' out of my truck. I watch as her ass hits the ground, pullin' out my phone.

"Damn, girl, you fucked up," he says, helping her up off the ground.

"I told you to come help me, Knutz. You want me to suck your dick and nuts real good, baby, huh?"

I let out a disgusted sigh. I glance at my screen. It's a text from my twins' fahver, Vernon. Baby Daddy Number Eight.

I WANNA C U

"Nah, you good," Knutz says to Dickalina. "Maybe in the mornin', baby. I'ma eat that drunk pussy though, aiight? You can swallow these nuts later."

I roll my eyes, textin' back. NIGGAH WHERE'S MY CHILD SUPPORT CK?

"Listen, motherfucka," I snap at Knutz. "Shut my motherfuckin' door!"

He lifts Dickalina up over his shoulder, shuttin' the door. "Cass—"

"Niggah, don't say shit to me," I snap, rollin' the window up in his face. Busted-ass motherfucka!

I GOT IT W/ME ALONG W/THIS BIG AZZ DICK ☺

I suck my teeth, textin' back. FUCK ALL THAT SMILEY FACE SHIT. BRING MY $!!!!!

Ten

"Damn, Cass," he says the minute I step out of my truck and walk toward him. He's leanin' up against the side of his Lexus. Tall, jet-black skin with thick waves and a nice juicy, black dick, he's looking real fuckable in his True Religion jeans, pullover and Timbs. He has a dark-colored fitted pulled down over his eyes. I swear if the niggah wasn't so fucked up in the head, he'd be a good catch. But there are three things wrong with his ass. Okay, four. One, he's a chronic liar. Two, he's a chronic manipulator. And, three, he's chronically full of shit. And four, the niggah's credit is all fucked up. I must have been trippin' off of some serious wet to have ever gotten caught up with his ass. And had his triflin' ass not been pokin' holes in the condoms I wouldn't be standin' here looking at his dumb ass now.

He licks his lips. "Took you long enough."

I roll my eyes, holdin' out my hand. "Whatever, Vernon. Give me my money." He grabs my hand instead and pulls me into him, reekin' of weed and alcohol.

"Fuck outta here. Let me get some tongue. I've missed you, girl."

He tries to kiss me. I frown, pushin' him back. "Wrong answer. I want my money."

He eyes me. "Damn, Cass. Why shit always gotta be about money with you? I'm tryna get some pussy."

I laugh in his face. "Niggah, it's *always* gonna be about money with me. And your deadbeat ass is already two months behind in your payments, so you might wanna make good on what you owe me tonight, or I'ma have you fucked up."

"See. Here you go threatenin' me with that shit again. And didn't you have to do anger management twice already?"

"Threat? Boo-boo, you know I don't make idle threats. I make promises. And I keep every one of 'em. And no, I ain't do no goddamn anger management, niggah. I know how to manage my anger just fine. Now where's my motherfuckin' money?"

"Damn, cut a niggah some slack. Shit's hard right now," he says, reachin' for me again. This time I let him pull me into him. Hell, the niggah has a nice hard body. "And so is this big-ass dick." He presses it into me, grabbin' my ass.

I slap his hands down, narrowin' my eyes. "Stop with the lies. I know your ass is workin'. Don't have me drag you into court for child support."

He eyes me, raisin' a brow. "Damn, you'd do me like that when you know I'm already on that shit with my other baby mothers?"

"Your other baby *muhvers* and your *five* other chil'ren ain't no concern of mine. My sons are."

"That's fucked up."

"No, *you're* fucked up."

"Yeah, aiight. Whatever. I wanna see my sons."

"Oh, now all of a sudden you wanna see your sons. Just a few minutes ago all you cared about was gettin' that dick handled."

"Yeah," he huffs, "until you fucked up the mood with ya bullshit. Now, fuck it. Let me see my sons. And I'm out."

"Niggah, stand in line. You ain't seein' them tonight. Not unless you peelin' off my money. I shouldn't have to keep goin' through this shit with you, Vernon. Your sons don't live off of air. It takes money to feed and clothe them and to keep a roof over their heads. I shouldn't have to use my other kid's child support checks to feed *your* sons, niggah."

He sucks his teeth. "Well, no one told ya ass to have a buncha babies."

I blink. "And no one told you to poke holes in the goddamn condoms, either. But that didn't stop you, now did it, motherfucka?"

"See. Here you go with the okey doke.If you didn't wanna be pregnant, then you shoulda had an abortion. But you didn't. So stop talkin' all that dumb shit. I ain't tryna hear all that, Cass. You know like I do you wanted to be knocked up."

This niggah's crazy!

"Niggah, get a grip. You punched holes in the goddamn condom, tryna trap a bitch."

"Yeah, whatever. You still coulda got ya guts scraped out if you didn't want any more kids. So save that shit. Let me see my sons, Cass."

I decide to let him think what he wants. I am not in the mood to argue with his nutty ass about this shit again. Not tonight. I glance down at my watch. It's a little after ten. "Uh, I don't think so. It's a school night. And you don't have my money. So if you wanna see your sons... you know, the ones you think I shoulda aborted, then you need to bring your ass around here at a decent hour and come with my goddamn money. Now either hand over my shit so I can ride down on your face real quick. Or get the fuck on and stop wastin' my time."

"Aiight, aiight, damn. I'm only fuckin' with you," he says, diggin' in his pocket and pullin' out a handful of bills. He hands them to me. "Here, this is all I got on me until next week."

I count out what he's given me, then count it again. All ones! "What the fuck is this shit?"

He frowns. "What the fuck it look like? It's money."

"No, niggah. It's bullshit. And it looks like you tryna play me. That's what it looks like to me."

He huffs, shakin' his head. "See. This shit right here is why ya ungrateful ass can't keep a man."

"Niggah, what the fuck you think thirty-seven motherfuckin' dollars is gonna do for your sons? Not a goddamn thing!"

He frowns. "Then give the shit back. That's the problem with you stupid bitches, you ain't ever satisfied."

I slap him. "Get the fuck off my property."

His jaw clenches. "See. Here you go with ya hands, again. You always buggin'; for real, Cass. And then you wonder why I left ya crazy ass."

I put a hand up on my hip. "Oh, puhleeze. Be clear. *You* left me because I *let* you leave. I was done with your triflin' ass after the first three weeks. But, it's mighty funny Mister 'That's Why I Left You' that your black ass keeps comin' back for *me*." I throw the money in his face. "Take your ass back home to that fat, bald-headed, flat-ass bitch you fuckin'."

"Bitch, suck my dick with that dumb shit."

"Oh, motherfucka, I see you wanna get it poppin' out here, huh? I'ma show you how I'll suck your dick, niggah." Before he knows what hits him, I whip out my can of mace and do him real dirty.

"Aaaaah, fuck! Shit! What the fuck!" He coughs and gags, droppin' down to his knees.

"You bring your black ass over here for some pussy," I say, kickin' him. "But don't have my motherfuckin' money"—I kick him again, then slap him—"then got the nerve to think you can talk all slick to me. Motherfucka, I've been good to you. You asked me to stop givin' that fat bitch of yours a hard time, and I did. But now I'ma take it to her goddamn face for her not knowin' how to keep a leash on your black ass."

I spray him again. Then crack him upside the head with

the empty can. Got his ass down on the ground crawlin' and howlin' like a wounded hyena for someone to come get me off of his ass. I don't know why these niggahs gotta take me there. I swear, a bitch can't go out and have a few drinks in peace without some motherfucka tryna serve it to me.

"And I'ma stomp ya ugly-ass sister's face, too, the next time I see the bitch." I run over and grab a stick layin' in the yard and start beatin' him across his back and head with it.

"Aaaah, shit! Someone come get this crazy bitch the fuck off of me! Yo, help! Aaaah, fuck! Shit!"

My front door swings open. Day'Asia, Joshua, Elijah, Isaiah, and one of the twins, Tyquan, come runnin' out of the house with baseball bats and kitchen knives ready to set it off. When they see that I have the situation under control, they stand and watch me stomp on him. Well, everyone except Tyquan. When he realizes it's his no-good daddy, he starts goin' off.

"Mommy, stop fuckin' my daddy up! Get off him! I know he ain't do shit to you! All he was probably tryna do is come see me and Fuquan. You always gotta mess shit up!"

I stop hitting Vernon with the stick long enough to yell at him. "Boy, get your grown ass in the house, talkin' shit to me, before I beat your ass next. Day'Asia, take his fresh ass back on in the house before I have to go to jail tonight." She yanks him by the arm and drags him back into the house with him talkin' shit all the way. I see

Fuquan, looking out of the livin' room window with his arms folded. He knows like I do that his daddy needs to be fucked up.

"Did that niggah put his hands on you?" Joshua, my fourteen-year old, wants to know, walkin' up on me with a knife in his hand.

"No, his ass ain't that crazy." I throw the stick down, pick up my things, then walk toward the house, leavin' him on the ground, coughin' and gaggin' and groanin' in pain. Sorry-ass motherfucka!

Five-thirty in the mornin', I'm up fightin' with these bad-ass kids of mine to get up and get ready for school. "Day'Asia, wake up," I say as I open her door and walk in. She groans.

"Aiight, Ma. In a minute."

"No. Your minute's up. Now." I close her door, then make my next stop to Marquelle's and Joshua's room. I'm glad Marquelle's at his fahver's house. He's one less person I have to yell at this mornin'.

"C'mon, Joshua, it's time to get up," I say, walkin' into his room. I gasp as he quickly throws the covers up over himself. I've walked in on him jerkin' off, again.

"Dang, Ma! Why can't you knock first?"

"Boy, don't talk shit. Bust your nut *before* six instead of playin' with your damn dick every mornin' and you wouldn't have to worry about me knockin'."

He sucks his teeth. "I'ma start lockin' my door, for real."

"You do and there won't be no door. Now finish up doing whatever you were doing with that little thing in your hand, then get your ass up. And I want that bed made today, if not you'll be sleepin' your ass on the floor. And you better wash them nasty-ass hands!" I walk out, shuttin' the door.

I make my way into the twins' room. "C'mon, Tyquan and Fuquan," I say, walkin' over to their beds and gently shakin' them, "get up, babies."

"Noooo," Tyquan says, pullin' his Spiderman comforter up over his head. "I don't want to."

"Ty, c'mon now, be a good boy and get up for Mommy."

Fuquan gets up without issue. I give him a hug and kiss, then tell him to take his shower. "That's Mommy's little man. You're such a good boy."

"I love you, Mommy," he says, rubbin' sleep from his eyes.

"I love you, too, Punkin. Make sure you wash your face and brush your teeth, okay?"

"Okay."

I take a deep breath, knowing it's gonna be one of those days. "Tyquan, c'mon," I say, yankin' the covers back. "Let's go."

"Leave meeeee alone! I'm not talkin' to you. You hit my daddy!"

I frown. Take another deep breath because I feel myself about to go the hell off. I yank him up by his collar and start shakin' him. "Boy, don't play with me. I don't give up fuck about you not talkin' to me. Ya black-ass daddy ain't shit. Now get your ass up before I fuck you up. And don't give me any more of your goddamn back talk. Do you understand me?"

His bottom lip quivers.

"I said, do you understand?"

He stares me down.

I shake him again. "Do you want me to punch your motherfuckin' eyeballs out?"

"N-n-no."

"Then get your ass up. And don't let me have to come back in here." I let him go, then walk down to Elijah and Isaiah's room. I call their names. Tell them to get up. Elijah is the only one who does. Isaiah doesn't stir. I stomp outta his room and into my bathroom.

"I'm sick of you motherfuckas in here doin' whatever the fuck you want. When I say get up I mean get. The. Fuck. Up. Y'all wanna stay up all motherfuckin' night, and think your asses don't have to get up for school..."

I fill a bucket with cold water, then go into the kitchen and dump four trays of ice cubes in, then march back into his bedroom. I yank the covers back and toss the whole bucket of water on him. "Get the fuck up!"

He jumps up, screamin'. "What the fuck?!"

"Don't you 'what the fuck' me, boy." I bang him upside his head with the bucket. "I said get your ass up. And I want all that water cleaned up, now!"

He sucks his teeth, mumblin' shit under his breath.

But he does what he's told. Next stop is goin' back to make sure Day'Asia's up.

"Day'Asia!" I scream, swingin' open her bedroom door, causin' it to hit the back of the wall. "Get your black ass up! And why the fuck is this room so nasty? There's no reason for you to be so goddamn triflin'."

She jerks up in bed. "Alright, dang, Ma! I'm up!"

"Don't 'dang, Ma' me. Get your lazy ass up and outta bed! And I want this room cleaned. And if I have to come back in here again, I'm gonna beat your ass sideways." I walk out.

One hour and fifteen minutes later, Day'Asia, Joshua, Elijah, and Isaiah have already left for school. And the twins and I are on our way out the door. "Stop it!" Fuquan screams at the top of his lungs. "Mommy, will you tell Ty to stop it? He's hittin' me."

"Ty, get your jacket on and let's go. And keep ya goddamn hands off your brother."

"Tattletale," he says to Fuquan. I hear a smack, then yellin'.

Fuquan runs into the kitchen and grabs a knife out of the drawer. "I'ma fuck you up!" he yells, chasin' his brother around the house. Tyquan runs out the door, laughin'.

I run out the door behind them, yellin'. "Fuquan! Fuquan! Get your ass back in this house with that motherfuckin' knife!"

"No!" he screams, chasin' his brother around the yard, wildly swingin' the knife. "I'm gonna cut his black ass open!"

"Fuquan! It's too early in the mornin' for this shit! Get your ass over here and bring me that goddamn knife!" He ignores me. I kick off my heels and chase him down, snatchin' him by the back of his hoodie. I dig my nails into his arm, clenchin'my teeth.

He is cryin' and cursin'. I don't know where the hell these bad-ass lil' fuckers get their filthy mouths from but it's outta control. "I told you to tell him to leave me the fuck alone!"

"Hahahahah, pussy," Tyquan says.

"Fuck you, bitch!" Fuquan yells back. "See, you don't ever say anything to that fucker!"

I smack him on his ass.

"What I tell you about your filthy-ass mouth? Don't have me wash your goddamn mouth out with bleach. Now get your evil ass in the house and wash your damn face and put some lotion on it, then change that shirt." Tyquan is still laughin'. "Tyquan, get your ass in the truck. I'm sick of this shit. Every goddamn mornin' I gotta go through this bullshit with the both of you. Keep it up, and I'ma put both of your asses in a home."

I go back inside and beat Fuquan's ass for pullin' a knife out on his brother and for having me chase him. "Now, I don't want any more shit outta you for the rest of the day. Do you understand me?"

He sniffles and coughs. "Yes."

I give him a hug. "You don't ever pull a knife out on your brothers, or your sister, you hear me?" he nods. "If they fuck with you, you beat them with your fists. You save the knives for a motherfucka out in the streets, you understand?"

He nods again. "Yes."

"Good. Now give me a hug and let's go."

I set the alarms, lock the double locks. Then head to the truck. I open the back passenger door and beat Tyquan's ass for makin' them late for school. "And if you go up in there and open your mouth, I'ma fuck you up some more. Now put your goddamn seatbelt on. I don't know why you kids gotta make me get ghetto every fuckin' mornin'."

"'Cause you are ghetto," he says.

"Boy, I'ma ghetto my fist in your mouth if you keep talkin' shit."

I slam the passenger door, then hop into the driver's seat. I start the engine and roll the windows down. Then frown when I realize somethin's wrong with my truck. It's drooping low in the back. *What in the hell?* I get out and check the rear tires and they're flat. Someone has either slashed 'em or let the air out of 'em.

"Motherfuck!" I snap, grabbin' my handbag and pullin' out my cell.

"Mommy, what happened?" Fuquan wants to know.

"Someone flattened my goddamn tires."

Tyquan laughs. "That's what you get!"

"Boy, shut your damn mouth before I punch you in it," I snap, waiting for Vernon's ass to pick up.

"Yeah?"

"Motherfucka, I know you flattened my tires."

He laughs. "I don't know what the fuck you're talkin' about."

"Laugh all you want, pussy motherfucka. But let's see how funny you think shit is when I beat your bitch's ass the next time I see her, okay? Then I'ma take a brick to your head. See you in court, niggah. Now laugh on that." I disconnect.

"I hope my daddy jumps on yo' ass," Tyquan says, kicking the back of my seat.

I swing around in my seat. "I mean it, Ty. Shut your ass up before I reach back there and punch your motherfuckin' front teeth in. I see why bitches be fuckin' their kids up and settin' their asses on fire and doin' all other kinda crazy shit to 'em. You about to take me there in one hot second. Now kick my seat again and I'ma break your goddamn ankles. Now try me."

Eleven

"Wassup, Cassandra?" Benji, the six-six, two-hundred-eighty-pound bouncer, says to me as he's scannin' me with the wand to make sure I'm not carryin' heat. It's Thursday night and The Crack House is about to be swarmin' with dicks and hoes. And after the damn mornin' I've had with my damn bad-ass kids I need to let it all hang loose. And anything's likely to pop off up in here tonight. Thursday to Saturday it's the only time they step up security and charge a twenty-five-dollar coverage charge. Ladies are free before ten. And I like being perched up at the bar facin' the door to see who's comin' and goin' before it gets packed. "We not gonna have any problems outta you tonight, are we?" His breath smells like hot shit.

I scrunch my nose up. "Niggah, damn. Whose funky ass you been eatin'?"

He frowns, givin' me a confused look. "What?"

"Your mouth, niggah. Smells like somethin' crawled up in it and died."

He ignores me, repeatin' himself. "Are you gonna be on your bullshit tonight, Cass?"

He's talkin' about the little situation that popped off up in here last month when I ended up havin' to take it to some young ho's head. This little, young messy, hot-in-the-ass ho jumped up in Dickalina's face—I know, I know. The shit had nothin' to do with me. Still, she started poppin' off at the mouth real greasy; makin' all kinda threats over some dumb shit that had to do with Knutz's no-good ass.

"You ugly bitch," she said in front of her little fan club—an entourage of about six hood rat bitches all in their early twenties. She had the neck-rollin' and her fingers all up in Dickalina's face. "Suck a dick and swallow! Knutz don't want your dumb ass, anymore. So you need to stop riding the niggah's dick with your nasty, stretched-out-pussy self. Yeah, he told me how loosey-goosey you are. Knutz don't even like fuckin' ya old ass. Why? 'Cause he's gettin' all this young, tight pussy; somethin' you wish you had. Now stay the fuck away from my man, Dickalina. Silly-ass bitch!"

That ho was really goin' in on Lina like she had snatched herself the million-dollar door prize. And although, it didn't have shit to do with me, I thought the whole thing was funny. 'Cause I knew, whether it was true or not, that Dickalina's dumb ass was gonna believe whatever game Knutz spit outta his mouth. And she did; hence why she's still with the no-good motherfucka.

"What the fuck you laughin' at, bitch?" Miss Hot-in-the-Ass snapped, givin' me the evil eye. "You can get it too, with ya ho-ass. Yeah, I know who you are with ya trampy ass."

Wrong! Now it was obvious that the bitch hadn't Googled me, or done her homework around here because had she, she woulda known that I am not the one to fuck with. So she had to get schooled. See. Unlike Dickalina, I'm not gonna go back and forth with some ho; especially some live firecracker. Nope. I'ma stomp her fire out real quick. And that's exactly what I did when I reached over the bar and grabbed that bottle of Ciroc and took it to her damn head. She didn't know what hit her until she hit the damn floor. I knocked her ass out, then turned around and finished drinking my drink. And I dared any other bitch to say another motherfuckin' word sideways to me, at me, or anywhere around me. They didn't. They dragged that bitch on up outta here and went on about their business.

I suck my teeth. "Niggah-bitch, how am I supposed to know? Do you see a crystal ball growin' outta my forehead?"

He laughs. "Yeah aiight. Take ya evil ass on, wit' ya sexy self. But don't have me toss ya ass up outta here tonight, Cass."

"Then make sure you keep them slimy bitches you let up in here in check," I say over my shoulder.

"I'm dead-ass. You start any shit tonight and your ass is gonna get banned from comin' up in here. You always wait until the weekends when I'm working to start shit up."

"Well, it's Thursday, niggah. The weekend doesn't start until tomorrow night. Dumb-ass."

"Yo, you know what the fuck I mean."

"Whatever, Shit Breath. I do what I do. If a bitch steps outta pocket, you already know I'ma tear this motherfucka up. You should know by now I don't mind gettin' arrested, or goin' to jail. I'll be bailed out before the ink dries. So save your energy. Just lock nine-one-one on speed dial, and do what you gotta do."

He shakes his head, wavin' the dude who was in back of me up to get frisked. A double-chinned chick with bad skin and a fucked-up weave is sittin' behind the bulletproof glass, eyein' me. I stop in front of the booth and open up my bag, fishing out a card. I slide it to her. "Sweetie, you need to hit up my girl, Pasha, down at Nappy No More and let her handle that weave. 'Cause that mess you got goin' on is dead wrong, sugah-boo." She rolls her eyes, buzzin' me in. Oh, well. I tried.

As soon as I walk through the door Maino's "Million Bucks" starts playin'. Whew, every time I hear this shit it makes me wanna lick all over them sexy tats on his body and fuck the skin off his dick. "Aaah, shit..." I snap my fingers and pop my hips through the door.

"Damn, do that shit, ma," one of the regulars sittin' at a table not too far from the door yells over the music. "You workin' that shit, baby."

"Whew, goddamn! She gotta ass on her," I hear someone else say. I glance over my shoulder and see that it's a niggah I ain't never seen before. From what I can see, he's a tall, brown-skinned niggah, rockin' a pair of baggy jeans, a red and white striped button-up with a red fitted on his head and Timbs on his feet.

I spin around and give them a little extra treat, shakin' it all fast and nasty-like. He's sittin' at a table with two other niggahs. They howl and clap, egging me on.

Buddha spots me as I dance. I pretend I don't see his frontin' ass. Niggah still hasn't called me. And all that does is make me wanna get in his boxers even more. He's sittin' up at the bar, alone. It's still kinda early so there are still a lot of seats empty around the bar. Buddha's eyes roam my body as I dance, stoppin' every so often to twirl my hips, then booty clap it a bit. Once it gets packed up in here, I'll turn it up on blast and really work the floor. And by the end of the night I'll have every motherfucka up in here droolin'. And ready to make it rain up in this bitch. I always do.

As the music fades, I pop my hips over to the bar, sittin' my Chanel bag—compliments of another one of my young sponsors—up on the bar.

"What's good, Ms. Simms?" he asks as I saunter over to him. "You lookin' real good tonight. How you?"

I ease up on the barstool, then lean into him. "I'm good; *very* good. But you wouldn't know that 'cause you keep runnin' from me."

He laughs. "Nah. I'm not runnin', ma."

I roll my eyes. "Niggah, quit. When you gonna stop playin' games and lick my pussy and eat this ass?"

"Nah, no games, Ms. Simms; real shit. I'm sayin'...you

sexy as fuck. But I told you I don't want no heat from Jah. Even though we ain't cool like that anymore, me and Jah used to be mad tight, feel me? I mean, if you wasn't his moms, I'd definitely be wit' it."

"No, that's what I'm tryna do. *Feel* that dick. And I already told you Jah'mel's ass is locked up. So what that got to do with you and me? Besides, he ain't my pussy's keeper. And what he doesn't know won't hurt him."

He nods his head. "True, true. But you know muhfuckas stay runnin' they mouths."

"Well, they can't run their mouths unless a muhfucka's givin' them somethin' to tell.

He grins. "True."

"Whatever, muhfucka," I say, playfully mushin' him in the side of his head. "You actin' like you're scared of pussy."

"Nah, never that."

"Well, then you're scared of all of *this* pussy?

"Oh, damn. You think?"

"Niggah, I know."

"Yeah, aiight. I already told you what it was. What you drinkin' tonight?"

"Hmm, I wanna sip on some cock cream, yours for starters." I lick my lips.

Big Mike, one of the bartenders, catches my eye and gives me a head nod. I wave him over, eyein' him as he makes his way over to us. They call him Big Mike 'cause everything on him is big—big head, big eyes, big nose, big lips, big hands and fingers, big feet, big balls and an extra big dick. The only reason I haven't fucked him is because he's my third son's daddy's relative.

Big Mike smiles at me. "Wassup, Cassandra? Where's ya girl tonight?"

I flip my wrist. "Where else, sniffin' up underneath Knutz's musty balls."

He laughs. "Yo, you ain't right."

"Well, I ain't wrong, either."

"I heard that. What can I get you tonight?"

"Let me get a Cum Cannon. Go heavy on the nut tonight." Code for extra Bailey's and Crème de Cacao.

"Comin' right up. Oh, I got that new Crack Pipe on deck if you wanna hit that, instead."

I snap. "*What?* I know you're not standin' here tryna play me, Mike. You and I go way back, niggah. I smoke weed. Not crack! Take that shit on somewhere else, comin' to me with that. Your motherfuckin' fat-ass mammy and stank-ass sister smoke that shit, niggah."

Buddha laughs. "Oh, shit. She just went in, son."

Big Mike starts laughin' too. "Yo, Cassie, yo' ass is crazy as hell; for real, baby. Now you know I wouldn't play you like that. I already know how you get down. I'm talkin' about the new drink we're featurin' tonight."

I place a hand up over my mouth, feeling bad that I called his mother and sister out like that. "Oops. Well, why you didn't say that shit in the first place? My bad." I ask him what's in it. He tells me Wild Turkey, 151, and Rumple Minze—a peppermint liqueur. I frown. "Uh, I'll pass. I can think of somethin' a whole lot more excitin' to get strung out on."

He laughs. "It's all good, baby." I apologize for gettin' at his mom like that. "Yo, you know I don't sweat shit like that, baby. We cool. How's my lil' cuz doin'?"

"Da'Quan's fine." He's my nineteen-year-old. And Big Mike happens to be Darryl's nephew. "I'm tryin' to keep him from lettin' them fast-ass hoes out there get him caught up. I keep tellin' him to keep that long dick of his in his pants and that head on his shoulders in them books."

"That's wassup. He's still at Howard?"

"He sure is. He has two more years to go. And I'm not about to let him fuck it up on some wet pussy." Out of all of my boys, Da'Quan and my seventeen-year-old, Marquelle, are the two who I know are gonna do somethin' really good with their lives. I am so proud of 'em both. And I will stomp a hole in any bitch who tries to bring either one of 'em down. Then I'ma stomp their asses out for lettin' 'em.

He smiles. "Yo, that's wassup. Stay in my lil' cuz's ass." He digs in his pocket, pullin' out a wad of money. He peels off three bills, then slides them to me. "Give him this. And tell him I said to hit me up when he gets a chance. I wanna rap to him."

"I sure will," I say, foldin' the Benjamins in half, then again. I stuff the money down in my bra. "Now hurry up with my drink. I need my throat coated with somethin' thick and creamy." I shoot a look over at Buddha.

Big Mike laughs, shakin' his head as he walks off.

"Yo, you wild for real for real," Buddha says. "You spazzed out on dude real quick."

"Mmmph. He'll get over it. Big Mike knows how I am. And if you got ya mind right, you'd know too."

He slings back his shot glass. "Aaah. I know how you get down; you real thorough with yours."

"And you know I like the young boys, too."

He nods. "Yeah, I heard."

I eye him as he tosses back another shot glass, then licks his lips. He chases it back with his Heineken. "Uh-huh. And what else you heard?" He shifts in his seat. I can tell I've put him on the spot. I smile. "It's cool. You can tell me."

"Nah, you cool peeps. I've never heard anyone say anything sideways about you. Know what I'm sayin'?"

"Buddha, baby. It's okay. I know niggahs talk. They're worse than bitches." I lean in closer, slide my hand between his legs on the sly, then whisper in his ear. "I know you've heard I have some real good pussy, and a deep, fat ass. You heard I like to be fucked in all three holes, haven't you? Keep it real."

He rubs his chin. Openin' and closin' his legs. "Yeah, sumthin' like that."

"And you not curious?"

"I ain't sayin' that."

I rub his dick until it thickens. "So what's the problem?

"You already know what it is."

I suck my teeth. "Niggah, man up. And handle this pussy like I know you can. I don't have on any drawers."

He grins. "Damn, ma," he says, glancin' around the bar. He takes a swig of his beer. "Why you fuckin' wit' me like this?"

"I wanna fuck you. Don't you wanna feel your dick deep in my ass?"

He fans his legs open and shut. His dick is extra bricked. "Word is bond, you got me wantin' to get into sumthin'. Shit."

"Let me make you feel good," I say to him as Big Mike walks back over with my drink. I slide my hand up on the bar.

Red Café's "Fly Together" starts playin'. I hop off the barstool and start hoppin' and droppin' it. I grab my drink from off the bar, and pull him by the arm. "Dance with me."

He glances down in his lap. "Nah, no dice, ma; not yet."

I laugh, shakin', bouncin', and poppin' my ass to the beat with him takin' in my every move. The way he is looking at me, I can tell I got the niggah thinkin', got him wonderin', about burying his dick in me. My pussy and ass are on fire! I dance up a light sweat, slowly twirlin' my body. He watches me watchin' him. Then tosses back another shot of Rémy, chasin' it with another swig of his beer. I lick my lips, purposefully, when he slides his hand down in his sweats. To handle that hard-ass dick, I'm sure.

I dance over to him and whisper in his ear, "I want

your balls deep in my ass, Buddha. Let's stop playin' this game. I know you wanna fuck me. So let's do this, *tonight*."

He grins. "I'm not playin', niggah. I want some dick—yours."

He glances around the bar, guzzles down the rest of his beer, then brings his attention back to me. He grins, standin' up. "Aiight. Fuck it. Let's roll."

Twelve

Buddha and I can barely make it through the door of the nasty little hole in the wall motel he's rented out. But, who cares? Big Booty's here for the dick. Not the décor. And I plan on fuckin' this young niggah *down.*

I watch as he reaches behind him and lifts his shirt up over his head, then slides outta his sweats. I take his body in. His arms are muscular and toned. There's a curly patch of hair in the center of his chiseled chest; strands of hair around his dark nipples. Heat shoots through my pussy as I glance down at the trail of hair that runs down his rippled stomach into his boxers. I lick my lips. This motherfucka's body is sick. *And now for the moment I've been waiting for,* I think as he steps outta his boxers. My eyes light up as his long dick swings and bounces, freely. It is a big, juicy beef sausage that hangs over balls the size of extra-large brown eggs. And tonight, a bitch wanna scramble 'em up right!

My asshole and pussy clench in anticipation. "Oooooh, that's a nice, big dick," I say, walkin' over to my handbag and pullin' out a bottle of Astroglide and two condoms—one for my ass and the other for my pussy. I will let him fuck me in all three holes because I know, understand, the art of fuckin' a niggah so good that you not only have him beggin' for the shit again, but willin' to do almost anything you want to get it. When I am done riding Buddha's cock, I will not only have him eating my ass, but outta the palm of my hands, too.

He gives me a cocky grin like, "Yeah, bitch. I gotta big dick. Tell me somethin' I don't know."

"I'ma call you lil' daddy tonight," I tell him, walkin' up on him, then droppin' down to my knees.

"Oh, word? I got ya lil' daddy, aiight"—he grabs at his dick—"right here."

I take his dick in both hands. "You better hope"—I kiss the tip of his dick—"you"—twirl my tongue around it—"can"—lick along its right side—"hang"—lick the left side—"with me, lil' daddy"—I look up at him, cuppin' his balls—"'cause I'ma fuck and suck the shit outta you."

He palms the back of my head, winds his dick into my mouth. "Aaah, shit…I got you, ma."

I take the niggah by surprise and swallow him whole. All eight inches down in one gulp. His knees buckle. After all the men I've had to use to get what I've needed, I learned how to suck and fuck a niggah outta his mind, and his money. I press my nose deeper into the curly patch of pubic hair, allowin' my throat muscles to massage the head of his dick.

"Aaaaah, shit, baby...damn, suck that dick...oh, shit... godd-dddddddamn...uhhh..." The niggah starts to stutter. "Fffffuck...aaaaah, shit..."

I moan. The sweet, musky man scent from his pubic hairs is turning me on beyond belief. My pussy is wet and drippin' juices. I take my right hand and reach in back of me, sticking a finger into my ass. I moan. Bob my head back and forth, pullin' his dick up outta my throat every so often to tease the head with my tongue, then gulp it back down. He squats, thrusting his hips into my face. I moan again. My pussy skeets as he skull-fucks me. I suck him harder, creatin' a vacuum while makin' wet, sloppin' sounds. Hoover, Bissel, Dirt Devil, Eureka...none of them vacuums on the market could suck a dick up better than me.

I make the niggah sing out. "Oh. Oh. Oh. Oh, fuck. Oh, fuck, fuck, fuck. Uh. Uh. Uh, shit."

My pussy is aflame. I'm ready to fuck. Ready to feel him stretch this ass open. I pull off his dick slowly, suckin' all the way up, lickin' the shaft, then tonguin' the slit and lappin' up the precum oozin' out. When I finish, I smack my lips, pullin' my mouth off and standin' up. I grab him by the neck and bring his lips to mine. I kiss him. I can tell I've caught him off-guard with this. But I don't care. If I suck your dick there are three things you will do. Eat my pussy, eat my ass, and kiss. Lucky for him he responds back; his tongue slippin' deep into my mouth.

I push into him, forcing him to walk backward toward the bed. I shove him, and he falls back on it. "Oh, shit… it's like that?"

"Shut up, niggah," I say, crawlin' on top of him, pinnin' him down. "Yeah, it's like that; makin' me wait for this dick, niggah, like I'm one of them dumb, silly bitches you fuck."

"My bad, ma." He opens his mouth to say somethin' else and I shut him up with another kiss, savorin' the remnants of booze and weed on his tongue. His dick is pressed up against his stomach. I position my pussy along its shaft, then slide back and forth; up and down its length. I wet his shaft up, then grind on the head.

He grunts. "Yo, you 'bout to make me nut."

"Grab my ass, niggah."

He does. I lean forward and kiss his neck, his shoulders. Breathe in the mixture of cologne and weed that clings to his skin. He closes his eyes and quietly moans in the back of his throat. "You feel how wet my pussy is?"

"Yeah, ma…"

"You like how I'm grindin' it all over your dick?" I slide the mouth of my pussy over the head of his dick, again, and milk him.

"Oh, shit yeah…goddamn, ma. Aaah, fuck…that shit feels good… Aaah, shit. Pussy real hot, ma. Feels like that shit's suckin' my dick…"

"You think you can handle this big, wet, pussy?"

He groans. "Fuck yeah…"

"I'm about to give you somethin' them young bitches will never give you."

"Oh, word? Mmmph…I wanna fuck, ma. You got me horny as fuck…got my shit hard as hell…I wanna feel my dick in that pussy."

I keep grindin' and slidin' up and down his cock until I coat it with a thick, creamy nut. I lick and suck his shoulder. Then run my tongue from his shoulder to his muscular chest, feeling another nut buildin' up in the back of my deep, steamy asshole.

I finally let go of his wrists, slidin' one hand between my legs, using two fingers to press on my clit while my other hand pinches his left nipple and my tongue circles around his right one. I stop what I'm doin', lookin' up at him.

"Be clear. I usually run a niggah's pockets before I give him any of this sweet pussy and ass, but I've had my eye on you since you were sixteen, niggah. I've been waiting a long time to fuck you."

He grins. His eyes are half-closed, enjoyin' the wet slide and glide my pussy's doin' over the head of his dick. "That's wasssup, ma."

"Mmmhmm. Yes, it is. But know this. You will eat this pussy and ass before you put your dick up in it. And if you don't know how to do either, you're gonna learn tonight."

"Nah, I got you, ma. I love eatin' pussy…"

"And ass?"

"No doubt."

"Good." I shift my body around into the sixty-nine position. "Then start eatin', niggah." I lower my pussy down on his lips. And his mouth opens wide, welcomin' its sticky heat. He sniffs in its honeyed scent, stickin' his tongue in my slit. I purr and smile. My pussy hums; my heart racin' with anticipation. "Slap my ass, lil' niggah," I urge before slippin' his dick back into my mouth.

He smacks it, softly.

"Harder! Make it shake, niggah."

He smacks it again. "*Oooh*, yes, that's better. Slap it like I stole somethin' from ya bald-headed, crusty-ass momma! Make my ass pop, motherfucka." He hits it again, this time hard. And my clit jumps. "Beat that ass up, niggah. Make it sting."

He smacks both of my cheeks, causin' me to wiggle my ass. My pussy makes swish-swishy sounds as he slurps it, jabbin' his tongue in and outta it. "Yeah, lil' daddy... you're a good pussy eater. Now work on my asshole. Get it nice and wet."

He moans, flickin' his tongue across my hole.

I moan back. And swallow him again, suckin' harder than before. He bucks his hips upward, gruntin' as I swallow his dick balls-deep. He has a mouthful of ass in his mouth, his tongue teasin' and relaxin' my hole.

"Yeah, lil' daddy...get that hole open nice and wet for this dick." I spit on his cock and jerk him off. "I'ma bury this big-ass dick, niggah deep it my ass. You wanna stuff this dick in my ass, niggah?"

He grunts again, grabbin' a handful of ass and pullin' it open as wide as it will go, darting his tongue in and out of it. My pussy starts to bubble up and boil over. Steam and juices splatter out onto his chest as I press down on my swollen clit.

A few seconds later, he slips a finger into my ass, then pulls it out and slides in two. Twistin' and pumpin' them in and outta me. As Buddha finger-fucks me, I bob my head up and down on his dick while humpin' his face. Waves of pleasure vibrate in the pit of my pussy, then explode, causin' my body to jerk.

I glance over my shoulder. Tell him to let go of my ass. Then bounce this big booty on his face and make it clap around his head. I'm suffocatin' him. He gasps, grabbin' my ass, then gulpin' in air.

"What, you can't hang with all this fat ass, niggah?" I pull open my asscheeks for him. His tongue goes around and around in tight wet circles toward my asshole. The tip of his tongue runs against it. My pussy aches for his tongue, his fingers; his dick. My asshole too. I reach beneath me and ease the aching in my clit, takin' his dick into my mouth.

Buddha's slurping and lickin' and fingering my ass while I'm slurping and lickin' and gulping his cock, hands free, while I play in my pussy. "I wanna feel your dick in my ass, lil' daddy... You ready to fuck me in it?"

"Yeah, ma...word is bond. You got my shit bricked."

We shift positions. I am now on my knees. Back arched,

ass raised high, ready and waitin'. I watch him over my shoulder as he tears open a condom with his teeth, then rolls it down on his cock. I pull open my ass as he grabs the lube. He squirts some over his cock, then into my hole. I moan in anticipation. Big Booty wants the dick, deep.

"Hurry up, niggah. Feed my ass that long, thick dick."

"I got you, ma. I'ma 'bout to give you all da dick you want."

His thick head nudges its way into my asshole, and I shiver in anticipation. But a bitch is gettin' antsy. He's takin' too long to mount this ass and fuck it. He inches himself in back of me, runs his dick along the crack of my ass, grinds on it. I grind back on him, slippin' two fingers upward into my wet pussy. "Niggah, will you hurry up? Put your dick in. I want you to pound my ass raw."

He stabs his cock deep into me. "Yesssss, that's it. Take my ass, niggah…oh yes…don't be scared to beat it up. They don't call me Big Booty for nothin', baby. Handle this ass like a real niggah."

He fucks me fast. Pounds me mercilessly, reaching his hand under me and toying with my clit. I pinch my nipples. I am moaning. He groans, thrusting into me again and again. "Daaaaamn, ma…aaaah, shit…goddamnit-motherfuck…ass is good…"

I grin. "Beat it up, niggah…yeah, you got all that dick in this ass, baby…Big Booty loves it in the ass, niggah… aaah, yesssssss…What's my name, niggga?"

He grunts as my hole clenches around his shaft. "Big Booty, ma...aaah, fuck...daaaaaaamn..." His body jerks as he tightly grabs my waist. "Mmmmm...aaah...mm-mmph..."

"Give me that nut, lil' niggah...got that asshole wide open...come all up in Big Booty, baby..." I am jabbing two fingers upward into my pussy, rapidly stroking my G-spot. "There you go, lil'-niggah...fuck that hot ass... ooooh, yes...I'm gettin' ready to come..." His cock pulses and I can feel the spasms shoot through me as he pumps harder inside of me. Seconds later, he pulls outta me and peels off the condom, coating my ass and back with his sticky cock cream. As he is comin', his body shudders and I squirt a horny stream of steamy juices, soaking the sheets beneath me.

He kisses me on the back of the neck, then grinds his cum-soaked dick into my ass. My asslips pucker in disappointment that he doesn't shove his dick back in. I clench and unclench my muscles, jiggling my ass for him.

"Slap it, lil'-niggah," I say over my shoulder. He slaps it, then smears his nut all over my ass with his fingers, spelling out his name. I smirk. "Oh, what you doing, lil' niggah, tryna mark ya territory?"

He laughs, collapsing beside me, catching his breath. "You da truth, ma, real shit."

I roll over onto my side, facing him, and deliberately let my gaze travel down to his cum-glistened dick. It looks so...tasty. And I have the urge to suck it clean. But I resist, for now. I take his cum-glazed fingers and slip them into my mouth, suckin' them clean. His nut tastes bitter.

He shakes his head, eyein' me.

"What? Why you shakin' ya head like that?"

"Real shit, you dangerous, ma. That was good as fuck."

"Oh, you liked that ass, huh?"

"Hell yeah...that shit feels like a pussy, nice and wet and hot, yo."

I roll over on my back and lift up my legs. "So imagine what this wet pussy feels like." I bend at the knees, pullin' open my pussy. "Fuck my pussy now."

Ten seconds later, he is hoppin' up and rollin' on another condom, sliding his dick into my pussy and fuckin' me relentlessly. And I. Am. Loving. It!

"Fuck, ma," he breathes. His body is gleamin' with sweat, his hips viciously thrustin' as he works my pussy over. I lift my legs around his waist, raking my nails down his muscled back. "Daaaamn, this pussy's...so...fuckin'... deep..."

"Uh-huh, uh-huh...mmmhmmm...come for me, lil' niggah...big-ass dick...mmmmm..."

It doesn't take long for his body to start jerking and he is yankin' his young, horny dick outta my wet, gushy pussy, leaving it feeling empty and alone, snatchin' the condom off and nutting all over my stomach and titties.

"Listen, ma, I wanna—"

I place a pussy-scented finger to his lips, silencing him. "I'ma keep lettin' you fuck me, under one conditions."

He arches his brow. "Oh, word? What's that?"

"If I ever need you to handle somethin' for me, that you handle it."

"No worries. *Anything* you want or need, ma. I got you."

He pulls me into his arms and I smile, snugglin' against him.

Exactly what I thought!

Thirteen

It's three A.M. when I pull into my driveway, well-fucked and exhausted. Buddha gave me what I needed. Some young, hard dick and a good deep fuckin'! And now I'm ready to hit the sheets and sleep like a baby. The front door opens, and Darius walks out as I am climbin' outta my truck.

"I hope you had a good time," he says, eyein' me. He says this with attitude, but I don't pay the shit no mind. I'm in too good of a mood to set it off on his ass. "The bar closed two hours ago."

I narrow my eyes at him.

"I'm just sayin'...you know I gotta go home now and hear Shenille's mouth the rest of the night if she hasn't locked me out." Shenille's his ghetto-ass, live-in baby momma who I can't stand. The bitch tries to control Darius and uses their son as bait to keep him with her. Desperate-ass hoes like that bitch make me sick.

I pull in my bottom lip and think before I scream on him. One for puttin' up with a bitch who keeps lockin' him out of a spot he pays all the bills at. And, two, for questionin' me like he's my goddamn man! I decide to give him a pass.

"It's late as hell and I ain't beat to be up beefin' wit' her ass. I gotta open the shop mad early in the mornin'."

Darius and two of his friends from the projects opened a barbershop, Gutter Cuts, over in Irvington last year and it's been goin' really good for them. But for a hot minute, I was kinda worried his ass was gonna end up being a damn bum-ass niggah like his fahver—Baby Daddy Number One, in and outta prison. When he was fifteen and sixteen, his ass stayed in trouble with the police. And when his ass got sent down to Jamesburg for eighteen months, I just knew he was gonna come back out and keep doin' dumb shit until he ended up somewhere doin' football numbers. But so far he's done me real proud, with his sexy, chocolate, broad-shouldered self. Like Jah'Mel, he's tall like his fahver and has his dark skin tone and dimpled chin, but he has my round brown eyes, nose and mouth. All eight of my baby daddies are at least six feet tall and packin' over eight inches of dick. Well, except Day'Asia's sorry-ass fahver. And I already told you about his ass. Anyway, speakin' of these baby daddies, Darius' and Jah'Mel's fahver, Cecil—well in the streets niggahs called 'im Trigger because he loved poppin' off guns and pistol-whippin' anyone who crossed 'im—was my first real fuck. I was twelve. He was all of sixteen.

Yeah, I had let boys at school play with my titties and

grind up on my ass. And I had even jacked off a few cocks. But to actually have my pussy pulled apart and stretched to the seams by a hard, thick dingaling was all new to me, thanks to Trigger. He sucked on my young tender titties, licked my swollen pussy, and showed me what sex was all about. Trigger mighta been sixteen, but he was goin' on damn near thirty—the streets can do that to you—and had fucked a lot of older bitches who loved young cock so he was real experienced in the sheets. He taught me how to suck a dick; taught me how to take a dick; taught me different positions. Then the niggah taught me that good dick don't mean shit if the niggah it's attached to ain't shit. Still, he had me wide open. I didn't give a shit about anything. All I wanted was Trigger and his dick. It didn't matter that I'd get my ass whooped with extension cords every time I cut school or snuck outta the house to be with him. He made my pussy feel good. He made me feel wanted. And that's all I cared about.

Three months later, I was knocked up with Darius. And he was locked up on aggravated assault charges. Six months later, he got released from juvenile justice and I was right back with him, legs up over his shoulders, bein' fucked down into his twin mattress. And two days after my fifteenth birthday, I gave birth to Jah'Mel and Trigger's ass was bein' sentenced to five years in prison for gun-related charges.

A few months later, Beulah tossed me out on the streets.

From that moment on, I was too busy tryna figure out how I was gonna manage with two damn kids to give any more thought about a niggah named Trigger and his super-sized dick. No, a bitch had babies to feed, and I needed to do whatever I had to.

I sigh, reachin' out and strokin' the side of his face. "Darius, I love you, boo. Thanks for watchin' the kids for me. Now go on home to that crazy bitch of yours before I go the fuck off on you. And if she does happen to lock you out, just bring ya black ass back here and go to sleep. You know you *always* have a place to stay if that ghetto, hoodrat bitch tosses you out. Now good night! I'm goin' to bed."

And instead of goin' upside his head, I kiss him on the cheek.

"Good night," he mumbles in back of me as he heads to his Lexus. I throw my hand up and head for the door. Darius might talk shit, but he always comes through for me, even if I have to threaten his black ass. Well, also because he knows I have no problem jumpin' up on his goddamn ass and punchin' him up if need be. And dare him to raise a hand to me.

Once I am in the house, I lock the door, set the alarm, then take my ass into my bedroom and strip outta my clothes. I take a nice long shower, dry off, lotion my body in some smell goods, then step into a silk teddy. I might sleep alone, but I'll be damned if I'm not smellin' good and sleepin' in somethin' sexy every night.

My cell pings as I climb into bed. It's a text from Buddha wanting to make sure I got home safe. I text him back, lettin' him know I did, then close my eyes and replay my night with him over in my mind until my pussy starts to tingle as I pinch a nipple. I work out a sweet, sticky nut, slippin' my fore and middle fingers into my ass while using my my other hand and fingers to play with my clit and pussy. It doesn't take long before I nut all over my fingers, then pull both sets of fingers out of my pussy and ass, and lick them clean. I close my eyes and drift off to sleep.

Six a.m., I am up racin' around the house tryna get these kids up and ready for school. Luckily, today is one of those days where I ain't gotta do a buncha cussin' and hollerin' and threatenin' them. Everyone gets up and does what they're supposed to without me havin' to turn up the ghetto switch.

By seven, Marquelle, Day'Asia, and Joshua are already at their bus stop waitin' to get picked up. Elijah and Isaiah are playin' PS3 until it's time for them to leave. And the twins are sittin' at the kitchen table eatin' their breakfast.

I narrow my eyes, starin' at them. This shit is too damn good to be true. Now I start wonderin' if they plan on killin' me in my sleep tonight. *Mmmph. I better lock my bedroom door tonight and sleep with my gun under the pillow.*

At eight-thirty, the twins have gotten on the bus and I have the whole house to myself. I decide to shower, dress, then head on down to the salon to get me a mani and pedi. Shit, sugah-boo, you never know when a niggah's gonna wanna suck on these fingers and toes so you gotta always stay on point.

"Heeeeey, girl," Miss FeFe sings out as soon as I walk through the door. Ooh, chile, Nappy No More is hot 'n poppin' this mornin'. *They must be runnin' some kinda special for all these bitches to be up in here on a Wednesday.*

"Miss FeFe," I say, liftin' my Chanels up over my eyes and restin' them up on my head. I have my weave pulled back into one long braid hangin' down my back. You can't tell me shit! I pop my ass over to the counter. "What is goin' on up in here today, sugah-boo? Y'all givin' out free milk and cheese today?"

She laughs, wavin' me on. "Girl, we started back our Nappy on the Go specials—a mani/pedi, full-body massage, facial, and hair—again, so it's been packed for the last two days."

"Oooh, I know that's right. Y'all shuttin' shit down. Got the block hot, boo."

"You want me to pencil you in for a special? Pasha doesn't have an openin' for another two hours, but by the time you finish gettin' the works she'd be ready for you."

"Oh no, girl, I don't need all the extras today." I run my hands over the sides of my hair. "The peas in the kitchen ain't poppin' yet, so I'm good. I just need these hands and feet handled."

One foot forward, standin' in a pair of six-inch Manolos, I profile for the two hatin'-ass hoes sittin' in the waitin' area who've been starin' me down since I walked in. I feel like turnin' around and tellin' them to eat my ass out, but I ain't tryna get ugly up in here today. One of 'em I know from the Crack House; the other I've never seen before. Either way, I know the bitches are over there talkin' sideways about me. And I don't give a hot goddamn!

I glance over my shoulder at them, shootin' them both a look to let 'em know that I see 'em watchin' me. I let my grey crocodile Bottega Veneta hang in the crook of my arm, then shift my weight from one foot to the other, archin' my back so that my juicy ass is all popped out 'n puffy for 'em. Bitches wanna stare, then I'ma always give 'em somethin' to stare at. I smack my ass in their faces for effect, then swivel my neck back to Felecia. "Ooh, Miss FeFe, I see y'all have special seatin' for the hoe's club up in here today." I gesture my head over in their direction. "But I'ma let 'em get their hate on without any drama from me."

She shakes her head. "Girl, I can't with you. Not today."

I toss my long Pocahontas braid. "Well, let me go to the back and say hi to Miss Pasha. Call me when they..." my voice drifts when the door opens and in walks Jasper and two of his cousins, Stax and Jaheem. They look more like brothers than cousins. And all three of them are fine and crazy as shit. Jasper's dark chocolate self is lookin' mighty tasty. And so does Jaheem. But the niggah who really gets my juices percolatin' is Stax's sexy ass. Six-feet-six of muscled milk-chocolate. Mmmph. I'd fuck that niggah and swallow his babies for free. Yes, lawd. Plus I heard he has a big-ass dick and huge cow balls. And a big-dicked, big-balled niggah is always a nice treat.

I swallow back drool.

They speak to all the chicks sittin' in the waitin' area, practically poppin' they titties out for attention. "Wassup, Felecia?"

"Ain't nothin'," she says. "How you?" I eye her as she talks to him. Felecia's a real sneaky bitch. Pasha better watch her ho ass around Jasper 'cause if she hasn't fucked him, she definitely wants to. I can smell her wet, horny pussy way over here. She can front if she wants. But I know that lil' skinny dick niggah, Andre, she's so in love with ain't hardly fuckin' her right.

Jasper eyes me. "Yo, wassup, Cass? Ain't seen you in a minute. What's good wit' you? I see you still laced up."

"You know how I do it, boo. Keepin' it real classy ghetto."

Jasper laughs. "I heard that."

I eye Stax. He grins at me as I lick my lips. "Yo, you mad funny. Wassup, Cass?"

I walk up on him and run my finger along his forearm. "Oooh, you don't even wanna know, boo. But I can show you better than I can tell you." I cut my eye over at the hater squad, then back to Stax. If Stax's a dog, he keeps his shit real low key 'cause I've never heard about it. But these other two—Jasper and Jaheem...mmmph, dog central! The niggah Jasper done ran through half of the hoes in Essex and Union Counties. And Jaheem ain't too far behind him. Nasty, no-good niggahs!

Why Miss Pasha married Jasper's ass still boggles my mind. I know his ass gotta big dick, like the rest of the niggahs in his family, but still...he ain't shit. Felecia claims he beats her. And she's scared of him. But I can't see Miss Pasha lettin' no niggah willie-whoppin' her upside the head. But, then again...who knows what is goin' on behind them closed doors?

Anyway, I don't know how much of what Miss FeFe and her messy ass said is true since the bitch rattled that off after she had tossed back a round of drinks at the weddin' reception. And that's exactly why I'd never tell the ho my business. The bitch can't hold her liquor or her tongue, and that's a real live situation for me. Anyway, Miss Loose Lips made me swear to never repeat it. And so far I haven't. But, if the bitch ever presses me wrong, I will. And I ain't gonna do it behind her back. Oh, no, sugah-boo. That's not how I do mine. I'm right up in ya goddamn face!

He laughs again. "Yo, Cass; for real for real, you shot out, baby."

"Mmmph. I'm dead serious, Stax. You need to stop playin' games, boo. Anyway, where's ya crazy-ass baby momma at?" I had heard that he wasn't fuckin' with her ghetto ass anymore. But shit, that don't mean he ain't still fuckin' her when his dick gets hard and horny.

"You know I don't fuck wit' Mariah like that no more."

"Oooh, for real. Mmmph. I had no idea. What she do? Don't tell me you caught her out there with her other baby daddy 'cause I ran into them over the summer in Times Square, lookn' real lovey-dovey."

He frowns. "Oh, word? Nah; that's news to me."

"Oops. I ain't one to gossip so you ain't hear that from me."

"Nah, it's all good. It is what it is. She can do her. Like I said, I don't fuck wit' her like that, so it's whatever. We just cool for my daughter, feel me?"

I keep flirtin'. "Oh, you have no idea how bad I'd love to *feel* you, boo. Now I know for sure you need to let me nurse ya love wounds. I'll have you feelin' like a new man."

Jasper shakes his head, laughin'. "Yo, Cass, word is bond, you my muthaeffen peeps, yo. You just don't give a fuck."

"Nope, why should I? Life's too short to be fakin' 'n frontin'."

"That's real shit," he says back.

Jaheem speaks to Felecia, then eyes me up and down, rubbin' his dimpled chin. "You lookin' real good, Cass. I can't get no love."

The niggah grins and licks his lips. Damn him!

I toss my braid. "Of course I am. And no, you can't get no love. Where's your wife at?" I walk off before he can speak, leavin' him, Jasper, and Stax eyeballin' my bouncin' ass as I walk toward the back. "Hey, Miss Pasha, girl," I say, shiftin' my handbag from one arm to the other.

"Hey, girl," she says as she sits her client up from the sink. She wraps a towel around her head and blot dries her long, wavy hair. Ooh, the bitch's hair is luscious. I've seen her here a few times in the past, too. Pasha looks at me. "I know you're not in here already to get your hair done again. It still looks good. And I'm lovin' how you workin' that braid."

I toss my head, swingin' my braid. "Yessss, sugah-boo. I'm lovin' it too. And no, I ain't here to have nothin' done to it. I'm here to get these hands and feet laid out."

"Oh, good. Did Felecia tell you about our house specials?"

"You know she did, Pasha Girl." I glance up at the large mani-pedi board up on the wall that lists prices and whatnot. "I think I'ma get me that lemongrass and sea salt treatment, then let them toss a lil' sake and ginger up on these suckas."

She chuckles. "Oh, you'll love it, girl. We even wrap your feet in natural sea paper, then give you a warm ginger compress that you can take home with you to use again."

I purse my lips. "See, Miss Pasha, this is why you stay gettin' my coins. You know how to do it right."

"We always aim to please, girl. I saw you up front cuttin' up with Felecia."

"Uh-huh. You know how I do. Pasha girl, Miss FeFe's

a damn hot mess. And that husband of yours knows he has some fine damn cousins. Whew. That sexy-ass Stax makes me wanna chew the nut outta his dingaling."

Everyone in earshot laughs. I glance at the chick sittin' in Pasha's chair. Miss Luscious is some kinda gorgeous. And one thing about Big Booty, baby, I gives out compliments where they're deserved.

Pasha looks over at Felecia, shakin' her head as she takes a sip of her Ocean Spray cranberry juice. "Girl, take a ticket and stand in line. You along with practically everyone else want a taste of him."

"And what about you, Miss Pasha Girl? You want some of that dingaling, too?"

She chokes and coughs. "Girl, you a mess."

I purse my lips. "Mmmph. But I see you ain't answer the question either." I eye the Miss Cutie-Boo Pasha has in her chair as she turns her chair around, facin' the mirror. Cutie Boo eyes me back. "Girl," I say, flickin' my bangs, "what you mixed with, Indian?"

"No," she says with sass in her voice. "Why?"

"Ooh, no, Miss Girl," I say, waggin' a finger at her, "put the weapons down. I'm only givin' you a compliment, Hon. I know all that thick 'n wavy hair ain't no weave so I was wonderin' if you were Indian or somethin'; that's all."

"Oh. I'm Puerto Rican and Black."

"Oh, you a Blatino. I knew you were mixed with somethin'. Anyway, boo, you 'bout to make me wanna start lickin' kitty-cats. And everyone knows how much I love the dingdong."

There's more laughter throughout the shop.

I ask her where she's from. "Brooklyn," she says, eyein' me. Her 'tude is still kinda stank, but I ain't concerned. "And thanks for the compliment. I guess."

"Chanel, girl," Pasha says, wavin' me on. "Pay this nut no mind. Cass is certifiable. But she's one of my most faithful and loyal customers."

The Chanel chick chuckles. "Oh, it's all good. I can rock wit' the best of 'em; trust. Like I said, I'm from Brooklyn. All day, e'eryday, so it is what it is." She glances at me. "I remember seein' you in here the last time I was here."

"Uh-huh. I remember seein' you too, boo." I tell her she was with another Indian-lookin' chick all dolled up in designer wear and jewels who leaped up on some Spanish ho and did her face in.

She laughs. "Oh, yeah, that was my girl, Kat. I had to turn her on to this spot, but she ended up havin' to turn it out. I felt so bad that day."

Miss Pasha tells her to not worry about it. That it's water under the bridge. I glance around the salon and count four beefy security guards posted up on stools.

"And I see you keepin' it real airtight up in here these days with all this fine-ass security."

"Girl, I had to. Too much craziness was goin' on."

"Yes, chile, it goes down at Nappy No More. Why you think I stays up in here? I don't wanna miss a drop of juiciness."

She laughs. "Girl, you're a mess."

Miss Luscious drops her eyes to my bag. “I’m lovin’ the Bottega.”

“Ooh, yes, sugah-boo. You know ya designers, I see.”

She chuckles. “I’ma label whore, sweetie. So, yes, I can spot the hotness a mile away. And can smell a fake even further. And that right there is official.”

“And you know this, Miss Cutie Boo. Yes.”

“Yeah, girl,” another chick says, sittin’ in Rhodeshia’s chair. “I was eyein’ that bag too.”

Pasha shakes her head. “Oh, y’all haven’t seen anything. This chile is the queen of handbags.”

“Yeah, and for a chick who don’t work,” Rhodeshia butts in as she parts her client’s hair down the middle. “You stay killin’ it.”

I frown. Oh, this bitch done crossed the line. She’s comin’ at me like we from the same block. “Wait a minute, *bitch*. You don’t know me like that. Ho, how you know I don’t work? You and I ain’t ever toss back drinks or suck down the same dicks so that says somebody been runnin’ they mouths about me. So I wanna know who you been sittin’ around talkin’ shit about me to?”

Pasha eyes me. “Cass, please, girl. Rho didn’t mean no harm.”

“No, Miss Pasha, girl. I don’t mean no harm, either. I want this ho to tell me how she knows I don’t work. Apparently she ain’t get the memo. But, I’ma give her a pass today.”

The Rhodeshia bitch quickly apologizes, then starts

flappin' out lies." My bad, girl. I thought I heard you mentionin' it the last time you were in here; that's all. But, you're right. I don't know if you work or not."

I shift my handbag to my other hand. "Bitch, lies. But you lucky I'm in good spirits today. Otherwise I'd be moppin' that mirror with your face."

"Thank God for small miracles," Pasha says, wavin' over one of her nail technicians who's sittin' at the nail booth.

"These hoes stay tryna do me." I shoot Mis Rho-Ho a dirty look. "I know one thing, let me find out you and Miss FeFe been meddlin' in my shit and I'ma turn the gas up on ya ass."

"Wassup, Pash?" the skinny chick says. She's wearin' a buncha bright colors; a fuschia tie-die shirt that is tied in a side knot showin' off her bellyring. And some kinda lime-green, pink, orange, and purple wrap skirt. I glance down at her feet. Mmmph. Pink satin baby dolls.

"Trish, can you fit Cass in? She wants the lemongrass and ginger wrap."

"Sure. I—"

I cut Miss Rainbow Bright off. "Wait a minute, Miss Pasha, girl. Don't be pushin' me off on no one. I don't want Miss Fruity Pebbles doin' me. Give me Anna. You know I ain't lettin' anyone fuck with my hands and feet."

Miss Rainbow blinks.

"Cass, girl. I promise you. You'll be in good hands."

I tilt my head. "I know I will. That's why..." I pause as

Jasper, Stax and Jaheem walk over to Pasha's station. They speak to everyone. Every ho up in here tries to get cute and sexy with it. I eye 'em all like, "Bitches, please!"

I watch as Jasper walks over and kisses Miss Pasha on the cheek. And for split second I think I see her cringe. But I ain't one to gossip. And I can't be too sure if she did or not so I ain't sayin' nothin' else about it. One thing Big Booty ain't is messy, okay. So we gonna leave that alone.

"Yo, wassup Pash?" Stax says, foldin' his thick arms over his chiseled chest.

Pasha smiles. "Nothin' much, Stax. What's up with you?"

"Chillin', baby girl. You know how I do it."

Baby girl? It's how he says it that makes me raise a brow. Oh, and don't think I don't catch how he looks at her—how he always looks at her anytime I see the two of them around each other. Even at the weddin', I caught him watchin' her on the sly. Mmmph. Stax ain't foolin' no one. That niggah wants her ass. And he ain't tryna give up the dingaling to any other bitch but Miss Pasha. And, yes, I'm hatin' 'cause I want me some of that dingdong, too.

Pasha shifts her eyes, then speaks to Jaheem who's too busy eye-ballin' me. He speaks back. "I'm good, baby girl. How you?"

"As you can see, busy, busy, busy."

"Yo, that's wassup. I ain't mad. Make that paper, fam."

"Yo, let me holla at you real quick," Jasper says, lightly

tuggin' on her sleeve. She tells him to give her a few minutes to get Miss Luscious under the dryer. I tilt my head and watch the bitch eyein' Jasper, and how he's eyein' her back. Oh, no! He waits 'til Miss Pasha's back is turned, then winks at her on the low. I scoot over and block her view of him. I don't think so, bitch.

I narrow my eyes at Jasper, then look over at Pasha. I decide to turn up the switch 'cause I don't like what's goin' down. "Ooh, Miss Pasha, girl, I see how Miss Cutie Boo over here's eyein' ya man. You might wanna hurry up and take him in the back before Miss Thingaling over here tries to slip him her number."

"*Whaaat?*" Miss Cutie Boo snaps. "What the fuck is you tryna say? I'm not thinkin' 'bout her man. So don't do me, bitch."

I turn to her. "Umm, Sugah boo, I already said it. I know a thirsty ho when I see one. And I *will* do you, bitch. Now try it." I turn back to Pasha, placin' a hand up on my hip. "Pasha Boo, these bitches in here are shameless and downright scandalous, startin' with the one in your chair. And you know I don't do messy."

Stax walks back out to where Miss FeFe is, clearly not interested in what's poppin' off back here. Jaheem stares at me, shakin' his head as Pasha looks from me, to the Chanel bitch, then over at Jasper.

Miss Luscious leans up like she's ready to get outta her seat. "Bitch, you don't know who the fuck you messin' wit'. I will take it to ya ugly-ass face, ho."

I laugh. "And I'd like to see you try it."

"Look, now," Pasha says, jumpin' in. She holds Cutie-Boo back. "Both of you stop. Chanel, girl, go on over and sit under dryer number four, please. I'll be back to check on you in ten minutes."

The bitch gets up, poppin' shit about how a bitch don't want it with her. How she'll bring the heat up in this bitch and wreck shop, blah, blah, blah.

I clap my hands. "Bring the heat, sugah-boo." I clap again. "Bring. It. Ya ass just mad 'cause I called you out on ya sneaky shit. Be real, bitch. You were eyein' her man. And you licked ya goddamn lips at him. And I peeped it. But I ain't gonna stand here and argue with some lyin'-ass bitch. I know what I saw."

"Yeah, whatever," she says, sittin' beneath the dryer. She pulls out her phone and starts talkin' real loud. "Oooh, bitch, I wish you were here right now...I'm over in Jersey gettin' my hair done at the spot I took you to...uh-huh, where you beat..."

I turn to Pasha. "Pasha, girl. You know I pay attention to every-damn-thing goin' on. And trust me, boo. That bitch wanna fuck ya man, or run his pockets. And Jasper's ass is with it. Now go 'head, niggah, and say I didn't just see you wink at her ass on the low."

Jasper's jaw tightens. "Yo, Cass, get da fuck outta here wit' that dumb shit, yo. Ya crazy ass is always somewhere tryna start shit."

"Niggah, ya lyin'-ass ain't slick. But, whatever. I know what I saw." Anna waves me over. I turn back to Pasha.

"Ooh, girl. Miss Anna's ready for me." I point over at Jasper, eyein' Pasha. "Watch him, girl. That's all I'm sayin'."

The Chanel bitch eyes me. And I laugh in her face, walkin' off, shakin' my ass over toward Anna. I overhear her sayin', "Ugly bitch. Tryna serve it to me.…uh-huh… Kat, girl, these Jersey bitches don't even want it…Bitch, please…you know I'm tryna keep it cute…but I will yabba dabba do that ho…Bitch, when is you comin' back to the east coast…?"

Ooh, she's lucky Miss Pasha's my girl. I would tear this shop up today. I don't give a shit where that bitch is from. I'ma Brick City bitch, okay? And we hit hard. Brooklyn or not, she's in the wrong hood tryna eye-fuck anyone up in here.

Fourteen

"Aye, yo, real shit. Why da fuck you ain't been answerin' ya phone, or hittin' my text back, yo?"

I shake my head. This crazy coon's been blowin' my shit up for a whole week and I've been iggin' his ass. I got too many other things to handle than to be dealin' with this niggah and his needy ass. Shit, he acts like he's my only goddamn sponsor. And the only reason his black ass won't show up at my doorstep is 'cause he ain't tryna disrupt his lil' happy home, like I give a hot fuck.

"Niggah, don't call here tryna do me. I don't answer to you."

"Yeah, whatever. Ya ass real type funny-style for real for real, yo."

"Yup, I sure am. So why the hell you still callin', niggah?"

"Yo, you already know what it is. 'Cause ya freak-ass know how'ta handle a big-ass dick. And I like beatin' that back up; what da fuck you think?"

"Mmmph. Yeah, I can handle a dick. But that shit don't give ya ass the right to think you own me."

"Yo, I ain't tryna hear that dumb shit. Answer ya shit when I hit you up."

I laugh at his crazy ass.

"Yeah, keep laughin', Cass; real shit. I got sumthin' funny for ya ass. Aye, yo. I meant to get at you 'bout that stunt you pulled down at the shop the other day. That was some real foul shit, yo. You stay showin' ya ass; for real for real. Why you always gotta try 'n blow a muh-fucka's spot up."

I frown. "Niggah, get a grip. I do what I do. Niggahs don't wanna get called out, then they should know how to fuckin' move. All that winkin' shit at some other bitch ain't it. Now what?"

"Yo, why da fuck you care?"

"Niggah, I don't. But that shit's nasty and disrespectful."

He snorts. "Yeah, right. And da shit you doin' ain't. Save that shit for someone else. Ya ass just like bein' messy 'n shit."

"Whatever, niggah. I know if I saw the shit one of them nosey-ass hoes up in there saw it, too. And that shit ain't cool."

"Yeah, aiight, whatever, yo. You need to mind ya mutha-fuckin' business."

"Bitch, how 'bout you mind yours. It is my business when the shit's done in front of me, or around me. So, like I said, get a motherfuckin' grip."

"Yo, and how da fuck you gonna be all up on my fam like that and I'm standin' right there. Yo, you real foul, yo. That was some real dirty shit, Cass. I'm tellin' you, yo. You really tryna get fucked up; real shit."

I laugh. "Hahaha. Niggah, puhleeze. We both know you ain't tryna take it there so bite a dick and chock. You not my man. And I don't want you to be. I don't know what part of the memo got ya ass confused. But I told you, I'm not ya goddamn wife. You put ya hands on me and you gonna know what it's like to be fucked real good. And I do mean, deep and good. Now you got one more time to threaten me and I'ma show you just what the fuck I mean, niggah. So do ya'self a favor and save that shit for ya wifey-boo."

"Yo, fuck outta here wit' all that dumb shit. You heard what da fuck I said, yo. Don't play me like that shit again."

"Bitch, eat the inside of my asshole. You don't run me, niggah."

He laughs. "Yeah, aiight. Pop that shit if you want. Let me come through and get some pussy. You was lookin' mad right in them jeans last week. All that thickness stuffed up in them shits. Had my dick all hard 'n shit."

I start hummin' Mary J's "Mr Wrong." And this niggah right here is all kinds of wrong. But the dick is oh so right. And his paper is nice and long.

"Yo, why is you hummin' 'n shit all up in my ear, yo? I want some pussy."

"And I want three grand."

"Yo, I ain't got it right now."

"Oh, well. Then you need to call me when you do. So 'til then this pussy's not available to you. And you know I don't do layaway or credit. So..." I have another call comin' through. I glance at the screen. Oooh, it's Miss Pasha. "Okay, I'm done. Call me when you got ya paper up and you ready to fuck."

"Yeah, aiight, yo. I'ma—"

I shut him down, clickin' over to Pasha. "Hey, Pasha, girl."

"Hey, girl. Did I catch you at a bad time?"

"No, girl. You actually saved me from talkin' to one of them no-good niggahs. What's doin', boo?"

"I wanted to talk to you about the other day when you were down at the shop."

I purse my lips. "Uh-huh. What you wanna know, Miss Pasha?"

"The one thing I've always admired about you, girl, is that you don't give a damn about what people say about you. And you don't bite your tongue, which is why I have a lot of respect for you. I mean, you are a little extra at times, but at the end of the day, I feel like I can trust you."

Well shit. Now she got me feelin' all guilty 'n shit. And there are three, well four, things Big Booty don't do: guilt, drama, dirty dick, and a man beatin' my ass, okay.

"Aww, Miss Pasha, girl, that's sweet, boo. But you ain't gotta spoon feed me no sugar, hon. Let's get right to the point. You wanna know if that pretty Indian bitch you had in ya chair was tryna do Jasper, right?"

"Well, I know you really had a strong opinion about what you saw. And, of course, he denies it."

I huff. "Miss Pasha, girl. Believe what you want, boo.

You know I ain't ever been one to be a messy bitch, or a lie. I don't make shit up, boo. And you should know this. That niggah Jasper is a goddamn lie and so is that China, bitch—or whatever the fuck her name is—he was winkin' at. The bitch slid her tongue outta her mouth at him. And I peeped the shit through the mirror. That's why I moved over and blocked the bitch's view. I can't stand a messy bitch."

She sighs. "I know. And I'm glad you put them both on blast. I didn't appreciate that shit from either one of them one bit. And I did tell Chanel her business was no longer needed or wanted at my salon."

"Well, good for you, Miss Pasha. That bitch was sneaky. And so is your man, boo. And I ain't ever been one to be all up in ya business, Miss Pasha, boo. But, why the fuck did you marry his ass?"

"It's complicated," she says. I can hear the baby in the background fussin', half-cooin', half-cryin', tryna get her attention I'm sure.

"Mmmph. Well, I don't know how complicated it is, Miss Pasha, girl. And I ain't one to gossip. But Miss FeFe says he beats on yo' ass, boo."

"She said whaaat?"

"You heard me, girl. She told me that the night of your weddin' reception while her drunk-ass got all liquored up. She told me that he whoops the hot dog shit outta you, and you scared of him."

"I don't believe it," she says, soundin' hurt.

"Believe it, sugah-boo. That bitch can't be trusted either. She done told me some other shit, too, about you."

"Other shit like what?"

"See, now, Miss Pasha," I say, ploppin' down on my bed. I kick off my heels. "You tryna have me get messy. But you ain't hear none of this shit from me 'cause, boo, if you wanna confront her about it and she steps to me, I'ma do her up real good."

"Oh, no, girl. Trust me. I appreciate you telling me all this. I've been kind of feeling like things aren't right between us, so whatever you tell me is going to stay strictly between us."

"Mmmph. Well, Miss Pasha, girl. Your feelin's are right. Miss FeFe has dragged you for filth, boo." I tell her everything Miss FeFe done told me about her. From how she got her windows smashed out to the crazy phone calls; from that niggah walkin' up in her salon tryna disrespect her to bein' attacked out in her front yard and not wantin' the police called. I let her know it all.

"That dirty bitch," she hisses. "All this time I thought she had my back. But something in my gut kept telling me not to trust her ass."

"Pasha, boo, the only thing Miss FeFe is tryna have is your man, trust me. And if she don't want Jasper, you can trust and believe she damn sure wanna be up on his big-ass dingdong—oops, girl," I quickly say. "I don't know if Jasper has a big dingaling or not. I only know what the hoes out in the streets say."

"It's fine, really. I already know what they say out in the streets. And Jasper's given out more of his share of dick so the rumors ain't a lie."

And you still married his no-good ass. Mmmph.

"I still can't get believe Felecia has told you all those things. And stands here, smiling all up in my damn face."

"Uh-huh, boo. That's how them messy bitches do it. But you gotta keep this shit tucked on the low. Fish the bitch."

"This shit has me sick to my damn stomach."

"Oooh, poor thing. I hate to be the bearer of bad news, boo. But you my damn girl, Miss Pasha, and it was time I told you what was what. I ain't been tryna feature Miss FeFe every since she told me all this shit about you. That bitch really thinks you mighta been out there suckin' all kinda dicks behind Jasper's back. I'm tellin' you, Miss Pasha, girl. That bitch is scandalous, boo. And I wouldn't put it past her if she's been fuckin' Jasper, too."

She gasps. "Oh God! I know Felecia likes to run her mouth, but I don't think she'd stoop that low."

"Well, believe it. That ho will drop down in the gutter for a ride on his dingaling. The bitch talked greasy about you and I heard the shit come outta her mouth with my own two ears. And ain't shit wrong with my hearin'. So I know she'd snake her way into ya sheets too, boo.

"This shit is crazy. We've always been very close."

"Uh-huh. And the bitch is jealous of you. Always has been. Even when we were in elementary school the bitch was hatin' on you. But I always kept the shit to myself 'cause I ain't wanna be wrapped up in nobody's family drama, girl."

"Oh, trust me. There'll be no drama. Everything you're telling me is confirmation of everything I already thought or felt. Booty, I mean Cass, you have no idea how much having this conversation means to me. It has definitely been an eye-opener."

"Well, in case you still have some doubts. Keep ya eyes open wide and watch that bitch."

"Oh, trust me. That's exactly what I plan on doing."

"Mmmph. And if you wanna set that bitch up, let me know. We can reel her in and do her ass up real dirty."

"I will. Thanks again, girl. Look, I need to get off this phone. I hear Jasper coming in."

"Go do you, boo. And Miss Pasha, boo?"

"Yeah?"

"I don't know if you were suckin' a string of dicks or not on Jasper's cheatin' ass. And I don't care. But I think it's time we shut these niggahs' playhouses down. One by one, boo. Niggahs gotta be taught, boo."

She lowers her voice. "Sadly, I think you might be right. We'll talk soon."

We disconnect. I get up and shut my bedroom door, then head to my bathroom to smoke me a blunt before these damn kids get home from school and I gotta deal with their mess.

I light the blunt, then take a long, deep pull on it,

blowin' a cloud of smoke into the air. I stand up and pull off my jeans, then step outta my lace panties. I unhook my bra and let my titties bounce free. I shimmy my shoulders and watch 'em sway. Mmmm, I want some dingaling. But of course callin' a niggah to fuck me is outta the question since that'll mean I'll have to give the niggah a free round of pussy. Oh, no. Buddha's ass was the last niggah who I'm givin' some free pussy to. And I let that niggah fuck me real good in all three of my holes. Next round he pays for.

I take another pull on the blunt, holdin' my head back and closin' my eyes, replayin' that night with Buddha in my head. *Oooh, that big dick niggah did me right, goddammit!*

Proppin' a leg up on the toilet seat, I reach between my legs and start playin' with my clit, surprised that my sweet juices are already seepin' outta me.

I take another pull off the blunt. *Mmmm, long-dick motherfucka.* I slip a finger into my hot, moist pussy, thrustin' my finger in and outta me. I blow out smoke, slippin' two fingers in now. I gasp. *See what you do to my pussy, motherfucka? See how wet you got it, niggah? Oooh, you got some good dingaling...uhhh...*

I imagine standin' up on the sofa, bent over and bracin' myself on the back of it, shakin' my ass in his face. I look over my shoulder. Tell him to eat my ass; to get it wet and ready for the dick. He slaps it a few times, causin' it to sting. I make my ass clap for him. Tell him to slap it again. And he does 'til it stings.

I slap my ass, hard, pretendin' it's Buddha. *Oooh yes, niggah...*

I slap it again, spreadin' my legs wider. I push my fingers knuckle-deep into my pussy, thrustin' 'n twistin' them in and out. I moan.

Fuck me! Fuck me, lil' niggah!

I imagine him pullin' open my ass and buryin' his face in between my cheeks. His tongue feelin' like heaven as he flaps it up and down, swirlin' it around and around my hole before stickin' it in.

Oh, yes...eat that ass, baby. Get it ready for that long dick...

My body starts to tremble. Pussy juice squirts all over my hand. "Ooooooh, yesssss!" I hiss. *Give it to me, goddammit! Do me right!*

I reach under my sink and pull out a red wooden box. I take another pull from the blunt, holdin' the weed smoke in my lungs 'til I find what I'm lookin' for inside the box. I slowly blow out smoke as I pull the clear, eight-inch, pink glass dildo with the ridges outta its black velvet sheath, then reach in back of me and slide it in my ass, deep.

I gasp.

Ooooh, yessss...

My ass muscles clutch as I imagine Buddha pullin' open my cheeks and workin' his Mandingaling into my hot valley, slowly; easin' me open.

Mmmmm...

I reach into the box again and pull out a seven-inch

vibrator. I turn it on high, then remove my fingers from my pussy and replace 'em with the vibrator. I bend all the way over and work both holes. The half-smoked blunt danglin' from lips. The hum of the vibrator beats up against the pressure of the dildo rammed in my ass, sendin' waves of sensations through me.

Oooooooh yes, dirty motherfucka. I am cummin' and cummin' and cummin'. *Yesssss, niggah. Stuff my ass while you fuck my pussy...*

I shut my eyes tight. Then out of nowhere, that niggah Buddha was with down at the Crack House—the Hill Harper look alike, pops into my head. I see the niggah grinnin'. *Sneaky bastard! You probably gotta little-ass four-inch dick, niggah...*

Mmmm...

Yeah, you got one of them shorty stumpy dicks; don't you, niggah?

I try to remember what the fuck the niggah's name is.

BJ?

CJ?

DJ?

Then it hits me. *AJ!*

Talkin' 'bout you like your dick...

My eyes pop open.

My mouth drops open. The burnin' blunt hits the floor.

Ohmymotherfuckin'gawd!I know where the fuck I remember that niggah-bitch from.

Fifteen

Two days later, I'm steppin' outta my truck on my way into Dickalina's buildin' when I hear someone say, "Yo, ma, what's good?"

I hate the projects. I lived over in buildin' four for almost sixteen years until I moved out almost two years ago. And, before then, I didn't think I'd ever leave here, or hate comin' back. I really thought that this was my life. That this was all I'd ever wanna know. Then somethin' changed. I woke up one day ready to get the fuck out. I'm not sure if it was because I wanted the twins to be able to play outside and not have to worry about them gettin' shot by a fuckin' stray bullet that had me ready to box my shit up and bounce. If it was because the elevator had broken and I had to climb up twelve flights of pissy-ass stairs, again, for the fourth day in a row that made me say I was done with this shit. Or if it was the night I caught Day'Asia's hot ass in the stairwell at two o'clock in the mornin' suckin' some fifteen-year-old niggah's dick that I said I had enough. All I know is I knew it was time to go. Four months later, I found me a five-bedroom house with a finished basement across town that took my section-8 voucher and was out. And I don't miss this shithole one bit.

I glance over my shoulder. "Do I know you?"

"Nah, but I'm tryna change that. Let me holla at you for a minute."

I stop and turn to face him as he's walkin' up on me. He's a tall—like six-six or some shit—brown-skinned niggah with a big nose and thick lips. I don't recognize him from any of the buildin's here. And it's obvious he doesn't know me either, comin' outta his face like this. Everyone in these projects knows me and my kids so he's definitely new to this part of the hood if he's steppin' up to me like he's King Ding Dong.

I place a hand on my hip.

He grins.

"Damn, ma. You got a bangin' body."

I blink. "How old are you?"

He squares his shoulders, pops out his chest, then deepens his voice. "Seventeen, why, wassup?"

"Ain't shit up. Not with you bein' seventeen. So, no, you can't holla at me. I'm old enough to be your momma, niggah."

He grins, lickin' his lips. "That's wassup. I'm grown, ma. I'll be eighteen in two weeks. I don't fuck wit' broads my age, anyway, so it's all good. I like 'em older. What, you like twenty-five, twenty-six?"

Okay, the lil' niggah's cute. But, uh…I glance down at his feet. Mmmph. He has on a pair of dusty-ass Timbs.

I decide to not tell him that a niggah wearin' rundown footwear will never, ever, have a chance with me, no matter what his age. Besides, talkin' all sideways to this young niggah isn't smart, especially since I don't know who he is, or who he's related to. "No, lil' niggah. I'm old enough to be ya mammy. So why you ain't got ya black ass in school?" He tells me school isn't his thing. That he has all the education he needs, right here on the streets. That he's about makin' his paper. "Oh, so you one of them lil' high-school dropout niggahs who wanna hug the block instead of gettin' an education, huh?"

"Yeah, sumthin' like that. I'm doin' me; that's all."

"Well, you keep doin' you, boo-boo. But, you *won't* be doin' me."

He laughs. "It's all good. You still sexy as fuck. So if you ever change ya mind, holla at ya boy."

"Boy, puhleeze."

"I'm sayin', ma."

"Whatever, lil' niggah. And I ain't ya ma. You live over here?"

"Nah, my peoples do." I ask him who they are and what buildin' they're in. I almost faint when he tells me he's related to Knutz's ass. That he's his nephew.

"Say no more. You'll never sniff this pussy. If you related to that crazy niggah, then you must be three screws this side of retarded, too."

He laughs. "Oh, daaaayum; that's foul. But, nah, I'm not as bad as him."

"Mmmhmm. And who are you?"

"Killah," he says, smirkin'.

Yeah, okay. This lil' niggah crazy, too. "Well, listen, Killer..."

"Nah, not Killer. It's *Killah*."

"Okay, *Killah*. It was nice chattin' with you, boo. But I'm on my way up to see the woman your uncle beats up on. You know Dickalina, right?"

He frowns. "Yeah, she's cool peoples. But I ain't know my Unc beats on her."

I shrug. "Well, now you do. But if he ever puts his hands on her around me, I'ma have his hands chopped off; make sure you let him know that. Look. Do me a favor and keep an eye on my truck until I get back. Do you think you can do that?"

"Yeah, I got you, ma." He says this as another young boy—well, he looks young—walks up to him and gives him a fist pound. "Yo, what's good, Eli?"

"Chillin' son. I see you out here doin' ya thing-thing." He eyes me with his cute self. He's dark-skinned with deep brown eyes and has his hair braided in fresh cornrows. I glance at the thick chain draped around his neck, then look down at his feet. He's wearin' a brand new pair of Jordans. "Recruitin' some new cougar pussy, I see."

"'Cougar pussy'? Lil' niggah, puhleeze. How old are you?"

He licks his lips. "Old enough. And, for da record, ain't nuthin' on me lil'. Believe that."

"Allllrighty then. This is my cue to leave before I have to school ya young ass."

He laughs. "School me, baby. I'm always up for learnin'."

I walk off, wavin' him on.

"Aiight, ma, later," Killah says.

"Damn, son. She gotta fat ass," Mr. Old Enough says. "Word is bond."

I glance over my shoulder at the two of them. "Make sure you watch my truck, and don't worry about how fat my ass is, *son.* 'Cause ain't either of you lil' niggahs gonna ever get any of it."

"Yeah, aiight, ma," Killah shouts. "I got you. But, as soon as I turn eighteen, I'ma be checkin' for you again, so be ready; real shit."

"Not with them old-ass boots you got on," I say, walkin' up to the buildin' and through the double glass doors. I throw up a peace sign, then bounce and shake my ass into the buildin'.

Surprisin'ly the elevators are workin'. I step in, then press the button for the eleventh floor; glad the lobby isn't packed with niggahs as it usually is. Once I get to Dickalina's apartment, I press down on the bell. Someone is blastin' "Rack City" by Tyga. I roll my eyes, pressin' down, long and hard, on the buzzer.

"Who the fuck is leanin' on my motherfuckin' bell like that?" someone yells, lowerin' the music.

"It's Cassandra. Open the goddamn door."

I hear the locks click. Candylicious opens the door. "Oh, it's you," she says, smackin' her greasy dick suckas together. "What you want?"

I frown. See. This lil' bitch is too damn grown. And I don't know why she likes to try me. For the last six months or so she's been sayin' real slick shit and I've been lettin' it slide. But I'm thinkin' she's not goin' to be satisfied until I wreck her face. "Candy, don't fuck with me. I will beat your motherfuckin' ass and you know it. What the fuck you mean, what I want? Obviously I'm not here to see your bald-headed ass. Where's your ugly-ass mammy at?"

I brush past her.

She sucks her teeth. "Damn, you don't have to get all sensitive. I'm only playin'. She's in the kitchen."

"Ho, you play in ya pussy. You don't play with me. That's the problem with you dumb-ass, lil' bitches. Y'all think everything's a damn game. I'm not your motherfuckin' friend. Now say somethin' else slick and see what I do to you. Anyway, shouldn't your retarded ass be in school?"

"I'm suspended."

"For what, bein' stupid?"

She sucks her teeth, then mumbles somethin' under her breath as she points the remote toward the stereo. The music blares out of the speakers again. I walk down the hallway into the kitchen. Dickalina is standin' over the sink washin' some chick's hair. She's leanin' back in the stylin' chair Lina found at a yard sale last year. Penelope, a.k.a. PennyLou—a skinny, big-tittied chick from over in buildin' six—is at the kitchen table sittin' under a hair-dryer. Dickalina has turned her kitchen into her very own mini-salon where she's been doing hair for the last eight years.

"Hey," I say.

"Hey," Dickalina says dryly, glancin' over her shoulder. But I don't pay the shit no mind. I sit my bag on the table, pullin' a chair out, then takin' a seat.

"Girl, I ain't seen you in a minute," PennyLou says, eyein' me. "What you been up to?"

"Not a damn thing, girl. It's school time now so chasin' behind my bad-ass kids is all I have time for. I just got finished droppin' the twins off to school this mornin' with their bad asses."

She laughs. "I heard that. So I see you finally comin' through to let Lina lay ya hair right."

I frown. "Lay my hair right? Girl, puhleeze. I wish I would. Lina's my girl and all, but she knows the only place I go to get my hair laid is down at Nappy No More."

Lina grunts. "Mmmph. Fuck her. The bitch's too grand to let her girl hook her up. She'd rather give them high-priced bitches down at that salon her money than help her homegirl out. And the bitch knows I ain't workin'."

I plop my handbag up on the table. "Ho, the last time I let you run your hands through my hair my shit fell out in clumps. I had to wear damn headwraps and wigs fuckin' with you. Had me looking like a damn man in drag."

PennyLou and the girl gettin' her hair wash laugh.

Dickalina shoots me a scowl over her shoulder. "Ohmygod, Cassie. I can't believe you still on that shit. That happened, what, like fifteen years ago?"

"Try twenty. But who's counting? The point is you fucked up my hair."

She rinses chick's hair. "You need to get over it. You know I was still learnin' about hair back then. But can't a bitch out there fuck with me now. And you know this."

Okay, I won't lie. Dickalina can slay the hell outta some hair. But, still…I'm not lettin' her do my shit up in no damn dirty-ass kitchen.

I wave her on. "Oh, Lina, puhleeze. Suck a dick, boo. I told ya ass to go get your license, then get ya ass into a shop and I'd come through and let you hook me up. But noooo, you'd rather do hair up in some makeshift shit. Sorry, I'm not doing that."

"Bitch, what the hell I need a license for? I already have a shop."

I look around the kitchen. There are dirty dishes stacked up on the stove. The recyclables can is overflowing with beer cans and liquor bottles. "And where might that be? Did I miss the openin' or somethin'?"

"No, ho. You're sittin' in it."

"Bitch, puhleeze."

She rolls her eyes, suckin' her teeth. "PennyLou, reach over there on that cart and hand that ho a flier and one of my new business cards."

PennyLou reaches over and grabs one of the colored fliers from the stack and a white card, then hands them to me. I blink. The flier reads:

DICKALINA'S SWISH 'N SWIRL SALON
THE ONE STOP POP 'N DROP SHOP
CUM THRU AND LET DICKALINA DUE YOU UP WRITE

APPOINTMENTS ONLY
ACCEPT CASH AND EBT PAYMENTS

I'm speechless. "Dickalina's *Swish 'n Swirl*? Girl, what kinda hot-ghetto shit is this? This looks like an ad for a cock-wash and ball gargle instead of a damn hair salon. What, you gonna be suckin' dick and tongue-curlin' balls, too?"

PennyLou snickers. "Oooh, you wrong for that."

"No, this damn flier is wrong; all wrong. And who the hell wrote this mess up, anyway?"

"Bitch," she snaps, "you're such a damn hater. I wrote it. Why?"

"Mmmph. Then Candy isn't the only one who's retarded in the room. Her damn mammy is, too."

She swings chick up in her chair. "Bitch, get the fuck out! Your hatin' ass always gotta have some fucked-up shit to say. I'm sick of you talkin' shit about me and my kids and my gawtdamn man. Now get the fuck out!"

I sit back in my seat. She knows I'm not leavin' up outta here until I'm good and goddamned ready. "Well, excuse me. No need to get all sensitive on me."

"And there's no need for you to be a damn hatin'-ass, evil bitch, either. But I see that ain't stoppin' you. If you don't wanna be down with Swish 'n Swirl, then don't. But keep your gawtdamn comments to ya'self."

I put my hands up. "Okay, okay. Geesh. From now on, I'll keep my trap shut."

She rolls her eyes. "And now your black ass is lyin'."

I laugh.

"Bitch, I don't see shit funny. We 'posed to be girls, and all you ever do is talk about me. You don't ever look out for me. You know the only money I get up in here is my welfare check and whatever little scraps Knutz gives me." I roll my eyes. "Not a word, ho. And I mean it."

I laugh. "I'm not sayin' a thing. Carry on. Obviously you have some shit to get off your chest. And that's what girls do."

"Yeah, and girls have each other's backs, too."

Knutz must not have come home last night. I count to ten in my head. Decide to let her have her moment. "Sooooooo, PennyLou, while Lina's gettin' her nut off, what you been up to?"

"Chile, tryna find a j-o-b; that's about it. Fuckin' probation officer is bein' a real cock sucka. A bitch can't even get a job at McDonald's, that's how bad it is out here. I told them I'd scrub toilets if I have to. I just need a damn job."

"I heard that. Times are definitely hard. That's why I keep me a few sponsors on deck to help out."

"Shit, girl, that's what I need. A few good men to pay off all these damn fines I have. And my fuckin' probation officer is ridin' a bitch down like a hard dick. Talkin' about she's gonna violate me if I don't get a job in ninety days and start payin' my fines. I felt like tellin' her ass, 'Bitch, eat my ninety-day cycle.'"

I ask her what she's on probation for this time. She says for stolen checks. Says she wrote and cashed six-thousand dollars' worth of checks usin' a fake ID down at one of the check cashin' spots where she had a connect.

She eyes me. "Cassie, you stay lookin' good, girl. When you gonna invite me over to your place for drinks?"

I tilt my head. "PennyLou, boo. Did I ever let you up in my place when I lived over in buildin' four?"

"No."

"Okay. Then what makes you think shit's changed now that I've moved out? You know we don't roll like that. I mean, we cool in the streets and whatnot. And yeah, I fucked your brother a few times, God rest his dead, big-dicked soul. But that's as far as it goes. I ain't never been one to entertain a buncha nosey-ass bitches anyway. And definitely not a thievin' one."

She twists her face up. "Umm, whatchu tryna say, ho?"

I stare her down. "I already said it. No nosey bitches allowed. And no damn thieves."

She rolls her eyes. "First of all, I don't steal from everyone so let's get that straight."

"That's nice. And you won't get the chance to steal from me either."

"Cassie, girl. I wouldn't do you like that."

I laugh. "Lies. Yes, you would. And you know it. A desperate bitch will steal from her own damn mammy if she thinks she can get away with it. The first chance you got. You'd steal the drawz off me if I had any on."

She waves me on. "Whatever. I see you still think you better than everyone else."

"Yup. Glad you realize it." I glance over at Dickalina. "Lina, I met your nephew, *Killah*, downstairs. He's a real piece of work. The niggah was practically tryna get some pussy from me."

She sucks her teeth. "That horny niggah ain't no nephew of mine. He stays tryna fuck. And don't even get me started on his triflin', trigger-happy ass. That lil' niggah is wild. And now Knutz got him hangin' all up under him, like he's his damn mentor or some shit. I told his ass I don't want him stayin here, but Knutz moved him up in here anyway, talkin' about it's only for a few days."

I roll my eyes. "Girl, how the fuck is you lettin' Knutz move anybody up in here when he don't pay the rent? That makes no sense to me."

"See, bitch. There you go steppin' all outta pocket again. Stay in ya lane, boo."

I tilt my head, and stare at her. This bitch is dumber than a box of crayons.

"Anyway, Knutz does what he wants around here. He's so fuckin' hardheaded. He knows I'm not even supposed to have his ass up in here. And now he wants to let that lil' crazy-ass niggah stay up in here, too. He's really tryna fuck up my Section-8."

I grunt. "Bitch, he's only fuckin' up what you let him fuck up. I see where the problem is. It's you. Not Knutz. You the one who stays fuckin' with his nutty ass."

"I know that's right," PennyLou says, shakin' her head under the dryer. "It couldn't be me. I'd have that niggah out on his ass. Everyone knows how that niggah gets down."

"Mmmph," I grunt. "I'm keepin' my trap shut on that one 'cause I'm not tryna get cursed out again. But you don't need no young, hard, horny cock up in here any-damn-way, especially when you have two hot-in-the ass daughters flouncin' around up in here. Next thing you know they'll be up in here fuckin'. That is, if they haven't already."

"Wait a minute. Why in the hell is you always callin' my daughters hot-in-the ass, when your daughter is just as hot in the ass as mine, if not hotter?"

"Lina, puhleeze. Grip a dick, bitch. Yeah, I know Day'-Asia's a lil' ho-ish, but at least I admit it. You, on the other hand, wanna deny the facts that your daughters are sluts."

She stops what she's doin', placin' a wet hand up on her apron-covered hip. "Oh, you wait one damn minute now, bitch. You really done gone too far. I know Candy and Tina aren't the most innocent girls out there, but they damn sure ain't sluts, either. But, mighty funny Day'Asia was the one suckin' a string of dicks in the stairwell. And we all know that's why you rushed to move the hell up outta here, but I guess she ain't no slut, now, right?"

"Yeah, Day'Asia was the one who got caught. But don't get it twisted. Clitina was the head ho in charge of the dick suckin' committee. But I ain't one to gossip. Anyway, why is Candy's grown ass home from school?"

She sucks her teeth. "Her ass done cursed out the principal. Now they want her to see a shrink when ain't shit wrong with my baby."

"What you mean ain't shit wrong with your *baby*? Chile, face it. There are two things wrong with that lie. First is, Candy has a grown woman's pussy with lots of cock mileage on it, so she definitely not a damn baby. She lost that title the first time she popped a dick in her mouth. And the second is, she's eighteen still in tenth damn grade. Now either she's borderline retarded or she's just plain ole stupid, either way...I don't mean no harm here but there's somethin' definitely wrong with that picture. And you need help ya damn self if you can't see it."

"Bitch, ain't shit wrong with Candylicious. She's lazy and don't wanna do the damn work; that's it. I keep tellin' her ass if she'd just study harder she could pull those Eff's up to Dees."

"Girl, I done heard it all. What you have in here to drink?" I glance down at my watch to make sure it's after twelve. I don't like to toss a drink back before noon. "I think your ass needs to see—" I stop midsentence when my cell starts ringin'. It's from one of the kids' schools. I take a deep breath. Answer in my professional voice. "Hello?"

"Miss Simms?"

"Yes. Who's speaking?"

"It's Vice Principal Wiggins over at Eastside Charter Academy. I'm callin' about your son, Isaiah..."

"Yes. What about him?"

"We need you to come pick him up from school. He's being suspended for the rest of the week."

"*Whaaaat? Suspended?* What the fuck you mean he's suspended for the rest of the week? What his black ass do this time?"

"Miss Simms, please calm down."

"Calm down? Oh, I'm calm. I'm calm. I'm soooo fuckin' calm. Now what the fuck he do 'cause you know I'ma turn that school out?"

"Please, Miss Simms. That's what I'm hoping to avoid this time. I don't want to have the police and DYFS called out here again. That kind of disruption is always upsetting to the students."

"And gettin' a call at"—I glance at the time—"twelve-thirty in the afternoon from you is upsettin' to me. A bitch can't even go out and have some chill time with her girl without some shit happenin'. I'll be right there." I get up from the table. "Isaiah done got his black ass suspended. Now I gotta go down to the school and act a damn fool. I'll talk to you later, girl."

Dickalina grunts as I walk outta the kitchen. "Mmmph. But my girls are the ones fucked up. Yeah, okay. Call me later and let me know what his bad ass did this time."

"Kiss my ass, Dickalina," I say, headin' toward the door.

"I love you, too, bitch," she says back, laughin'.

I smack Candy upside the head as I walk by. "Oww!" she yelps, jumpin' up from the sofa. "Why the fuck you hit me?"

I swing open the door, then turn to face her. "For bein' so goddamn ugly. Now buck, booga, so I can whoop the shit outta you."

She rolls her eyes, suckin' her teeth as I slam the door in her face.

Sixteen

I don't even pull into the parkin' space good or get outta my truck before I see Wiggins' big-dick self racing out of the school's doors toward me. I step outta the truck, frownin' at his ass.

"Uh, when the fuck you start meetin' me outside? This better be some new shit y'all doing down here with all the parents who have to pick up their kids 'cause if you only doing the shit to me, I'ma light your ass up, Wiggins. And you know I will."

"Now, now, Miss Simms, there won't be any need for all that. I just thought I'd remind you to please try to keep it together when you get inside. There's a certain etiquette that we like to maintain at all times at the Academy and I'm hoping—"

"Wiggins, cut the shit, niggah. The only thing you need to be hoping is that I don't tell your wife how many times I let you fuck me over the summer and how many times I *might* ride down on your cock this school year. I don't need you to remind me of shit. What you tryna say? That I'm some hood-ghetto bitch or somethin'? I pay tuition here like every-goddamn-body else. Don't have me drag your rusty ass into court for discrimination and sexual harassment, bitch."

His eyes pop open. "Miss Simms, please. Lower your voice; all that is unnecessary. You gave me your word that our indiscretions from this past summer would never be spoken of out in public. So, please." He looks around to make sure no one else is in earshot. "Let's keep this strictly about Isaiah. We all know how passionate you can get when it comes to your children's misbehaviors."

"Passionate? Niggah, my pussy don't get wet over no shit like that. You know I'm only passionate about good dick. I don't know what kinda sick games you into, but you better watch your step. Or I'ma have your ass under investigation. Let me find out you up in there gettin' *passionate* with one of these kids and I'ma have your goddamn head."

He blinks. "Miss Simms, I assure you I was not speaking of being passionate in a sexual sense. I merely meant you care deeply for your children and you don't take lightly to any of their bad behaviors. I wish we had more concerned parents like you."

I put a hand up on my hip and pop my lips. "Oh. Then why ya stupid ass didn't you say that shit in the first place instead of takin' me there?" I see the principal bitch starin' outta her window. She moves back when she sees me looking at her. I frown. "Now what the fuck Isaiah do this week?"

He clears his throat. I stare at his shiny forehead. The

niggah's forehead is so damn greasy I could fry a damn chicken up on it. "Well, uh, he…let's see how I can delicately put this…"

"Wiggins, will you just say it and stop with all the fuckery? I got shit to do."

"Well, uh, I'm sure you know Isaiah is an intelligent young man with so much potential."

I roll my eyes. "Is he being nominated for a school award or somethin'? If not, get to the goddamn point, Wiggins."

He pulls out a handkerchief and wipes his forehead. "Isaiah stood up on his chair, unzipped his trousers and exposed himself, then told the teacher to perform fellatio on him."

I feel my knees buckle. "That lil' motherfucka did *whaa-aaat?!* He told a teacher to do what? Suck his goddamn cock? Is that what I heard you say?"

"Miss Simms, please try to stay calm."

"Stay calm? How the fuck you expect me to stay calm, hearing my motherfuckin' son is up in there tellin' teachers to suck his dick?" *I hope that motherfucka used lotion this morning and didn't pull out no ashy-ass dick or I'ma really beat the skin off his ass for embarrassing me.*

"I know this news is upsetting. And I hope you understand our concern here as well. We think it's…"

"Wiggins, I'm not tryna hear shit else you have to say." I start walkin' toward the school. My heels click across the concrete. "I'm goin' in to get my son. You can stand out here and bullshit if you want by your damn self."

He quickly follows behind me. “Miss, Simms, please. Remember to stay calm. We have him sittin’ in the disciplinary room. Why don’t I have you take a seat in my office while I have one of the aides bring him down to us? Then we can discuss disciplinary action further.”

I stop, puttin’ a hand up in his face. “There is nothin’ else to discuss. I will take him home, you will suspend him for how many days, then he *will* return to school. And he will think twice before he ever pulls his goddamn dick out again.”

“See, that’s the part you wouldn’t let me finish. Principal Lewis wants to expel him.”

I tilt my head. “Expel him, for pullin’ out his dick? Are you serious?”

He nods. “I’m sorry. It’s considered gross sexual misconduct. Isaiah won’t be allowed back into school; at least not until there’s an evaluation done on him.

“An evaluation? My son doesn’t need a goddamn evaluation. What he needs is his black ass beat down to the white meat for pullin’ some stunt like that.”

“We’re concerned that Isaiah might have learned this kind of behavior from…” He looks away.

“Say it, bitch,” I snap, shiftin’ my handbag from one hand to the other. I feel like swingin’ it upside his goddamn head. “You think he learned pullin’ his dick out from who, *me?*”

“No, no, I’m not suggesting that. But he had to learn it somewhere.”

“Oh, I know you’re not suggestin’ he learned it from

me 'cause you already know what's between my legs. And it ain't no damn dick. So suspend him for the rest of the week, then allow his ass back in school next week."

"My hands are tied."

"Well, you better untie them," I hiss. "Let the bitch try it and I'ma tear into her asshole and yours. And I mean it, Wiggins. Now try me."

I'ma beat the shit outta Isaiah! "Now let's go inside and handle this. And, no, I'm not gonna tear your damn office up like I did last year, if that's what you're worried about."

He chuckles nervously. "Will we need to call the police or DYFS?"

"You can call whoever you want."

As soon as we step into the school's entrance I make a beeline into the principal's office. Her dick suckin' secretary, Rebecca—a short, stumpy bitch with extra big titties and a wide ass, quickly hangs up the phone when she's sees me. Wiggins tells me he's goin' to get Isaiah and bring him down to the office. "Yeah, you do that."

"Oh. Hello, Miss Simms," Becky the Cock Bobber says, pastin' a phony-ass smile on her face. "Is Principal Lewis expecting you?"

I sneer at her frog-eyed self. "No, the bitch ain't expectin' me. She's hidin' from me, I'm sure. Call her and let her know I'm here to see her and I'm not leavin' until I do."

She buzzes her office. "Hi. Miss Simms is requesting to speak with you....No, you have a two and a three o'clock...no, she said she wants to see you *now*...okay..."

She hangs up. "Principal Lewis said she'll be out in a minute."

I roll my eyes.

It takes the bitch almost seven minutes to come out of her office, wearin' a beige pencil skirt with a matchin' blazer over a pale pink V-neck blouse. I eye her shoes. Four-inch leather Gucci pumps. She parts her dick-suckin' lips into a wide, phony smile.

"Hello, Miss Simms. It's always a pleasure."

"Girl, stop with the lies."

She blinks. "Okay, then how can I help you?"

"Ummm, Principal Lewis," Cock Bobber says, cuttin' her eyes at me. "Should I have Mister Wiggins paged?"

She looks from me to Cock Bobber. "No. I'm sure this won't take long. What can I do for you, Miss Simms?"

I plop my handbag up on the counter. "What is this shit about you wantin' to expel my son from school? You must really wanna see me set it off up in here, don't you?"

"Miss Simms, that won't be necessary. What Isaiah did this morning was unacceptable and simply can't be tolerated here."

"LaQuandra," I snap, rollin' my eyes. "Cut the formalities with your phony ass."

She looks over my shoulder, then cuts her eye over at Becky the Cock Bobber. "Miss Simms, I won't tolerate profanity from you. If you wish to speak to me about your son's behaviors, then fine. But I will not allow you to be verbally assaultive to me."

I huff. "Ho, when I assault you, you'll know."

She sighs, shakin' her head. "Okay, that's it. I see some things never change. You're still making threats and always looking for a fight. Well, save it. I'm not moved by your hood tactics. Isaiah is being suspended, following a review hearing."

I give her an incredulous look. "A review hearin' for what?"

She tilts her head. "To determine if he's appropriate to return to this school or if he's in need of somethin' a bit more structured, and self-contained."

Oh, this bitch is goin' too far now! "Self-contained? Uh, Boo-Boo, what exactly are you tryna say?"

"I've already said it."

I pull in my bottom lip, tryna keep from takin' it to her damn face. "Well, say it again 'cause I'm not understandin' what the fuck you're tryna say."

"Bottom line, Cassandra. I will not allow any form of gross conduct, be it sexual or otherwise, here at Eastside Charter."

"Bitch, puhleeze. Gross conduct, my ass. You might have gone out and got you a few college degrees. And, yeah, you got ya'self some fancy clothes with a new nose job and ya ass and titties lifted, but you still the same old hoodrat bitch from the projects, *LaQuaaaaaandra.* You've always hated me, bitch. And now you wanna take it out on my son."

She laughs. "You're more delusional than I thought,

Cassandra. The fact remains, you're an unfit mother. And Isaiah is being expelled. Whether you believe it or not, I'm concerned for his well-being. We all are. Fact of the matter is if he's learning that sort of lewd behavior at home, then I can only imagine what else he's being exposed to there. Face it, Cassandra, you're a bad influence. I don't know why DYFS hasn't taken those kids from you by now. You really need to give custody to—"

Before she can finish her sentence I rear my hand back and whop her upside her head, then punch her in the face. I've had enough of all this talkin' back and forth. A bitch's ready to fight!

"Aaaah! No the fuck you didn't put your motherfuckin' hands on me, tramp-ass bitch!"

Becky screams for assistance through the intercom, but it's an ass-whoopin' too late. LaQuandra and I start scrappin' like two crusty, crackhead hoes on the streets. She starts swingin' her arms wildly.

"I'ma kill you!" she screams at the top of her lungs. The tension between me and this ho has always been thick ever since we were kids. But shit really turned ugly between us when her hubby—well, her boyfriend at the time—got me pregnant. Dumb bitch still married his ass.

"Bitch"—I punch her upside the head—"you've always hated the fact that I fucked Isaiah and gave him the son you couldn't. You empty, rotten-pussy bitch!"

I swing her into the counter, then we start tearin' the office up. "Ohmygod! Ohmygod! Principal Lewis! Miss Simms! Someone help! They're fightin' in here!"

Wiggins scurries into the office and tries to pry us apart but we're too much for him to handle by himself.

I punch LaQuandra's mouth in, and blood gushes everywhere. She starts swingin' her arms like a wild woman. "You're a dead bitch, Cassandra! Do you hear me?! DEAD! You put your motherfuckin' hands on me! Your ass is goin' into a body bag, bitch!"

So much for the bitch's Miss Prim and Proper act; she's quickly slipped back into being the ghetto-trash bitch she is. I let her keep yellin' out threats as I punch and slap her. She claws my face. But I am so goddamned pissed that this bitch was questionin' my parentin' and threatenin' me with DYFS after all I've been through with that fuckin' agency. My two oldest were taken from me when I was fifteen—Darius was only two and Jah'Mel was only a few months old—because I had gotten locked up for stealin', and Beulah fuckin' refused to take them in; her own great-grandchildren. I never forgave that old, selfish, hateful-ass bitch for that.

I spent two months locked up as a ward of the state, then another four months fightin' to get my kids back when I got out. But the blessin' came when the Family Court judge on the bench that day happened to be the same old nasty fuck who I'd rode down a dark alley with—on more than one occasion—and sucked his dick in the front seat of his Cadillac just so I could make a few dollars to buy milk and Pampers for my kids. And that day in court I knew justice would be served. And dished up well, or I was gonna turn it up. The nasty fucker looked like he was about to shit himself and pass out when I came through his courtroom with my court-appointed Public Pretender.

Long story short, he not only emancipated me, but gave me my sons back. And yes…I knew I'd owe him, big time. But it didn't matter. I woulda fucked the whole court house if I had to in order to get my sons back. Two nights later, I paid up. I met him at a rundown motel in Newark—and let him run his fifty-five-year-old dick in me, fuckin' me in all three holes. And I swore then, I'd never let anyone else take my kids from me.

So for this bitch to threaten me with DYFS, she had crossed the motherfuckin' line. I wish a bitch would! I take damn good care of my goddamn kids. They want for nothin'. So for this ho to part her cum lickers to say I should give Isaiah to her and his fahver is ridiculous. And she needs the shit beat outta her for even thinkin' it. Bad-ass or not, he's mine. And I'm responsible for his ass until he's eighteen. But until then, I'ma beat the snot outta him for fuckin' up my goddamn day.

"Bitch," I snap as four teacher's aides rush into the office to break us up. "The only thing dead in the room are your insides. You'll never get my son, so you better go adopt another pet."

"Miss Simms! Principal Lewis!" Wiggins yells as he and the aides try to pry us apart. "Stop this madness." But neither of us stop goin' at it like two wild whores in heat. Her nails graze the side of my face as she slaps me and that only pisses me off more. I punch her as hard as

I can, causin' her to grunt and stumble backward, then I lunge at her, grabbin' her by hair and wrappin' my hands up in it.

He grabs me by the waist and I snatch a chunk of the bitch's weave outta her head as he yanks me. "Both of you are makin' a spectacle of yourselves."

"Motherfucka, you think I give a shit about bein' a goddamn spectacle? Get your motherfuckin' hands off'a me."

She screams, holdin' her head. "Get that crazy whore out of my office!"

"Bitch, the only one crazy in the room is *you*. You will never raise my son! Always the stepmother, never a mother." Cock Bobber and Wiggins give us both a confused look. "Oops. The secret's out. Yeah, this stuck-up bitch is Isaiah's stepmother." Her eyes pop out in shock. "Yeah, I fucked her—"

"You fuckin' dirty bitch!" she snaps, tryna lunge at me. But she's quickly held back by one of the aides.

"Principal Lewis, the police are on their way," Becky the Cock Bobber announces.

"Fat bitch," I snap, tossin' LaQuandra's weave pieces in her face. "Eat a dick and choke! I don't give a fuck about no cops comin'. I'll be bailed out before the ink dries. Dumb, trick-ass!"

She blinks, shocked.

Big dick Wiggins tries to calm me. "Miss Simms, please. Let's not make this any—"

"Fuck you, niggah. Let's go tell ya wife how many times

you sucked these guts out. How 'bout we do that, huh, niggah-bitch?"

Everyone in the office's mouths drops open. I can see the blood drainin' from his face as the po-po make their way into the buildin'. Eight deep! But I don't give a fuck! I smile to myself when I see three officers I know walkin' in.

They separate the two of us, takin' our statements. LaQuandra tells 'em I attacked her and the Cock Bobber cosigns the shit. I admit to goin' upside her head. But because I have a scratch on my face and neck, they have to arrest her ho-ass, too. And she's sick! Good for the bitch!

Before I let them arrest me, I call Darius to come to the school and pick up his brother since he's also listed as an emergency contact, then hold my arms out in front of me and let them cuff me. As they're escortin' me outta the buildin', I see Elijah and Isaiah and go off. "Niggah, you see what the fuck you caused?! I'm gettin' arrested 'cause you don't know how to fuckin' behave in school. I'ma beat the skin off ya back when I get home for pullin' out your goddamn cock in class! You lucky they have me in handcuffs or I'd do you right here. Your brother's comin' to pick ya black ass up!"

Wiggins tries to usher Isaiah back into his office and Elijah tries to run outside after me, but two aides grab him and hold him back. "Why you pig fuckers lockin' my mom up?" Elijah wants to know, then he starts yellin' at

Isaiah. "See what you did, asshole!" Next thing I know he's goin' after Isaiah.

"Elijah!" I scream, cranin' my neck as the cops are tryna haul me out. "Drag his ass!"

Once I'm in the backseat of the squad car, the dark chocolate officer with the dark brown eyes, thick nose and juicy, pussy-eatin' lips, waits until his partner goes back inside to use the bathroom, then looks at me through his rearview mirror, shakin' his head. His voice is low. "Damn, Cass. When you gonna stop all this dumb shit? You too fuckin' fine to be carryin' on the way you do. "

I lick my lips, then lean up in my seat and whisper, "Niggah, don't worry 'bout all that. When you gonna come by to eat my pussy in the backseat of this squad car, again? You know you miss this pussy all up on ya tongue, niggah."

"Yo, c'mon, Cass. Don't start. I'm serious. The judge is gonna get tired of seeing your ass in his courtroom. You keep fuckin' around and he's gonna lock ya ass up. Then what?"

I sigh. "Then I'll do the time."

He shakes his head. "And you gonna end up losing ya damn kids. Listen. Speaking of which, we need to talk about Joshua. I've been tryna put this off, but after today I can't anymore."

I blink. Joshua is—as you already know, my...*our*... fourteen-year-old son. Yes, this niggah is Baby Daddy Number Five. And one of the few niggahs that pays his child support on time every week and spends time with his son. "You've been tryna put off what, Julius?" I ask, feelin' my pressure startin' to rise.

"I want custody of Joshua."

"You can have joint custody, but that's it. My son is not livin' with you."

"*Our* son," he corrects, raisin' a brow. "And I'm takin' you to court for full custody. It's time he lives with me. You still wanna run the sreets and be wild. He needs stability and structure."

"Niggah, you a goddamn liar. I've raised him for the last fourteen years and all of sudden you wanna step in like Captain America. I don't think so."

'Listen, the fact is you keep too much shit goin'. Josh needs a more stable home environment, Cass. You still wanna run the streets and shit."

"Niggah-bitch, this has nothin' to do with what the fuck I do on my own time. I take damn good care of my kids, and you know it. Ya black ass just don't wanna pay all that child support. That's all this is about. Well, guess what, niggah? You ain't gettin' my son. And now I'ma drag ya ass back into court for more money; watch me."

"Ya ass is crazy, Cass. I pay close to nine hundred dollars a month so you better enjoy it while you can 'cause I'm gettin' my son and you won't be gettin' shit else."

I glare at him. "You'll get Joshua over my dead body, niggah."

"Be careful what you wish for," he says as his partner opens the passenger side door and slides in.

He revs the engine, then peels outta the parkin' lot, headin' downtown. He keeps eyein' me in the rearview mirror, and I'm eyein' him back.

This niggah's crazy if he thinks I'ma ever let him take Joshua from me. I'll let a train full of niggahs fuck me before that happens. I'll pay someone to body him, first. And I mean that shit!

I lean all the way back in my seat, lift my legs up and plant my feet up on the partition, spreadin' open my legs and showing my bald snatch. "What, niggah…you want some'a this hot pussy? Is that why the fuck you starin' so goddamn hard." His partner tries not to look back at me.

"Get your feet down," he barks, mean muggin' me all crazy and whatnot.

"Fuck you, little dick," I snap, kickin' the partition. "Yeah, bitch… I know all about that lil'-ass, piggy dick you got. And I heard you come fast, too, you worthless fuck!"

He glares at me. "Yo, you heard what the fuck I said. I'm not gonna tell you again."

"What the fuck you gonna do, bitch?" I kick the partition again. "Suck a tampon, punk-ass niggah!"

"Yo, man," Julius says, glancin' over at him. "Don't crank her up. Just ignore her crazy ass."

He turns back the fuck around and keeps his eyes forward as Julius hits the siren button and presses the pedal to the metal. The niggah knows he'd better hurry up and get me to the station and outta this car and away from his ass before I say a whole lot more.

"Both of you pussy-ass niggahs can eat my ass."

I kick the partition again.

Julius shakes his head, lettin' out a disgusted sigh, like I give a fuck.

Bastard!

Seventeen

"C'mon, Cass…damn," he whispers all throaty and whatnot as I unfasten his belt buckle, unzip his pants, then fish out his thick, throbbin' cock. "You tryna get me fired 'n shit." He feebly pushes my hand away; tries to lift my face from his crotch. But I know it's all an act.

"What, you don't want this fat-ass dick sucked?" I ask, lickin' the sticky precum that oozes outta his piss slit. This niggah might not be shit. But his dick is hella good! And he knows it. But I know that his ass is weak…for good pussy and good head, which is why he really isn't stoppin' me from havin' at his cock. His mouth is sayin' one thing, but his body and dick are sayin' somethin' else, as always.

And I'm here to give it to him. Besides, if I don't get a dose of dick before I get home I'ma end up killin' Isaiah for bringin' all this damn drama in my life today. So I need me some dingaling and a good fuckin'!

He moans, leanin' his head back. "You know I do, damn…fuck… I have'ta get back to the station soon."

I flick my tongue over the head, again. "It'll only take five minutes if you stop playin' around, niggah." I wrap my warm, wet mouth over the head. Allow my tongue to swirl over it. I look up at him and bat my lashes. "C'mon, daddy...let me eat the nut outta this dick real quick."

"Shit!" He lifts his head up from the headrest and looks around to see who's outside, then glances at the clock. He's thinkin', wonderin' inside his horny-ass head if he can turn down a dose of this bomb head game. His dick, swollen and hard, throbs in my hand. Even if he wants to, we both know his dick won't let him. The niggah is a slave to it. He's a freak like me, which is why he can't stay away from me. No matter how much shit he pops; no matter how hard this niggah tries to fight it, he always finds himself—his rock-hard dingdong—stuffed between my lips—mouth, pussy, or ass, whichever I decide to give him. Right now, I want his nut down in my throat. I flick my wet tongue back over the head, then slip it into my mouth, teasing him. "Fuck...uh, shit..." He lifts his hips up from the seat and pulls his pants and underwear down. "Make it quick, Cass. But this isn't gonna change what I said to you earlier."

I eye him, knowin'ly as I twirl my tongue around his dick. "What won't change? Me suckin' ya dick all up in ya squad car? You gonna stop fuckin' me?"

"Nah, me wantin' custody of Joshua."

Niggah, you fuckin' with the wrong one!

"Oh, that," I say, smirkin'. "Julius, you do whatever you feel you gotta do. And I'ma do what I gotta do. But, for right now, all I want is this big dick down in my throat."

"Oh, word? You got my shit hard as fuck."

I cup his small, hairy balls and gently juggle them in my hand, then roll 'em between my fingers. I throat his dick, then reach up with one hand and twist his nipple. He grunts. "I love it when you suck this dick, Cass...aaah, fuck..."

I know you do, niggah!

He reaches over and hikes up the side of my skirt, rememberin' from earlier today that I don't have on any drawers. He smacks my ass, causin' my pussy to clench. I wanna fuck him! But I hate his ass right now. All six-feet of him! Still...I love the niggah's dick! And right in broad daylight, I have his ass moanin' and groanin' and gruntin' as I greedily suck him down balls-deep in the school's empty parkin' lot next to my truck.

I pull his dick from outta my throat, then slap it. Softly at first, then hard, causin' it to spring back at me. I slap it again. He grunts. I slap it again, this time squeezin' his balls. "Aaah, shit, fuck...you about to make me nut..."

I know what he wants better than he knows it. It's always been like that from the moment I met him. I was twenty-one and hot in the ass, pussy, and throat with five kids and four baby daddies. It was a Saturday night and I was up in the club—on the dance floor—doin' what I do best, shakin' it, droppin' it, poppin' it, and clappin' it. All eyes were on me, "the bitch wit' da *phat* ass" as I bounced it up on some niggah who didn't know what the fuck to do with it. I was too much for him to handle, and he finally backed off, leaving me to continue my show—alone.

With a drink in one hand, I lost myself in the music, slippin' back to my days as a stripper—when I was one of the highest-paid, well-sought-out hoes on the stage. Niggahs would line the stage and pack the club just to see me make this ass pop and clap. And there was a part of me that missed that adrenaline rush that came along with bein' up on the stage in front of hundreds of horny motherfuckas, whistlin' and howlin' for more while lettin' ones, fives, tens, twenties, and fifties rain down on me. That night at the club I was dancin' fast and hard and real nasty, then hip rolled it into slow, seductive, hypnotizin' moves. Yes, a bitch was real frisky and feelin' herself, but so what. I knew I was workin' the floor. And I had almost forgotten where I was until I felt someone dancin' behind me, grindin' all up on my ass like he owned it. When I spun around to face the intruder, it was this niggah, standin' in back of me, drunk and grinnin'.

"You sexy as fuck," he yelled in my ear over the music.

"Yeah, and?" I said with a buncha sass. "That still doesn't give you the right to ride up on my ass like you got it like that."

"I wanna take you home wit' me and fuck you all night."

"Niggah, you wouldn't know what to do with a young

bitch like me." I spun around on my heel, then bent over and popped it up on his crotch. The minute I felt his dick stabbin' the seam of my ass, I werked it, twerked it and damn near made him squirt in it. I reached around and grabbed his arms, wrappin' them around my waist, then practically let him fuck me on the dance floor. I had motherfuckas who were tryna get at me all night, but had been igged or dissed, feelin' some kinda way.

I threw this ass up on him, rump-shaked it until he bucked at the knees, then spun back around to face him, grinnin'. "I made you nut on ya'self, didn't I?"

He stared at me with a goofy-ass look on his face. His eyes were glazed from booze and lust. He folded his hands in front of him, seemingly embarrassed that I called him out on it. "Nah, I can't come like that."

I rolled my eyes. "Lies. You ain't gotta front. I already know I made ya drawers sticky, niggah."

He smirked. "I ain't had no pussy in two weeks."

I rolled my eyes up in my head. "Just what I thought, niggah. Ya horny ass can't hang with me; nuttin' all quick and shit." I walked off the dance floor.

"Aye, yo, wait up," he said, gently pullin' me by the arm. "You gotta name?"

"You eat pussy?"

"Hell yeah."

I tilted my head and eyed him. He was sexy as fuck. "Come outside and eat my pussy real quick. If it's good, I'll tell you my name after I cum on ya tongue."

Ten minutes later, I was in the backseat of his black Jeep with my legs up over his shoulders and his tongue shoved deep into my pussy. His tongue work was delicious and it wasn't long before he had his dick in me and was fuckin' me deep, hard, and fast.

Julius was twenty-three and fine with a hard, horny dick that wanted to be sucked and fucked. The niggah had heard through the street news that I had some real good pussy and took it up the ass so he wanted to sample it for himself. And after two weeks of reckless fuckin', I got pregnant.

That night at the club when his boys pointed me out on the dance floor he walked up behind me and started dancin' up on me, I let him think I was caught off-guard. What he didn't know was that I had been watchin' him from the minute he stepped foot into the club. That I was on the prowl that night for some dick; that all of my hard, nasty dancin' that night was to reel the niggah in, like now…

I rapidly suck and pop his cock, slather it up with a buncha spit, then gulp it down into my throat as I slide a hand between my legs and start playin' with my clit.

"Ohh, fuck, baby…I can't keep fuckin' with you like this…You trouble, Cass…aaaah, shit…you 'bout to make me nut…"

I remove his dick from outta my throat and start jacking it off, flickin' my tongue over the head. He grabs a chunk of my ass, then slaps it. "Nice, big, juicy ass…"

I grin. "You wanna put your dick in it?"

"What you think?"

I cum all over my fingers, then remove my hand and put 'em up to his lips. I slip them into his mouth, watch him as he sucks each finger clean. "I think Mister Officer's ready to fuck. You had my pussy real hot when you arrested me today, niggah."

He grins. "You had me heated when you hiked ya legs up in the backseat and was tryna show ya pussy. But I ain't gonna front. That shit had my dick hard as fuck. But, yo, that was fucked up what you said to my partner."

"Fuck that lil'-dick niggah. I don't give a fuck about him. He ain't shit. His crooked ass."

"C'mon, chill with that. Look. I gotta get back to the station. You gonna finish suckin' this dick so I can bust this nut real quick, or what?"

I run my tongue down the left side of his dick, swirl my tongue over the head, then lick down the right side. "The whole time I was down at the station I kept thinkin' about you rammin' this fat dick in me. I was pissed at you, but fuckin' horny at the same time. Now I wanna ride down on this dick real quick. I want you to slide ya nightstick into my pussy while you fuck me in the ass, then hose me down with that hot, creamy nut..."

He looks around the parkin' lot. "C'mon Cass, I can't fuck you out here, like this, in broad daylight."

"Yes, you can, niggah." I sit up and twist my body toward him, lifting my left leg up on the seat and showing him my pussy. I smack it, then pull my thick lips apart. "You're an officer of the law. You can do whatever the fuck you want. Now drive this cop car around the back and protect and serve me like the naughty lil' police officer you are." I pop my clit. "Come arrest this wet pussy, Mister Officer."

He stares at me, then down at his hard dick, shakin' his head. "Shit." He starts the engine, then drives around to the back of the buildin'. "I can't keep fuckin' with you like this, Cass. You gon' fuck around and get my ass fired."

Yup, that's exactly what I'ma do if you think I'ma let you get full custody of my son, bitch. I'ma ruin ya fuckin' career if you even try it!

I grin, lickin' my lips. "You know you love this pussy, niggah, that's why you keep comin' back for it." I lean forward in his lap and swallow his cock whole. Two minutes later, I'm fishing a condom and lube outta my oversize bag. I roll the condom down on his cock. Squirt a glob of lube on my fingertips and smear it over my hole, then squirt some over his dick. Once the head pushes its way in, it doesn't take long before he has every inch shoved in my ass.

"Oooh, Julius…I love it when you fuck me in ya cop car, niggah. Feel how hot you got my ass? You like how that ass feels around ya dick, baby?"

He grunts. "Aaah, shit…Cass, you gonna fuckin' get me fired. I can't keep fuckin' you like this…shit feels…so…fuckin'…good…"

The wetness of my pussy splashes out as I rub my clit

and ride down on his dick. Yeah, takin' it in the ass hurts—at first, but once ya asshole's been trained to take it—a bitch can eventually gobble up any size, like me. The pleasure of being filled—stuffed and stretched—is like no other.

I clench my pussy muscles as I feel fire shot through my ass. "Mmmmm…oh, yesssss, niggah…this dick feels so good in my ass…You like fuckin' me in ya cop car?"

"Yeah, baby…aah, fuck…I'm gettin' ready to nut…oh, shit…"

"Oooh, yessssss….cum for me, daddy. Bust your nut all up in me…"

I toss my head back, clench my asscheeks, then explode from my pussy and my asshole as he floods the condom with his hot nut.

We cling to each other for an extra moment, his tongue slippin' into my mouth as we both try to steady our breathing and pulses, the way we used to when we were young and horny and didn't know the difference between being in love and being in lust. Even now the line is drawn in the sand, yet we continue to cross it. The difference is I know when and when not to step over it. Lucky for me, this niggah doesn't.

I lift up and his dick slips outta my ass as I slide back over to the passenger side. "Damn, that shit was good," he says as he slowly pulls the condom off. I lean over and suck his sticky dick clean. "I gotta stop fuckin' with you, Cass, for real. Your ass is trouble."

I sit back up in my seat, lickin' my lips as he pulls his boxers up, then his pants. "Oh, you have no idea," I warn, eyein' him as I open the door. I smile, steppin' outta the car and shuttin' the door. "Try to take my son from me, niggah, and I promise you I'ma make sure your whole world is turned upside down."

He laughs. "Yo, can't we ever just fuck and keep it at that without all the extras?"

I suck my teeth. "Niggah, fuckin' you has nothin' to do with what I just said."

He starts the engine. "Then we good, baby. As long as you know all that shit you talkin' doesn't faze me, we should have no problems. We can still fuck, but at the end of the day I'm still takin' you to court. And I'm gettin' custody of Josh; end of discussion."

I feel like reachin' back into the car and punchin' the shit outta him, but I refrain myself and give him the finger, then mush him in the head instead. "Thanks for the dick, niggah."

He watches me, shakin' his head as I throw my hips in gear and start walkin' back to the front of the buildin' to my truck, ass bouncin' every which way with each step.

Eighteen

It's almost five-thirty in the evenin' when I finally pull into my driveway behind Darius's Lexus. I get outta the truck and strut toward the house with a purpose: to whip the skin off of Isaiah's ass. All of my kids know I don't play when it comes to school. I send their asses to school to get a goddamn education, not be disrespectful and definitely not bullshit around. "Where the fuck is Isaiah?" I yell the minute I step through the door, then slammin' it. I toss my handbag on the sofa. Roll up my sleeves, ready to bring it to Isaiah's ass. The house is quiet. "Where the fuck is everybody at?"

"Yo, Ma," Darius says, walkin' into the livin' room. He comes over and gives me a hug and a kiss. "You aiight?"

I eye him. "Yeah, I'm alright. Why wouldn't I be?"

"I'm sayin', Ma. After what popped off down at da school and whatnot, I figured you might wanna lil' sumthin'-sumthin' to calm ya mind." He pulls out a bag of weed and hands it to me, grinning.

"Oh, I'm calm," I say, stuffin' it in my bra while headin' toward the stairs. *But I'ma be even calmer once I smoke this real quick*. "Where's Isaiah? He has an ass whoopin' on reserve."

Darius comes up on me and drapes his arm over my shoulder. "Yo, Ma. Let me holla at you, for real. Relax, aiight. I know you real aggie and all. But before you start spazzin' out on Isaiah, I handled his lil' ass for you. I promise you, he won't do nuthin' stupid like that again. I yoked him up real quick. So, let it ride, aiight? Can you do that for me? He knows his lil' ass is gonna be on punishment. So you ain't gotta go stompin' him out, feel me?"

I put a hand up on my hip. Tilt my head, then take a deep breath. "Niggah, I spent almost two goddamn hours down at the police station in handcuffs for goin' upside that bitch's head all behind his black ass. And you think I'm supposed to let that slide? No, I'ma fuck him up 'cause he shoulda kept his motherfuckin' dick in his pants."

"Yo, c'mon, Ma."

"C'mon, hell." I look up and see Isaiah standin' at the top of the stairs, lookin' all scared and shit. "Get yo' ass down here, and come get this ass whoopin'. Because if I have to come up those stairs to give it to you, it's gonna be worse. You had no goddamn business doing what you did."

"I'm sorry, Ma. I promise I won't do it again," he says, wringing his hands as his leg shakes. "Darius already beat me for it."

"Well good. 'Cause now I'ma beat yo' ass for gettin'

suspended and for having me break two goddamn fingernails banging that bitch in her head. And now I gotta sit home with ya black ass. So get down here."

Joshua and Elijah come runnin' upstairs from the basement, swingin' open the door with Fuquan and Tyquan behind them. "Hey, Ma," Joshua and Elijah say, goin' up the other flight of stairs.

"Hey," I say back.

Tyquan runs over and wraps his arms around my waist. "Momm- mmmmmmy, you home! I thought you was in jail."

I hug him. "I was. How's Mommy's lil' handsome man doing?"

"I'm fine. Why you get locked up?"

"Because your brother, Isaiah, pulled his goddamn dick out in school and I had to beat up his fahver's bald-headed wife."

"Ewww, that's nasty; why he do that?"

"'Cause he wants me to fuck him up."

"Oh, maaaaaaan," Fuquan says, foldin' his arms across his chest. "I thought they were gonna keep you locked up."

I stare at him, not sure if I should laugh or be insulted. I shake my head. "Boy, shut ya fresh mouth up, and get over here and give me a damn hug before I swing you into that goddamn wall." He shuffles over to me and gives me a half-ass hug. "Why you so evil, boy?"

"You evil," he says, shrugging away from me.

Outta all my kids, I already know Fuquan's gonna be

the one who tries to bring it to me. And I'ma have to bury his ass when he does.

Darius plucks him upside the head. "What I tell you 'bout ya mouth, boy?"

"Owww!" he yells. "Why you hit me, Fucker!" Darius laughs and that only pisses him off more. He balls his fist and starts punchin' him. "I'ma fight yo' ass."

"Darius, why you gotta get his ass cranked up. You know he's half crazy. Isaiah, get yo' ass down these stairs, boy. I ain't forget 'bout fuckin' you up. I'm gonna change my clothes and when I come back out you better have ya black ass down here ready for ya ass whoopin'."

Darius stops wrestlin' around with Fuquan's bad-ass and stares at me. "Yo, Ma. I told you I handled it. Chill." He lets Fuquan go and stands up.

I place a hand up on my hip. "Okay, Mister I Handled It, did you handle what the hell I'ma do with him durin' the day, too? 'Cause I'm not about to be stuck sittin' up in this house babysittin' his nasty ass, and he's definitely not ridin' no-goddamn where with me."

"He can come down to the shop with me during the day," he says. "I'll put him to work. Yo, Isaiah, get down here. I'll keep him busy. He can sweep up the hair."

"Boy, you hear me callin' you," Darius says, snappin' me outta my thoughts. "Get ya butt down here."

He takes his slow sweet time comin' down the stairs, then peers around the wall. I glare at him. "Boy, get over here," Darius says to him. "What you gotta say to Ma?"

He lowers his head. "I'm sorry."

I narrow my eyes, clenchin' my teeth. "Boy, I wanna wrap a cord around ya neck and swing you through the goddamn streets for doing that shit. Why the fuck you do it? And before you shrug ya goddamn shoulders and say you don't know, you better think long and hard." I place a hand on my hip, waiting to see if I'ma have to punch him in his mouth or not.

His lips quivers. "I got really mad."

"Why'd you get mad, Isaiah?"

"'Cause Missus Lambert never picks me in class. She picks the other kids to do stuff and always acts like I'm not there."

I frown. "What the fuck you mean, Missus Lambert don't pick you?"

Tears start fallin'. "When I raise my hand to answer questions or to go to the board, she won't pick me. She told the class that if they wanna end up in jail or dead to look at me."

My eyes pop open in disbelief. "Say *whaaaat?!*" I snap, shakin' my head. "That bitch said what?" He repeats what she said. "Are you makin' this shit up, Isaiah? 'Cause you know I will tear that ho's ass up."

He shakes his head. "No. She said it. And the kids were laughin' at me."

Oh, I'm steamin' now. You don't fuck with my goddamn kids. I don't give a fuck who you are. And you don't make them feel like they ain't shit. When I was their age, I didn't have anyone encouragin' me, or tellin' me I could be a lawyer or a doctor or the next top supermodel. No one made me feel special. No, I had a grandmother who kept tellin' me I was gonna end up bein' a junkie-whore like my mother. That I was worthless like her; that I would be found somewhere dead.

No, Beulah didn't have a goddamn kind word for me. And she didn't give a damn about me. All that old bitch cared about was gettin' her monthly check from the state for me. I had to look for encouragement in the goddamn streets, in the backseat of some horny niggah's car, or in some alleyway, or abandoned buildin'. I never wanted to be a junkie bitch. So I wasn't gonna allow shit Beulah said about me make me become that. And I be goddamned if I'ma let some bitch or no-good niggah try that shit with any of my kids.

I feel all the blood rushin' to my goddamn head. I'm ready to go off. I pull out a chair and sit. "Come here," I say to him. He moves slowly over to me, and starts crying. "Stop crying. I'm not gonna hit you." I pull him into my arms and give him a kiss. Then I grab him by the shoulders and look him in the eyes. "Do you wanna end up in jail or dead?"

He shakes his head, wipin' his tears. "No."

"Then fuck what that bitch said. That ho don't know shit. You stay in school, get good grades, play sports, stay focused and outta trouble, and you can be the next president of the goddamn United States if that's what you wanna be. I don't send you to school to curse out teachers. You know I didn't raise you to be disrespectful to adults. And you had no goddamn business pullin' out ya motherfuckin' cock. But did you have on clean drawers and was ya body lotioned?"

He nods. "Yes."

"Mmmph. Ya black ass better be glad 'cause I woulda really beat yo' ass for havin' on dirty drawers or showin' off an ashy-ass dingaling. But don't you do that shit again, you hear me?"

He nods, again.

"Good. Ya ass is still gonna be on punishment, though. And where the hell you see someone pullin' out their damn dick and tellin' someone to suck it, anyway?"

He shrugs.

I eye him. "Don't do it, boo-boo. I will take it to ya throat boy, and you know it. So you better say it."

"At Daddy's."

"What? You saw ya fahver do some shit like that?"

He shakes his head. "No, I was watchin' it on a movie." I ask him what kinda movie. He tells me that when he was stayin' at his fahver's over the summer that he found videos of people havin' sex and watched them while his fahver and that bitch LaQuandra were asleep.

"And where'd you find these movies?"

"In the closet. They were in a box on the floor, and I wanted to see what they were doing."

I sigh, decidin' to deal with this later. "Did ya fahver call here?"

"Yes. He wants you to call him."

I roll my eyes. "I'ma call him later. But, first thing tomorrow, I'ma be down at that school, again, draggin' that bitch outta the classroom."

Shit. I forgot I can't go up in the school 'cause that punk-ass bitch LaQuandra got a restrainin' order on me. "On second thought, I'ma meet that teacher bitch out in the parkin' lot."

I stand up, eyein' Elijah as he comes down the stairs. "Elijah, did you have homework today?" I gotta stay on Elijah's ass when it comes to his schoolwork; otherwise he'll end up with a buncha damn D's and F's on his progress reports for homework. I try not to be too hard on him since he's my eyes and ears when I'm not around. Don't shit get past him that I don't hear about. He sits back, takes in everything. Then, the first chance he gets me alone, he gives me a minute-by-minute report. So I can't fuck him up too bad. But he knows I'll rock his goddamn ass if his homework isn't done.

"Yes. I already did it," he says, shiftin' his eyes.

"Where is it? Go get it and let me see it." He looks at me all crazy and whatnot. And I know he's lyin'. "Elijah, don't do it. Don't get fucked up tonight. Go get that goddamn homework—you know, the shit you didn't do, but shoulda did the minute you walked through this door—before I turn the ghetto switch on and fuck you up. I see all of you lil' fuckers musta really thought I was gonna be locked up for a few days, didn't you? Well, guess what? I'm not. Now go get that homework and get yo' ass over at this table and get it done." As Joshua is comin' down the stairs, I add, "And, Joshua, you help him."

He sucks his teeth, goin' into the kitchen.

"Did you hear me?"

"Yeah."

"Josh! Don't have me bang you in ya fuckin' mouth. What I tell you about *yeah*-ing me? You kids gonna fuckin' respect me around here goddammit. Or I'ma put your black asses out. Do you hear me?"

"Yes, Ma. I heard you."

I glance over and see Darius playin' Xbox with the twins and smile. "Darius, I need to see you in my room," I say as I'm walkin' down the hall. That's code for let's spark a blunt and talk.

"Aiight, I got you."

A few minutes later, he's sittin' in my leather recliner chair with his feet kicked up on the ottoman, passing me a blunt. "Yo, wassup with the stash I gave you?" he asks, blowin' smoke up in the air.

"Boy, please. I'm savin' that for a rainy day." I take a deep pull, then hold the smoke in my lungs, blowing it slowly out. "These goddamn kids stress me out. That fuckin' bitch down at the school today really tried my nerves."

I hand him back the blunt.

"Who?"

"Goddamn LaQuandra, talkin' 'bout I'ma unfit mother and need to have my kids taken away from me."

He shakes his head, takin' two pulls from the blunt, then passing it back to me. "Do you think I'ma fucked up mother?"

"Nah. You holds it down, Ma. I mean, yeah, you get a lil' reckless at times..."

I raise my brow, snatchin' the blunt from him.

"I'm sayin', Ma. You go in hard. And sometimes you real extra wit' it. But you def not an effed-up mother. Shit, we've always had food to eat and clothes on our backs. I can't front. You always kept us laced in that hotness. And you stayed on my ass to finish school. You handle ya handle, Ma; real talk. And you ain't no joke. Shit, you fucked me up a few times, so I already know what it is."

I laugh, wavin' him on. "Boy, hush. I ain't never really fuck you up. I let you get away with a lot."

"Yo, Ma. Stop." He takes off his fitted, pointin' to a scar above his hairline. "Then how I get these stitches in my head?"

I close my eyes, leaning my head back in my seat. He was sixteen, and thought his ass was grown. I had walked in on him and three of his friends up in his room, drinking and smoking weed and I went off. Instead of him apologizing, he tried to step to me like he was a grown-ass man, poppin' a buncha shit. So since he wanted to show off in front of his niggahs, I gave 'em all a show. I snatched the bottle of Alize they'd been drinkin' from off the dresser and went upside his head with it, knockin' his ass out. He woke up in the hospital with a slight concussion and thirty-eight stitches to the head.

He laughs. "Yo, Ma. You was dead wrong for that. And then you told 'em down at the hospital that I had gotten jumped."

I laugh with him. "Yup. I sure did. Shit, I didn't feel like goin' to jail that day. But I bet you didn't try 'n talk shit to me again after that, either. Did you?"

"Hell nah. Beetle 'n 'em still clown me about that shit 'til this day."

I shift in my seat, takin' another pull from the blunt, then handin' it back to him. Besides the fact that Beetle is one of the barbershop owners, and is one of his best friends, if he ever found out I sucked and fucked Beetle's fat, juicy dick last summer, he'd be ready to kill his ass. They've been friends since sixth grade, and he spent many nights at our apartment. So he was like family. But, last summer, Beetle stepped to me all grown and sexy, talkin' about how he'd been feelin' me. And I quickly forgot his ass wasn't no damn kin of mine and handled him. Whew, the sex was all that! And we fucked for about two months before I had to cut him off.

"You know Beetle's always askin' about you. He keeps sayin' he's gonna stop by to see you."

I bet he does. That niggah's probably still thinkin' about this pussy and ass. I smile, passing the blunt back to him. "Tell him I said hi. I need to come down to the shop one of these days, soon."

"Yeah, you do." He glances at his watch. "I gotta bounce. I'ma hear Shenille's mouth. She stays snappin' if I'm out too late."

I frown. "Tell that bitch to call me if she gotta problem."

He sucks his teeth, shakin' his head. "See, Ma. Here you go." He stands up, talkin' one last pull from the blunt, then passing it to me. "I wish you'd try to get along with her."

I finish off the blunt, then stub it out in the ashtray, standin' up. "Shenille's a sneaky bitch, okay? You know how I feel bout sneaky bitches. And I'm not gonna be phony about it. But as long as she treats you right and she makes sure my grandbaby comes to spend time with me, then I won't have to fuck her up."

He smiles. "Yo, Ma. I don't know what I'ma do with you; you a real piece of work." He hugs me, kissing me on the cheek. "But I wouldn't trade you in for the world. I love you."

"I love you, too, niggah. And you know I'll go to jail behind a bitch fuckin' you over." He laughs, shakin' his head. I watch as he walks out, closin' the door behind him. I roll another blunt, then smoke half of it before goin' out to check on these kids. I quietly open the door and creep up on Elijah and Joshua fiddlin' with their cell phones instead of doing homework. I go off. "Elijah! You supposed to be doing ya goddamn homework, not fuckin' around on that phone. What I tell you about being on that phone when you have homework." I snatch his phone outta his hand, then throw it across the room. It smashes into the wall.

"Maaaaaaaaaaaa!" he shouts. "Why you do that? I *am* doin' my homework. I'm almost done."

"I told you no phone unless all of ya school work is done, and that's what I mean. And, Joshua, you ain't no goddamn better. Give me ya damn phone, too."

"Awww, c'mon, Ma," Joshua groans. "I'm helpin' him. Isaiah, haven't I been helpin' you?"

"Nope," he lies, foldin' his arms across his chest.

I pop him upside the head. "Elijah, stop lyin' on ya brother. And hurry up and get that damn work done. I can't even unwind in peace around here." I hold my hand out. "Give me ya phone, Joshua."

He sucks his teeth. "C'mon, Ma. I was only readin' Day'Asia and Tina's status updates on Facebook."

I frown. "What updates?"

He smirks. "Clitina posted that she and Asia are on their way over to buildin' four to chill with some dudes."

"What? All this time I thought her ass was in her room. Did she come home from school?"

"I ain't snitchin'," he says, laughin'.

"Boy, I don't see shit funny."

Fuquan looks up from his Xbox game. "No, she ain't come home. That ho needs to get her life together, too."

I am too through with his grown-ass, fresh-mouthed self. "What I tell you about callin' your sister names?"

He shrugs. "Well, she is."

I roll my eyes and tell Josh to call Day'Asia's phone, then give it to me. "Yeah, what is it? Why is you sweatin' me, niggah?"

"Day'Asia, if I—"

"Who's this?"

"What the fuck you mean, 'who's this?' It's your mother."

"Oh," she says nonchalantly. "I thought you were locked up."

"Oh. And so thought that gave you the green light to just do whatever the fuck you want, hunh? You out tryna get your ho on tonight?" Fuquan falls out laughin'. I ignore his ass.

She sucks her teeth. "No."

"Mmmnph. Then why the fuck you ain't home?"

"I caught the bus over to Tina's so Miss Lina could do my hair."

I take a deep breath before I go off. "Day'Asia, if I gotta leave up outta this house to drive over to buildin' four to get ya black ass, I'ma beat the shit outta you. So you better get the fuck home, *now!* You have fifteen minutes." I disconnect the phone, stuffin' it in my bra. Josh looks at me. "You'll get it back when Elijah's homework is finished." He opens his mouth to say somethin' else, but I stop him. "Say somethin' else and I'ma smash this shit up against the wall next." I tilt my head, darin' him. "Just what I thought."

These damn kids know how to fuck up a damn high!

Nineteen

"Cass, we need to talk."

I frown, glancin' at the clock. It's midnight. *This niggah has gotta be kidding me!* "Isaiah, are you fuckin' crazy? Do you see what time it is? If you wanna talk to me you shoulda called me earlier, at a decent damn time."

"I told lil' Isaiah earlier to tell you to call me."

"Well, he did. And I didn't feel like talkin'."

He sighs. "I wanna know what happened between you and LaQuandra down at the school today?"

"Niggah, ask ya wife what happened. I'm sure she gave you an earful. She's the bitch who came outta her face all sideways at me."

He lets out another breath. "This shit's gotta stop between the two of you. Every goddamn time I turn around it's somethin'. I'm sick of being in the middle of y'alls bullshit."

I sit up in bed. "What? Niggah, what you mean 'y'all's bullshit'? If you was so damn concerned about not being caught up in the middle of shit, then you shoulda kept ya damn dick in ya pants. But you didn't. So don't blame me because you can't control that dog-faced bitch of yours.

I don't fuck with the bitch. That ho came at me, talkin' about DYFS should be called on me. The bitch tried to say that shit Isaiah did down at the school was some shit he learned here when come to find out he found a box of porno in the back of one of the closets over there. That's where the fuck he learned to tell some bitch to suck his dick. Not from over here, like that bitch tried to insinuate. So you make sure she knows that. Then the punk-ass bitch gets a restrainin' order on me, like I'm some damn threat. That hateful bitch was the one who threatened to kill me."

"Calm down, Cass, damn."

"Calm down hell, niggah. That bitch crossed the line. But it's all good. You tell that—"

I hear LaQuandra's voice in the background. "Isaiah, who are you on the phone with?"

"Cassandra," he tells her. I grin, knowin' that's gonna set her off.

Jealous bitch!

"At this time of night? What the hell you gotta say to that crazy bitch at this hour of the night that can't wait until tomorrow?"

He musta covered the phone or placed me on mute 'cause now I can't hear shit. *I should fuck him for the hell of it, then call her ass to rub it in her face. Fuck with me, bitch!*

I met Isaiah—Baby Daddy Number Seven—when I was twenty-five. On one of the hottest days in August. And, of course a bitch like me didn't make matters any better. I had on a pair of white booty shorts, a white gauzy-like blouse over a sexy white sequined bra and a pair of seven-inch red fuck me heels, cranking up the heat hotter than it already was. I had Joshua, who was ten months old, propped up on my hip, strutting across the campus to get over to the Student Center. I had gotten my GED a few months prior and was feelin' really good about myself. With seven kids, I was takin' two college courses, and you couldn't tell me shit. I was gonna be a nurse one day. Or work with kids, maybe.

But shit happens, and dreams get pushed aside. And then you find ya'self layed up with another niggah, knocked up again. Isaiah was that niggah. Anyway, he and some other niggahs were sittin' out on benches when I walked by. Of course, they started catcallin' and whistling. Yes, I knew what I was doing when I wore the skimpy outfit. Shit, I loved the attention. Still, I paid 'em no mind. Well, that is until this caramel-skinned niggah walked up beside me wearing a cut-off shirt and basketball shorts with a basketball up under his arm. I quickly sized him up. He was tall just how I liked 'em, had three tats, and was a real smooth talker.

I gave him my number. Two weeks later we were fuckin'. Problem was the niggah failed to mention two things. One, that he was only twenty; and, two, that he was already married—to LaQuandra. They had been married for almost a year. But by the time I found out, it was too late. I was already pregnant. I woulda had an abortion. But, he begged me to keep it. Said he didn't believe in abortions. I didn't either. Shit, I had enough babies to prove it.

Anyway, he told me that LaQuandra kept having miscarriages, and he really wanted a baby. But I wanted to go to college. Still, I kept it. And, when I gave birth to a son, he asked me to name it after him. And I did that, too; more so to piss LaQuandra off. To rub it in that ho's face that I gave her man somethin' she hadn't. And, ten years later, somethin' she still hadn't given him—a son.

Isaiah's voice comes back through the phone. "I'm sick of this shit."

"Fuck that crazy bitch," I whisper into the phone. "Come out and get some pussy. I know you want that dick sucked. It'll make you feel better."

"C'mon, Cass. Don't start that shit."

"What, you don't miss the way I suck that dick? C'mon, let me make love to that big dick with my mouth, lips, tongue, and hands, then slide you deep in my ass. I know you miss this big, juicy booty."

I got the niggah breathin' all heavy into the phone. Thinkin', I'm sure. About how he's gonna get outta the house to get some of this sweet 'n sticky. I know, and he knows, that flat-ass bitch ain't clappin' it around his cock like I can, like I have, like I always will. Yes, you heard it right. I'm still fuckin' Isaiah. Not because I have some emotional ties to him that I can't let go of. And not because I'm strung out on his dick, even though it is good. No, I fuck Isaiah, and three of my other baby daddies—like Julius and Vernon, because I can. Because those niggahs are weak for Big Booty, baby. They crave bein' all up inside this hot ass. They love it when I swallow them up into my asshole. And I love knowin' that I can fuck them, suck them, then look in their bitches faces and laugh to myself, or even tell 'em—if I choose to, which I never do—that I'm still fuckin' their men—the fahvers of my kids. I take great pleasure in knowin' that these silly bitches think they have their niggahs on lock. When in truth, I'm the bitch that keeps 'em all comin' back, wantin' more.

"Oh, now you whisperin' into the phone," LaQuandra snaps in the background.

"LaQuandra, take ya ass to bed. No one's whisperin' shit. Fuck. This bitch," he mumbles into the phone. "See what the fuck you did, Cass? Damn, did you have to go up in there and put your hands on her?"

"Oh well. She shoulda watched her mouth. You tell that bitch that if she doesn't let Isaiah back in school next week that I'ma press charges on her ass. And that bitch will be on the unemployment line. Now try it."

LaQuandra's carryin' on in the background. "I mean it, Isaiah. If you wanna be with that ghetto bitch, then you can have her. I've put up with her shit for long enough."

I grin. "Uh-oh, I better let you go. Sounds like there's trouble in paradise. My offer still stands, though. If you want some stress-free suckin' and fuckin', say the word. My legs and mouth are wide open for you."

"Shit. Listen. I'ma call you back in thirty minutes. Make sure you pick up."

"You can pack your shit and get out, Isaiah. Go stay with that bitch. What the fuck you need to call—"

The line goes dead, cuttin' off the rest of LaQuandra's rantin'. I don't know why these dumb bitches put their niggahs out, knowin' they're gonna let 'em right back in. All that dumb shit does is push his ass in between another bitch's legs, temporarily at the very least. *Like mine!* I get outta bed, smilin'.

An hour later, my phone pings. I reach over and grab it off the nightstand. There's a new text. Im outside

I text back, tell him to come around to the patio door. I creep out of my bedroom in a red lace bra and matchin' thong set and a pair of seven-inch black peep-toe fuck-me pumps with the red pencil heel. I slide open the glass door. Isaiah slips in and follows me back to my bedroom, sayin' nothin'. I can feel the heat of his stare on my ass and hips as they sway. He's pissed. At LaQuandra for givin' him grief. At me for bein' the cause of it. He will take his anger out on my pussy and my ass. He will piston-fuck me 'til he's released all of his rage.

My pussy spasms at the thought.

As soon as we're behind the closed bedroom door, he strips outta his clothes. His dick springs upward, already hard and ready. He's thought about how he's gonna beat this pussy and ass up on his way over here.

I drop down in front of him. There's no need for small talk. The message is clear: He came to fuck. I want to be fucked. I kiss the tip of his dick, flick my tongue over it, then take him into my mouth. No hands. I swallow him, cuppin' his heavy balls in one hand, then slidin' my other hand over his muscular ass, squeezin' his ass, then pullin' him deeper into my mouth. He thrusts his thick dick down into my throat. He is face-fuckin' me for his own pleasure. I am the stress reliever he needs for the night.

I flutter my eyes upward. He has his head back, his eyes closed and hands up on his hips. He grunts. "Fuck, Cass...damn, baby... oh shit...I wanna get up in that fat ass, baby..."

I grab him by the ass. It's smooth and muscled with a trail of hair along the center of his asscheeks. I pull him in deeper, squeezin' his ass. Ooh, his dick tastes good. His cock hairs tickle my nose.

"Yeah, suck that dick," he hisses, pumpin' his dingaling in and outta my mouth. "I'm sick of you fuckin' bitches stressin' me the fuck out...yeah, eat that nut outta my dick...fuck, Cass...aaah, fuck..."

I am makin' gulpin' 'n slurpin', 'n poppin' sounds with my mouth. I know that LaQuandra bitch ain't handlin' his dick right. She ain't keepin' him happy, or this thick, curved dingaling wet. He moans. Palms the back of my head and skull-fucks me. Spit is gushin' outta my mouth and runnin' down my chin and onto my titties as his dingaling stabs up the back of my throat. I neck him down 'til his left knee starts to shake, then pull his dick from outta my throat.

I lightly rake my teeth over the head of his throbbin' dick, then swirl my tongue over it one last time before climbin' up on the bed, lyin' on my back, then loopin' my arms under my legs and pullin' them back. I pull my thong over to the side, exposin' my wet pussy and asshole. "Come eat my pussy, then fuck me in this ass, niggah."

He walks over to me, his thick dingdong in his hand, and grabs my asscheeks, then squeezes. My asshole 'n pussy clench in anticipation. Outta all my baby daddies, Isaiah's the one who knows my body the best. He knows when and where and how to give me the dick 'n tongue without me havin' to tell his ass. And the niggah serves me well. He's the one I woulda married—not that I ever really wanted to be hitched to some niggah forever. But if I did, Isaiah is the one I woulda said yes to if he hadn't already been married to that horse-faced bitch, LaQuandra, with her flat-assed self. The bitch better be lucky I ain't tryna have no more kids, otherwise I'd be givin' this niggah another baby tonight; just to spite that childless bitch.

I feel like textin' the bitch and tellin' her to come watch me fuck my baby daddy real good. She betta be glad I ain't a messy bitch 'cause I'd do it for sure.

Isaiah reaches for my right titty and starts pinchin' my inch-long nipple while suckin' on my clit and usin' his free hand to slide two, then three, fingers into my pussy.

Yesssss, goddammit!

He slurps 'n moans, and says, "Aaah fuck, Cass…your pussy tastes…so good."

I buck my hips, offer up all of it to his tongue, his fingers, his mouth. "Get it. Get it…ooh, yessss…get all up in it, niggah. Do me right, goddammit…"

I fuck his face as he works a nut outta me. He won't stop 'til I am coatin' his tongue with my creamy goodness. He rapidly flaps his tongue over my clit, then stabs my slit with it. He twirls his tongue in, feelin' around the loose heat. "Yeah, you nasty motherfucka…get all that cream…lick it out, niggah…uh, uh, uh…

He knows what I want next. One finger, then two, then three, knuckles deep in my ass. He loves fuckin' me in my ass as much as I love bein' fucked in it. He understands, he appreciates, what havin' a hard dick stuffed inside of it does to me. He's experienced, firsthand, how much pussy juice I shoot when my asshole is bein' stroked just so. He knows how I nut outta my ass when it's bein' fucked deep.

He plunges his fingers in and outta it, suckin' my clit, lickin' my pussy. His hot tongue is long and firm and when he rolls it just so it feels like a finger. It feels so goddamn good slidin' in and outta my pussy. Oooh, yes, goddammit! He knows I am ready to feed him when I grab his head and wrap my legs around his neck. My body shakes as I pump my hips into his face and start skeetin' in his mouth.

"Yessss, goddammit…gulp up that sweet potato pie…"

He laps my pussy, darts his tongue in, then licks my asshole, causin' my pussy to shake. "Mmmmph…do me right, niggah…yesssss…"

He growls. "You ready for this dick, bitch?"

I moan, then rapidly start bouncin' 'n shakin' 'n clappin' my ass. He slaps me on it. And I moan again, workin' my clit with my fingers.

"Yeah, ya slutty-ass ready for all this hard black dick… get on ya fuckin' knees. I'ma fuck you in that big, fluffy ass…"

I roll over onto my stomach, then lift up on all fours, beautiful ass hoisted and ready. He reaches for the lube on the nightstand, opens the bottle, pours it between my cheeks, then uses his thumb to rub the bud of my asshole, before pressin' it in, teasin' me.

I wind my hips, glancin' over my right shoulder. "Give me the dingaling, goddammit. Feed this booty, niggah…"

He slaps my ass. It jiggles. He slaps it again; right cheek, left cheek. I let it clap for him. Then he slides his face back between my cheeks and eats my pussy from the back, nips my clit between his teeth, causin' my nipples to harden. Then he straddles my thighs and, in one quick thrust, stabs the head of his dick into my hole. He grabs my hips and pulls me back onto the length of him. All ten, thick delicious inches are buried in my ass. The pain, the pleasure, both shootin' through me; causin' my pussy to drip and my clit to swell. I am in heaven.

He holds onto my hips and rides me fast 'n hard. "You fuckin' bitches always stressin' me the fuck out…crazy-ass bitches…uhhh…fuck…I'm sick of you hoes…shiiit… aaah…"

"Yeah, niggah…talk that shit…you want me to whoop the shit outta that bitch…"

He slaps my asscheeks, hard, as his dingaling stings my insides so goddamn good. "Uh, uh...both of you... mmmph...bitches need to...aaah...get...mmmph... along...I'm...uhhhh...sick of this...shit...mmmph... fuckfuckfuck..."

"Yeah, get all up in that hotness...mmmph...I know that ughly bitch ain't handlin' this big dick...Ooooh, ooooh, fuck LaQuandra...I can't stand that bitch...oooh, oooh, oooh...beat that asshole up, niggah..."

He's behind me, strainin 'n pumpin'; sweat drippin' onto my back.

His dick stops movin' in my ass. Instinctively, I milk his dingaling with my ass muscles, then push myself backward onto it. I let myself fuck him, buckin', 'n rockin', 'n slammin' my hips, showin' him how much I want, need, him, his dick, inside of me stuffin' my ass. The sweet, delicious burn of my baby daddy's dingdong slicin' through my asshole, causin' my pussy to rapidly spasm. Oooh, yes, goddammit! He reaches beneath me and fingers my slippery clit.

"Aaaah, fuck, baby...goddamn...you know how to take this dick...you a fuckin' bitch, Cass...aah shit...nice, deep ass, baby...oooh...mmmph...ass is fuckin' good...aaah..."

He's rapidly fuckin' me, bangin' deep into me; his balls slappin' up against the back of my pussy. He pulls himself all the way out, then slams back in.

In.

Out.

Oooh, yessssss, godddamn it! This niggah is doin' me

right! He grabs a titty, squeezes and kneads and pinches my nipple—ping-ping-pingin' my spot, causin' a liquid fire to shoot outta my pussy, then my ass. I cry out. He cries out. Both of us wildly jerkin'.

I am cummin'. He is cummin'. He grunts, loudly.

"Aaah, shit...motherfuck you, Cass...crazy bitch...aaah shit...what the fuck you doin' to me...mmmph...it's comin', baby...Hmmhmmhmm...I'm gettin' ready to nut all up in this ass, bitch..."

"Yessss, baby daddy...with ya big-dick self...mmmph... give it to me, goddammit...mmmm...cheatin'-ass niggah...fuck me deep, motherfucka..."

"Aaah, shit, baby...talk that shit...I gettin' ready to bust...I want you to ride up on this dick, bitch..."

He pulls outta me, leavin' my pulsin' asshole gapin' and hungry for more dingaling. My pussy is so close to gushin' out hot juices, I need him back in me, now. My baby daddy kneels as I sit on his lap, facin' him. I raised my long, smooth legs and wrap them around his muscled body. He grabs my hips and rams himself back into me.

"Yessss, goddammit! Dick me right, niggah...long, black dick all up in this juicy ass..."

"Yeah, baby...nice, fat, hot ass...I'ma 'bout to bust this nut all up in this ass..." I put my arms around his neck, ridin' down into his lap, grindin' my pussy onto his stomach. "Yeah, baby...you gonna skeet your pussy juice on Daddy's stomach?" I moan. "That's right, baby... give Daddy that pussy cream...I want you to skeet on my stomach, nasty lil' bitch..."

"Uhhh, ooooh, long ass dick feels so good...you better tell ya bitch-ass wife...uhhh, mmmm...I want my son... oooh...back in school...uhhh...or I'ma...aaah...mmmm... beat...her...uhhh...ass..."

"Yeah, baby...both of you bitches crazy...mmmm... this ass is sooo fuckin' good..." I moan. Buck my hips. My pussy starts shootin'. "Yeah, baby...that's it...shoot that hot pussy milk all up on Daddy's stomach..."

I gallop up and down on his dingdong, grindin' my pussy and playin' with my clit.

"Oooh, ooooh, oooooooh..."

"You nuttin' out that ass?"

"Yessss...yesssss...mmm...tear that asshole up, niggah..." Isaiah rolls his head back as I clench my ass and ride him, grindin' into his hips and cummin' all over his dingaling. I pinch his nipples. He is shakin' and gruntin'.

"Fuck, Cass...aaaah, shiiiiiiiiit..." He deepens his thrusts. Pounds my hole for filth. I cum again and again and again. The whole bedroom smells of hot, sweaty sex. My asshole, my pussy cummin' in sync to my baby daddy's moans. He cums and cums and cums, his body jerkin'. "Ohshitohshitohshitfuckfuckfuck..."

After he finishes nuttin', he pulls out and collapses. I collapse beside him, pullin' off his condom, then tossin' it to the side. I lean in and take his dingaling into my mouth, suckin' the rest of his nut outta him. I watch the niggah's toes curl as I clean his whistle. I lick my lips when I am done, then reach over and slide my tongue into his mouth.

He catches his breath, pullin' me into his arms. "Damn, Cass... I don't know what the fuck you do to me. I gotta stop doin' this shit with you."

Niggah, puhleeze. I got you strung!

I grab his sticky dick. Stroke it. Rub his balls. "Lies, niggah-boo. You know ya black ass ain't ever gonna stop fuckin' me."

He sighs, kissin' me on the lips, then slippin' his tongue into my mouth. He pulls back and stares me in the eyes. "Yeah, I know. But I gotta stop. You trouble, Cass."

I grin, liftin' up and straddlin' him. I grind my still very wet pussy up and down along his growin' shaft. "Let me know how you make out with that, niggah."

He grips my hips as I lift up, reach behind me and slip the head of his hard dick into my slit. I use the mouth of my pussy to suck it. I watch as he closes his eyes, pullin' in his bottom lip. "Aaaah, fuck..."

I slide all the way down on his dingaling and fuck him raw. I fuck him until he shrieks like a bitch, moanin' out my name, tellin' me how good my pussy is. How juicy it is. How hot it is. How he loves the way it gulps up his dick. Yeah, sugah-boo, I'ma ho. But I'ma fine bitch with a string a niggahs who stay wantin' to fuck and give me whatever I want, includin' this niggah. Dog-faced LaQuandra might be his wife. But I'ma always be his baby *muhver*. And it ain't shit that childless bitch can do about it.

Twenty

"Isaiah, get ya ass up!" I yell, bustin' up in his bedroom. I bang the foot of his bed. He's been home for almost a week now, and this shit is wearin' my nerves. If Darius wasn't picking' him up and takin' him down to his shop every day, I'd be fuckin' him up for disrupting' my flow.

Lucky for his ass, we have a hearin' tomorrow down at the Superintendent's office. And I already told him if he doesn't get back in school I'm whoopin' the skin off his ass, so he had better go in there and fight for his life and save his ass from gettin' torn off. And I ain't go down to his school and beat his teacher's ass, yet. Oh, but, trust. That ho-ass bitch still gotta ass beatin' with her name on it. But I gotta get Isaiah's ass back in school, first, before I take it to that bitch's head. But I did call her ass up and let her know that if she ever says some shit about my son endin' up in jail or dead, again, that I'ma knock all her teeth in and snatch her tonsils out. Mmmph. Trick-bitch!

Anyway, I'm sure fuckin' Isaiah down real good helped

move this shit along with the hearin' 'cause knowin' LaQuandra's messy ass she woulda dragged the shit out. And she didn't show up for court yesterday, so the judge tossed out the charges. Surprise, surprise! I made sure Isaiah let that bitch know—since she still has a restrainin' order against me—that I was gonna file complaints against her punk-ass since she wanna get the courts 'n shit involved. I mean, really…who the fuck does that? Silly bitches do! But, I guess she got her mind right and saw the light. Trick bitch!

Whatever. All I know is, I need to get to Short Hills and pick me up some new heels and a handbag, then get down to the salon get my hair done for this hearin' tomorrow.

"Isaiah, wake up, damn it! Your brother will be here to pick ya ass up in about an hour. So you need to get showered and dressed." His head is wrapped under the covers. When he doesn't budge, I yank the comforter off of him. "Look boy, don't do me this mornin'. Everybody is up and outta this house—in school where they belong, except you. So I know you don't think you're gonna lay in bed and sleep all goddamn mornin'. Get ya black ass up!"

"Dang, I'm up," he groans, liftin' his head, then rollin' over and stretchin'.

"Don't you 'dang' me, boy. Do you want ya face slapped? You know I'm still ready to set it off on ya black ass for gettin' suspended and we only in the first month of school. So don't do me, lil' niggah."

I eye him as he gets outta bed. I see his lil' ten-year-old dingaling is kinda hard in his boxers. Oooh, I'm so glad he ain't gonna have no tiny-ass dick. "Am I goin' to my dad's this weekend?" he asks, tryna cover himself.

"Oh, boy puhleeze. Ain't nobody thinkin' about ya hard dick. I done seen it plenty of times. And you done pulled the goddamn thing out in school so don't even try it. And yeah, you goin' to ya fahver's. But, the minute his wife start talkin' shit about you findin' them nasty movies at her house you tell that bitch I said you ain't gotta listen to her ugly ass."

"LaQuandra says you don't like her and she ain't never do nothin' to you," he says, makin' his bed.

I put a hand up on my hip. "That flat-ass bitch is a lie! She ain't never liked me. Don't be listenin' to no shit that bitch says, Isaiah."

"Then why you attack her?"

"I ain't attack her."

He looks at me like he doesn't believe me. "Then why you get locked up?"

"I went upside her head for talkin' slick." I sit at the foot of his bed. Tell him to come sit next to me. "I'ma keep it real with you, okay?" He nods. "I was dead wrong for goin' upside her head like that at the school. No matter what, that's her job. And you were dead-wrong for pullin' ya dingaling out bein' disrespectful. When I heard you did that, I was embarrassed. That shit hurt me, Isaiah, 'cause you know I ain't raise you to be actin' like you some ghetto trash, pullin' out ya dick to nobody. All I kept thinkin' about is if you had on clean drawers and if you was ashy or not. And then when I heard you was bein' kicked outta school and that bitch was sayin' you should be taken away from me, I gave her a fist to the head. Don't no-goddamn-body threaten to take my kids away from me. I love y'all too goddamn much. And I ain't tryna let no other bitch raise you."

I turn my head for a quick minute 'cause I feel myself gettin' kinda choked up. Thinkin' about this shit got me wantin' to tear that bitch up again.

He rubs my back. "Mommy, you cryin'?"

I shake my head and sniff a lil' bit. "No. I'm mad at how shit went down. I'll kill a bitch over you. And that bitch took me there. I shoulda never fought her like that; not there. I shoulda kept it classy and just cussed her out. Then I shoulda waited for the bitch out in the parkin' lot, or went to her house and whooped her ass. That's how classy hoes do it."

He blinks, I guess tryna make sense outta what I'm sayin' to him. "But how come y'all always fightin' and sayin' mean stuff about each other?"

I blink. "What that bitch been sayin' about me?"

He shrugs. "Just stuff."

"Like what? You can tell me. I ain't gonna get mad." He stares at me, givin' me a "yeah right" look. "I'm not. But if you don't wanna tell me 'cause you wanna be on her side, then don't tell me."

"Mommy, I'm not on her side."

"Then tell me what that bitch says about me."

"But I don't want Daddy to be mad at me."

"You let me worry about ya fahver. Now tell me." He says sometimes he hears her sayin' to his fahver how I'm triflin' and how he needs to take me to court and get custody of him. How I don't deserve to be a mother. How his fahver shouldn't have to pay me all that child support money. I feel myself about to go off, but I keep it calm 'n classy. "And what ya fahver be sayin' when that bitch is tryna kick my back in, sayin' all this shit?"

"I only heard him tell her he ain't takin' me from you. And for her stop talkin' shit about you 'cause you a good mother."

I toot my lips up. "You goddamn right, I am. Do you wanna go live with them?" I ask this, holdin' my breath 'cause I already know if he says yes, I'ma go off.

He shakes his head and says, "No. I like goin' over there and stayin' sometimes, but I wanna live wit' you."

I let out a relieved breath, pullin' him into me. "I love ya bad ass to pieces."

"I love you too, Mommy." He hugs me back. "Mommy?"

"Yeah, boo?"

"Why she say you a man-stealin' whore?"

"Oh, see. Now that bitch wanna get down 'n dirty. She said that to ya fahver?" He tells me no. That he heard her on the phone sayin' it. I roll my eyes. "Boo, I'ma always keep it real with you 'cause that's how I do it. That bitch is jealous of me. Always has been, always will be. I ain't never tell you this 'cause I ain't think it was any of ya business. But since that bitch wanna talk all freely, I'ma give it to you straight. I was fuckin' ya fahver while he was married to LaQuandra. But I ain't know he was married 'til after I got pregnant with you."

"Oh," he says.

"See, boo, LaQuandra hates me 'cause I gave ya fahver somethin' she can't. A son. And my baby is fine and chocolately like his daddy. And that burns that bitch's asshole to shreds 'cause every time she looks at you she gotta be reminded that she ain't ever gonna push a baby outta her cootie-hole."

"How come she can't have a baby?"

"Because the bitch's insides are rotted."

He frowns.

"Look, I don't wanna talk anymore about that hatin'-ass ho. Tomorrow we gotta go to that school meetin' and you gotta get ya black ass back in school. So we gotta keep it classy and talk that talk. Tell them niggahs what they wanna hear. You understand?" He nods. "Good. Now give me another hug, then go get yo' musty ass in that shower and hurry up and get dressed before ya brother gets here."

He lifts up his arms up and starts smellin' his pits. "I'm not musty. I smell like fresh onions."

I can't help but laugh at his silly ass. "Boy, get yo' ass in that shower. And make sure you scrub around them balls real good. If you musty under ya arms I'm sure them balls startin' to funk up too. And make sure you pull open them asscheeks and get all up in there real good too. Niggahs gotta know how to wash that ass out good. And to keep them balls fresh. I don't want you ever droppin' ya drawers tryna serve up some dingaling and a bitch sayin' you funky. I'ma fuck you up if you do. You hear me?"

"Yes."

I watch as my baby bops his self into the bathroom, shakin' my head. *That bitch crazy if she thinks she's gonna ever get my baby.* I get up and walk out into the kitchen to fix him some waffles and scrambled eggs. Then unload the dishwasher. The alarm chirps just as the house phone rings. I already know who it is, on the phone and walkin' through the door.

"Yo, Ma, what's good wit' you?" he asks the minute I answer. "Why you ain't been up here to see me?"

I beat three eggs, add some cheddar cheese, green peppers, and onions, then pour them into a pan. "Jah'Mel, you know I don't jail with no niggahs, boo. Son or not, you know I don't do jail visits. Did you get the money I sent you?"

"Yeah, I got it, thanks." He laughs. "Yo, Ma, you know I don't really care about visits anyway. I just like effen wit' you. I'm sayin' though. How's e'eryone doin'? You good?"

Darius walks into the kitchen and kisses me on the cheek. "Who you on the phone wit'?" he wants to know, talkin' to me like he's my damn man or somethin'. I tell him it's his brother. "Yo, let me holla at him for a minute."

"Boo, you know I'm always good. Now when ya black ass comin' home?" He tells me his child support shit is handled but now he has to do another forty-five days for some traffic violations. "Mmmmph. I told ya ass to stop drivin' on the revoked list, but you so hardheaded."

"Yo, Ma, chill. I ain't call for no lecture; feel me? I know what I was doin'. And I'm cool wit' doin' da time."

I toot my lips. "Mmmph. Well, good for you. Now why that bitch, Frieda, ain't brought my grandbaby over here to see me? I done sent her three texts and I still ain't heard from her ass."

He sighs. "Yo, Ma. You already know what it is. How you s'pect her be around you after that shit you did?"

I roll my eyes. He's talkin' about the night I took it to her face for scratchin' his face and neck up 'cause he didn't come home one night. Coon, *boom!* That bitch clawed up the wrong niggah 'cause I hopped on her ass. Well, I asked her why she did it first. And when the ho started talkin' slick about how that was her man and how I needed to stay outta their business, I took it to her face.

"Mmmph. Well, she shoulda never put her hands on you. Anyway, Darius wants to speak to you."

"Aiight, cool."

I hand Darius the phone, then go check on Isaiah. He's dressed and stretched out across his bed watchin' TV. I tell him to come eat. He shuts off his TV and follows behind me. "Did you put deodorant on?"

"Yes."

"And you washed them balls like I told you?"

He laughs. "Yes."

"Niggah, I ain't laughin'. C'mere." I grab him by his arm and sniff him. "Now, that's how my baby's supposed to smell. Fresh 'n clean with ya fine self." I fuss in his hair. He has a mini 'fro. "You need a haircut." He starts talkin' shit about wantin' to let his hair grow 'cause he wants braids. I ignore his ass. Darius hands me back the phone while Isaiah eats his waffles and Darius gobbles up the eggs.

I walk back out into the livin' room so Darius ain't all up in my convo. "Jah, do you know some niggah named AJ?"

"Where he from?" I tell him Irvington. "Nah, I don't know. What he look like?" *Sneaky.* I give him his description. "Oh, hold up. I know who you talkin' about, now. Yeah, I know that cat. Why? That niggah ain't stepped to you, has he?"

I suck my teeth, rollin' my eyes. "See. Here you go tryna act like you my man."

"Nah, yo. You know I don't be diggin' that, Ma. It's bad enough you got my boys always tryna sniff up around you. Let me find out that niggah tryna get at you."

I laugh. Jah done fought more niggahs for tryna get up in these drawers than I can keep count. His ass gets crazy and overprotective when it comes to me. "Boy, stop. Them lil' fresh-ass niggahs only lookin'. Besides they ain't ready to handle real pussy work." Buddha's long dick flashes in my head. I press my thighs together.

He sucks his teeth. "Yo, Ma, you shot out; for real. You stay on that..."

"Aiight, Ma," Darius says, walkin' outta the kitchen. Isaiah is followin' behind him. "We out. I'll bring this knucklehead home around six."

"You a Butthead," Isaiah says back to him.

Darius grabs him into a headlock and they wrestle. "Yeah, aiight. I'ma kick ya butt if you get in any more trouble at school."

I tell Isaiah to come give me a hug, then kiss him on his cheek. "I love you, boo."

"I love you, too. Bye." Darius gives me a hug and a kiss, then walks out. I step to the window and watch as they get in the car.

"So why you ask me 'bout that cat, AJ?"

I plop down on the sofa, then kick my barefeet up on the leather ottoman table. "'Cause I wanna know what he's into."

"He ain't 'bout shit. Some low-level cat; flunky type niggah, lookin' for a come-up. Word is he pushin' some light shit, but nuthin' major. But you still ain't tell me why you wanna know all this? Is you diggin' cat or sumthin'?"

"No, I ain't *diggin'* him. But if I was, so the hell what. I'ma grown ass woman. And I don't answer to ya ass. So if I wanted to give the niggah some airplay, I would. But he ain't my type, so slow ya roll."

He chuckles. "Yo, I ain't tryna hear all that, Ma. I know

you grown. That still don't mean I won't rock that niggah's top when I get out if I hear he's tryna get at you. And even if he ain't tryna get at you and you pushin' up on him, I'ma still bring it to his neck."

I shake my head. "Jah, you need to stop actin' like you own me."

"Yo, go 'head wit' that,Ma. I ain't tryna own you. I'm lookin' out for you. And I don't want none of them grimy-ass niggahs tryna get at you; that's all. So yeah. You my moms and you gonna do what you do. But at da end of da day I'm da one who's gonna always have ya back."

I grin. "See, niggah. And that's how it's supposed to be. That's why I love ya black ass like no other. You need to hurry up and get ya ass home."

"Word up. You already know. Yo, what's good wit' Day'Asia? I heard she out there on some real foul shit."

"What kinda foul shit you heard?"

"That her and Candy supposedly out there trickin' wit' some niggahs from Elizabeth? All up in motel rooms 'n shit, drinkin' 'n smokin'. Real shit, Ma. Tell Asia I'ma bust her ass when I get home."

"Well, I don't know when she got time to be over in Elizabeth. But I don't put shit past Day'Asia. She probably doin' the shit durin' the day or right after school. I know her fast-ass likes to suck down on a dick, and she always wanna be all up under that retarded-ass, stink-bitch, Candy. So ain't no tellin' what them two doin' when she's not home."

"Ma, real talk. Word on the block is, Asia, Candy, and Tina are all hot like fire. You need to get in Asia's ass."

"Oh, don't worry. I'ma jump up on her back as soon as she gets home from school. I'm not havin' no hot pussy livin' up in here." I glance at the clock. It's almost ten o'clock. *Oooh, I gotta hurry and get the hell up outta here.* "Look, boo. I gotta get up off this phone. You need anything?" He tells me he's good. Tells me he'll call me one day next week. Tells me he loves me. Then this niggah opens his goddamn mouth and tells me he wants me to stop goin' down to The Crack House. "*Whaaaat?!* Niggah, boom! Now you crossin' the goddamn line. You don't tell me where the fuck to go. I keep tellin' ya black ass that I don't answer to you."

"Ma, I'm sayin'...you out there wildin' too. And you wonder why Day'Asia's so wild."

I frown, pacin'. "Niggah, I ain't wildin' shit. I go out to have me a good goddamn time. I take care of home, first. And if I wanna go out every now and then to have a few goddamn drinks, so what? It's none of ya motherfuckin' business. See, you gonna have me smack ya goddamn face up when I see you."

"Ma, chill wit' that crazy shit. Nobody sayin' you can't go out and toss a few back. But you out there bendin' over and pullin' shit outta ya ass 'n shit. That ain't a good look. That's all I'm sayin', Ma. Fall back from goin' up in there so much; that's all."

"Jah'Mel, eat the back of my ass, niggah. Don't worry

about what I'm doin'. You don't run me. And I don't appreciate you havin' motherfuckas reportin' back to you, either. What you need to be doin' is worryin' about what the fuck that bitch Frieda's doin' when ya black ass is locked up. And take yo' ass downtown to get that blood test like I told you, too. 'Cause, boo. I am ninety-nine-point-nine-nine percent certain that, you. Are. Not. The fahver."

Click!

Jah'Mel done hung up on me. Oh, well. Niggah so worried about what the fuck I'm doin' when he should be worried about what the fuck is goin' on in his own shit. I know that bitch Frieda been fuckin' on him. And I know that baby ain't his. I told his ass this. And the pussy-whipped niggah wanna believe *her* over me. So fuck him, too! I toss the cordless phone on the sofa and quickly hop up and go into my room to get showered and dressed so I can get down to the salon and hopefully get my shit did up right.

Mmmph. Tryna do me. Niggah, puhleeze!

Twenty-One

A week later, I'm on the phone fumin'! I gotta letter in the mail from Family Court, talkin' 'bout I gotta appear in court for a custody hearin'. And I'm hot that that motherfuckin' Julius is tryna do me. Motherfucka, *boom!* Not only is this niggah tryna take my son, but he's tryna cut into my goddamn money too. And Big Booty ain't havin' it, okay. I scream on him the minute he answers his cell. "Coon-bitch, motherfucka! What the fuck is this shit you tryna pull, niggah?"

He takes a deep breath. "It ain't no secret, Cass. I already told you what it was. I want my son; period."

"You can't have him, niggah! I gave birth to him! Not you, bitch!"

He stays calm, like he always fuckin' does. And it only pisses me off more. The niggah never raises his voice. He's one of them silent, crazy-type niggahs. Still, I don't give a fuck. "You gotta lotta motherfuckin' nerve, bitch, tryna take me to court. Pussy-ass bitch!"

"Listen. All that rah-rah you got goin' on ain't changin' shit, Cass. So cuss and scream all you want. I'ma still see you in court next week."

I try 'n keep from goin' gutter on his ass, but I'm so goddamn pissed that I don't give a fuck what comes outta my mouth. Still, I know if I crank it up to threats on the phone it'll fuck me up 'cause I know the niggah's recordin' me. This bitch thinks he can hook me. But he gotta 'nother thing comin'.

I take a deep breath. "Julius, have I ever fuckin' kept you away from Joshua?"

"Nah, you haven't. That's one thing I can honestly say, Cass. You've never been on that crazy shit when it comes to me seein' our son."

"Then why the fuck is you tryna finger-fuck me and take my son away from me, Julius?"

He sighs. "Cass, I'm not tryna take *our* son away from you. I want full residential custody. He can stay with you on the weekends, and alternatin' holidays."

My heart drops to my feet. I feel lightheaded. I'm startin' to feel like I'ma throw up. I ain't tryna be without my son. But I ain't about to beg no niggah, either. But I feel myself on the verge of beggin', pleadin' for him to not do this. I swallow. It feels like I have a hard dick down in my throat, pluggin' up my airway. And right now that's what I wish it was instead of the shit this niggah's tryna shove down my neck. "Niggah-bitch, boom! I'm not about to be no goddamn part-time mother."

"Look, Cass. I don't wanna beef with you about it. I know you're upset. You should be. But, let's face it. You brought this shit on ya'self with all the shit you keep going.

Besides, you gotta enough kids to deal with. Joshua will be better off with me. This way he can get the attention he deserves."

"Niggah, he deserves to be with his mother! And I don't keep shit goin', niggah. I mind my business. I don't do drama. And you know it."

He laughs. "Yo, Cass, stop. You have more assault charges and disorderly persons offenses than either one of us can keep up with. You stay in the middle of some shit. And I don't want my son around it anymore."

"Niggah, you a goddamn lie! I don't stay in shit. Bitches bring they shit to me. I don't go out lookin' for it."

"Yeah, that's the problem. Maybe you ain't out there lookin' for it. But you damn sure *out* shakin' ya ass and fightin'. You spend more time at the bars than you do at home bein' a mother. It's for the best."

"Niggah-coon, *boom!* You'se a goddamn lie. I'm home every damn day with my kids. I'm at every school function and parent-teacher conference. They come home to a clean goddamn house, and a house full of food. Don't do me, niggah!"

"Cass, I'm not sayin' you a bad mother. All I'm saying is, it's time for Joshua to live with me. I know you do the best you can. But, I'm sorry. It's not enough. My son needs a stable home; something you're not able to give him. We can hash out all the details in court."

Cop or not, if this niggah was standin' right here I'd take it to his goddamn face. But I know goin' upside his head would only make shit worse for me so I shake thoughts of clawin' his face up and lumpin' him up. But I swear, I wanna do this niggah real good. Big dick bitch!

I crumple the letter in my hand, then throw it across the room. "Julius, eat the inside of my ass, bitch. And eat it goddamn good 'cause I am goin' to bring you down, niggah. If you think I'ma let you take my son from me without a good fight, you gotta 'nother thing comin'. And you know I *love* a good goddamn fight so buckle up, bitch."

I hang up on his ass, then march out into the livin' room. I stand at the bottom of the stairs and call out, "Joshua! Get yo'..." I catch myself from goin' off on him 'cause I know he ain't the enemy. His fahver is. "Joshua!"

"Yes?" he says, standin' at the top of the stairs.

"Come here, boo. Come talk to Mommy."

He looks at me suspiciously before comin' down. He must think I'm tryna lure him into some kinda trap, then fuck him up or somethin'. I let him know he ain't gettin' a beat down. "Oh, okay," he says, soundin' relieved as he follows me to my room. I tell him to shut the door behind him.

I sit on my bed, then pat the space beside me. "Come sit, boo." I wait for him to sit, then shift my body, tuckin' a leg beneath me. I reach for his hands. "Do you know ya fahver wants you to live with him?"

His eyes widen, then he lowers them to his lap.

My heart drops. *That dirty motherfucka! Tryna backdoor*

me, goddamn him! I lift his chin up and look at him. In my head, I'm smackin' his damn face up 'cause he looks so much like his fahver. In my heart, I know he ain't the problem. That motherfuckin' Julius is! "You knew about this?"

He nods. "Yes."

"So you knew that motherfu…ya fahver was gonna take me to court and you ain't say shit, Joshua, why?"

"Daddy told me not to?"

"Oh, so you turnin' ya back on me, huh? You choosin' that coon motherfuc…I mean, ya fahver over me, is that it, Joshua? After all I've done, you tryna do me, too?"

"No, I'm not tryna do it to you, Mommy. I wanna live with you and Daddy. But Daddy said it's better if I live with him, and come stay here on the weekends."

"Do you wanna live with him?"

He nods. "Yes, sometimes I do. But I don't want you to be mad at me."

I gasp, clutchin' my chest. I feel like someone has set fire to all my Louis heels and red bottoms, then opened all of my handbags and tossed hot shit in 'em. "Why, boo? Why you wanna live with that motherf…ya fahver?"

He shrugs. And I feel like shakin' the shit outta him 'cause I know he knows why he wanna abandon me. "Don't do me, Joshua. I'm not gonna go off on you. I only wanna know why you wanna leave ya brothers and sister. I wanna know why you wanna leave me."

"I don't wanna leave you, Mommy. I wanna stay the

weekends with you and some of the summer. But…it's too many kids here. And Isaiah and the twins are always goin' in my stuff."

"Well, that's what brothers do, boo. They 'posed to go through ya shit and get on ya nerves. But you ain't 'posed to wanna turn ya back on 'em and wanna move out." I squeeze his hands tighter. "You ain't 'posed to do this to us, goddamn you. All my life I've fought to keep all'a you together 'cause I'm ya mother. You ain't 'posed to wanna break us up." Oooh, I feel so goddamn betrayed. Now I'm shakin' him. And he's lookin' at me like I'm crazy. I catch myself before I swing him into a wall, then grab him and pull him into my arms. I hug him, tight. "That ain't what brothers do, Joshua. They stick together. They ride or die with each other. Not run off. But I ain't mad at you. If you wanna go live with ya fahver and leave us, then you go right ahead." I choke back my anger at that no-good motherfucka. *Oh, he's fuckin' with the wrong one!*

"You promise you not mad at me, Mommy?"

I take a deep breath. Push back a tear. And you know I don't do drama or goddamn tears. "No, boo. I ain't mad at you." His eyes water with tears. I wipe them as they fall. Then kiss him on his forehead. "Mommy loves you, boo. And *anyone* tryna take you from me gotta pay. I don't give a goddamn who it is. But if you wanna go live with ya fahver, then I ain't gonna stop you." I let him go. Tell him he can go on back upstairs. He gives me another hug, then walks off toward the door. He opens it, then turns back to me.

"I love you, Mommy. And I'ma call you every day, okay?"

I nod, forcin' a smile. That's all I can give him. He done sliced me open, then snatched my heart outta my chest with this shit. And that motherfuckin' fahver of his gave him the blade to do it. He quietly closes the door behind him, leavin' me sittin' on my bed, starin' at the shut door.

"Cass," Dicklina says, snappin' her gum in my ear. I am layin' across my bed on my back starin' up at the ceilin'. "That's what you get for havin' babies wit' a motherfucka who wanna be a daddy. Shit, all these no-good, deadbeat niggahs you coulda had and you get one who wanna play fahver of da year. Shit don't make no sense."

I blink. I've been on the phone with Lina for the last two hours, ventin'. But now I see that this bitch is extra special and severely retarded and I had no goddamn business callin' her with this shit. "Lina, I'm glad the niggah wants to be in Joshua's life. I just don't want him tryna take him from me. I like things the way they are. But now this niggah wanna play dirty. And I'm not havin' it."

"Boo, and that's why I'm sayin' you shoulda got knocked up by a bum niggah. Bum-niggahs got that good dick, too, Cass. Shit, look at Candy and Tina's fahvers. They ain't seen't their daddies since they were two or three months old. And they don't want nuthin' to do wit' 'em either. And that's fine by me 'cause I ain't gotta worry about the dumb shit, or my girls bein' around they other bitches."

I frown. "Lina, you sound cuckoo crazy, boo. Kids need they fahvers in their lives. They just don't need the motherfuckas tryna take 'em away from good goddamn mothers."

"Mmmph. I guess."

I take a deep breath. This bitch ain't gotta clue. Both of our mothers were junkie-hoes. Hers to dope, mine to crack. She didn't know her fahver, but at least I knew mine. He was in my life. And I remember him givin' me a hug, and tellin' me he was gonna come back to take me for ice cream. But the niggah never did. A bullet got 'im in the head, first, for gettin' caught fuckin' some other niggah's wife. I was eight. My junkie mother didn't want him in my life 'cause he ain't wanna be in hers. I swore I'd never be like that. I promised myself that when I had babies I was gonna make sure my kids at least knew who their daddies were, even if the niggah didn't wanna know them.

Shit. I may have a buncha baby daddies, but at least I know who every last one of my kids' fahvers are. I know who I let nut up in this pussy and when I let 'em do it. Unlike Lina's ho-ass who had to pick a name outta a hat 'cause the bitch ain't know which niggah she was fuckin' was Candy or Clitina's fahvers 'cause she was fuckin' the fahver and his two sons. Sometimes they fucked her at the same time. Mmmph. Lina was a nasty bitch back in her day. Anyway, come to find out Candy was the old-ass fahver's baby. And Clitina's daddy is one of the sons. So they sistahs and cousins, too! Oooh, that ho was messy back then.

"Well, I know they don't. I could see if I was a triflin' bitch who ain't take care of her kids, but this niggah tryna do me like I'm hot trash or somethin'."

"Well, I ain't wanna say nuthin', Cass, 'cause I know how you get. But he kinda gotta point. You do be out in da clubs a lot. And you always complainin' about how bad they asses is. Maybe it's best Joshua go live wit' his daddy. Look on da bright side, that's one less child you gotta worry about feedin' and clothin' and hollerin' at."

"Bitch, ain't no goddamn bright side to that dumb shit you talkin'. That's my baby that motherfucka's tryna take from me. I don't give a goddamn how bad my kids might be, I ain't never wanna give 'em up to no-goddamn-body. And I ain't about to give 'em up now. And on that note, before I curse ya black ass out, eat the inside of my ass, bitch. I'm done with ya black ass."

I disconnect. That bitch done gave me a headache. I lift myself up from the bed. I feel so weak. I wanna call Julius's ass back and bring it to him good. But I know all he gonna do is not answer his phone or hang up on me.

I need a blunt and a good goddamn lawyer!

"I gotta get this money up," I think, pullin' out a blunt, then walkin' into the bathroom to get my get my head right. I spark up, take three pulls, then start scrollin' through my cell to see who I can call. Yeah, I got a couple of dollars I could use to pay for a lawyer, but why should I have'ta dig in my stash when all I have to do is lay on my back, or drop down on my hands 'n knees and arch this back. No. A smart bitch holds onto her change, and finds herself a niggah who's willin' to spend up his.

I go through my list of sponsors in my head. At the moment, I only have two. JT and Born. And JT has more money than Born. But Born won't be on no extra shit. He'll fuck me real good, drop them dollars, then bounce. The niggah JT is gonna wanna put more claims on me. I blow smoke up into the air, then call Born.

"Yo, wassup, ma? How you?"

"I'm okay, I guess." I sigh, then pause. "Umm, no, I'm not. I'm all fucked up, Born. I gotta get lawyered up, boo. And I need you to finance me, if you can."

"What you need?" Shit, I don't know since I ain't called around for one. But I know they pricey. I tell him ten grand. But I ain't 'bout to give no coon ten grand for shit. I'ma find me a lawyer for under five gees, then use the rest of the money to buy Marquelle, Isaiah, and Joshua new iPhones, then get me a new MacBook and a fifty-inch flat-screen for my bedroom. But he ain't gotta know all that. He whistles. "Daaayuuum, ma. I ain't got ten grand. But I can prolly hit you with like thirty-five hunnid."

I smile. "Okay, boo. Thank you. You always come through for me."

"You know I got you, ma. You my peoples. I can have that to you tomorrow mornin' sometime, aiight?"

"That works. And I'ma have you a dish of wet pussy for you when you do."

He laughs. "Aiight, that's wassup. I can always use some'a that."

"Uh-huh. I know you can." We talk a few minutes more. He tells me he'll text me in the mornin' when he's ready to meet up, then disconnect.

I wait 'til I finish smokin' before I call JT's ass. Crazy or not, the niggah's stacks are heavy, his dick is thick, and he don't ever tell me no. But fuckin' this devil-ass niggah and takin' his money comes with a price. And it's only a matter of time before the niggah tries to collect.

Twenty-Two

"Who else you givin' this pussy to, yo?" JT asks, throwin' me down on the bed, then pinnin' my legs back. I don't answer him. He rips my thong off, then slaps my pussy and clit. "Yo, you hear me fuckin' talkin' to you, yo? I asked you who the fuck else you fuckin'?"

Although a mixture of pain and pleasure shoot through me, I frown. This is the first time he's ever man-handled me like this. "Niggah, I don't answer to you and you don't own me. I fuck who I wanna fuck."

He rams his dick in my slit, pressin' his right hand into my neck. He squeezes. "Yo, fuck outta here. I own this shit..." He bites the side of my neck. "This pussy's mine, Cass." He rapidly bangs up my walls. Oooh, the dingaling feels soooo damn good. But I ain't diggin' him tryna choke me out.

"Get off...mmmph...my...uhhh...neck, niggah." I dig my nails into his hand. Slap him with my free hand. This only seems to make his dick harder.

"Oh, fuck, slutty bitch...I own this shit, yo...mmmm...

good-ass, muthafuckin' pussy…aaah…you gonna fuck 'round…mmmm…and have me…uhhh…kill ya muhfuckin'…mmmm, shitfuck…ass, yo…"

This niggah has a nutty look in his eyes. Everything about this niggah looks crazy. But he's fuckin' me so damn good. I try not to moan, but he's hittin' my spot. He pulls his dick out as I'm skeetin', slingin' me over onto my stomach. My pussy juice keeps shootin' outta me, then streaks down the inside of my thighs.

"Get on ya muhfuckin' knees, yo." He slaps my ass, hard. Makes it bounce 'n jiggle, then pulls my cheeks open and rams his dick back in. "I don't want nobody else hittin' this shit, yo." He yanks me by hair. "You hear me, yo?"

I hold back a loud moan. "Fuck you, niggah! I do what….w-want with…t-this…mmmph…pussy."

I throw my hips back at him. He stops pumpin' in and outta me. Tells me to fuck his dingaling. And I do. I give the niggah a good fuckin'. Watch him over my shoulder toss his head back, shut his eyes, and grunt. He has his hands planted up on his waist. Sweat is drippin' down his face and chest. Shit, for the ten grand this niggah done lined my handbag with the least I can do is give him his money's worth. The fact that—when this day with this niggah is over—I will have collected, between him and Born, over thirteen thousand dollars makes me hornier than usual. I coat his dick with my cream, makin' my ass clap. I wanna hurry up and make this niggah nut so I can get the fuck on with my day. I wanna get down to the salon and get my hair, nails, and feet did. Then buy me some new heels and a handbag for court.

"Fuck me in my ass," I tell him, knowin' he'll nut in five minutes...in two if I talk real gutter-slutty. "Give it to me good, niggah. Spit in my asshole and prison fuck my ass, niggah. Show me how they do it in prison, boo."

He reaches over and plays with my wet clit as he pounds in and outta my pussy. His sweat drips on my back. "Aaah fuck...mmm...you want me to bust ya ass open, huh? You want this big-ass dick in that phat ass? Mmmph... you'se a nasty freak bitch..."

"Yeah, Ja...uhh...oooh...give it to me..."

"I wanna keep fuckin' this pussy...aaahhh, shit..."

He presses my head down into the mattress, clamps his thighs around my hips and bangs my pussy up like a set of drums. "You like this dick slidin' in and outta you, huh? You like it when I'm fuckin' you deep in this wet pussy?"

In a flash I go from purrin' to full-fledged growlin' like some foamy-mouthed wildebeest. "Yesss, goddammit! Fuck me deep in it, motherfucka! Do me right, goddammit!"

"Yeah, baby...I love this dick in you...yeah, you love this dick, bitch...?"

"Yesssssssss, motherfucka, yessssssssss!

He pulls it out to the head, dips in and out nice 'n easy. Then speed-pokes my slit, causin' juices to splash out. I grab it, slurp it, with my muscles. "Ohhh, fuck...pussy so muthafuckin' good."

He slaps my ass, then rams back in, deep. The niggah wants me to beg him to feed my asshole his dingalaing, stretch it open 'til it whistles. He wants me to whimper and plead for the dingaling. But I ain't beggin' no niggah for shit. I don't give a fuck how good the dick is.

I moan. "Motherfucka...you ain't shit...uhhh...long dicked, bitch...ohhh, yessss...mmmm..."

He goes in with long, deep strokes, then pulls and short strokes my hole, then plunges back in deep. He keeps hittin' my spot. His dick strokes are relentless. The motherfucka is doin' me right, goddammit! He pulls back out to the head, sirs the tip in and out. *Slllurp, sllllurp, slllllllurp! Swish, swish, swish!* Jucies keep splashin' out. I am cummin' and cummin' and cummin'. I glance over my shoulder at him. The niggah is lookin' down, watchin' as his hard dingaling disappears inside of me.

"Aaah, shit..."

He slaps my ass.

"Muthafuckin' good-ass pussy...I'ma break my dick off in it..."

"Give it to me good, niggah! Punk-ass...oooh...yesss..." I am cummin'. I twist and shudder and buck, grabbin' and squeezin' my titties. I pinch and lick my nipples. I wanna cum outta my ass. I wanna ride this niggah's dick in my ass, but he's makin' me wait for it. And I know why. 'Cause he ain't ready to nut yet, and he knows once I have him trapped in this sweet chocolate, I'ma have him spent in no time. He knows he can't ever hold his nut when I have him gobbled up in my ass.

He finally pulls his dick outta me, opens my asscheeks, then works his dick into my ass. I press on my clit, wigglin' my ass. I wanna buck back on it, but I'm gonna keep it ladylike 'til the niggah gets it all in. His dingaling, my asshole, fit like a snug glove. I arch my back, toot my ass up. He speed strokes me. All the while sweatin' 'n gruntin' 'n poppin' shit about not wantin' to share this ass, pussy, or throat with any other niggah.

His balls slap against the back of my wet pussy.

"Yeah, Daddy, get it, motherfucka…mmmmph…fuck that ass, baby…uhhh…yesssss…oooh…get all up in that chocolate, boo…"

The niggah grunts 'n shakes. "Aaaah, aaaah, aaaaah… I'm cummin' baby…mmmm…mmmm….ya ass so hot… uhhh…"

Of course it is,niggah. It's hot from the ten gees I can't wait to spend.

"Yesss, goddammit…skeet in my ass, Daddy…give me that hot cream, niggah-boo…"

Two seconds later, he pulls outta my ass, snatches off the condom and tells me to hurry up and turn around. "Catch this nut, baby…" I wrap my mouth around his Mandingaling and suck the sap outta it. "Aaaaah shit… fuckfuckfuck…" His hot nut fills my mouth, then glides down into my throat. I keep suckin'. "Yeah, baby, gobble that shit up…"

When I am done cleanin' his dick, I climb outta bed,

grab my handbag loaded down with my ten gees, and head straight to the bathroom. Glad the shit is finally over with. This damn niggah ain't shit!

"Heeeeeey, Miss Pasha, girl," I say, walkin' toward her workstation. It's packed to the seams up in here today. And I'm pissed that I ain't get down here first thing this morning, or at least make me an appointment. "Where's Miss Messy today?"

She shakes her head, smilin'. She has Jasper's cousin, Mona, in her chair, textin'. Mona ain't really messy, so I can't say anthing shitty about her. But that sneaky niggah she married is. Mmmph. And he's some kinda fine, too. But his dingaling's longer than his money so there you have it. "Felecia has the day off," Miss Pasha says, swivelin' Mona in her chair toward the mirror. She trims the back of her hair. "What's going on with you?"

"Not a damn thing, hon. How you, boo?"

She glances at me through the mirror. "I'm good. Keepin' busy as you see."

"I see. You doin' it, boo. How many heads you got today?" She tells me she has two more after Mona, but they're only washes 'n wraps. "Ooh, you think you can fit me in? I gotta look right for the weekend, boo." She wants to know what I want done. I tell her I want my weave redid; that I wanna go Rihanna red 'cause I'm fierce and hot like fire.

She laughs. "Girl, you a mess. I'll fit you in between my next two appointments."

"Boo, you always do me right, goddammit." I glance at Mona. "Hey, Miss Mona. What, you not speakin' today?"

She looks up from her phone, eyein' me in the mirror. "Girl, no. I'm wrapped up in fussin' with Mario about some mess he done posted up on Facebook. I'm tellin' you, social media is the devil in disguise."

"Girl, what he do now?" Miss Pasha asks.

She sighs. "This damn boy posted up on his wall: where them—spelled d-e-m—hoes at. I told him to take it down."

That classic "Where Da Hoes At?" by Snoop Dogg starts playin' in my head. Oooh, I used to wanna smoke a blunt with that niggah, then ride down on his ding-aling. "*...She be lickin' my dick...because bitches ain't shit but hoes and tricks...they lick on the nuts and they suck a dick...Fuck a bitch, suck a dick...*" Yes, goddammit! I feel like poppin' my fingers, and droppin' it. That used to be my shit!

"Oh, no, girl," Miss Pasha says, cuttin' into the mini concert I was about to have in my head. "I don't blame you. I woulda told his fresh behind the same thing. These kids today are outta hand."

Miss Mona grunts. "Mmmph. Tell me about it. But I stay on Mario's butt. I'm not raisin' him to be disrespectful to women. I don't give a damn if Avery doesn't see anything wrong with some of the mess he says and does. I do."

"I heard that."

I shift my handbag from one arm to the other. "Well, Miss Mona, I hope Mario ain't still getting' his dinga-ling sucked down inside girls's bathrooms."

"Ugh, please. Don't even remind me. I've tried to block that horrible experience out of my head."

I chuckle. "Chile, I heard Clitina was suckin' his ding-aling like a pornstar. She had his knees buckin' and everything, girl. Oh, that lil' whore was tryna turn him out, boo."

She scrunches her face up. "Ugh, do you mind? I really don't need to hear this right now. But I was wondering who the lil' tramp was down on her knees since the school wouldn't say and neither would Mario."

"Mmmph. If he knows like I know he'll keep his ding-dong in his pants 'cause that lil' ho is suckin' for Jeezus, chile. She gobblin' up nuts for the Cum Gawds, boo. I ain't tryna sling no mud on her, but if he's still lettin' her sop him up in school, I hope he's double wrappin' it. Then again, he better use two condoms *and* Saran Wrap."

Miss Mona frowns. "Girl, I can't. I'm not even tryna go there. I already told him to keep that dick in his pants. But you know like I do, once you get a taste you end up wanting more."

"Uh-huh," Miss Pasha agrees. "And doing more to get it."

"Yes, Lawd," I say, pullin' out my cell as it rings. It's Buddha. "Sex is good. Thank you, Fahver. I stretch my hands out to Thee for blessin' us with good sex." I throw a hand up. "Oooh, excuse me one minute. Miss Pasha, I'ma take this call and head on upstairs to get my hands and feet did. Hello?"

"What's good, Miss Simms? I got that info you wanted."

I grin. "Oh, good, boo. Now what's with all this Miss Simms shit? You done been all up in my pussy and done tongued all through my ass. Ain't no need to be formal with me, boo."

"I feel you, ma. It's outta respect, though, feel me? Plus, I still ain't comfortable wit' gettin' it in wit'..."

I suck my teeth. "Niggah, stop worryin' about Jah. He ain't gonna find out. Besides, I done told you don't no niggah run this pussy. I do what I want with it."

"I hear you, ma. It's just that I ain't beat for no beefs, you feel me?"

I take a seat in one of the open massage chairs and wait for Miss Anna to get these feet right. "Yeah, I feel you, boo. And I'd love to *feel* that dingaling, again, too."

"Yo, that's wassup. I wanna give it to you, too; word. When you free?"

I glance at my watch. It's already after eleven-thirty. I'ma be cuttin' it real close today, so I ain't gonna be able to fuck him like I want. And Buddha's the kinda niggah I wanna give it to real good. I tell him tomorrow mornin'.

"Aiight, bet. Same spot?"

"Uh-huh," I say, lickin' my lips. "And you better do me right, boo."

He laughs. “I got you, ma.” We disconnect as Anna comes over to me. “Hey, Cass. You wanna full pedi?”

“Give me the works, boo.” I reach for a glass of champagne bein’ carried on a tray by a tall, shiny buffed, bare-chested chocolate-drop niggah. Oooh, Miss Pasha knows how to do it up. I grab a strawberry. Take a bite into it, then sip my bubbly. Now this is how a bitch ’posed to serve it. I lay my head back.

Oooh, Buddha’s gonna get fucked down real good. Yes, Lawd! Big Booty gonna tear that dingaling up, goddammit!

Twenty-Three

I hate goddamn courts, courtrooms, judges and motherfuckin' prosecutors—well, except for the three that I've fucked down real good. But that's another story for another time—and right now I am not diggin' this arbitration bitch one goddamn bit, talkin' down to me like I ain't shit. Miss Bitch is sittin' here on the other side of the table, lookin' all googly-eyed at Julius's ass 'cause he's tall and fine and chiseled and a motherfuckin' police officer. The niggah's played real dirty, too, comin' up in here in his uniform, lookin' goddamn delicious! But, right now, I hate his ass, too, goddammit! However, I'm keepin' it real classy in my slate gray wrap dress that dips just right in the front to let 'em see my titties pop without screamin' slutty. It grazes my knees just so to let these bitches see my smooth, shapely stockin'-less legs, and clings to my ass, lettin' all the big booty bounce, baby. I even pulled out some of my good jewels—three-carat tennis bracelet, two-carat studs, a diamond choker, and the two-carat engagement ring Julius gave me when the niggah thought

I wanted to be wifed up. I have my Birkin bag tossed up on the table to let this bitch know she ain't dealin' with no ghetto trash bitch.

Every so often I catch Julius cuttin' his eyes down at the ring blingin' on my finger, then lockin' 'em on my titties, rememberin'—I'm sure—the last time I had his dingdong slidin' in between these juicy cantaloupe-sized boobs. I flip my long weave over my shoulder like I'm the new ho for the next Pantene commercial.

"Miss Simms," Miss Bitch says, eyein' me, "as you are aware Mister Reeves has petitioned the court for residential custody of Joshua Simms? And it is my understandin' that you have agreed to allow the said child to live with his fahver. Is that correct?"

I cut my eyes over at Julius. I feel like cussin' him out. I bite my tongue. "No, I have not agreed to shit, boo."

Julius shakes his head, sighin'. "Yo, Cass, stop. Joshua told me you told him he can come live with me so why are you sittin' here tryna switch it up now?"

My heart aches. I wanna go upside his head so goddamn bad. "Nig...Julius, I never wanted you to take my...our son. But since you done got all up in his head tryna turn him against me, what was I gonna say, huh? You tryna do me, nig...Julius. And I don't agree to this shit."

Miss Bitch says, "Missus Simms, Mister Reeves has stated he is willing to allow you to have Joshua every other weekend and alternating holidays."

I blink. "Bitch, I don't care what he stated. I'm not an unfit mother and I'm not lettin' him take my son from me. And I'm not sayin' shit else until my lawyer gets here." Of course I don't really have a lawyer since I ain't wanna spend my money on one. But if need be, I'll shut this shit down to go scrape up one.

"Missus Simms, please let's refrain from profanity and name-calling. This is a civilized arbitration hearing. There's no need to be hostile."

"Boo, I ain't bein' hostile. *Hostile* is when I go upside his head, then start tearin' the courthouse up. Right now I'm lettin' you know I ain't interested in givin' him custody of my son. Now, bitch, what part of that don't you understand?"

"*Our* son, Cass, he reminds me as if I don't know the niggah'a his fahver. "And I'm not tryna take Joshua away from you or turn him against you. I'm tryna give our *son* a better home environment."

"Niggah-coon, *boom!* You talkin' like I keep a filthy house and keep mice and roaches for pets. Joshua wants for nothin', boo. And you know it. I don't neglect him or any of my other kids, so don't do me."

"I'm not tryna *do* you, Cass. I'm tryna do what's right for our son."

I hop up from my seat and Miss Bitch jumps as if I'ma leap up on her. "Niggah, I'm not tryna hear it. You and"—I flick my finger over at Miss Bitch—"this bitch can both eat the inside of my asshole. Take this shit to the judge 'cause I ain't givin' over my son to you or nogoddamn-body else without a fight. And you know I love a good goddamn fight."

"Alrighty then," Miss Bitch says, gettin' up from her seat. "Mister Reeves, looks like we'll be bringing this matter before the judge since this is not something that can be handled amicably. Both of you can expect a court notice in the mail within seven to ten days."

He shakes his head. "I told you she was difficult."

"Niggah, ain't shit difficult about me. I'm real easy-breezy and you know it. I ain't never kept you from havin' Joshua anytime you want him. I let you have him durin' the summer months and on any holiday except Christmas mornin' and Mother's Day—and don't look at me like I don't goddamn know Mother's Day ain't no real holiday. You just pissed 'cause you gotta pay child support. You wasn't even thinkin' about Joshua 'til I said I was gonna take ya black ass back to court for more money. Now all of a sudden you want him. You work long hours, Julius. How the hell you gonna take care of him, huh?"

Miss Bitch cuts in. "I'm gonna let the two of you take a moment to try and hash this out on your own. Mister Reeves, we'll be in touch." She glances over at me. "Missus Simms—"

"Bitch, *boom!* Don't say shit to me."

Julius watches her scurry up outta here. He waits for the door to close. "Damn, Cass. Why you always gotta be so damn ghetto all the time? We in a courthouse, sitting with an officer of the court, and you can't even control your damn mouth or your nasty-ass attitude." He shakes his head. "Then you wonder why I want my son outta that house. You're fuckin' outta control, Cass."

I tilt my head. "Niggah, you want outta control. Take my son from me and I'ma show you what outta control looks like, startin' with this." I pull out my cell, then press PLAY. The niggah's face goes blank when he hears his voice. I play a recordin' from one of our many times fuckin' up in his police car and him fillin' my ass up with the barrel of his gun while rammin' his dick in my pussy.

"Damn, baby…you like it when I slide this gun in ya ass, huh? Nice *phat*, juicy ass. Look how that shit opens up for my gun, Cass….you like ya ass stuffed…?"

"Yessss, goddammit! Do me right, niggah. Oooh, yesss. Fuck me with that gun."

"Yeah, baby…you wanna taste ya ass on my gun?"

I stop the recordin'. "And I have a whole lot others where that came from, niggah. And I got videos and photos, niggah, of you fuckin' me in ya police car. Or did you forget that shit?"

"Yo, you a fuckin' dirty bitch, Cass. You'd really try and blackmail me?"

"I don't do blackmail, boo. I do what I gotta do to keep my son. And if you wanna keep ya job, I suggest you tell Joshua that you've changed ya mind. That you think it's best that things stay the way they are. If not, I promise you. The Mayor, the Commissioner, the Police Chief, the Captain, Facebook, YouTube and every goddamn news channel will get copies of you fuckin' me down in ya cop car and you lickin' my ass juice off'a the barrel of ya own gun, boo. You 'posed to be on duty and you fuckin' me, ha! Nigga-coon, boom! Fuck with me if you want, Julius."

"Fuckin' bitch!" he snaps, grabbin' me by the arm. "You'd really try and fuck my career up?" He twists my shit. "Fuck with my job or my money, Cass, and…"

"And what, niggah? What you gonna do, bitch?"

The muscles in his jaw twitch.

"Get ya motherfuckin' hand off'a me!"

He lets my arm go. "Fuckin' crazy bitch," he snaps, swingin' open the door, then walkin' out. Just because this niggah's a cop, bitches think his ass is squeaky clean. Well, here's a goddamn newsflash for ya asses: Julius Reeves is just as crooked and dirty as his motherfuckin' lil' piggy-dicked partner. And he knows I know it better than anyone else. Let him go through with this custody shit. And I'ma drag his drawers for all to see.

I smile, walkin' out. I head toward the bank of elevators, decidin' to go up to the Prosecutor's Office to have a friendly chat with Lance Jefferson, one of the assistant prosecutors and past sponsors. Maybe I'll suck his dick for old time's sake; maybe I won't. Right now I need to ensure Julius doesn't get custody of Joshua. By any goddamn means necessary. And if Prosecutor Jefferson can't help me, I'm sure he'll be more than happy to find me someone who will. After all, I have dirt on his married ass, too.

Nigga, boom-boom! Fuck with me if you want.

Twenty-Four

"Bitch, why you ain't called me?" Dickalina screams into my ear the minute I answer my cell. This ho is so damn ghetto and loud. It makes no kinda sense. "I ain't talk to you in three damn days. Don't get cute, bitch, 'cause you done got ya ass some new silky yak hangin' down ya back. And I heard you done dyed ya shit blonde. Priscilla's sister Princess told me she seen't you comin' outta ShopRite the other day and you acted like you was too cute to speak."

"Well, I was. And I am. Shit, what the hell I wanna speak to her for? That ugly bitch looks like shit on a stick. Other than her havin' the same baby daddy as me...and I still don't see what the fuck he saw in her ass. It must have been one of them late-night, drunk fucks 'cause that bitch's ass is up on her back and she looks like her pussy stinks, but whatever. That bitch and me don't have a damn thing in common." I grunt, shakin' my head. "I should smack the shit outta her ass next time I see her for runnin' back reportin' to you like you my damn man. Tell that bitch I said to eat a dick and mind her goddamn business."

She laughs. "Girl, whatever. You still ain't say shit about why you ain't called me today? Why I gotta always call you?"

"Dickalina, puhleeze, boo. Tell me you done smoked dope today 'cause you talkin' real retarded right now. I ain't call you 'cause, bitch, I didn't feel like talkin' to ya ass."

She sucks her teeth. "Then why the fuck you answer the phone, ho?"

"Girl, you know, I'm real with my shit. I rather tell you to ya face, than roll you over into voicemail."

"OMG, fuck you, Cass. I can't stand ya ass sometimes. Anyway, you wanna run out for a few drinks tonight?"

I roll my eyes up in my head. "Bitch, are you a drunk?"

"Hell no!"

"Then there's ya answer. I was just out with ya black ass a few nights ago." Shit, Lina's my damn girl, but tonight I just want to get my drink on and chill and not have to hear her complainin' and whinin' about havin' to get home to Knutz's dumb ass. The niggah tells her she can go out, then texts her half the goddamn night, stressin' her about when she's comin' home. Who the fuck does that shit? A crazy-ass, insecure niggah, that's who!

My last six baby daddies tried to keep leashes on me like that and all that shit did was piss me off. And eventually dismiss their black asses. Shit, three of my baby daddies sadly thought I was gonna be their personal boxin' bags 'til I showed them I wasn't the one to be puttin' your hands on. I don't give a fuck if I have to fuck a niggah to sleep real good, first, then slice his ass. You better ask somebody. Baby Daddy Number Two, Darryl, got stabbed. Then Baby Daddy Number Three, Marcellus, got bit in his face for tryna do me. Still to this day, that niggah's walkin' around with my teeth marks stamped on the side of his face. And Baby Daddy Number Four, Mustafa, got hand sanitizer slung in his eyes, then hit in the face with a bat and got his nose broke and his jaw cracked. That niggah couldn't see, chew, or breathe by the time I finished with his ass.

Anywho…back to Dickalina. "Look, girl. Tonight I'm just gonna chill, so I'll catch up with you later. Right now I need to get up off this phone and get dinner started before all these kids get home."

"Uh-huh…well, if you change your mind, let me know."

I don't respond. I simply end the call. I glance up at the clock. It's almost three o'clock. I pull my hair up into a ponytail, then change into somethin' more comfortable so I can get dinner started. I don't give a damn what a bitch says about me, but what you won't ever say is that my kids don't have a hot, homecooked meal *almost* every night, or that they come home to an empty house. Nope. I see my kids off in the mornin', and I'm here to greet their asses when they walk back through these doors after school. Now what I do at night after their homework is done and they've had their baths is my goddamn business. But I always take care of home first.

The twins swing open the door, first. "Mommmmmy!" Fuquan screams as he storms through the house.

"Boy, don't come in here with all that noise," I yell out

while rinsin' dishes and stackin' the dishwasher. "I'm not in the mood!"

He stomps into the kitchen. "That stupid ho makes me sick!"

I crane my neck to look at him. "Boy, what I tell you about callin' people hoes?"

"Well, she is a ho."

I dry my hands and turn to face him. "Who?"

"Missus Sweeney," Tyquan answers as he walks in behind his brother. Mrs. Sweeney is one of the bus aides who sit on their school bus.

"Mind your business, punk," Fuquan snaps. "She ain't ask you."

"Well, I told her anyway, punk!"

I take a deep sigh. "Look, don't y'all start your shit. Come here and give me a hug," I say, walkin' over to them. Tyquan hugs me and gives me a kiss, then goes off to his room. But Fuquan's temper is flared up so high, he isn't interested in hugs or kisses. "Boy, give me a damn hug before I floor your ass." He reluctantly does. I kiss him on the cheek and he wipes it off. I ignore his evil ass. "I still love you, anyway. Now tell me what Missus Sweeney did. And watch what you say 'cause I don't wanna have to punch you in ya goddamn mouth. You kids' mouths are too damn fresh."

"She said I was actin' like a wild baboon on the bus, then pulled me by my ear and twisted it. And all the kids started laughin' and teasin' me, makin' monkey noises."

"That bitch did *what?*" I ask, placin' a hand up on my hip. "And why the fuck did she put her goddamn hands on you?"

"Because he kept standin' and turnin' around in his seat, horseplayin'," Tyquan says, walkin' back into the kitchen.

"I was not horseplayin', punk!" Fuquan screams at the top of his lungs. "So mind your stupid business!"

I take a deep breath, then smile at Tyquan, usin' my nice mommy's voice. "Thank you, sweetheart. But Mommy wants to hear this from your brother."

"But all he's gonna do is lie."

"Am not!"

"Will to! Because you like to lie."

"Look. Stop all this goddamn yellin' up before I beat the shit outta both of you. I'm tryna be goddamn nice up in this bitch, but y'all takin' me there. Now, Tyquan, do you have any homework?" He tells me no. I tell him to go take his ass into the livin' room and watch television and leave his brother alone. I bring my attention back to Fuquan. "Now what were you doin' on the bus? And don't you lie."

"I wasn't doin' nothin'. I was playin' my game and that asshole, Rasheed, kept blowin' spitballs at me because I wouldn't let him play it."

"Well, why didn't you tell Missus Sweeney on his ass?"

"I did. And every time she wasn't lookin', he kept doin' it. Then she told me to stop bein' a tattle-tale and worry about what's goin' on in my own seat. I got mad and got up and screamed in his face and told him I was gonna fuck him up if he didn't stop."

"Liar!" Tyquan yells from the livin' room. "Fu kept gettin' up out of his seat while the bus was goin' and Missus Sweeney kept tellin' him to sit down. And he wouldn't. He stuck his tongue out at her. Then told her to eat his ass."

"I did not!"

"You did so, liar!"

Next thing I know Fuquan runs out of the kitchen into the livin' room and jumps on Tyquan. The two of them start fightin'. And I have to run in and break them up. Now I gotta fuck 'em both up for not gettin' along.

"I'm sick of this shit! Y'all brothers, goddammit! And I'm not gonna have this shit up in here, both of y'all fightin' each other! Now don't have me goin' to jail today for breakin' your goddamn arms up in here!" I swing Fuquan by the arm and he flies into the recliner. "Now, Fuquan, I'm warnin' ya black ass. Don't have me goin' up in that school tomorrow ready to whoop Missus Sweeney's ass. Now tell me the truth. Did she twist your goddamn ears or are you just sayin' it 'cause you pissed at her?"

He folds his arms, then pokes out his lips. "I don't like her."

"Well, that's too goddamn bad. Now did she put her hands on you or not?"

I actually have to smack up his face a few times before

he finally answers me and admits he was lyin' on her. I beat his ass some more. That's one thing I don't play is that lyin' shit. Tell me the truth, goddammit! My kids know I will fuck a bitch up in a minute over them. But they also know I will fuck them up just as fast.

"And don't you ever let me hear about you cussin' an adult out again. I'm not gonna have no goddamn gutter mouth up in here. Do that shit again and I'ma snatch ya motherfuckin' tongue out. You gotta lotta damn nerve. You don't even know how to wash the shit out right and you tellin' some goddamn body to eat ya nasty ass out. Where the fuck you hear that nasty shit from, any-damn-way?"

"You," they both say.

I finish whoopin' his lyin'-ass, then go into my bathroom to light me a damn blunt. I take a few deep pulls to calm my nerves, then make myself a mental note to call Darius to bring me some more of this good shit when he comes over. I take two more pulls, then put it out, feelin' a whole lot more relaxed. I decide to save the rest for later. *These goddamn kids are goin' to drive me crazy,* I think, walkin' out of my bedroom, then goin' back into the kitchen to finish cookin' dinner.

The rest of the night it's quiet up in here. Actually, a little too quiet, which makes me get up and do a quick run-through to make sure the twins aren't tryna burn the house down. Fuquan is sleep. And Tyquan is watchin' cartoons. I check on everyone else. Day'Asia's in her nasty-ass bedroom runnin' her mouth on her cell, and on her laptop Skypin'. Elijah's playin' some game on PS3, waitin' for his fahver to come pick him up. And Marquelle, Joshua and Isaiah are all already out with their big-dicked daddies.

I head back to my room and call Darius to re-up my stash, then ask him to sit with Day'Asia and the twins.

"Damn, Ma," he says, suckin' his teeth. "Day'Asia's old enough to stay home and watch them by herself. When I was her age you had me watchin' Da'Quan and them all the time."

"That's because you were responsible. And I could trust you. Now how many times I gotta say this. You know I don't trust Day'Asia's ass up in here alone."

"Yeah, whatever. Shit's still retarded. No reason why she can't watch them."

"Darius, don't have me go off, okay? All I wanna do is go out and have me a few drinks without worryin' that my house is gonna be tore up when I get back."

"Well, why can't you get a bottle and drink at home?"

"See, now you're bein' too goddamn grown. I don't know why you wanna have me go off on you tonight. You know goddamn well I don't ask you for much. But when I do, I expect you to come through for me. Now if you're sayin' your black ass is too good to have my goddamn back, then say it."

He huffs. "C'mon, Ma, why you gotta always start talkin' reckless, callin' me niggahs and shit? You know I'ma come through. But, damn. I'm just sayin'. Day'Asia's ass is sixteen. She should be able to watch the twins for a few hours; that's all."

"No, Darius. The only thing I wanna hear you sayin' is when you gonna have ya ass here. I told you, I don't want her left up in here alone. I'd come back here and she'd have a buncha niggahs up in here and my babies tied up to a damn tree somewhere."

"I'm sayin', Ma. Don't you think I have a life, too? Why can't the twins go with Vernon?"

I blink. "Darius, don't do me, niggah. You have a life because I brought you into this world. And I'm kind and gracious enough to let you live. So don't try me. My babies ain't goin' over to no goddamn Vernon's house after he flattened my motherfuckin' tires. And the niggah still owes me money for child support. So hell no! Now please don't have me come over there and bust out them goddamn windows in that car I helped you buy. And you know I will."

He sucks his teeth again. Shenille's in the background poppin' shit as usual. I hear the trick-bitch talkin' shit about him havin' to come here to babysit every time I wanna go out.

I hear her say, "Tell her ass to watch her own damn kids for a change. Why you gotta always run over there every time she calls you? I'm sick of this shit. You need to man up, Darius. Stop bein' a pussy all the damn time and tell her ass no."

He tries to muffle her out.

"Darius, I know that bald-headed bitch ain't over there talkin' shit 'cause you know I'm lookin' for a reason to bust her in her raggedy-ass mouth. Let that bitch keep runnin' her mouth and I'm gonna have her goddamn EBT card shut down. And you know I know that bitch is out there sellin' her stamps for money so you had better put a muzzle on that ho real quick."

"C'mon, Ma, chill."

"'Chill' hell. Put that ugly bitch on the phone."

"Look, Ma. Damn. Why you gotta disrespect her like that?"

"Oh, you takin' up for her ass? Niggah, why *you* gotta let her disrespect *me?* I'm your mother. You know what Darius? Fuck it. You stay right over there with that gorilla-faced bitch of yours. And the next time you gotta get bailed outta jail, you make sure you call that bitch. I'll find someone else to sit with your brothers and sister. Since you gotta life. But you had better hide that mother-fuckin' car because when I'm done with it, not even the junkyard is gonna want it."

"Fuck, Ma! Let me go. I said I'll be there around ten, damn. And, Shenille, will you shut the fuck up! Both of you about to drive me fuckin' crazy!"

"No, niggah!" Gorilla-Face shouts. "You don't tell me to shut the fuck up! You shut the fuck up! When you gonna grow a set of balls and stop bein' a bitch? I'm sick of you lettin' her run you. If her ass ain't have all them goddamn kids..."

"Oh that bitch want her face knocked off. You tell that ho I'ma—"

"Yo, Shenille, shut the fuck up, bitch!"

"Bitch? Who you callin' a *bitch*, niggah? You can pack your shit and get the fuck outta my goddamn house..."

"Look, Ma, for real. I gotta bounce before I end up in fuckin' jail tonight. You done got this bitch cranked up and now I gotta hear her shit."

"Mmmhmm. And tell that whore I'm gonna give her that ass-whippin' she keeps askin' for real soon. I don't know why you kids stay testin' me. There's no way you should be givin' me so much backtalk, Darius, when I ask you to sit with your brothers and sister. And you damn sure shouldn't be lettin' no bitch ever talk slick to your mother, or come between us either."

"Aiight, aiight, Ma...damn. I said I gotta go." Even though his attitude is on high and he's tryin' very hard to keep from goin' off on me, the one thing he won't do, or has ever done—yet, is hang up on me. And he knows that'll I'll keep talkin' shit to him on the phone just to piss off that bitch he's laid up with off even more. But lucky for him I have another call comin' through. I glance at the screen. It's Dre—six-foot-three and loaded with thick, black dick, callin' to eat this ass again, I'm sure.

"And bring me some more of that purple when you come to-night," I say before disconnectin' and clickin' over to the incomin' call. "Yes, how can I help you?"

"I'm good, baby."

"I didn't ask you how you were. I asked you how I can help you."

"I wanna see you."

I roll my eyes up in my head. "Why? It's not like I'm givin' you any pussy."

He laughs. "I'm not callin' for that."

"Yeah, right. Then why you callin'?"

"I was thinkin' about you; that's all."

"Mmmhmm, is that so?"

"Yeah, I don't want you to think it's always gotta be about sex."

"Then, uh, what the hell you think it's gonna be, boo-boo?"

"I don't know. I thought maybe we could chill out; spend some time together."

I yawn in his ear, then pick my cuticles. Oooh, I need to get down to Pasha's soon. "Oh, ain't that special."

"Yeah. What you cook?"

Is this niggah serious?

"What I cook? I made *me* and *my* kids some smothered chicken, sautéed spinach, and baked sweet potatoes."

He makes smackin' sounds in my ear. "Mmm-mmm, damn. That sounds good. I need to slide through with a movie and come get my grub on."

"Niggah, you better slide your ass on over to Wendy's or White Castle, then hop ya ass on over to CityPlex 12 if you tryna see a movie."

He laughs. "It's like that? I can't eat?"

"Yeah, you can eat this pussy, then tongue fuck this ass. But that's the only meal you can get outta me. And that ain't for free. I don't feed no niggah, boo. And I ain't givin' out no free happy meals. You got the wrong one."

"Oh, word? So, hypothetically, if I came through and was hungry, you wouldn't feed me?"

I frown. See. I knew it was a mistake givin' this motherfucka my number. And it was an even bigger mistake to let him eat my ass out that one time after a night of tossin' back Toe Lickers down at the Crack House. But the niggah has a wicked tongue game. Whew! That long-ass tongue of his snaked its way into my asshole, twirled around in it, then made sparks shoot through my pussy as he strummed his fingers across my clit. Oh, yes...if I could cut his tongue out and carry it around in my purse I would. And although I was only able to run his wallet for five-hundred dollars, it was still enough to get my weave done, buy Marquelle those hundred-and-fifty-dollar Jordans he wanted and fill my Rover up. But for this niggah to think he could get a hot meal. Mmmph.

"Hell no," I snap, pullin' off my clothes, then walkin' into the bathroom and turnin' on the shower. "What I look like takin' food from outta my kids' mouths to feed some man? No, boo. That's not what I do. I fuck, I don't feed."

"Damn, that's foul."

"No, what's foul is you not makin' sure ya ass ate before you got here; *hypothetically* speakin', that is, since we both know you're not steppin' foot up in here, any-damn-way."

Now, I like to do a lot of fuckin' and cussin' and drinkin' and smokin'—and, yeah, fightin', too. But there are two things I don't (and won't) do: Put a niggah before my kids, or take money or food from them to give to his ass. There's already enough dumb bitches out there who do that stupid shit. And my name will never be added to the list. No thank you!

He laughs. "It's cool. But, damn. How you expect to get a man if you ain't even tryna feed 'im?"

"Boo-boo, I don't want a man. And I ain't lookin' for one. I want his hard dingaling and his dollars; that's it. All that extra shit, save it for them thirsty bitches, lonely for a man. The only thing I'm tryna do is fuck 'n shop, niggah."

"Yo, Cass, see. That's why I fucks with you; you straight raw with it. But, damn…you really wouldn't feed me?"

"Is my ass flat?"

"Hell muthafuckin' naw. You already know."

"Mmmph. Then there's your answer."

He laughs. "For real, Cass, when you gonna stop playin' games and let me spend some time with you?"

"I'm not playin' games. As soon as you open your wallet and let me run through it, then we can talk. And this time I'ma need more than five-hundred bucks. You know how I do it, boo. Time is money, and money is time. If you can't finance me, then niggah, you definitely can't fuck me."

"Damn, you drive a hard bargain. Don't you get child support for all them kids you have?"

I twist my face up. *This niggah can't be serious? I know he's not tryna clock my goddamn coins.* "Niggah, don't calculate my money. What the fuck does that have to do with you?"

"I'm sayin'. Why everything gotta always be about money with you? Why can't we spend time together because we enjoy each other's company?"

"Boo-Boo, you dialed the wrong number. I don't enjoy you. I enjoy gettin' what I can out of you; that's it. If you lookin' for a love connection you had better head on over to eHarmony or Match-dot-com. And if you lookin' for freebies, then you better hop ya cheap ass up on Craigslist."

I end the call, then step into the shower. I'm ready to get my drink on, dammit!

Twenty-Five

Oooh wee! I'm on my third Cum Cannon, feelin' right, god-dammit! And The Crack House is startin' to get crowded. The drinks are flowin' heavy. The deejay is tearin' it up. And security is on high-alert up in this piece tonight as it is every Thursday, Friday and Saturday night. And I'm lookin' real sassy in my orange sleeveless, knit, cowl-neck mini dress. I got my brown leather, six-inch platform slingbacks on. My smooth honey-coated skin is oiled up 'n shinin'. My pussy's floral fresh. And asshole's Fleet-rinsed and ready. What you say? Calves, POW! Waist, POW! Booty, POW! POW! POW! Oooh, yes…Big Booty's lookin' delish!

I throw my right arm up, pumpin' a fist into the air, then start slow humpin' in my seat, twirlin' my pussy up on the barstool when Grace Jones' "Feel Up" starts playin'. I glance over toward the deejay's booth and give Slick the middle finger for tryna crank me up tonight. He makes me sick with his long, skinny-dick self. Ooh, but that six-foot, cocoa-brown niggah with the light-brown eyes and wavy hair fucks like a savage. Hot 'n nasty 'n real sneaky with it. I fucked him twice. Once when I was sixteen, workin' the poles. Then, again, when I was almost nineteen. I needed a couple of dollars to feed my babies, and Slick was always right there with his dick in his hand, tryna get up in this pussy. So I did what I had to do. And when shit got hectic and I needed a place to stay with my kids, Slick took me in. And I didn't have to fuck him, although I probably woulda.

I close my eyes and slip back to my days as a stripper. I was sixteen. And I had no damn business strippin' in no club. I was stacked like a twenty-year-old, workin' the pole down at this gutter hole called Heart Throbs in downtown Elizabeth. The owner, Jam—who was about forty-five at the time, knew my real age but he didn't give a damn. As long as I kept the room burstin' at the seams, kept it rainin' up in that motherfucka, and didn't hit any of the back rooms to suck dick or get fucked, I could make my paper. And that's exactly what I did. I was young and had body for days, and knew how to use 'em both to get what I needed. Makin' sure I didn't end up sleepin' outside on a park bench or under a bridge somewhere with two small kids was my only concern. So I did what I had to do.

Mmmph. Heart Throbs kept me and my babies fed. And it allowed me to have a roof over my head. It's also where I met Darryl Jennings—big dicked, dark-chocolate niggah and Baby Daddy Number Two—who ate my pussy and fucked me nonstop. I met him three months after I started workin' there. He was twenty-two and one of the regulars, who came through three nights out of the week; specifically for me. He was a big-spender and tipped well. And, after two months of makin' twenties rain down on me, he made it known he was diggin' me.

The niggah started waitin' for me after shows, makin' sure I got home safe. Then it went to him takin' me out for breakfast after the shows to dinners on the nights I wasn't workin' to buyin' shit for me and my sons. Oh, you couldn't tell a bitch like me shit. I had snagged me a real live baller. He hustled hard, played hard, and fucked harder. And out of all the bitches he coulda had, he wanted *me*.

Before I knew it, I was movin' out of the one room I was cramped in with my two kids into a two-bedroom apartment. The niggah kept me stuffed with dick. Kept me and my sons laced in all the fly shit. And kept my handbag lined with paper. Then somehow it all went funky. I shoulda listened to my gut and kept it movin', but I was real grown and hot in the ass. You couldn't tell a ho like me shit. I had a thing for older niggahs. And he was checkin' for me hard. So, I igged that little voice in my head that told me to seal my pussy up and bolt the other way. But the niggah knew my weakness. Money, big dick, and long tongue. He served all three. And served 'em well! Eventually, I got pregnant. And shortly thereafter, he tried to use my face as his personal punchin' bag. The niggah thought he owned me. And thought I owed him. In some ways, I guess I did owe him somethin' for rescuin' me from a fucked-up situation. But I didn't owe him my life. And I damn sure wasn't gonna let him tear my face up or let the niggah control me. The last time that motherfucka put his hands on me, I waited until he least expected it and slammed a knife down into his right hand, then took off runnin'. I was seventeen with three kids. And Slick was right there for me. He had my back. And 'til this day, he always has.

I open my eyes and peep his pencil-dick ass grinnin' at me. I stick my tongue out at him. Niggah still fine as shit, mmmph!

"Feeeeeeeeeeel UP!" I sing out, throwin' both hands up in the air. "Feel Up! Feel Up! Aaawl shit…Don't start none, won't be none, goddammit!"

Slick knows I'm about to light the bar up. He flicks his tongue back at me, laughin'. Oooh, this niggah knows how to do me right! He knows this shit right here is my goddamn jam! The bass line starts workin' me over. I grind my pussy harder into the stool. Slick licks his lips. I roll my eyes at him, then turn my back on him. He knows the beat is about to have me bring it up in this bitch tonight. But I swear I ain't come here to twerk it. I came to get my drink on, then take it on in. But goddamn him!

"Ooooooow!" I swing my right arm up in the air, sway to the beat a taste, then hop off the barstool. "Damn you, Slick! Yesssss! Yesssss!"

The niggahs who know me up in here all wait and watch with their drinks in their hands 'cause they know I'ma 'bout to crank up the Booty heat. "Aaah, yes!" I hop up and down, then kick my right leg up, toot my lips up and start swingin' my head from the left to the right. My silky weave sways across my ass.

"Aaah, shit, yeah...do that shit, Booty!" someone yells out.

"Bounce that ass, baby..."

"Goddamn, her body's the truth..."

I act like I don't hear 'em. Shit, truth is, I ain't payin' these niggahs no never mind tonight. I close my eyes. Belly-roll it, hip roll it, then lean forward and booty pop it. I start feelin' up my body, grabbin' 'n squeezin' my titties. I back it up from the bar. Give myself room to spin around. I run my hands through my hair and start goin' at it hard when Slick plays Joe Budden's "There's Some Hoes In The House."

"Aaaaaaah, yessssss...hot hoes in the house...you lil' dick motherfuckas can't handle this...where the big-dick niggahs at! Owwwwl!"

I dip down low, then roll it back up. The Crack House is about to come alive. Niggahs got their eyes locked on my ass. Hatin'-ass bitches ice-ballin' me. But I don't give a fuck. I'm in my zone. "Goddammit, Slick!" I scream over the music. "I need my throat wet! Someone get me another Cum Cannon! Owwwl...smoke a niggah's dick! There's some hoes in this house...Jerzee's here, bitches!"

Big Mike comes from around the bar and brings me a drink. He's the only niggah I'd trust to not try 'n drug a bitch. "You doin' it up, baby," he says into my ear as he hands me my glass.

"Big Mike, you lucky you my baby daddy's nephew 'cause I woulda been fucked you down by now, niggah. Wet that big dick right on up."

He laughs. "Yo, Cass. You wild as hell, baby."

"I know I am. Now back it up from outta my space and let me get my dance and drank on."

He keeps laughin', shakin' his head as he walks off. He knows I love talkin' shit to him. And the niggah knows I mean everything I say. I would cream all on his cock, then suck it clean, goddammit!

I toss back my drink, then hand my empty glass to some niggah all up in my face, starin' me down and lickin' his lips when Ester Dean's "Drop It Low" starts playin'. "Aaaaah, shit...y'all tryna make me get my Ester on..." I dip 'n bounce real low, swayin' my head from side to side and causin' my hair to sweep the floor. I pop back up, then bend over and grab my ankles, lettin' my asscheeks peek out from under the hem of my dress. I start poppin' it. Niggahs start hootin' 'n howlin'.

By the time Pussy's "Suck My Pussy" starts playin' I'm all sweated out and ready to come outta my dress and drawers. But I'm so caught up in the music and moment, that I don't really give a damn. Niggahs are winkin', grinnin', and lickin' their lips as I shake up the booty heat.

After about six songs, I finally shake my ass back over

to my seat where I stay perched, poppin' shit to the niggahs who are all up in my face and tossin' back the drinks. Tonight may be free drinks for the ladies, but I never have to pay any-damn-way so it really doesn't matter.

Big Mike hands me another drink. "You were tearin' it up out there."

I reach for a napkin and pat my forehead, then the back of my neck. Sweat is just rollin' all down my back. "You know how I do it, boo. Ooh, it's hot as hell in here."

He laughs. "Nah, that's all you. You hot like fire, Cass."

I wave him on. "And I'm ready to burn somethin' up tonight."

He laughs, walkin' off to help another customer at the other end of the bar. I swivel my barstool so that I am facin' the door as I place the straw to my lips and take slow, deliberate sips. I catch the eye of that sneaky-lookin', Hill Harper look-alike watchin' me from the other side of the room. He gives me a head nod. With his fine ass! I roll my eyes, then wrinkle my nose the minute I see Shuwanda and Alicia walkin' through the door.

These nasty-freak bitches! Mmmph. I knew they'd be all up in each other's faces, again. Images of the two of them chowin' down on each other's pussy's flash in my head. *Ugh!* I toss back my drink, shakin' the thought.

"Hey, girl," Shuwanda says, walkin' over to me with a phony-ass smile on her face.

I frown. "Bitch, don't speak to me. You know I don't like you. Now move along."

She laughs. "I will when I'm good and ready. I know

you don't speak to me. That's exactly why I fuck with you."

I decide to ignore this bitch, lookin' over at Alicia. "Ooh, girl. I heard how Chauncey dragged ya ass all through Pasha's shop and busted ya face open a few months ago. A mess, boo. I'm so pissed I missed that shit." I laugh. "Girl, what he do? He knocked out like three of your front teeth and broke ya nose, too, right? Speakin' of which, how is that sexy-ass Mandingalo, doin'? I'm sure you missin' all that hard cock. Oooh, Courtney is some kinda fine. Too bad you couldn't keep him."

She rolls her eyes. "Fuck you, Cass. Messy bitch."

"No, sugah-boo, you the messy one. How you gonna be on your knees suckin' some stripper-niggah's dick at a party, then get put on blast all up on Facebook? If you gonna be a whore, be a smart one." I shake my head at her.

Alicia smirks. "Whatever, Cass. Say what you want, shit happens. I see you got that ugly scar off the side of ya face. KiKi really did your face real dirty when she sliced you down to the white meat."

She's talkin' about the young bitch who came to my doorstep and slashed my face with a razor. And yeah, she did my face in lovely. Sliced the side of my face with a razor real good. But she got one even better. Me and five of my kids stomped that ho's ass. Beat her face in until her head blew up like a pumpkin. We tried to beat her face off. Broke her eye sockets, nose and knocked teeth out. And, yes we posted it all up on YouTube and Facebook for all to see. And what? And yeah, we all got arrested and charged with aggravated assault. But, guess what? I didn't give a fuck. That ho had crossed the line, comin' to my door confrontin' me about ridin' down on her niggah's dick.

And, yeah, I got ninety-seven stitches to the face. But that didn't change shit. I still kept fuckin' with her man's young ass, and runnin' his pockets. I fucked him because I wanted to. And because he had some good damn dick! And I dismissed his ass and sent him on his way when I got bored. But guess what? It was her niggah who hustled up the ten grand to get that scar removed. Plastic surgery is where it's at, sugah-boo. And a bitch is good as new.

I pull open my handbag and take out my phone, settin' it up on the bar. "Hahaha…real funny, bitch. And you see what happened to her ass. Pumpkin-head bitch got her ass stomped in. You must wanna be next. Oh, wait. You already know what it's like to get stomped. Matter of fact, didn't they have to carry ya ass out on a stretcher. Poor thing. Mmmph. But I'm glad to see you standin'. I know you glad you finally got all those knocked out teeth replaced."

"Cass, you're such a ghetto bitch. I don't even know why I'm standin' here wastin' my time fuckin' with you."

"Ooh, Alicia, don't do it to ya'self, boo. By the way, are you still with Courtney? Oh, wait. Not. I forgot. He dumped ya ass when he found out what a triflin' bitch you are. I'm sure he's happy not to be fuckin' with your whorish-ass anymore, nasty cum-slut."

Her mouth drops open. "The only whore here is you."

I ignore the comment, shiftin' my body around on the barstool. "Pussy eater, *boom!* I wasn't the one who got caught suckin' dick, sugah. You were. And then ya nasty, desperate ass done sucked down on Melvin's ashy-ass dick. Ugh, ya ass really done fell off. 'Cause anyone who fucks a niggah after"—I flick my hand over at Shuwanda—"they done run all up in this bitch, is a straight up whore."

Shuwanda starts neck-rollin' it. "Bitch, how about you try spendin' more time at home raisin' ya bad-ass kids instead of poppin' ya ass up and down in the bar and mindin' everyone else's business all the damn time? How about you do that for change, ho?"

I laugh. "Slut, *boom!* Both of you bitches are sickenin'. One minute the two of you bipolar hoes are airin' each other's business out, then the next minute you clit-lickin' whores all coochie-crunch. You confused, dizzy bitches deserve each other. Now get the fuck outta my face."

Shuwanda shifts her cheap handbag from one arm to the other. "Whatever, Cass. You always somewhere startin' shit with ya miserable ass."

I laugh, peepin' the edges of her handles all frayed up. This ghetto, low-budget bitch is hot trash! She has the nerve to have a matchin' scarf wrapped around her head. "The only miserable one in the room is you, sugah-boo. By the way, cute bag."

She smirks. "Of course it is."

This bootleg bitch really thinks I don't know fake shit when

I see it. Bitches kill me tryna pass off knock-off shit like it's official. I shake my head. "Mmmhmm...downtown Newark and Chinatown specials; cheap wears and knock-off handbags. You're real fly with it with ya Fooey Futon danglin' in the crook of ya arm. A real Daffy's girl; frontin' like you're doin' it up. Bitch, puhleeze."

"What?!" she snaps, plantin' her fist up on her hip. "Cassandra, I know you don't even wanna go there with me."

I gulp down the rest of my drink and feel like bangin' my glass in her face, but I'ma keep it real classy-ghetto tonight. "Boo-boo, puhleeze. I didn't stutter. You heard what I said. We can go there all night if you want. 'Cause the truth of the matter is you can't bring it to me, boo. No matter how hard you try. Yeah, I have a buncha kids by different men. And yeah, I live in Section-8 housin'. And *whaaaat*, bitch? You still see me pushin' a Range Rover, don't you, ho? And you see my kids stay fly every damn day. And you see this thousand-dollar bag on my arm, don't you? So where you tryna take me, huh, sweetie? No motherfuckin' where; that's where. But, you can take your—" My cell pings. "Saved by the bell, ho." I grab it from off the bar.

"Whatever, bitch. Alicia, I'm gettin' away from this ho before I have to turn it up in here."

I laugh in her face. "Let me see you try it." She huffs, walkin' off.

Alicia eyes me. "You know that's fucked up, right?"

I shrug, glancin' at my screen. "Fuck that nasty, cum-guzzlin' bitch. And fuck you too."

"Fuck you, bitch!"

I crack up. "Boo, you wish you could fuck all this goodness. But guess what, bitch? Ya dick ain't big enough. Now get the fuck away from me before you find ya'self eatin' glass."

She frowns, stormin' off.

I have a text from Elijah. Asia gotta boy n her room n door is closed.

I blink to make sure I'm readin' the shit right. *What the fuck!* I frown, textin' back. Where's Darius?

Elijah texts back. he left

Oh, hell motherfuckin' no. I yank my bag off the bar. *I'ma beat that lil' ho's ass tonight. Then I'ma cuss Darius out for leavin' up outta there!* I specifically asked his ass to keep an eye on things. And the motherfucka dips. Then he doesn't even call me to tell me. *Oh, I'm goin' to jail tonight.* Where r the twins?

wit darius

I sigh. Somewhat relieved he didn't leave the eight-year-olds in the house. Still, I'm pipin'-hot mad and ready to go the hell off!

I don't waste no time racin' up outta the bar, hoppin' in my truck and screechin' my tires outta the parkin' lot. I call Elijah's phone, then black the minute he answers. "Who the fuck does Day'Asia have up in my motherfuckin' house?"

He whispers into the phone. "You remember Pissy Sissy when we lived in buildin' four?" He's talkin' about Priscilla Keyes, one of the hoodrat hoes from around the way, who everyone calls Pissy Sissy 'cause she smells like cat piss. Bless her lil' smelly heart! "It's her brother," he says.

"Which one?"

"The one with the crooked eye."

"*Whaaaat?* That cockeyed motherfucka is around your brother, Da'Quan's, age. How long he been there?"

"Like twenty minutes. He came ten minutes after Darius left. Mommy, you better hurry up before they start doin' stuff in there."

I press on the gas, speedin' through red lights and stop signs. I don't give a fuck! I'll run a motherfuckin' pedestrian down dead tonight. "Where's Joshua and Isaiah?"

"Joshua went with his dad..."

I frown. *What the fuck Julius doin' comin' to get my son without clearin' it with me first? I see I'ma have to curse that niggah out again.*

"...and Isaiah's in his room 'sleep."

"Don't say a word. I'll be there in a minute."

"I won't," he says, his voice goin' lower. I almost have to strain to hear him. "But hurry. She just came out of her room and went into the kitchen. Now she's goin' back into her room with three beers."

I don't wanna hear shit else. My stomach is in knots. I need to call my bank to make sure I have enough money for bail. I tell Elijah to make sure the patio door is unlocked for me. Then remind him to keep his goddamn mouth shut. He promises.

I disconnect. They done fucked up my groove and I'm pissed the fuck off!

Twenty-Six

It takes me exactly ten minutes and seven-seconds to get to the house. As I creep up to the house, I shut off my lights. There's a dark-colored BMW boldly parked up in the driveway. *Oh, this bitch is real grown 'n hot with it, bringin' her niggahs up in where I pay motherfuckin' rent!*

See. Her ass thought she was real slick. Askin' me a buncha goddamn questions earlier about what I had planned for the night. I knew her sneaky ass was up to somethin', but I couldn't put my finger on it. That's why I asked Darius to keep an eye on her ass. Then I told Elijah to be on the lookout as well; just in case. This lil' grown bitch keeps the switch flipped on sneaky. I block the niggah's car. His ass ain't goin' no-motherfuckin'-where tonight!

I walk around to the back of the house, slippin' off my heels as I quietly slide open the glass door. Elijah is sittin' at the dinin' room table, waiting. His eyes are wide with excitement. His ass loves drama. I put a finger up to my lips, walkin' toward the hall closet. I pull out my locked box, open it with the key I keep hidden, then pull out Old Faithful and load it. Then I stand there for a hot minute, starin' down the hall at Day'Asia's door. Fuck knockin' on it. Fuck yellin' out her name so she can scramble around and hide shit. No, this calls for street action. I take off runnin' down the hall and kick in her door, causin' it to fly off the goddamn hinges.

"Surprise, motherfuckas!" I yell, wavin' my gun in the air. "Don't fuckin' move. Or I'ma blow both of your motherfuckin' heads off."

This little bitch got the lights on low and motherfuckin' fuck-music playin' low in the background. I smell her hot pussy in the air. It smells like clambake 'n shrimps up in here. I'm too goddamn through!

"Oh, shit. Fuck!" Cockeye says as I flip on the lights. He's butt-ass naked; dick bouncin' everywhere. Day'Asia's fast-ass is in a red thong. *A goddamn thong!* Some shit I didn't buy her at that. I'm standin' on his pants. He tries to grab his boxers.

"Oh, no, motherfucka! You stand there naked or you're goin' outta here in a body bag! Now try me."

He drops them. I quickly glance down at his hard dick and almost get weak. Now I'm really heated. But I don't know what I'm more pissed about. The fact that this cross-eyed niggah has a long, black dick, or the fact he was fuckin' my daughter with it. Either way, all I see is red as he tries to cover it with his hands.

Day'Asia throws her hands up over her titties. "Mommy, we wasn't doin' nothin'. I swear."

I point the gun at her. "Bitch, puhleeze! Then why the

fuck you in here all naked? I can smell ya steamin' pussy way out in the livin' room, smellin' like goddamn clam juice."

She blinks.

"Yeah, I said it. Rinse ya goddamn pussy out good before you wanna get it fucked."

"But we weren't doin' anything."

"Don't you stand there and lie to me. I will blow your top off tonight, sweetie. Lights off, music playin', candles lit, you only in a goddamn thong...where the fuck you get that shit, anyway? And this niggah here naked to the bone; y'all were gettin' ready to do a whole lotta nothin' up in here."

"Mommy, please...we didn't—"

"Bitch, I told you to shut the fuck up! And I'm not gonna tell you again!"

"M-M-M-Miss-Miss Simms, I-I-I can explain," Cock-eye offers as he tries to stutter his way out of a bullet to his face.

I aim the gun at him. "Shut the fuck up, niggah! You in my motherfuckin' house, gettin' ready to fuck my motherfuckin' daughter...you can't explain shit to me. The only thing I wanna know is. Did you put your dick in her? And if you open your motherfuckin' mouth with a lie, I'ma get charged with a body tonight." I place a hand on my hip. "Now talk!"

"No, word is bond, Miss Simms. We didn't fuck. I'm mean, I didn't. I swear. We were gonna, but...I swear on my seed. We—"

"Mommy, please. I'm sorry. Put the gun—"

Before she can open her mouth to say anything else, I leap over and backhand her. She falls back into the wall. "Shut the fuck up. Next time, I'ma pistol whip your ass up in here." Now I'm not really gonna shoot my baby, or his ass. But, I'd mace both of their asses down real good. But they don't know what I'd do at this moment. And the poor, slutty thing pisses on her nasty-ass self. Bless her lil' pissy-ass heart! I feel like clawin' her damn face it, then punchin' her in her throat. She's crossed the goddamn line, fuckin' up in here! And not havin' her pussy fresh. Oh, I'm goddamn through.

She slides down the wall, cryin' and holdin' her face. Like I give a damn! "Get ya goddamn stinkin'-ass pussy up off my carpet before you stain it."

Cockeye looks over my shoulder and I follow his stare. Elijah and Isaiah are standin' in back of me gawkin', takin' everything in. "Y'all go on and take your nosey asses upstairs before I fuck both of you up, next."

They take off runnin'. "Hahahahaha, Mommy said she's gonna blow his cock off. And shoot up Asia's nasty stink-box. Her pussy smells like clams."

"Elijah!" I yell. "Stop makin' up shit. 'Fore I beat yo' ass!"

I stare Cockeye down. "Niggah, you tried to run your dick up in the wrong pussy. How old are you?" He tells me he's twenty. "Twenty? Niggah, have you lost your motherfuckin' mind? She's sixteen!"

He frowns, shootin' a look over at her. "*Sixteen?*" he

repeats, soundin' shocked. "Yo, I ain't know she was only sixteen. She told me she just turned eighteen."

"Well, she told you a motherfuckin' lie!" He cut his eye over at Day'Asia. She looks at him, then me. I narrow my eyes at her. "Don't say shit. I feel like crackin' your skull open."

"Can I put my clothes on, now?" Cockeye has the audacity to ask.

"Hell no," I snap, yankin' his boxers outta his hand, then snatchin' the crumpled sheet from off the bed and throwin' it at him. "Put that on if you wanna cover up. As a matter of fact, go sit your ass out in the livin' room until I'm finished with Miss Hot in The Ass over there. Then you can leave." He stares at me as if I'm crazy. "Niggah, I'm not playin'. You do know who my sons are, right?"

He nods. "Yeah. Miss Simms, I don't want no problems."

"Oh, too late, niggah. You shoulda thought about that before you snuck yo' ass up over here and climbed up in my daughter's bed. Now you got problems. And just so you know. I've blocked your car in. So if you're tryna go somewhere, you're gonna be goin' on foot. Now go take yo' ass on out in the livin' room and wait until I'm finished. Then I'ma give you your shit and send you on your way."

I keep the gun aimed at him. He shoots a look over at Day'Asia, shakin' his head. "I don't believe this shit," he mumbles, wrappin' the sheet around him, then walkin' past me.

"Elijah and Isaiah, y'all block the door and make sure this nasty niggah doesn't try 'n leave up outta here."

"Okay," they say. "We got it covered." I hear Elijah talkin' shit to him, laughin'. But I'm too focused on beatin' this little ho's ass to be concerned.

"You stay right there," I tell her. "And if you fuckin' move, I'm promise you tonight will be your last night breathin'. Do you understand me?"

She looks at me, scared shitless. *Good!*

She nods. "Yes."

I walk out into the livin' room. Tell Elijah and Isaiah to go up-stairs until I call them back down. Cockeye is sittin' in the dinin' room. "Niggah, I told you to go sit yo' ass in the livin' room. See. You hard-headed. That's why your little bad-ass stayed in trouble and always in and outta jail."

He locks his eyes on the gun in my hand, then looks up at me. "Miss Simms, I swear to you. I thought she was eighteen. If I woulda known she was only sixteen I woulda stepped off when I ran into her."

I put the gun to his head. "Did you fuck her?"

He shakes his head. "No. The only thing we did was fool around."

I frown. "Fool around how, niggah? You eat her stank-ass pussy and suck all over her titties? She suck that big-ass dick of yours?"

He blinks. I got the niggah shook. Good! "And you better think long and hard before you speak 'cause you done tried to run ya dick up in the wrong one. Now open your mouth." I rub the barrel of the gun over his lips. "Open your mouth, niggah, or I'ma bang your teeth in."

"Miss-Miss Simms...rrreal shit...we didn't ffffuck."

"Open. Your. Mouth." I cock the gun back. "I'ma count to ten, then I'ma shoot your head off and splatter your goddamn brains all over the room. One, two, three..." He opens his mouth and I slide the barrel in.

"Did she suck your dick?" He swallows hard. The niggah's sweatin' bullets. "Motherfucka, don't think I won't blow your brains out in here. Answer the question." He tells me, again, that he didn't know she was only sixteen. He pleads. Tells me I gotta believe him. I do. Still I wanna toy with the niggah some more before I run down on Day'Asia's ass and beat her down. I get up in his face. And speak real low. "I'ma tell you what we gonna do." I pause, narrowin' my eyes. "We gonna act like this never happened, understand?"

He rapidly nods his head. Sweat is pourin' down his face. "Cool. I can do that, ma'am. It never happened."

"Good. Now this is what you're gonna do for me. How much money you have on you?"

"I got like three, four, hunnid in my jeans pocket."

"Good. I want it for all my pain and sufferin'. And then I want you to bring your black ass back here tomorrow mornin' at nine. So I can collect the rest. You got that?"

He nods again. I pull the gun from outta his mouth.

"And if you don't show up here at exactly nine, I'ma

have my crazy-ass sons beat yo' black ass after I fuck your mother up, *word is bond*, niggah. And them I'ma hunt ya baby muhver down and fuck her up. You got that?"

He nods. "I got you. I'll be here. I'm not gonna front. I don't want no problems; real shit."

"Good." I step back. Tell him I'll be right back, then walk back down to Day'Asia's room. Lucky for her, she's in the same spot I left her in. I grab Cockeye's clothes, then walk back out into the dinin' room. I tell him to stand up and give me the sheet he has wrapped around his body. He removes it, tryna cover his cock.

"Niggah, I already saw your dick. Remember, you were tryna *fuck* my sixteen-year-old daughter with it, niggah-bitch." I hand him his boxers and watch as he slips into them, runnin' his pockets. I pull out two condoms, a driver's license, and four-hundred-and-fifty dollars. I fold the money and stuff it down in my bra, tossin' him his jeans. He puts them on, then finishes puttin' the rest of his shit on. I keep my eyes on him as he stuffs his feet into his Timbs, then grab my car keys and walk him outside.

I memorize his license plate as he gets in his car. I back my car away from the driveway, then get out as he backs up. "What time you gonna be here tomorrow?"

"At nine-thirty."

"No, niggah. Nine."

"I got you."

"Oh you gonna get me, all right. And if you don't show up, I'ma have yo' ass hemmed up for tryna rape my daughter."

He blinks. "Yo, I ain't—"

I put my hand up, cuttin' him off. "Oh yes, the fuck you did, niggah. You tried to rape her. And trust me. I will make sure yo' black ass gets fried for it. Now don't have your ass here in the mornin' and see what I do for you."

He wipes his sweaty forehead with the back of his sleeve. "I'ma be here, Miss Simms. I don't want no problems."

"Good. Now get the fuck up outta here."

He backs outta the driveway, then peels out down the street like a damn maniac. I wait for his car to disappear in the night, then go back into the house and beat the shit outta Day'Asia for a) disruptin' my goddamn night, b) for sneakin' a motherfucka up in this house, c) for wearin' a goddamn thong, d) for not washin' her pussy out, and d) for tryna be so motherfuckin' grown.

Twenty-Seven

At exactly nine o'clock, Cockeye rings my doorbell. But I make the niggah wait, peekin' through the curtains at his young, horny ass. I take him in, *all* of him in, startin' downward to his brown Gucci sneakers. *Hmm, they gotta be size twelves, or thirteens.*

Booty gotta thing for niggahs with them nice, big feet. Yes, lawd!

I lick my lips.

If this niggah got nice feet, I might suck them toes. Well, after I wash them down real good.

My eyes journey up to the way his designer jeans hang just so. Loose fittin', but still up on his waist. A brown and beige Gucci belt is holdin' them up. Unlike them ghetto bitches who think a niggah wearin' saggin' pants with his ass hangin' out is sexy, I think the shit is triflin'. His brown long-sleeved T-shirt has Gucci scrawled over his chest. The niggah's thin, but from what I remember from last night, chiseled.

My eyes travel up to his side profile. Mmmph. This cocoa-brown niggah got the nerve to be kinda sexy from the side. A brown and tan Yankees fitted is pulled down over his eyes. But I can tell his head is freshly lined 'cause the niggah's goatee and mustache are piped out nice 'n fresh. *Oooh, let me find out this lil' niggah tryna impress me.*

Flashes of him standin' butt-ass naked in Day'Asia's room last night pop into my head and I feel heat shoot through me. I was so goddamn mad and turned on after seein' all that dick that niggah has hangin' between his legs that I—after I beat the shit outta Day'Asia's fast ass—had to ride down on one of my dildoes to take the edge off. Mmmph. And the niggah-bitch was tryna fuck Day'Asia with all that cock meat. Not on my watch, goddammit!

Oh this niggah gonna learn today! And I'ma learn him good.

I finally swing the door open when he rings the bell, again. I step back and let him in, wearin' a white chiffon and sequin lace-front flyaway with matchin' thong and a pair of seven-inch platform heels. "Don't open your mouth to say shit."

He blinks, tryin' not to stare at my hard nippes pokin' through my "Fuck 'Em" wear.

I shut the door behind him, lock it, then slowly turn to face him as I place a hand up on my hip. "I'm glad you came through and didn't have me have to hunt you down."

"I-I-I..." He pauses, takin' a deep breath, then wipin' beads of sweat from his forehead with his hand. "Whew, it's gotten hot all of a sudden."

"That's the heat from my pussy, niggah. Now what you got for me?" I walk up to him, holdin' my hand out. "And relax. I'm not gonna fuckin' bite you. Well, maybe I will. But I'm not gonna kill ya ass."

He lets out a nervous chuckle, reachin' into the front pocket of his jeans and pullin' out a wad of rubberbanded money, then handin' it to me. I can tell the niggah's extra nervous. And he should be. "H-here you go."

He watches as I count out the money—seventeen-hundred dollars, in all hundreds. I stare him down, countin' in my head. Mmm, the four hundred and fifty I got from his ass last night and now this piece of change is gonna get stashed right into my emergency "handbags and heels" fund for those last-minute fashion emergencies. Still, I need a lil' somethin'-somethin' for now. "Niggah, I know you don't think this is gonna do me right after the shit you tried to pull up in here last night."

"M-M-Miss Simms, on e'erything, I swear on my moms I ain't know Asia was only sixteen. What I gave you is all I-I-I have on me r-r-right now. But how much more you want? I can hit you wit' about five stacks later on tonight when I make my rounds. No frontin'. I'll come through wit' it."

"Oh, I know you gonna *come* through, lil' niggah." *Right up in my ass!* I eye him, lettin' my gaze roam his body. His long, black dick pops into my head. And I grin. "How much dick you got?"

He gives me a confused look. "Huh?

"Niggah, you heard me. I asked you how many inches that long, black dick of yours is. You know, the one you were tryna rape my daughter with."

He puts his hands up. "Whoa, whoa...I-I wasn't tryna rape her."

"Niggah, I know what I saw when I kicked the door in. You had my baby pinned down to the bed with her drawers ripped off, tryna stuff her pussy with your goddamn dick. That's what the fuck you did. Now that's my story, and I'm gonna stick to it. That shit you pulled traumatized me, niggah. So you gonna have to compensate me for my pain 'n sufferin' if you want me to forget about what I saw."

"Real shit, Miss Simms, I ain't tryna get hemmed up on no bullshit rape charge. And you know that's what that is."

I tilt my head, ploppin' both hands up on my hip. "Niggah, don't do it. You know one of my baby fahvers is a police officer, right?"

"Nah, I ain't know."

"Well, now you do. And you already know how I do mine. I shuts it down, so don't do it, boo. And I have no problem sendin' ya black ass to jail so some big-burly niggah can run a shank in you and gut ya asshole out. Now try me. And ain't LuAnn your mother?"

"Yeah."

"I know she is. And you remember when I snatched her wig off and dragged her knotty-headed ass up and down the playground in back of buildin' eight, don't you?"

He removes his fitted. "Miss Simms, I don't want no problems wit' you."

"Oh, I know you don't. That's why we're gonna handle this like two adults. Now, answer my question. How many inches is that dick?"

He shrugs. Tells me he's never measured it. But knows it's big. That he can only fit extra-large condoms. My pussy lips pucker. "And you wanted to come up in here and try to rip my daughter's pussy open with it, didn't you?"

"Nah, real shit, Miss Simms. I ain't tryna toss shit up on Asia, but she's mad wild out there; especially when she's wit' that chick CandyLee."

"CandyLee? Who the fuck is a CandyLee?"

"Candyilicious. But she's CandyLee in the streets."

I roll my eyes up in my head. "Well, what does she have to do with you tryna fuck Day'Asia, niggah?"

"No lie. When the two of them together they are hot like firecrackers. And like I said, Asia told me she was eighteen. I'da never got at her if I knew she was only sixteen. But she was talkin' like she was mad ready for the getdown. But I ain't know. On e'erything, Miss Simms. I only eff wit' chicks my age or older."

"Is that so? And who are you again?"

"Bunz…I mean Benjamin."

I frown. "Benjamin, mmph. Who the fuck gave you that old-ass name?" I put a hand up, stoppin' him from openin' his mouth. "Never mind. I already know crack snatched ya momma's ass. So I'm not gonna say nothin' bad about ya bald-headed mammy. So, let it go." He blinks. I tilt my head. "What? Did I say somethin' to offend you?"

He bites his bottom lip. "Nah, I'm good."

"Mmmph. I bet you are. And why the hell they call you *Buns*, any-damn-way?"

"It's Bunz wit' a zee."

"Whatever, niggah. Why they call you that?"

He rubs his chin. "Well, uh, 'cause...when I was younger I used to always grab on girls' with them big booties and wanna hump on 'em."

I smirk. "Oh, so you an ass man, uh, lil'niggah?"

He nervously laughs, shiftin' his weight from one foot to the other. "Sumthin' like that."

"Well, what the fuck was you tryna stick ya dick up in Day'Asia's ass for when all she got is big-ass titties? The ass you shoulda been tryna fuck is"—I turn around, glancin' over my shoulder, then smackin' my ass—"this one right here. Now if *you* want me to drop this rape shit, then *you* drop ya goddamn drawers and come do me right."

His eyes pop open.

"I ain't playin', niggah. You wanna fuck lil' girls 'n shit. Well, let me show ya black ass how'ta be a man and fuck a woman. Now drop. Them. Drawers."

He looks at me, tryna figure out if I'm serious. "M-M-Miss Simms, word is bond. I can't do you like that. I mean, damn...whew. Are you serious?"

I walk up on him, take his right hand and shove it between my legs. "Feel that heat?"

He pulls in his bottom lip, noddin' his head. "Yeah."

"Then you should know I'm not playin'." I grab the front of his jeans and grab his dick. It's already hard... brick hard. "Oooh, looks like somebody's ready to fuck."

"Damn, M-Miss Simms. Yo, this ain't right."

"No, lil'niggah. What's not right is you tryna fuck a lil' sixteen-year-old girl's pussy to shreds." I stare him in his crooked eyes, but quickly shift my gaze. Lookin' in them starts to make me dizzy.

Oooh, I'ma have to fuck this niggah with my eyes closed, or let him hit it from the back. Ain't no way I can look him in his crooked eyes tryna get my nut off.

"This is what I want from you, Bunz with a zee." His dick has stretched down the right side of his leg. "I want you to fuck me with this big dick."

His leg shakes. "Damn."

"No. Not 'damn.' Yes."

"Mmm, shit. Yes..."

"You like that, lil' niggah?"

"Hellz yeah. But, damn. Yo, I can't."

"Oh, yes you can. And you will. What, you scared? You ain't ready to handle no real pussy, are you?"

I flick my tongue over his lips, take his hands and place them up on my titties. I tell him to squeeze 'em, pinch 'em. I unzip his jeans, then slide my hand in, strokin' his thick dick over his boxers. "You tried to fuck the wrong lil' ho, Bunz with a zee. And now," I squeeze his dick, "you gotta pay, niggah. Big Booty gonna stretch her pussy all over this dick, then fuck the shit outta you."

He moans. "Damn. Shit. Real shit, I ain't know."

I place a finger to his lips. "Sssh...I know you didn't, lil'niggah. That's why I'ma fuck you real good instead of havin' you fucked up. You wanna feel ya dick in my pussy?"

I speed stroke his Mandingaling. "Hellz yeah. Oh, shit. Mmm-mph..." I remove my hand from outta his jeans, then grab him by the belt and pull him down the hall toward my bedroom. As soon as we're in my room, I shut the door, walk over to my stereo and slip in my Big Booty "Fuck Me Down" mix CD, then turn to face him. I'm gonna fuck his young ass to one of the instrumental CDs I had Slick hook me up with. I snatch open my flyaway, then let it slide off my shoulders.

Wiz Khalifa's "On My Level" starts playin' low.

His eyes buck. "Oh, shit..."

"You like what you see?" I cup my titties, lift 'em up to my lips, then flick my tongue over 'em. He starts grabbin' at his hard dick. Tells me he digs what he sees. Of course the niggah does. They all do.

"I hope you ate ya Wheaties, lil' niggah, 'cause it's gonna be a long mornin' for your black ass. Take off everything except them drawers."

It doesn't take long for his horny ass to kick off his sneakers, strip off his Polo shirt and unbuckle his belt. The big double-G's on his buckle hit the floor with a *thump* when he drops his jeans. I watch as he steps his feet outta 'em, standin' in the middle of my bedroom in a pair of white Ralph Lauren boxer briefs; the head of his long black dick hangin' outta the edge of 'em. I lick my lips, eyein' the sticky drop of precum leakin' from his piss slit.

My cunt flutters.

I tell him to sit on the bed as soon as Dr. Dre's "Kush" comes through the speakers. I bounce and shake my ass, then catwalk it over to his cross-eyed ass. "I'ma 'bout to uncross ya eyes, niggah. Give it to you real good." I get up on him, quickly spin around, then bend over and toss my ass all up in his face, grabbin' my ankles. My ass shakes and bounces to the beat. I pop each cheek one at a time, then reach back and pull 'em open.

"Lick my pussy, niggah."

He does what he's told, slidin' his tongue into the back of my pussy, gently at first. then he slides it in again, faster, in and out. I moan, bouncin' my ass and windin' my pussy all over his lips, nose, and chin while grabbin' at his tongue. Oooh yes...the pleasure of his licks, his tongue, vibrates through me. I moan. He moans. He is lovin' the taste of my pussy. And I am lovin' him tastin' it. I reach back and grab his dick, then strokin' it over his boxers. He grunts. His dick is so hard it can cut through diamonds. I run my fingertips over the head of his dick, smearin' his sweet 'n sticky, then slip my fingers into my mouth. Mmmm, yummy!

Cockeye groans. I tell him to slap my ass. He does. Tell him to slap it again. He does. I wind my hips. Let the niggah know, Big Booty's ready for his tongue in my other hole, the sweet chocolate hole that melts in a niggah's mouth and all over his dick. He licks and laps around it, gettin' it wet 'n ready. I grin when he tells me my ass tastes like candy. I slide my right hand between my legs and give my pussy a three-finger fuck while usin' my left hand to stroke my clit. I don't tell him I'm gettin' ready to shoot him some candy-rain 'til my pussy skeets in his face.

I turn around and stare at him. Pussy cream glazes his nose, his lips, his chin. I lean forward and lick it all up, peel outta my sticky thong, then push him back on the bed and sit on his lap. I take my naked pussy and rub it up and down his long dingdong through his boxers. Wiggle my ass back and forth, then reach back and part my asscheeks, slidin' his Mandingaling between them. My pussy's so wet. It soaks the front of his boxers.

Chris Brown's "Wet the Bed" starts playin' and I grind my pussy slow 'n nasty along his hard dick.

He grabs my titties and starts squeezin' 'em. "Aaah, shit…damn, ma…mmm…why you teasin' me?"

I lift up, turn to face him, then drop down on my knees and tug at his wet boxers coated with my pussy juice and stained with his precum. He lifts his hips and I yank them down, takin' him deep into my mouth. Each time I let his Mandingaling hit the back of my wet throat, he groans. I gulp him down good. Suck his dick until he's singin' out, "Ohfuckohfuckohfuck…shitshitshitshit…I'm gettin' ready to nut…uh, uh, uh, uh…"

I moan. "Oooh yes, lil'niggah. Give momma that sweet, creamy dingaling juice."

"Uh, uh, uh…"

I quickly place my mouth back over the head of his dick

and fiercely suck him until I am garglin' back his hot nut. When I'm done, I lick my lips. He's lookin' at me dazed.

By the time I'm finished with this niggah I'ma have him pussy-whipped, ass-whipped and throat-whipped. I snap my fingers in his face. "Niggah, you ain't even get this pussy yet and you already outta it. You better get ready to reup 'cause this party's just gettin' started. And you ain't leavin' up outta here until you do me right goddammit!"

It only takes five minutes or so before his dingaling is stretched out 'n bouncin' for action. I tell his ass to lie back on the bed, then roll a condom down on his dick. I straddle him, then lean forward and softly suck on his nipples. He closes his eyes. And I'm glad 'cause his cockeyed ass makes me dizzy lookin' in 'em. I kiss him as I reach back and guide his horse cock to the back of my pussy. I work it between my wet cunt lips until the head finds my wet hole. I sit down on it, then slowly work his dingaling into me. Mmmmm...he feels soooo good. Once I have it all in me, I start gallopin' up and down on it, real fast 'n nasty, slurpin' him in, buryin' him deep. Titties bouncin', ass clappin', I Kentucky Derby his ass down into the mattress. Giddy-up on his dingdong 'til I got the niggah's eyes rollin' back in his head. "Oooh, this big-ass dick...tryna fuck my goddamn daughter...not on my watch, niggah...ooh, yes...you fuckin' her momma's pussy now, niggah-bitch...this is how grown women ride a dick..."

"Aaaah, shiiit, yo...pussy's so wet..."

"Uh-huh...you like this juicy pussy don't you lil' niggah?"

He grunts and groans. "Yesss...oooh, shit..."

I pound my pussy down on his dingdong. "Cock-eyed bastard, you still wanna fuck Day'Asia?" I reach under me and squeeze his balls, sloshin' my pussy juice all over his cock. "Big ass dick...uhh...you like stretchin' out lil' sixteen-year-old pussy, niggah?"

"Aah...uh, uh, uh...ohfuckohfuckohfuck...hellz no... fuck..."

"You see Day'Asia, niggah...you better run...mmm... ya black... oooh...ass...aaah...the...mmm...other way." I lift up on his dick, ride the tip of his dingaling fast 'n real nasty, swirlin' my wet pussy all around it. "Ooh... you ever...try to put...mmm...this big dick...up...mmm... in her...aah...again...I'ma have...oh, yes...ya goddamn... uh...meat...sliced off...down to the gristle...mmm... now do me right goddammit, so I can toss you the fuck out!"

Twenty-Eight

Seven o'clock Saturday morning, I am up, showered, dressed and ready to get Day'Asia's cocksuckin' ass down to the clinic before all them damn niggahs pile up in there. "Day'Asia, get up, boo, so we can get down to the clinic," I say all nice 'n sweet. Her head is under the covers. She doesn't budge.

"C'mon, Asia, get ya ass. You know it's a mess down there on the weekends. And I'm not in the mood to have to curse one of those ghetto bitches out this morning. So, let's get a move on it." She still ain't movin'. "Day'Asia!" I yell, smackin' her upside the head and yankin' the covers off her. "Don't lay there like you don't hear me. Wake ya ass up!"

She groans, poppin' her head up. "What?"

"Girl, don't *what* me. I said get up."

"Why? It's Saturday. I'm tired."

"Wrong answer. You wouldn't be tired if you didn't have ya ass up on Skype all goddamn night. Now get up and let's hit this clinic since your ass likes to fuck. So get up so we can go handle your situation."

She snaps her neck in my direction. Stares at me and frowns. "I'm not pregnant."

"Well, I'm glad you don't think so. That saves you from gettin' a beatdown." I toss the EPT test at her. "Now get up and piss on the stick."

She sits up in bed, foldin' her arms. "Ohmygod, Ma, I don't need that. I *told* you, I'm not pregnant."

I walk over and shut her door. I don't need Elijah's nosey-ass creepin' around tryna get his eavesdrop since he's the only one up in the damn house. I stand in the middle of her nasty-ass bedroom with my hand up on my hip. "And I *told* you, you better hope you're not. 'Cause if you are, boo-boo, I'm goin' to jail and you're goin' up outta here on a stretcher 'cause I will beat it out of you."

She sucks her teeth. "Dang, Ma, you always talkin' crazy. You never trust me."

"Oh, see. Now I understand why you like to test me. You didn't read the memo, did you, sugah? I talk crazy because I *am* crazy. So Day'Asia, please don't try me this mornin'. Get your ass up."

"Ma, I'm not havin' sex like that."

I take a deep breath. "Listen, bit..." I stop myself from callin' her a bitch. I'm tryna keep it light this mornin', but this lil' heifer is really 'bout to take me there. "Day'Asia, I'm not gonna do a lot of back and forth with you. I don't know how much sex you're havin'. But I know your sneaky ass just had some long-dick niggah up in here the other night tryna get ya back blown out, so don't give me this bullshit about you ain't fuckin' like that. 'Cause I done heard you and Candy's whore-asses are real live campfires, lettin' niggahs roast their dingalings all up in you, so all that shit you talkin' about never trustin' you means nothin' to me."

She huffs. "I'm not even a big ho like that."

"Well, if you kept your legs shut, your ass wouldn't be any kinda ho. But since you spreadin' them high and wide, lettin' any ole type of niggah slam his cock up in you, then we need to get your ass down to the clinic. I can't trust you. Ho or not, I won't stand for you fuckin' any niggahs in here. You wanna fuck. You fuck out in the woods, or go to his place. And you better have ya ass back here before curfew."

"Ma, for real. I'm not havin' sex like that. I'm not a ho."

I sit on the edge of her bed. "Let me tell you somethin', Asia. If you're not fuckin' like that, then good for you. But, you're sure on your way to becomin' a ho whether you wanna be one or not. I can't stop you from bein' one, either. It's your body, do with it what you want. If you wanna fuck the whole damn projects, do you. But I'ma tell you this. You won't be bringin' no motherfuckin' babies up in here. And if your hot ass gets AIDS you not stayin' up in here, either. You like dick, don't you?"

"Ohmygod, Ma. I can't believe you're sayin' all this stuff."

"Girl, don't sit here and try 'n act all shy and shit. I know you're a hot-ass. I gave birth to you, boo. So I know you keepin' them drawers creamy. But know this, we're the only two with pussies up in this house and I need to make sure yours ain't gettin' more dick than mine. And how the hell you gonna be fuckin' and not rinse your pussy out, huh? Your pussy stinks, Day'Asia. You're sixteen damn years old. Your pussy should not be smellin' like a goddamn fish market. Now get yo' ass up so you can go get ya insides checked. Is ya pussy leakin'?"

She gives me a confused look.

"Do you have a discharge?" She shakes her head no. I tell her to take them drawers off and let me see. Now the ho looks at me like I'm crazy. And I feel like punchin' her in her throat. I get to cursin' her out 'til she peels them drawers off. I'm sick! Her drawers are all stained up. "What the fuck?! I have a whole goddamn box of pantyliners in my bathroom closet; why the fuck ain't you usin' them like I told you to?"

She shrugs. Tells me she keeps forgettin'. And I slap her damn face. "Get yo' black ass up and get in that shower and scour out ya goddamn stankin'-ass pussy for I beat the rot outta you. You think I want some-motherfuckin'-body talkin' shit about ya goddamn pussy stinkin', huh? Do you know how embarrasin' that shit is? I feel like stompin' the funk outta you. And how many niggahs you done let run up in you? And don't lie."

She shifts her eyes. She mumbles, "Like five."

I blink. "See, you already lyin'. Now let's try it again. How many?"

"Like six."

"What do you mean, 'like six?' First it was five, now it's six. Does that mean you're not really sure if it was five or six or not?"

"No, it was six. Me and Bunz ain't get a chance to do anything 'cause you kicked the door in on us."

I frown. "So then his ass woulda been fuck partner number seven, right? And what kinda niggah calls himself 'Buns'?'"

"It's Bunz with a Zee."

His long dick flashes in my head. I press my legs shut. "What-ever. So how many niggahs' dicks you done sucked?"

"Ohmygod, Ma. Why you askin' me all this?"

"See, you already done fucked up. I'm tryna have a civilized conversation with you, Asia, but you about to have me turn the ghetto switch on real quick. Don't 'ohmygod, Ma' me. Answer the question, Day'Asia. How many niggahs you done sucked? I'm not gonna go off on you. So tell me."

She shrugs.

"Bitch, what the fuck you shruggin' for? You wanna do grown things, then be real with your shit. Now how many damn cocks you done shoved down in your goddamn throat? And don't lie or I'ma fuck you up this mornin' 'cause you know I'm still hot about you havin' that cross-eyed niggah up in my goddamn house with his big-ass dick swingin'. Some motherfuckin' Buns, Bunz, or whatever the fuck he goes by. So don't have me set it off on your ass. Is that what you want, Day'Asia? You want me to stomp a hole in your ass this mornin' 'cause you know I will."

She shakes her head. "No."

I stare at her. "Then how many dicks have you sucked?"

She looks up at the ceilin'. I can't believe this nasty-ass heifer is actually lookin' up as if she's tryna count the string of dicks in her head. "Ten."

Well, I done heard it all now. I have a goddamn mini-super head livin' under my roof. "Ten? Oh, so you a regular ole lil' cum-guzzler, huh? You swallow, too?"

"Ewww! Ohmygod, Ma…no! That's nasty. I spit."

I-I-I'm shocked! How dare she? Oooh, I feel like slappin' her goddamn face off. One: She's suckin' dick and wastin' good nut; two: she's sixteen and done already sucked off ten different niggahs and done let six niggahs fuck her; and three: she's suckin' and fuckin' and don't have a goddamn thing to show for it. This lil' bitch gonna end up bein' another damn Dickalina if I don't school her ass, real fast.

I take a deep breath 'cause I done promised her I ain't gonna go off. "Day'Asia, let me get this right. You done let six niggahs pound your pussy out already, right?"

She nods.

"And you done sucked at least ten different niggahs off, right?"

She nods, again.

"These niggahs you sucked, were they the same niggahs fuckin' you or different ones?"

"Different ones," she whispers.

"What? Speak up."

"Different ones."

I narrow my eyes. "So let me get this right. My sixteen-year-old daughter done had some kind of sex with at least seventeen different niggahs is that what you're tellin' me?"

"Yeah."

"Don't 'yeah' me, ho."

"Yes."

"Mmmmph. You takin' it in the ass, too?"

"Ohmygod, Ma! Noooooo! That's goin' too far."

"So, why are you out here doin' all this fuckin'?"

She shrugs, again.

I reach over and slap the shit out of her. "Don't fuckin' sit here and act like you don't know why you're doin' all this fuckin'. You know exactly why ya nasty ass is fuckin'." She grabs the side of her face. Balls her fists up. "Bitch, I wish you would. You better unclench those goddamn fists right now or I'ma take that as a sign that you wanna take it to the streets. And you know I love a good fight, so act like you wanna leap."

She unclenches her hands. "I only wanted to know what it felt like," she says, tryna hold back tears.

"And it felt good to you, didn't it? That dick made your pussy hum, huh?"

She squirms. Tells me she got tired of hearin' all the

lil' fast-ass girls she hangs out with talkin' about how good dick was so she wanted to see for herself. "Mmmmph, so you a follower, huh? If them dumb bitches tell you they got HIV or AIDS, you gonna wanna see how that is too, I guess."

"I'm not stupid, Ma. I don't go out and do everything my friends do."

I lean up in her face. "Lil' girl, you *are* stupid. You stupid for fuckin' and suckin' a buncha goddamn niggahs in the first damn place. There's no damn reason for you to be sluttin' it up the way you are. You're a pretty girl, Day'Asia. When I was your age, I had to ho it up to keep a damn roof over my head. I sucked and fucked a niggah because he had somethin' I needed or wanted. And trust me. It had nothin' to do with his goddamn dick. I've sucked and fucked a buncha niggahs to make sure you and your brothers never had to go without. Have you ever not gotten what you've wanted?"

She shakes her head. "No."

"Exactly. So there's no goddamn reason your dumb ass is out here ho-in' it up for no damn reason." I shake my head. "I feel like bustin' you in your motherfuckin' face."

When I caught her ass in that stairwell down on her knees she told me that was her first time doin' it. But I saw the way she bobbed her head back and forth over that motherfucka's cock. She was suckin' his dick like she had a degree in cock suckin'. And now her ass is fuckin' like a pornstar. Mmmph.

"Get your ass up. You're gettin' the Depo shot. You can get AIDS. And you can get herpes, and any other STD out there if you want. But the one thing you won't do is get pregnant; not on my watch, boo. When you turn eighteen you can have all the babies you want. But until then, every three months you and I got a date down at the clinic to get that damn shot. And you better hope I don't decide to shove an IUD up in your nasty ass, too. Now get up."

She sucks her teeth, gettin' out of bed. She snatches the EPT box up, stomping toward the door. I follow behind her. Tell her to use the bathroom in my bedroom. Tell her that she is to keep the door open while I watch her piss. She doesn't like that. But I don't give a fuck. "You can stomp all you want. But you better hope that test comes back negative, or you will be stomped down."

Twenty-Nine

I eye Chunky Monkey—well, his name is really Christian, Chris for short—up in the deejay's booth. Oooh, his ass is too fine for his own damn good. Light-skinned with fine silky hair that he always wears in a ponytail. Nice smooth skin, perfectly straight, white teeth. And he has beautiful green eyes. Oooh, and you know he done made himself a buncha pretty babies, too. Mmmph. Yes, Lawd! His nasty ass has about fifteen—no, excuse me, sixteen, damn kids by three different hoes. And two of 'em are hot ghetto trash. But you know I ain't one for slingin' shit up on anyone, so I'm not gonna say no more about them hoes; other than they love them some six feet tall, lil' dick Chris. Mmmph, and I know for a fact that—him havin' a lil' itty-bitty, short dinga-ling—is true since I jerked it off up in the deejay booth a few years ago. That fine niggah is all balls, and no damn dingdong. Oh, it's tragic! But he's so fuckin' sexy to look at. So I talked real dirty in his ear and let him finger-fuck me in my ass while I jacked him off with a smile.

Anyway…the niggahs in the streets call his sexy-ass

Chunky Monkey, and not 'cause he's all fat and nasty with it. Shit, the niggah's body is all that. But the reason they call him Chunky Monkey is 'cause anytime you see him he's eatin' a pint of Ben & Jerry's Chunky Monkey ice cream. Or he's somewhere smearin' it on some pussy and lickin' it off 'cause the niggah loves eatin' pussy. And I know that to be true, too, since I let him chunky my monkey with his long tongue twice. And oooh, he did Big Booty right, goddammit!

But that's beside the point. Saturday night is his night to spin the beats at The Crack House. And it's instrumental night. And his ass always serves it up right, okay. He catches my eye and grins, givin' me the thumbs up. And I roll my eyes, givin' him the finger, like I do Slick every time he's up in the booth. Chunky gets on my damn nerves with his pretty-faced self. He and Slick are always tryna set me off on the dance floor. Sexy-ass fuckers!

He laughs, then gets on the mic and says, "Aiight, Cass. I see you, baby. Lookin' good, ma-ma..."

Mmmph. Long Pocahontas braid swayin' past my ass. Chinese bangs sweepin' my forehead. Diamond hoops blingin' in my ears. Python Birkin bag in the crook of my arm. Six-inch black Louie heels on my feet. Sexy black dress with the back cut-out and thigh-high split on both sides, showin' off my thighs, smooth back and ass crack. I can give you a mouthful of nice titties, but it's my greatest *ass*et that does 'em all in. Ass 'n hips. Pow, Pow! Who shot ya? Big Booty, sugah boo! So you damn right I'm lookin' damn good. No, motherfuckin' damn good!

Shit, I hate to say it. But I really am that diva-bitch, sugah-boo. Even with my Section-8 and EBT card havin' self, I stay sponsored up. I'ma hood celebrity, sweetie. When I step through the door they roll out the red carpet. And everyone up in this bitch knows Big Booty likes to bring it, serve it, do it up right, goddammit!

"That's right, sexy ma-ma, I see you," Chunky says, grinnin' as if he can read my thoughts. "We *all* know how you do it down here at The Crack House, baby, so I'ma 'bout to turn it up real quick; just for you."

I wave him on as Rick Ross's "9 Piece" starts blastin' through the speakers. Fuck a damn nine-piece. Give me a nine-inch—*long* and *hard*, and I'm good. I strut over toward the bar, iggin' the few niggahs tryna get my attention. Ain't no need to be eyein' me 'cause I'm not doin' 'em unless they buyin' drinks, or they one of my sponsors. Otherwise, I ain't got nothin' for none of 'em. Not tonight.

But I do stop and talk to a few of Darius' boys, with their fine, fuckable selves. It's three of 'em sittin' at one of the tables near the door, poppin' bottles of champagne. I can see it in their eyes that they're all blazed 'n bubbled up real nice from blunts and bubbly. "Damn, Miss Simms, you stay lookin' fly; for real for real," the one everyone calls Scooter says. He's tall—exactly how I like, maybe six-three, thin and chiseled. And you know what they say about them thin, boney-ass niggahs, don't you? Mmmph. They all dick, shugah. And so far I ain't been wrong yet.

I eye him. "Scooter, boo. I'ma always keep my sexy on high, baby. I'm too damn fly not to."

I see the lust in his eyes. "I heard that. And you doin' it, ma-ma."

Beyoncé's "Ego" starts playin' and before I know it, I'm swayin' side to side to the tempo, then droppin' down low and poppin' it back up. Shit, I have a lot to celebrate. Day'Asia's ass ain't pregnant. And hopefully she ain't got AIDS. But, her pussy's all crusty 'cause she gotta bad yeast infection. Mmmph. Whatever. Ain't my pussy. I told her stank-ass to take them pills and keep her goddamn legs shut.

I twirl it a taste, then two-step and finger pop it. All three of these niggahs got they eyes locked on my body. Scooter slowly licks his lips, makin' my pussy clench. He knows he's some kinda sexy with his rugged, tatted-up self.

Oooh, I gotta hurry up and get away from this niggah before I forget I'ma lady and give his ass a lap dance up in this bitch.

"Look, let me get movin' along. I'm tryna keep it classy tonight. And I ain't about to have none of you fine-ass niggahs sidetrack me and have me out here turnin' up the ho-meter."

They laugh. Tell me I'm shot out. But that doesn't

stop any of them horny niggahs from eye-fuckin' me. I know, and they know, I could fuck every last one of 'em—*down*, if I wanted. I turn to leave and can feel their eyes bouncin' up 'n down like lil' ping pong balls tryna keep up with the shake in my ass.

Chunky, I mean Chris, plays Lil' Wayne's "6 Foot 7 Foot" as I hoist my ass up on an empty barstool and bop to the beat. Big Mike comes over, smilin'. "Wassup, Cass? What can I get you tonight?" I ask him what tonight's specials are. He tells me Wet Drawz and Dirty Drawz.

I frown at the thought of tossin' back a pair of dirty draws. And I know there's a few hoes up in here wearin' a pair of cum-crusty, pussy-juiced drawers right now tryna be cute; just like Day'Asia's ass. Stink bitches!

"What's in those Wet Drawz?"

"Absolut Peach Vodka, Peach Schnapps, and a splash of grenadine syrup, shaken then poured over ice."

I smack my lips. "Ooh, that sounds tasty. Let me try one of them Wet Drawz, then. And hopefully by the end of the night, my drawers will be wet, too."

He laughs, shakin' his head. "Yo, Cass, you somethin' else, ma-ma."

"I know I am. Now hurry up and bring me my drink so I can wet my throat."

"I got you," he says before walkin' off to handle thangs behind the bar.

I decide to hit the bathroom real quick to make sure all things are in place. Face, hair, waist and ass. I sashay my hips into the four-stall bathroom. Give myself a once-over, then blow myself a kiss. Oooh, I'm so sizzlin' hot. I can't stand the heat! I fuss with my bangs, then apply a coat of gloss up on my cherry-painted lips. I like to keep my lips sweet 'n juicy at all times.

I step outta the bathroom and start headin' back toward the bar when someone grabs me by the arm. "Aye, yo. What's good wit' you? You lookin' damn sexy tonight."

I yank my arm back, and black, "Niggah, do I know you? Did I suck your dick? Did I fuck you? Hell no! So don't put ya goddamn hands on me."

He puts his hands up. "Aiight, aiight…my bad. I ain't mean no harm, ma."

"And you don't mean me no good either, lil' niggah."

"Yo, I'm not tryna disrupt ya night. I only wanted to say wassup to you."

"Then say 'wassup', but don't touch me 'cause you were about to have me turn the gas up in here, niggah, comin' at me like that. I was about to take a torch to ya ass."

"Oh, nah, nah…it ain't that serious. I don't want no problems, ma. I spotted you when you walked through the door and wanted to holla at you, that's all. Let me buy you a drink."

I eye him up and down, tiltin' my head. Pink Polo shirt, baggy jeans, crisp white Louie V sneaks. Dreds done up right. Oooh, and the niggah got the nerve to be lookin' real tasty in his pink.

I decide to lower the gas a taste, since I wanna know more about this niggah. "AJ, right?"

He grins. "Oh, you remembered. That's wassup."

"Niggah, puhleeze, don't go bustin' a nut over it."

He laughs. "Nah, never that."

I twist my lips up. "Uh-huh, that's what your mouth says, lil' boo."

"And that's what it is. And for the record, ma, e'ery-thing on me ain't little."

"Prove it. I don't usually fuck short niggahs but tonight might be ya lucky night."

He grins. "And it'll be a night you'll never forget, ma. I fuck hard, believe that."

"And you probably nut quick, too."

He laughs "Nah, but I nut a lot."

Oooh, this lil' niggah real cocky with it. I step into him, then lean in and brush my glossy lips against his ear. "Niggah, I. Will. Fuck. The. Shit. Outta. You." I flick my tongue, then whisper my number into his ear. "I'm gonna give you a chance to prove ya'self. Make sure you have ya dollars up, niggah."

He grins. "Yeah, aiight. I got you."

I get ready to open my mouth to tell him to pull his dick out and let me see it since he wanna talk so much shit. But I see Jasper and Stax headin' this way and decide to let it go.

Whew, Stax is dipped and rolled in sexiness. Yes, Lawd, Big Booty wanna do him right. But I know the niggah has eyes for Miss Pasha on the low, so I'm not even gonna waste my time fantasizin' 'bout havin' his dingaling stuffed in my holes.

Stax smiles at me. *Oooh, this fine niggah better be glad I ain't real messy 'cause I'd lean in and tell his ass if he doesn't give me some of that dingdong that I'ma tell Jasper how he stays eye-fuckin' his wife.*

"What's good, Cass?" he says to me, steppin' up and givin' me a hug. "I see you keepin' it sexy as always."

"I sure am," I coo, runnin' my hand over his rock-hard chest, although that's not really where I want my hand to be. Shit, Big Booty wants to run her hand between his legs and grab his dingdong and cup them balls. But, I ain't tryna play myself like some thirsty slut. Now I might toss back a few gin 'n juices every now and again, but slut-juice ain't ever on the drink list.

I lick my lips. "And you'd know how good I was if you stopped playin' games, Stax, and get with the program."

He laughs, releasin' me from his hug. "Yo, Cass, real shit, baby. You a real trip."

I peep Jasper and the AJ niggah choppin' it up, givin' each other dap. Then catch Jasper whisper some shit into his ear. Bells and lights start goin' off in my head. *Mmm-hmm, Jasper's no-good ass got this niggah pushin' weight, I bet.*

Jasper eyes me. "Aye, yo, wassup, Cass?"

I look him up and down, then sweep my bangs across my forehead. "You tell me. Where's Pasha?" He tells me she's home where she's supposed to be. I blink, twistin' my lips up. "Mmmph. Poor thing. Well, look. It's been cute, but I need to bounce it back on over to the bar 'cause all this chit-chat is startin' to cut into my drink time. Y'all niggahs do what you do." I shoot a look over at Sneaky Ass. "And I still want that drink, niggah."

He laughs. "I got you. And I still want what we talked about."

"Niggah, puhleeze," I say over my shoulder, catchin' all three of them with their eyes locked on my ass. "You wish."

Chunky starts playin' "Ether" by Nas and I'm too through. *Now this niggah knows I'm 'posed to have my tank full before he starts doin' me.* I put a hand up on my hip, then bounce and sway to the beat, just a taste 'cause my tank's on E and I'm still tryna keep it hood classy. But, damn him! I love me some instrumental night down at The Crack House. Yes, Lawd! They do me right!

I toot my booty back up on the barstool, finger poppin' it as Big Mike slides me my drink. I take a few sips of it, then start twirlin' my pussy up on the stool. "Aaah, yes, goddammit! This that grown 'n sexy shit."

I take a few more sips, then toss it all back. Shit, I'm tryna get right, quick. I order another. After my third drink, my tank still ain't full, but them Drawz done worked their way through me and got me ready turn it up a notch. I grab my glass from the bar and hop off the barstool when the instrumental to Nas' "Oochi Wally" starts playin'. "Oooh, yes, do me right, Chunky, goddamn you!"

I throw my right hand up in the air and start oochie-coochie-wallyin' it up, bendin' at the knees, pumpin' 'n humpin' my hips to the beat, makin' believe I'm naked, tossin' my pussy at the niggahs watchin' me. Chunky plays Juvenile's "Back That Azz Up" and starts smilin' when he catches my eye. I give him the finger again, doin' what the song says do: back all this ass up!

By the time the instrumental to Tupac's "I Ain't Mad At Ya" starts playin', I'm on my fifth drink and ready to do the ballroom hoochie-coohie up in this bitch. I grab my skirt and start snappin' it up and down, to the left, then to the right, like I'm a bullfighter, swayin' to the beat, showin' the niggahs gawkin' my toned legs and givin' 'em a glimpse of the red lace thong I have my pussy wrapped in. "Chunky, damn you," I yell, windin' my hips. "Do me right, goddammit..."

I toss both hands up and swoop 'em around in the air. Then Chunky flips the switch and starts playin' "Tonight" by Fabolous and I start dippin' down real low. "Aaaah, shiiit, goddammit! Do me right, do me right!" I'm steppin' side to side, then swayin' to the beat, titties bouncin', ass snap, crackle 'n poppin'. Oooh, you can't tell me shit. "Goddamn you, Chunky Monkey!"

Oooh, he's tryna do me right. When he starts playin' the Ciroc Boyz Anthem, I am sweatin' like a race horse. Three songs later, I'm swirlin' my ass back up on the barstool, sippin' on my seventh drink. My tank is full. I'm in high-gear. And I'm feelin' right, goddammit! The place is packed somethin' fierce, drippin' with dick, dollars and potential new sponsors. And I am lovin' every minute of it.

I cross my legs and strike a "I'm-the-sexiest-bitch-up-in-this-piece" pose while runnin' my tongue over my straw, wishin' it was a hard dick. I take a slow sip of my drink, bobbin' my head to Waka Flocka's "No Hands." I sit my drink up on the bar and start bouncin' in my seat, pumpin' my hands in the air.

"Yo, baby," this deep, dark dreamy, panty-wettin' voice says in my ear, causin' me to jump.

"What the fuck?! Is you..." My voice fades, lookin' into a delicious slice of heaven, grinnin' at me. Sweet damn ding-a-ling-a-ling! This niggah coulda been my next baby daddy if I didn't already tie and knot up my tubes. Oooh, he's fine dark chocolate. And Big Booty love her some dark chocolate niggahs with them heavy dingdongs. Yes, Lawdy! And he has that fresh I-just-got-outta-jail-and-wanna-fuck look which makes my pussy lips pucker a bit. But there's somethin' in this niggah's eyes that makes him look extra crazy. Like he's the kinda niggah that'll break a ho's jaw and punch her in the titties, then kick her pussy in right out in the streets and not give a fuck.

"Yeah, I am."

I scrunch my face up. "You are *what?*"

"Tryna fuck you." He stares me down when he says this. "Deep in that fat ass of yours." The niggah doesn't blink.

"And who the fuck is you?"

"Legend," he says in his deep voice. He licks his lips, glancin' down at my thigh while runnin' his big hand down my back as Cassidy's "Aim for Your Head" starts playin'. I bite down on my bottom lip. This niggah smells like trouble, looks like trouble. And I hope I don't gotta take a bottle to his goddamn head tonight. "But niggahs out in the streets call me L."

"Well, I don't care what they call you out in the streets, niggah-boo, you don't know me like that. So get ya goddamn hands off my back." I tell him this, but I ain't crankin' up the noise. I keep it real calm 'n steady 'cause I done told y'all I'm tryna keep it classy tonight. But, I can already tell I'ma have to help get this niggah's mind right in a minute.

He removes his hands. "Yeah..." He pauses when Big Mike sits another drink in front of me. "Hey, Playboy, put whatever this fine, sexy thang's drinkin' on my tab. She drinks on me tonight, all night." He tosses a crisp hundred-dollar bill up on the bar.

Big Mike gives him a head nod, then eyes me and winks. Dark Chocolate waits until he walks off to continue tryna crank it up. "Now back to you, sexy thang. You real feisty; just how I like 'em. I've been watchin' you on the dance floor all night bouncin' that phat, juicy ass and them melon titties, teasin' niggahs. You got some real live moves, baby. And it looks like you know how'ta handle a dick, too."

I lift my drink off the bar, take a sip, then eye him. "Niggah, I do. But you ain't gonna know about it. So all that 'she drinks on me tonight' shit ain't gonna earn you no pussy."

He laughs. "I can tell you got some good-ass pussy."

"Yeah, niggah, I do. But you won't know about that either."

"Oh, yeah? Is that so? And what if I told you I take what I want."

I twist in my seat. For some reason, I believe this niggah means what he says. I can see it in his eyes. He kinda reminds me of Knutz with that glazed, empty "I'ma-walkin'-cuckoo-clock" look in his eyes. *Oh, yeah. This niggah is good 'n goddamn crazy, for real!* And I don't see a goddamn thing funny about the shit he's talkin'.

"I wanna take you outside and fuck you in the backseat of my whip and pour Hennessy down ya back and let that shit roll down into the crack of ya ass, then slurp it up. You got my dick rocked the fuck up and I wanna feel your tongue on it, then that juicy ass sittin' down on it. My dick needs you, baby. Let me take you outside and fuck the shit outta ya freak ass."

I blink, then gas it up on his ass straight to ghetto. "Niggah-bitch! I don't know who the fuck you think I am, but I ain't some hoodrat, hooker-bitch you can talk shit to! Who the fuck is you, threatenin' to take my pussy? Niggah-bitch, puhleeze. Do you know who the fuck I am, bitch?! Obviously not. I will have you stomped up in this bitch tonight, pussy-ass coon!"

He grins, lickin' his lips again. And that only pisses me off.

I toss my drink in his face and the next thing I know,

Big Mike and three security goons pop outta nowhere and surround us. "Yo, e'erything aiight over here, Cass?" Big Mike asks, eyein' this nutty-ass niggah. "Yo, my man, is there a problem here?"

"Nah, we good," he says, reachin' over the bar and grabbin' some napkins to wipe his face and the front of his designer shirt. "Just a lil' misunderstandin' between me and this sexy thang."

"Niggah, puhleeze. Misunderstandin' my ass. You came outta ya face all wrong, bitch. Tryna play me for some low-budget hood ho. Niggah, you can't even lick my goddamn drawers without showin' me that cream, niggah. Tryna do me. Niggah, puhleeze. You ain't even let me get my throat wet real good before you start comin' at me."

I look over and see Scooter and his boys up and on ready to set it off. Scooter makes his way over to me. "Yo, Miss Simms…" He eyes Crazy Ass. "…we good over here?"

"No, we ain't good. I want this coon-bitch outta my goddamn face." Big Mike and his goon squad tell him to bounce, or get his shit and hit the door. He puts his hands up. Tells them he wants no problems. That he only wants to have a good time. He apologizes to me. Then the crazy niggah pulls in his bottom lip and winks at me as he steps back.

As he walks off, I yell out, "And bitch, I'ma still drink on ya fuckin' tab, all goddamn night!" I follow him with my eyes 'til he gets lost in the crowd, then tell Big Mike to fix me two more Wet Drawz. "And make it heavy on the Drawz and less wet"—meanin' more Absolut and less goddamn Schnapps—"'cause that niggah done worked my nerves."

Oooh, but his chocolate ass done got my drawers real juicy!

Thirty

"Yo, was you poppin' shit the other night, ma, or are you really 'bout handlin' a dick?"

I'm half asleep when I answer my cell so my brain isn't on alert, yet. I don't know whose number this is, or what niggah this voice belongs to. "I glance at the clock, frownin'. It's two in the goddamn mornin'. "Who the fuck is this?"

"It's AJ, yo."

I blink. "*AJ?* Niggah, how you get my number?"

He laughs. "You whispered that shit all sexy in my ear down at the club. Had my dick all hard'n shit da whole night."

Oh, yeah I did give this niggah my number last week. Shit. I ain't think he was gonna remember it. But I'm glad he did. And not because I wanna ride down on his ding-aling. I want info outta this niggah. So instead of cussin' his ass out for bein' dead wrong for callin' me this time of night, I bite my tongue and kick up the charm.

"Took you long enough to call, niggah. But why the fuck is you callin' me this time of night? You must be tryna get some pussy."

"Yo, you already know. You was talkin' some real good shit. I'm tryna hit that deep."

I roll my eyes, sittin' up in bed. I reach over and flick the lamp on. "You eat pussy?"

"Nah, ma…I ain't wit' that."

"Well, do you lick ass?" Now I already know if a niggah ain't eatin' pussy, he ain't lickin' no ass either. But I wanna hear what this coon gotta say. And if you ain't doin' both, you definitely ain't gonna be freaky enough for me.

"Nah. I don't get down wit' that either. But I'll fuck you in it." Mmmph. This corny-ass niggah ain't ready for a bitch like me. I ask him how big his dick is. He tells me he has nine thick, hard, inches.

"Niggah, if you ain't eatin' pussy or lickin' out no ass, ya dick game better be bananas."

"No doubt. I puts in that work, yo. So wassup. Can I get up in them hips and stroke up ya insides or what?"

"Niggah, you gotta stroke up that cash, first. You got that money up?"

"Yeah, no doubt. I gotta lil sumthin'. How much you tryna trick a niggah for?"

"Well, if you were eatin' pussy 'n ass I woulda gave you a discount sampler, but since you ain't puttin' out no tongue work, you gonna have'ta hit me with…mmmm…"

Louie V gotta sexy pink belt I want, then I saw a pair of aviators I also want and this cute lil' Keep It Twice monogram bracelet they got. I start calculatin' in my head: *Six-hundred-and fifty-five plus six-hundred-forty-*

five plus three-hundred-seventy. I tell him I want two grand, but I really only need seventeen hundred to get my trinkets. The extra three hundred is the tax for him not eatin' pussy or lickin' ass. But if what Jah said about this niggah is true, then I know he ain't gonna be able to hang 'cause his pockets light.

"Daaaaaaayum, that's kinda steep for some pussy. I can see if you was askin' for a few hunnid, but two gees? You buggin' wit' that."

I laugh. "Niggah, if you broke, say you broke. You ain't gotta front. But I ain't buggin' 'bout shit. Ain't no shame in my game, boo. If you can't afford me, then so be it."

"Yo, ain't nobody frontin'. And ain't nobody say I couldn't *afford* you. I'm sayin' how I know you even worth that kinda paper?"

"Niggah, you don't. But that ain't stop you from wantin' to fuck me. Now did it?"

"Nah, but still. I ain't that kinda dude to be trickin' up that kinda paper for no ass. Fuck that."

I keep laughin'. "Okay, if you say so. But I ain't givin' you none of this pussy, boo."

"Oh word? It's like that?" I can hear the disappointment in his voice. Niggah, boom! Like I give a fuck. "You suck dick, ma?"

"I sure do."

"How much you tryna run a niggah for some dome? I wanna feel ya lips 'round my dick."

I smirk, gettin' outta bed. I walk to my closet and pull

a blunt outta one of my hidin' spots. *Niggah, you 'bout to get more than these lips.* I pop my bare ass into the bathroom, then shut the door. "You like gettin' ya dick sucked?"

"Hell yeah, ma. What muhfucka you know don't like his top spun? I'm always lookin' for a good head doctor."

Uh-huh, niggah. I just bet you are.

I spark the blunt and take a pull, then blow smoke up into the air. "Is that so, lil niggah?" I sit on the edge of the oversized tub with the claw-feet, crossin' my legs. "Mmmph. You ain't ready for no real neck work, boo. And ya paper's light. So you tell me. How much *can* you afford to trick up for some of this wet throat?"

See. This niggah's real cocky with his shit, so I know he ain't diggin' bein' called out like that. But he's either extra cheap or extra broke. And, trust. A cocky coon like him ain't ever gonna admit to bein' broke. "I'll hit you wit' like a few hunnid, but that's all."

I laugh. "Niggah, you must want the Walmart special for a *few hunnid.*"

"The what?"

"You heard me. You tryna play me cheap, boo. That means you only get a tongue lap. No mouth, just tongue over the head, then down the sides of ya shaft, and maybe over ya balls a few times. And that's that. If you want lips 'n mouth, you gonna need to run a lil' deeper in them pockets. You wanna push ya dingaling down in my throat, then you need to bring it right. And if you wanna get that dingaling cream slurped outta ya piss slit, then you definitely better get ya money up and do me right. Do me right, niggah or don't get done; simple as that."

"Damn, yo. You got my shit hard as fuck. Ya mouth's real reckless, yo. But you a sexy bitch. And you nasty as fuck. I peeped that shit the night I first saw you all up on my niggah Buddha's ass."

"Uh-huh. I sure am. And I like nasty niggahs who know how'ta fuck. How you know Buddha anyway?"

"We cool from back in the day. And we did a few county runs together. But I ain't tryna talk about him."

I roll my eyes. "Well, what you wanna talk about?"

"You. Me. I wanna fuck, and I want my dick sucked."

"Then you need to pay, boo. Or get the fuck off my phone. I got bills to pay, niggah. And I got kids to feed. So if you wastin' my time, then you cuttin' into my money. Or in ya case, my goddamn sleep." I take two deep pulls, hold the weed smoke in, then push it outta my lungs. This niggah is startin' to bore me, but I wanna see his ass.

"Listen, ma. Real shit, you right. My paper ain't right like that. I gotta lotta fines 'n shit suckin' my pockets dry. But, I'm diggin' you. And I wanna get at you."

"You gotta lil dick, don't you? Keep it real, niggah."

"Hell naw, my shit ain't lil'. I gotta fat-ass dick, ma, and I know how'ta use it."

I laugh. "In other words, that's code for my dingaling is short 'n stumpy."

He laughs with me. "Yo, you funny as hell. Yo, c'mon. Let me get at you."

I finish smokin' my blunt down to the gristle, then toss it in the toilet and flush. "You got ya own spot?"

"Nah, I live wit' my peoples."

"Oh, yeah? Where at?" He tells me over in a new development off Martin Luther King Blvd. in downtown Newark. Not too far from Essex County College. "So, how we gonna do this then 'cause I got kids and you ain't comin' up in here?"

I wash my hands and start brushin' my teeth. He tells me we can roll over to his man's spot and chill there. That he has a room that he can use. This niggah is suckin' horse shit if he thinks I'ma be stretched out somewhere knowin' another niggah's up in there.

I frown, walkin' back into the bedroom, then crawlin' back in bed. "Niggah, boom. You must think I'm some kinda crazy. I don't know you like that. You won't have me somewhere bein' tag-teamed."

"Nah, ma. I wouldn't do you like that."

I laugh. "Niggah, I know you won't. 'Cause you ain't gettin' the opportunity to. So look"—I glance over at the clock—"it's almost three o'clock in the mornin' and I gotta be up at six to get my kids ready for school. So call me when you can afford a room at the Marriott or Sheraton, and you got some paper to spend."

"Yo, what you doin' tomorrow night?"

"I don't know. Why?"

"Meet me down at the club. I owe you some drinks."

I laugh again. "Drinks ain't gonna get you no pussy,

boo. But I tell you what. You pull ya dick out and let me see what you workin' with and if I like what I see, I might give you a sampler."

"Oh, word? And what's that?" I tell him I might straddle up on it and ride down on the head and milk his nut out. Now he laughs. "You shot da fuck out. But know this, if you ride the tip of my dick, you gonna wanna slide down on all of it. It's that good, ma."

"Mmmph. Whatever." We talka few minutes more, poppin' shit about his dick work, then make plans to meet down at The Crack House for drinks. "Niggah, I think you all mouth, but we gonna see. I'ma guzzle ya wallet up at the bar, so make sure you got ya money right to keep the drinks flowin'."

He laughs. "Aiight, ma. I got you. And hopefully you'll be swallowin' this dick by da end of da night."

Nine p.m., I'm lookin' right in my black, short knit, scoop neck dress. I slip my manicured feet into adobe-colored five-inch Stuart Weitzman platform, peep-toe pumps. It's my first time wearin' the three-hundred-and-eighty-five-dollar heels and I'm hopin' these bitches don't hurt my feet. I don't usually like wearin' heels under four-hundred dollars. But these were cute. *Do me right, goddammit!*

I spray a few squirts of Signorina between my titties, then along my wrists and crotch area, then grab my twelve-hundred-dollar Clara Kasavina clutch. These ghetto bitches around here ain't ready for Miss Kasavina's pieces. But I am. And I serve 'em well. I open it and toss in a small tube of anal lube, a mini-remote butt plug and some lip gloss, then snap it shut.

I give myself a once-over in the mirror, then hit the lights off and swing outta the room toward the livin' room. I stop dead in my tracks when I see Clitina's ass sittin' on the sofa in a leopard print catsuit and a pair of black hightop Converses. Her hair is dyed cotton candy pink and she has pink lipstick slathered up over her dingaling coolers.

I frown.

"Ummm, Clitina, what the hell is you doin' here?"

"Hi, Auntie Cass."

"Don't 'hi, Auntie Cass' me. I asked you why you here?"

She looks over at Day'Asia. "Ma, I was gonna ask you if Tina could spend the night."

I blink. "Ummm, noooooo, she may not. I'm 'bout to go out and I'm not gonna have her hot-pussy self up in here while I'm out. So c'mon, boo. Get ya shit. You comin' with me."

"Puhleeeeze, Ma, can she stay?"

"Please, Aunt Cass. I'm locked outta my house. I promise you won't have any problems outta me."

"Where's ya mother at?" She tells me she's out with Knutz. I roll my eyes. "And where's Candy?" She shrugs. Says she's not answerin' her cell. That she hasn't seen her all day. I huff, pullin' out my cell. I scroll through my numbers, then press Dickalina's. "Ho, where you at?"

"I'm out wit' my boo."

"Bitch, I ain't ask you who you with. I wanna know where you at so I can drop Clitina there."

"What? Oh, no. You ain't about to fuck my night up. Me and my man is havin' a nice romantic dinner down at Joe's Crab Shack. Why she ain't home?"

"Bitch, she ain't home 'cause she's here at my house and I'm gettin' ready to go out."

"Well, why can't she stay there?"

"Ho, I told you I'm gettin' ready to go out. What the hell I look like leavin' two hot pussy hookers up in here? There'll be in here tryna fuck all through my house. Oh, no, sugah boo. Day'Asia's hot ass is enough to have to keep up with. I'm not about to be stressin' over what the hell Clitina's doin' too while I'm out."

"Well, she ain't got no key. And me and Knutz aint' gonna be home 'til late." I tell her not to worry, then disconnect. I make Clitina get her shit, load her ass up in the car, then speed off in my truck toward the Garden State Parkway northbound toward Clifton.

When I get almost to our destination, I lower the radio, turn on the interior lights, then ask, "Clitina, you fuckin', boo?"

She looks at me. "Ewwww, Aunt Cass, nooo."

"Girl, don't ewwww me. Are you ridin' or suckin' down on the dingaling?" She says no. But I know the lil' ho's lyin' through her crooked-ass teeth. "Listen. You ain't gotta lie to me. If you ho-in' that's you. But I'ma keep it real with you, sugah-boo. You ain't movin' right. The niggahs you toppin' off and throwin' the pussy to ain't respectin' ya ho, boo. The word on the street is, you, Candy, and Day'Asia are faster than Amtrak. Y'all lettin' niggahs ride all through ya asses. Now you ain't gotta say if it's true or not. Just know, I know you a whore, boo. I can smell ya hot pussy a mile away, but that ain't my business. Day'Asia's stank pussy is. But I'ma say this, sugah. You need to cool ya jets and let the smoke settle out ya ass 'cause you sizzlin' boo. And it ain't cute. You understand me?"

She nods. "I do. But we ain't really havin' sex like that. I mean, we be chillin wit' dudes, but we ain't havin' sex wit' all of them." I ask her what they be doin'. She says they drink and smoke with 'em.

"Clitina, boo. I know you half-retarded, but you much smarter than Candy 'cause she's a full-blown retard. But there's hope for you, boo. All you gotta do is shut ya legs, keep the dingalings outta ya throat, and get ya goddamn mind right. Instead of bein' the bitch on fries, or askin' to take a ho's order, you can be the bitch givin' orders. But you gotta wanna do better, boo. Otherwise you ain't gonna be shit. You ain't gonna be nothin' but a ran down, broke-ass ho with dried up cum stains on ya pussy 'n face. Is that what you want for ya'self?" She shrugs. And I feel like smackin' the shit outta her. "Bitch, what the fuck you shruggin' for? You 'posed to know, boo. You 'posed to have a damn plan. Fuck for a purpose, not for a wet ass! Geesh. You young bitches got shit backwards."

I pull into the parkin' lot of the Crab Shack and feel like tellin' this dumb bitch to get the fuck outta my truck, but I don't. I keep it classy and walk her inside. I wait 'til I know she's found Dickalina, then bounce. I don't give a fuck about Dickalina screamin' out my name, cussin' and yellin' about fuckin' up her night and not havin' room on Knutz's bike to ride Clitina home. Not my motherfuckin' problem.

I slip back behind the wheel of my truck, then press the CALL button on the steerin' wheel. I wait for the voice to come through the speakers. "Wassup, ma?"

"I'm on my way to the club now."

"Aiight, bet. I'll be there."

"Good. And then we gonna go somewhere and fuck real good, boo. My asshole wants another round of that long dingaling."

He laughs. "I got you, ma."

"Niggah, you better."

Thirty-One

Thirty minutes later, I'm finally pullin' up into the parkin' lot of The Crack House. I freshen my lips with a coat of peach gloss, then step outta my truck. I'm hot like fire and about to shut the spot down. Can't tell me shit, sugah-boo.

I see Slick up in the DJ booth, spinnin' the beats. He winks at me when he sees me walkin' through the club. I toss a hand up at him. "Amen" by Meeek Mill is playin'. I lightly bounce my way over to the bar 'cause I ain't tryna sweat up my drawers just yet.

"Bad bitches in the buildin'…Preach, godddammit…" I finger pop it, hoistin' my hips up on a barstool. "Big Mike," I yell over the music, wavin' him over to me. He smiles at me.

"Wassup, Cass, baby?"

"Wet my throat, niggah. What's on the menu?" He tells me the drink specials are Blue Balls and I'll Take Ya Man. I ask him what's in the Blue Balls. He tells me Bombay Sapphire Gin, Blue Curacao and Grenadine. "Let me try that."

"Yo, her drinks on me," I hear over my shoulder. I

look the niggah up and down. I can't lie on the lil' niggah. He's lookin' real tasty in his baggy jeans and white Polo pullover. A thick 18kt white gold chain hangs from his neck. I glance at the diamond encrusted dog tags, then up at him. "I ain't think you were gonna show up."

"Niggah, I'm real with mine. I told you I was gonna drink ya wallet up."

He laughs. "Yo, I got us a booth. C'mon."

I toot my lips. "Well, all right now. Do me right, goddammit." He tells Big Mike to bring my drink over to the table, then leads the way. I finger pop, then drop it one time when Jadakiss's "Respect It" starts playin'. "Yesssss, goddammit! Oooh, they shittin' on this! Owwww!"

He waits for me to finish my booty pop, then steps back for me to slide in the booth. I let the niggah know I ain't interested in bein' blocked in. I tell him to slide in, let me sit on the end. He does. There's already two bottles of Veuve Cliquot already on the table. "Yo, you sexy as hell."

"I know I am, boo. Tell me somethin' I *don't* know."

He laughs as the cocktail ho—some big titty boo with a cute face and small waist—brings me my drink. He eyes her as walks off, then says, "Yo, why you ain't bagged up?"

I raise a brow. "Niggah, the only thing baggin' me up is Gucci, Louie, Prada, and my damn kids."

He pours himself a drink "I heard that. So, what was all that good shit you was talkin' last night?"

I lift my drink to my lips, eyein' him over the rim. "I already told you what it is,niggah. Pull ya dick out. If I like what I see *and* feel in my hand, then I might top you off. But that's it 'cause you ain't gettin' no pussy unless you comin' at me with that paper."

He laughs. "Yo, I ain't worried about that." He says this, but the niggah don't budge with unzippin' his pants and pullin' out the dingaling. So I take it as a red flag that the motherfucka is only talk. But I'ma keep it classy and keep the shit to myself.

He tosses back his drink, then pours himself another round. I toss mine back as well, then tell him to top my glass off with some of the bubbly. We bug out 'n bullshit and toss back four rounds of drinks, and now I'ma feelin' extra frisky. But not enough to wanna toss this niggah some free pussy. I run my hand up in his lap, and start feelin' for his dingaling.

He pours himself another drink, then leans back and spreads his legs. He tries to reach for my titties, but I slap his hand away. Tell the niggah that unless my pussy gets wet and starts poppin' while I'm playin' with his dingaling, then he ain't touchin' up on me unless he's payin' for it.

"Yo, fuck all that, baby," he says. "I wanna fuck."

I unbuckle his belt, unfasten and upzip his jeans, then snake my hand down in his pants and massage his dick over his boxers. He closes his eyes. So far I ain't impressed with what I'm feelin'. But I'm thinkin' maybe he's a grower so I keep workin' him in my soft hand. It finally starts to thicken and stretch. And now I wanna see it.

"Yo, I wanna fuck."

"Yeah, and you like this dick sucked, too. Don't you, boo?" I squeeze it. Run my fingertips over the head, smearin' the precum into his skin.

"Hell yeah. You gonna let me fuck you?"

I pull my hand outta his jeans, then place my fingers to his lips. "Lick my fingers, niggah." He frowns. Tells me he ain't into tastin' his own dingdong. I'm done. "Then you can zip that shit right on up. And while you're at it, why don't you go back and find the rest of ya dick." He gives me a confused look. "Ummm, apparently you done lost about three inches off ya dick somewhere."

He starts laughin'. "Yo, get da fuck outta here. What you mean, I done lost about three inches?"

I eye him as I lift my glass to my lips, then sip. I hate a niggah who lies on his goddamn dick. I mean, really. Niggah, *boom!* Don't give me no imagined shit, or tell me shit you fantasize about havin'. Give it to me real. If you gotta small dick, then say it, shit.

I set my glass down, then lean into him. "Listen. I hate to bust ya bubble, and I don't mean no harm, niggah-boo. But...this just in: ya dingaling ain't nine-inches, boo. So whatever instrument you used to measure ya shit was defective." I reach for it, again, and start rubbin' it. It's still extra hard and very thick...beer can thick. The kinda thick that can rip the seams down the middle, but won't gut the floors. "It's real fat, niggah. But nine inches it definitely ain't."

I know most niggahs get real sensitive when a bitch

starts goin' in about their dick strokes and sizes can but, oh well. Niggahs gotta know. And I can tell I done bruised the niggah's ego, and now he's feelin' some kinda way. Whatever. Truth is, I don't give a fuck. He ain't my man. And we ain't fuckin'. Shit, the niggah ain't even pulled out no paper.

He frowns. Then tosses back his drink.

"So how big you think my shit is?" he asks, soundin' all fucked about the news.

"I've handled a lotta dicks over the years, boo. So if I had to guess, I'd give you six-and-a-half tops. And that's what you need to be proud of. Embrace ya fat-ass ding-aling, niggah. And stop with the lies."

He reaches for the bottle, puts it to his lips, and tosses it back. He wipes his mouth with the back of his hands. I can tell the niggah's feelin' right. "So, you sayin' I gotta lil' ass dick; is that what you sayin'? Shit, I ain't ever have no complaints."

I shrug. "I ain't complainin' either, boo. Like I said, it's real fat. I just don't like it when niggahs lie on their shit, that's all. But, anyway, niggah…I figured out where I seen you before."

He raises his brow. "Oh, word? Where?"

I lean in and nip at his ear. "You were the niggah who walked up in Nappy No More and put the owner on blast. You called her out about suckin' ya man's dick."

He grins. "Oh, daaayum. Right, right. Yeah, I did go up in that spot. Yo, that was a minute ago. Yeah, my man said that bitch was a real live cock and cum freak. What, you cool wit' her or sumthin'?"

I shake my head. "Not really. I mean, she does my hair." I tell him I was sittin' in her chair when he came up in there and tossed filth on her. I tell him how it made my pussy pop. "Oooh, you was so bold and sexy comin' up in there grabbin' ya dick, askin' her if you could get ya dick sucked."

He laughs. "Nah, I asked for one of her deep throat specials. Damn, I can't believe you'd remember some shit like that."

"Boo, who wouldn't? I remember that like it was yesterday. You turned the salon out that day, niggah. Oooh, that was messy, boo. I knew that bitch was a whore. Tryna act all uppity 'n shit. But you did her in real good that day, boo."

He keeps laughin'. The niggah's eyes are all glassy so I know he's liquored up real good. "Yeah, that bitch is a real cum whore. She was toppin' off mad niggahs on da low, too. She called herself Deep Throat Diva or some shit like that."

"What? No, she didn't call herself some shit like that." I repeat the name. "Mmmph. Ooooh, that's a real dirty bitch. *Deep Throat Diva*, mmmph!" I pour him another drink, then pour myself one, too. We click glasses, then toss 'em back. "Mmmph. That messy bitch shoulda had her ass whipped for that." I reach for his dingdong. Stroke it.

He laughs. "Real shit, she did. She got fucked up real good."

"Oooh, noooo, boo," I coo, reachin' for his dick. I stroke it. "What happened? How she get it?"

He glances over his shoulder. Then back at me. He's liquored up real good. "Yo, I shouldn't be tellin' you this shit, yo."

"Niggah-boo, puhleeze, you safe with me, Daddy. I ain't messy like that. Besides, who I'ma tell? I don't even like that bitch like that. So fuck her. I'm glad she got served."

He pours another drink.

I lean in and whisper in his ear, "I wanna fuck you, boo. All this talk done got my pussy real juicy. Let's go somewhere and fuck. I wanna give you some pussy, boo."

He grins. "Yeah, yeah…that's what the fuck I wanna hear, ma. Let's get the fuck up outta here. I'ma take you back to my man L's spot and shove all this muhtafuckin' fat-ass dick in you."

L? Where I hear that name before? I think, slidin' outta the booth. He slides out, then stumbles a bit. Yeah, this niggah's tanked up real good. "I'ma stretch the fuck outta that pussy, ma. Fuck it real good. I'ma hit the bathroom, then meet you outside."

"Don't keep me waitin'," I say, shakin' my hips through the club. It's packed as shit in here. When I get around the club, I spot Knutz at the bar all up in some brown-skinned bitch's face. I can't tell who it is since her back is to me. And it really doesn't matter since that shit ain't my business. I shift my eyes and catch Buddha lookin' at me. He smirks, givin' me a head nod. I flick my tongue at him, walkin' outta the club. As bad as I wanna fuck him, again, tonight's not the night. AJ's the only niggah I got on my mind.

I disarm my alarm, then slide behind the wheel of my truck, lockin' the doors. It's almost one in the mornin'. I crank the engine, then drive off just as AJ is comin' outta the club. *Niggah, we ain't fuckin' tonight. But I promise you, I am goin' to fuck you.*

And when I'm done with his ass, he's gonna know he's been fucked real good.

Thirty-Two

Day'Asia's rude ass comes bargin' into my room while I'm in the middle of a juicy conversation with Miss Pasha. Oooh, Miss Pasha is my boo, even if she is a messy cum whore. But I can't even get into it right now 'cause Day'Asia's ass done disrupted my goddamn groove.

"Ma, you have some money? Me and Tina wanna go to the mall."

"Excuse me one minute, Miss Pasha, girl," I say as I stare Day'Asia down. I blink. *This lil' ho must think I'm some kinda special or some shit.* "And how you gettin' there Asia? And who else is goin'?"

"Samara gonna drive me, Tina and Weena."

I frown. "*Weiner?* What the hell kinda name is that? What kinda bitch names her child after a goddamn hot dog?"

She sucks her teeth. "It's Roweena, but we call her Weena for short. And it's with an *a* at the end, not *er*." She spells it out for me.

I tilt my head, takin' in the ho-wear she has on. She's

standin' in my room wearin' some kinda black and white pinstriped shirt dress that's barely coverin' her ass with a wide red belt and a pair of red and black peep-toe "fuck me" pumps on. Shit I know I didn't buy. She looks a hot damn mess!

"What circus you tryna go to today, Day'Asia? Steppin' up in here lookin' like a goddamn clown with that shit on."

She rolls her eyes. "I'm goin' to the mall."

I bunch my brows together. "Mall, my ass. Not dressed like that. You must think I'm some kinda stupid, Day'Asia, don't you?"

She sucks her teeth. "No. I don't think you're stupid."

"Oh yes, you do, lil' girl. You ain't goin' to no goddamn mall in that getup. Ya ass wanna be out trickin' for dick with that damn Clitina. Not today you won't. Now go take that shit off and clean your goddamn nasty-ass room 'cause I know it's filthy."

"Ma, please. I already told them to come get me."

"Well, that's too damn bad."

She stomps her feet. "Ma, please. I promise I'll clean my room this weekend. And I'll do Isaiah and Elijah's chores for a week, too. I wanna go to the mall. I don't see what the big deal is."

"Day'Asia, I said no."

"Ma, puhleeeeeze, can I go?"

I take a deep breath. "Asia, no."

"Why?"

"One, because I said so; two, because you're dressed like

you tryna slut the night away; and, three, because you not ridin' in no car with some girl named after a damn hot-dog. Now get the fuck outta my goddamn room before you see ya self on the floor!"

She slams my door. "I'm fuckin' sick of this shit! All I ask for is a goddamn few dollars so I can hang with my girls and she wanna give me shit..."

I scream at the door. "Bitch, who is you cursin' at, huh, ho?! Miss Pasha, girl, let me call you back. I need to whip some ass up in here."

"Okay, girl. Go handle your situation. Call me when you can." I tell her to give me twenty minutes and I'll call her back, then end the call, stormin' outta my room.

"Day'Asia! Day'Asia!" I scream, stompin' through the house.

"She left," Elijah yells out from the livin' room.

"Oh no the fuck she didn't." I run to the front door and swing it open just as she's gettin' ready to climb in the backseat of some car with Clitina and two other hoes. "Day'Asia!" I run up on the car and grab her by the back of her damn weave. "Oh, no the fuck you not leavin' up outta here after I told ya black ass you couldn't go out!" I swing her around and she tries to push me off of her.

"Get off of me!"

"Oh, you wanna fight, huh?"

"No, but you ain't gotta be puttin' ya hands on me either. You stay lettin' Marquelle and them do whatever they want, but I can't do shit!"

I slap her face. "Who the fuck is you talkin' to like that? I told you ya ass couldn't go and you tryna step out anyway. Like fuck me, right? Get yo black ass in the house 'fore I fuck you up out here. Don't you ever fuckin' disrespect me!"

"Asia, girl," a dark-skin chick sittin' in the front passenger seat says, gettin' out the car. She's wearin' blue contacts and a long black weave with blue streaks in her bangs "You ain't gotta put up with this shit. Get your shit and come stay at my house."

I blink. This fresh-mouth ho can't be no more than fifteen or sixteen, talkin' all kinds of reckless and sideways. "Oh, lil' girl. You better jump back in ya lane and mind your goddamn manners."

The heifer has the audacity to put a hand up on her hip and swirl her neck. "Bitch, you don't tell me what to do. My name ain't Day'Asia. You better check my birth certificate. My name is Roweena and I will smack the shit out you. Asia, you better tell her, girl. I'll give her what I give mine. And you know how I do it."

She slams a hand up on her narrow hip, starin' me down like she tryna prove a point.

"Weena, girl, I know. But I got this," Day'Asia says.

"No, lil' girl, what you got is an ass whippin' comin'. Now get your ass in the house."

The hotdog ho snaps her fingers. "Look, Asia, you need to handle her. I know she's your moms and all, but we got shit to do. And this bitch is crazy tryna set it off and block our flow. You don't even gotta put up with it."

I shoot her a nasty look. "Oh, you real grown, huh?"

"Yeah, *bitch*. And what?"

"Weena, girl, don't," Day'Asia warns her. "Just let it go."

"Oh no, girl. I got this. You know I don't like her ass anyway for how she treats you and shit, so fuck that, girl. I got ya back. Ya mom needs to catch it real good, then I bet you she'll get her mind right instead of treatin' you any ole kinda way."

I blink. "Day'Asia, take yo' ass up in the house, now!"

"Ma, please."

"Don't fuck—"

Slap!

The lil' ho hauls off and slaps the shit outta me so hard I'm seein' stars. But it don't stop me from leapin' up on her ass and beatin' her like a grown woman. I swing the bitch into the car door. Day'Asia's screamin' for me to stop. Clitina's jumpin' outta the car and screamin' for me to get off of her. And the other bitch in the driver's seat is screamin' for the bitch to fuck me up.

"Bitch! You slapped the wrong one!" I punch her in the forehead and her head snaps back, then I hit her in her goddamn throat. The ho gasps for air. I punch her in the chest. And then it's on.

I hear someone across the street yellin', "Fuck that little bitch up, Cassandra. I saw what the disrespectful bitch did to you."

Someone else is yellin' out, "Stomp her ass, Cass!"

"Ma! Stop! You're gonna hurt her!"

Day'Asia tries to pull me up off of her, but I elbow

her. And she backs the fuck off. "Bitch!" I scream at her. "Don't put your motherfuckin' hands on me! I'ma fuck you up.... next for...bringin' this...shit to my...goddamn... doorstep!"

Whap!

Pop!

I punch the Weena bitch in the face. "I'ma knock your goddamn eyesockets out!" *Whap!* I keep punchin' her. She tries to fight me off of her, but she came for the wrong one.

"Aaah, pleeeeeeeease! Asia! Tina! Samara! Y'all help me! Jump this bitch!"

I dig my nails into the lil' hoe's face, then claw her up. "Yeah, bitches jump me! Bring it! Stinkin'-ass bitch gonna put yo' goddamn hands on me. Oh, no, bitch, you gonna get an ass whippin' you will never forget!"

I swing her down to the ground and start stompin' on her, then grab her by the hair and wrap my hands around it. I drag her ass up and down the driveway and out into the street. "You lucky I ain't tryna kill ya black ass, bitch, for comin' at me like you some grown-ass woman." I punch her again. I'm yankin' her head, and hookin' off on her at the same time. "I'ma snap...ya motherfuckin' neck...fresh-mouth, lil' bitch!"

She is screamin' bloody murder. "Y'all get this crazy bitch off of me! Don't just stand there! Help me, goddammit!"

Clitina knows better. And Day'Asia knows she done set

it off so she damn sure ain't gonna try to stop shit now.

"Aah! Samara! Call my mother. Tell her to hurry up and get over here to kill this bitch!"

Now I hear Elijah's voice. "Whoop her ass, Mom!"

Then Isaiah's. "Fuck her up!"

Then the twins. "Yeah, Mommy jumped on her ass. Fuck her up good! Kick her in the balls, too!"

I hear one of them say, "She ain't got no balls, dummy!"

I drag this hotdog ho all through the grass, then back onto the driveway, then once I have her in the middle of the street, I let the bitch go. She is screamin' at the top of her lungs, like somebody's tryna kill her ass. I tell her to stand up and fight me like a real woman. She's all scraped up and bloody and cryin'. I don't give a fuck!

"Oww! Oww! I promise you, bitch! I'ma get my mom and aunts to fuck you up! Watch! They gonna kill you, bitch!"

I stand over her with a hand up on my hip, waitin' for her to get up. But the bitch doesn't move. "You still talkin' shit, huh?" I reach down and slap the shit outta her. She grabs her face and starts cryin' louder. "Yeah, Saaaaaaaamara!" I yell toward the car. "Call this dirty-bitch's motherfuckin' mammy so she can get it too!" I reach down and punch her again. "Put your mother-fuckin' hands on me, ho. And think you was gonna get that off. Bitch, please. Rude bitch! I don't give a fuck how old you are. I fight kids, too." I kick her. "Now get the fuck up and fight me like a real bitch!"

By now the whole block is lined with nosey-ass neighbors all up in the mix. But everyone on this block knows I don't start shit, but I will damn sure finish it.

I overhear someone say, "Somebody needs to call DYFS on her."

"Bitch, call DYFS!" I yell into the crowd. I start pacin' the street, wavin' my arms like a wild woman. "I don't give a fuck! Let this be a lesson to any motherfuckin' body else whose child thinks they gonna step up to me like they grown and put their motherfuckin' hands on me or talk shit. Step to me and I'm gonna beat your face off! I'm goin' to jail tonight for this bitch right here. And I don't give a fuck 'cause she's goin' too!"

I can hear the sirens in the background. I walk off, leavin' the ho in the middle of the street. Clitina and the Samara bitch run over to help her up. "Isaiah, call Darius and tell him to get over here. And Day'Asia, I want you outta my motherfuckin' house by the time I get released."

She's standin' there lookin' all pitiful. "Wh-where I'ma go?"

"Take ya black ass to the mall. I don't give a fuck where you go! You bring this shit to me! Got this hotdog bitch tryna bring it to me! You go stay with her disrespectful ass. And then you didn't jump on her ass when she put her goddamn hands on me. Oh, no, your black ass can sleep on the streets for all I care! You turned your back on me, bitch! And I don't play that shit! Now get the fuck outta my face before I put you in a body bag!"

Three cop cars pull up to the house, blockin' the driveway like somebody's gonna try and run off. Stupid, pussy-ass bitches! I ain't gotta run no-motherfuckin'-where. I stay with bail money, okay.

Thirty-Three

"Ho," Dickalina huffs into the phone. It's two days after that lil' Roweena bitch slapped me and I'm in Day'Asia's bedroom rippin' pictures and posters off her walls. I've been cleanin' her room out and throwin' shit out all mornin'. "You dead wrong for puttin' Asia out like that, Cass. You need to really get over ya'self and let that child come home."

Mmmp, this ho got some nerve callin' me with this shit, like she some good samaritan. Booga-coon, *boom!* Day'Asia turned on me. Stood there and let some lil' hoodrat bitch slap me and she ain't do a goddamn thing. Oh, no, boo-boo. You do some shit like that, I'm through with you. And Day'Asia Martinique Simms is dog shit to me. That's how bad she done fucked up! And I'm not tryna hear nothin' else about it.

After all I've done for that lil' ungrateful bitch, she goes and does some shit like that. Mmmph. I've let her ass get away with a lotta shit, but that right there…no thank you! I promise you this, if she wants to get back up in here, she'll have to fight her way back in. And I mean that!

I tear down the rest of her posters of Trey Songz, DJ Khaled, Pusha T, and Kirko Bangz. This girl is hot, nasty trash to me, just like all this shit that is goin' out on the curb.

"You of all people know how it feels to be put out on the streets so why you do that shit to Asia like that?"

"Bitch, is she sleepin' on the streets?"

"Well, no. She's here with me."

I sit on the edge of her bed. "Then what the fuck is you talkin' about? I was thrown out with two damn babies, okay? So don't compare me to her. I was never disrespectful to Beulah or any-damn-body else. My mother was a goddamn junkie who turned her back on me, but I bet you when she was out in the streets and someone was talkin' shit to her or about her, I jumped on their asses. I don't use drugs. I keep a roof over her head and food up in this house. I'm good to Day'Asia. That bitch gets anything she wants and she gonna give me her ass to kiss. I don't think so. I'ma loyal bitch. You stay loyal to me, I'ma stay loyal to you. You turn ya goddamn back on me, then damn it, I'ma turn mine on you."

"Well, that shit makes no sense. Why…"

I sniff, sniff again, then frown. It smells like stale pussy funk! I get up from her bed and get on my knees and look under her bed. *Oh, hell no!*

I stand up. Drag her mattress off the bed, then flip up her boxspring. This nasty bitch got crusty and bloody drawers all up underneath her bed. I'm too through!

She knows I don't do filth! You can say what you want about Cassandra goddamn Simms, but you'll never say I keep a nasty, dirty, or funky-ass house. Day'Asia's lucky she's not here. I swear for gawd I'd make her eat every goddam nasty-ass pair of drawers in here, lick all through these crusty-ass crotches, then chew these drawers. All ten of them!

"Damn, bitch. I'm talkin' to you and you act like you ain't got shit to say. It's fucked up what you doin', Cass. You have no business puttin' her out. She's a girl. Anything can happen to her."

"Well, too goddamn bad. She shoulda thought about all that before she turned on me." I walk outta her room and go into the bathroom to grab a pair of gloves, then go into the kitchen to get a two large Ziploc bags. I'm gonna seal her bloody drawers and send them right on over to Dickalina's. This bitch is disrespectful and she leavin' bloody drawers around here. First she tryna fuck in my house, then lettin' some bitch disrespect me. Oh, no...her ass ain't comin' back up in here.

She huffs. "Well, how long are you gonna let her stay out on the streets? She needs clothes for school, Cass. She ain't been to school in two days."

"Oh, well. Not my problem. Her ass ain't up in there tryna learn shit any-damn-way, bringin' home a buncha goddamn Cee's and Dee's. She wanna be like Clitina and Candy's asses."

"Bitch, what is you tryna say?"

"Uhh. I done said it, boo. What part didn't you get? That she ain't tryna learn shit, or that she wants to be stupid like your two daughters? I mean, c'mon Lina, pay attention to what I'm sayin'."

"Bitch, my kids ain't stupid. They just a lil' slow; that's all."

"Yeah, and fast in the sheets; all three of them. Candy, Clitina and goddamn Day'Asia, three fast-assed hoes."

She huffs. "Look, you know I love Asia like she my own, but I can't have her stayin' here too long."

"Then put her ass out."

I walk back into Day'Asia's room and start pickin' up her filthy drawers by the edges and droppin' them in the Ziploc bags.

"Now you know good and damn well I ain't puttin' my goddaughter out on the streets. But she can't stay here forever. You need to let her come home."

"Ha! No, boo. What I need is a stiff damn dick. Day'Asia made her choice. She chose her friends over me. And now I've made mine. The lil' bitch can rot for all I care."

"You ain't shit, Cass. For real. What kinda mother puts her damn child out on the streets?"

"The kinda mother whose child turns her goddamn back on her. And I don't want no bitch who ain't got my back around me. Day'Asia was 'posed to sling that lil' bitch down and stomp her teeth out for disrespectin' me and she didn't."

"Oh, bitch. Get over it."

I take a deep breath. "Look, Lina, I'm really tryna be nice today. But you pushin' it. Do ya'self a favor. Don't call here tryna do me. Just mind your goddamn manners, okay? If you wanna let her stay with you, then let her. But don't call me with no shit 'cause I'm not tryna hear it. Her ass is on Depo, so she's good for three months. You ain't gotta worry about her ass gettin' pregnant."

"Bitch, you—"

"Mommy," Tyquan says, runnin' into the room. "There's some ladies here for you."

"Well, who are they?"

He shrugs. "I don't know. One's fat and one's skinny."

Now who the fuck is at my door without callin' first? I stop what I'm doin', walkin' over to the window, forgettin' that Day'Asia's room is in the back of the house. *Shit, I can't even see who it is.* "Lina, I gotta go see who's at my damn door this time of day lookin' for me. You can come over and pick up a few things for Day'Asia. But don't you bring her ass with you. That disrespectful lil' bitch is only gettin' the basic shit," *yeah like these dirty-ass drawers,* "all these high-priced clothes I paid for ain't leavin' up outta here. So she had better start trickin' for dollars."

"Well, that's so nice of you. I'll come by later and..."

I end the call, then walk down the hall toward the livin' room. I peek through the livin' room curtains. *Oh these bitches got some nerve,* I think when I see a white state car up in the driveway. I tell Isaiah and Elijah to take the twins downstairs to the basement to watch TV and not to come back up until I call them. As usual Fuquan starts talkin' shit and I let him know I'm gonna beat his ass as soon as I'm done with these heifers at my door.

He sucks his teeth. "I don't like you."

"Boy, don't start ya goddamn shit. Now take ya black ass downstairs. I gotta put my happy-clown face on for these bitches and I don't need you wreckin' my motherfuckin' nerves. Now try me."

"C'mon, boy," Isaiah says, snatchin' him by the shirt and pullin' him down the stairs. I wait for him to shut the basement door, then swing open the front door.

"Yes? How can I help you?"

"Hello, Miss Simms?" A thin dark-skinned woman says, lookin' like a burnt toothpick. Her hair is in extensions and pulled up into a ponytail.

"Who wants to know?"

"We're with the Division of Child Protection and Permanency," the brown-skinned chunky one says. She's wearin' the hell outta a real cute, short 'n sassy hairstyle. And her face is beat to perfection.

"Well, I think you have the wrong house. No one here needs protection."

"Miss Simms, may we come in?"

"Uh, no, you may not. Now who are you again?" They introduce themselves. Miss Toothpick says her name is Arletha Jenkins-Smith. Miss Chunky says hers is Loretta Sanchez. I place a hand up on my hip. "Mmmph. And how can I help you bitches?"

They both blink. Toothpick raises a brow, then slams

a hand up on her hip. I can already tell she'll light the party up if need be. My kinda worker 'cause the last one who came here was some scaredy-cat bitch who couldn't take a good cursin' out, but this ho right here looks like she'll bring it. "Look. We're not gonna be any more of your bitches today, okay? Now we're here regarding your daughter, Day'Asia Martinique Simms. Now may we come in?"

I smirk. Ooh, I'ma fuck with these hoes today. "Umm, no, ma'am, you sure can't. You can say what you have'ta say right there on the stoop. Now state your business, then be on your merry way. Please and thank you."

Miss Chunky says, "We received a call that you put your daughter out."

I nod. "Yes, ma'am, I sure did. I sure did. Anything else?"

"And why did you do that?" she wants to know.

"Because the bitch disrespected me and I'm not havin' that."

"Well, first of all," Miss Toothpick states, neck-rollin' it. "Maybe if you knew how to talk to her instead of referring to her as a *bitch* and whatnot, she wouldn't disrespect you. And second of all, you're still legally responsible for her. Therefore, putting your child out on the streets is against the law."

"Listen, gutter rat. She ain't out on the streets. She's over in the projects with her godmother. So talk what the fuck you know, ma'am. Thank you very much. And second of all, I pay the bills up in here so I do the fuck what I want. Anything else?"

Miss Chunky says, "Miss Simms, there's no need to get defensive. We're simply here doing our job."

"Well, your job is done. Day'Asia ain't comin' back up in here. Now move along."

"Then we'll file charges against you," Miss Toothpick threatens like that's supposed to scare me.

I laugh in her face. "Bitch, I don't give a fuck. I don't get a welfare check for her ass and her no-good fahver don't pay child support. So take the bitch. I don't give a hot fuck about no charges. What they gonna do, lock me up? Ho, puhleeze. Lock me the fuck up! I'll eat that shit upside down. So do what the fuck you gotta do. I need a damn vacation any-damn-way."

"Miss Simms," Miss Chunky says, "I understand your frustration."

"Frustration? Oh, no sweetness. I'm not frustrated about shit. But what I am is tired of you DYFS bitches ringin' my damn doorbell with nonsense."

"Miss Simms, I wouldn't call having to come out to your home as nonsense when we've had multiple phone calls, particularly around allegations of abuse, made against you over the years. Most recently less than a month ago an investigator was out here for allegations that you attacked one of your sons. And now this. I hope you realize if you are arrested and charged all your other children will be removed from your home as well and placed in custody, or with family members. Most likely bein' split up."

Miss Toothpick smirks. "And trust me. We *will* take your kids; all of them."

"Bitch, eat the inside of my asshole. You don't fuckin' threaten me. Do what the fuck you gotta do."

Miss Chunky snaps, "Look. Are you going to allow your daughter back in the home or not? We're not about to stand out here all day going around in circles with you. So, it's either *yes* or *no*."

"Umm, did your mammy drop you on that big-ass head of yours or were you just born special? I already told you, n-o. Which part of *no* do you not understand? The n or the o? Would you like me to spell it out on your forehead in crayon for you?"

Chunky takes a deep breath. "We also heard reports of you attacking a fifteen-year-old girl out on your lawn."

"Bitch, you stupid as hell. I ain't attack no girl. The lil' bitch slapped me and I whooped her ass. And the last I checked, that ain't no DYFS matter, so next."

I tilt my head.

"See, girl," Toothpick says to Chunky. "Let's go before I forget I'm still on the clock. Because this chick is really pressing it."

I open the door and step out. "Is that supposed to be some kinda threat? 'Cause you can jump off the clock and get punched up if it is."

"Take it however you want. Every worker who has ever come out to do an investigation on you has said the same damn thing. You're combative, uncooperative, and downright belligerent. And all the Division is trying to do is our damn jobs and maybe help your trifling ass be a better parent, if that's even possible, so you can keep your kids."

"Bitch, how about you help ya'self to a meal. Skinny bitch. You can't help me. And I'ma damn good parent. My kids want for nothin' ho, believe that. They stay fed, fly, and always fresh, so don't do me. I'm not some ghetto-trash bitch who don't take care of her kids. Now get the fuck on before I forget my manners and fuck you up."

Miss Chunky opens her mouth to speak. "Miss Simms—"

I put a hand up in her face. "Not a word, Hippo."

She blinks, puttin' a hand up to her chest. Somethin' catches her eye and she glances over at the window. I look myself to see what the fuck she's lookin' at. And of course, the twins are in the window makin' faces at them, stickin' their tongues out and puttin' their middle fingers up.

"Just look at 'em," Toothpick says, shakin' her head. "It's no wonder these kids are out of control. Look who their role model is." She eyes me. "Abusive and neglectful parents like you don't deserve to have kids. And the first chance we get, we will be removin' them."

"You'se a goddamn lie. I don't abuse my kids. And I don't neglect them. I fucks them up. Big difference, ho. And when they outta pocket, I beat them the fuck down. And make sure you document the shit just the way I said it. I fucks. Them. Up! And what? I'll let the judge know the same damn shit. And you ain't takin' my kids no-damn-where, so dream on, bitch." I step back into the house, keepin' my eyes on them. "Now like I said, Day'Asia ain't comin' back up in here unless I want her to. And today, I don't. So press whatever charges you gonna press. 'Cause. I. Don't. Give. A. Fuck!"

I slam the door in their faces.

Thirty-Four

Four hours later, I'm relaxin' outside, sittin' at the bottom of the porch steps in my yard wear: a pair of black booty shorts and a white tee with the words: HOT LIKE FIRE written across my titties in red letters. I've tied a knot in the back of the shirt to show off my pierced belly button. And I have on a pair of kitten heels.

I'm sippin' a glass of Remy, flippin' through a copy of some book, *Brick*, I found in Day'Asia's room—written by some Allison Hobbs chick—while keepin' an eye on Isaiah and Elijah washin' down my truck. I told them if they do a good job and not start no bullshit I'ma buy them new iPads this weekend. So far they ain't workin' my goddamn nerves. The twins are out with Darius. And Marquelle and Joshua are out with their fahvers.

I slide my right foot outta my shoe, brushin' grass from between my toes, then slidin' my foot back in my shoe. I glance at my chipped fingernail and frown. *Oooh, not cute! I need to get down to Miss Pasha's first thing tomorrow.*

Fuckin' around in Day'Asia's nasty-ass room, draggin'

her shit out to the curb for the trash, I've broken a goddamn nail. That lil' disrespectful heifer really fucked her drawers off with me. I meant what I said, that bitch ain't comin' back up in here. And if she does, she'll have to fight her way back in. Then, she'll sleep her ass on the floor. That bitch had it good up in here, but she fucked up. And she gonna learn today, goddammit! You don't bite the hand that feeds you, or the one that's wiped ya black ass when nobody else would.

Gonna turn on me, mmmph. Bitch, boom! Ya stank ass is shit to me.

I pick up my cell. I have a text from JT. I grin. *This niggah's real lucky I ain't one of them grimy bitches.* YO. I WANNA C U. U FREE?

I text back: No

FUCK! I WANT SUM PUSSY

My cell rings. I know this crazy niggah ain't callin' now. I glance at the screen, rollin' my eyes. It's Vernon. *Mmmph. I should let the shit go into voicemail.* "What?"

"We still beefin'?"

"Niggah, you slashed my motherfuckin' tires. But you lucky I ain't seen you or that bitch of yours, yet."

He sucks his teeth. "See. Here you go wit' this dumb shit. Ain't nobody slash shit. Did you see me do it? No. So quit accusin' me of shit."

"Niggah, I know you did it. So I'm not even gonna waste my time goin' back 'n forth with you about it. Now what the fuck you want?"

"I wanna pick my sons up this weekend. My fam's

throwin' a surprise birthday party for Nana and I want the twins to be there with all of their brothers and sisters, and the rest of the fam."

Awww, I always did like his grandmother. Miss Vee, short for Viola, don't play. I ask him how old she's gonna be. He tells me ninety-six. Tells me that his family's gonna have a mini-family reunion to celebrate her birthday. "Good for her. Tell that old bitch I said happy birthday when you see her. Is she still only seein' outta one eye?"

JT sends another text. WHEN U GONNA B FREE?

He sucks his teeth again. "Yo, ya disrespectful ass is fuckin' ridiculous. You need ya muthafuckin' mouth knocked in for that foul shit, yo."

I'M NOT, I text back.

"Mmmph. And who's gonna do it? You?"

"Look, I ain't call for all this dumb shit. Is you gonna let me come get my sons or not?"

YO, STOP FUKKN AROUND. IMA HIT U UP LATER

"Not."

"Yo, you crazy as hell. How you gonna keep me from my sons?"

"I'm not keepin' you from ya sons. If you wanna see them, you can make an appointment and come here to see 'em. But you ain't takin' 'em nowhere 'til I see some money from ya ass."

I text back: WHATEVER

He sighs. "Whatever, yo. You the only one who wanna be on that dumb shit. My other baby mothers don't ever pull no dumb shit like this."

"Well, that's them bitches. But my sons need to eat and they need new clothes. And I keep tellin' ya black ass that I shouldn't have to spend my other kids' money to take care of your responsibilities."

"Yo, c'mon, Cass. Cut a niggah some slack. I'm out here every day tryna find work, shit's real hectic. I'm doin' the best I can."

"Then get out there and suck some dick, niggah. 'Cause I need money to take care of ya kids."

"Yo, fuck outta here wit' that gay shit. What da fuck I look like?"

"Like a niggah suckin' dick tryna get money up to take care of his goddamn kids, that's what, niggah."

"You know what, Cass. Stop bein' a bitch and let me have my sons for the weekend. Damn. Why everything gotta always be complicated wit' yo' ass?"

"Bring me money, niggah, and you can have your sons for the weekend. No money, no sons. Nothing's complicated about that."

He sighs. "So what you sayin' is, I gotta pay to see my own damn kids, right?"

"No, niggah. Since you only wanna play daddy when it's convenient for ya ass, I'ma let you rent ya sons for the weekend. That's what I'm sayin'. You're three months behind in your child support. Pay up, or get lost."

"Fuck! I'ma bring ya monkey ass the goddamn money when I come pick them up on Friday. Have my mutha-fuckin' sons packed and ready. And, first chance I get,

I'm takin' your grimy ass to court for custody, bitch."

I laugh. "Coon, boom! Eat my ass, niggah. Ya bum ass don't even wanna work. You'd rather mooch off some dumb bitch instead of gettin' yo' lazy ass a job. Niggah puleeze! Ain't no judge givin' you my sons. So eat shit and choke, niggah."

He disconnects. I crack up laughin', pressin' my legs together. The niggah got my pussy hot talkin' all reckless to me like that. I text JT back.

U GOT SUM $$ 4 ME?

Now watch he call, I think settin' the phone on the step next to me. "Isaiah and Elijah, y'all stop dickin' around hurry up and finish washin' that truck."

"We almost done," Elijah says, chasin' Isaiah with the hose around the other side of the truck. I shake my head, watchin' them laughin' and splashin' soap suds everywhere.

My cell rings. It's JT callin' like I knew he would. "Yes?"

"Aye, yo, why e'erything gotta be 'bout fuckin' money?"

"Niggah, 'cause you know the rules. You fuck me, you finance me."

"Yeah, aiight. What time you gonna be free, yo?"

"I told you I'm not. If my sons' fahvers come get them, then I might be..." My voice trails off when I hear bells ringin', soundin' almost like an ice cream truck, and see some chick ridin' up on the handlebars of a bike. Well, at first, that's what I think I see 'til I realize the bitch ain't sittin' on handlebars. She's posted up inside a big-ass wire basket with a black and pink helmet on. I squint. And almost fall out. It's Dickalina. And Knutz is pedalin' a Beach Cruiser bike up in my driveway. The bike is spray painted brown and the wheels are painted orange. And it has orange and white tassels hangin' from the handlebars. And there are cards stickin' outta the spokes of the wheels. Lil'Kim is playin' outta a set of tiny speakers that are in the basket with Lina.

Knutz rings the bell again.

I blink.

OhmyGaaawd, I have seen-it-motherfuckin'-all now!

"Look, I gotta go. I'll call you later."

"Yeah—"

I disconnect.

Knutz pedals on up to me, brakin'. "Hey, girl," Dickalina says, holdin' a clutch in her hand. I'm sure somethin' she done picked up outta Marshalls or T.J. Maxx; her two favorite stores. I turn my nose up.

"Hey," I say back, placin' a hand up over my face like a visor, blockin' the sun. I blink, blink again. This bitch has on a tiny denim mini-dress with no drawers on. And I can see her hairy pussy. And the bitch is wearin' leopard print kitten heels. I'm too through.

"Ugh, bitch, you are so disgustin'," I snap as she hops outta the basket. "How you gonna be all up on some bike in that short-ass dress? I can see all up between ya legs. And it ain't sexy or cute. Ugh. Who keeps a hairy pussy? That is so triflin'."

Isaiah and Elijah laugh. "Ewww, Miss Lina gotta fur coat on her vajayjay."

"Don't let me beat y'alls asses, goddammit," I snap. "Finish washin' that goddamn truck, then take yo' fresh asses in the house and stay outta grown folk conversation. You goddamn kids too damn grown."

Lina huffs, hoppin' outta the basket. "Knutz likes it hairy." She turns to him, pullin' her helmet off. "Ain't that right, boo?"

I peep the get-up he has on and wanna scream. The niggah is wearin' a pair of camouflage carpenter pants and a black blazer over a green tank top. There's a set of silver dog tags hangin' around his neck. And wrapped around his waist is a goddamn nylon camouflage fanny pack. A fanny pack! What kinda niggah rocks a *fanny pack?* I glance down at his feet. He's wearin' a pair of crisp white K-Swiss with orange stripes. He has his hair all done up in zig-zag cornrows, too. Oh, this niggah just knows he's doin' it up real right.

He grins, liftin' his black aviator shades up and sittin' them up on his big-ass head. "Yeah, I love my baby's kitten furry."

"Aww, he's so sweet." She walks over and kisses him on the lips. I frown.

He eyes me, lickin' his lips. "Wasssup, Cass?"

"Niggah, don't speak to me." I shift my eyes back to Lina. He shakes his head. "And why the hell are you out in them damn shoes?"

She looks down at her feet. "And what da hell's wrong wit' my heels? I see you have on da same damn things, but I guess it's okay 'cause you da shit, huh? Cass, you make me sick wit' ya hatin'-ass."

"Bitch, I wear these heels to cut grass in. I wouldn't be caught dead wearin' these out in the streets."

She twists her lips up. "O-M-G, who the hell cuts grass in kitten heels?"

"I do, boo. Now what?" I catch Knutz eyein' my sexy toes. I frown. "Illllll, niggah, get up off my toes."

He laughs. "Yo, Cass. Why you so fuckin' mean?"

I tilt my head. "Umm, why you so triflin'? And who you snatch this bike from? 'Cause I know the shit's stolen."

He removes his jacket, drapes it over the handlebars, then folds his arms across his hard chest, flexin' his bulgin' muscles and showin' off his jailhouse tats.

Lina huffs, slammin' her clutch against her leg and her right hand up on her hip. "Look, bitch...don't be tryna get it crunked wit' my boo. We had a good damn day and I ain't tryna have you ruin it, tryna be messy. We done ate a delicious meal down at Je's, rode around downtown, and now we on our way back home for dessert."

All this with ya ass stuffed in a wire basket on a stolen bike? This bitch talkin' like the niggah done took her ass to a five-star restaurant or some shit. Yeah, Je's is a real cute lil' soul food spot over on Halsey Street, but the shit ain't fine dinin'. I mean, really. If the niggah was gonna do it up he shoulda took her ass to The Cheesecake Factory or some place classy like that. Mmmph.

"How romantic," I say sarcastically. "Now why are you here?"

"Uhhh, hello. You tossed ya daughter out, remember? And I'm here to pick up some things for Asia since you won't let her come back home, where she belongs. So don't start no shit. But, anyway…and why you got all that stuff out at the curb?"

I roll my eyes. Dickalina could be a fly-ass bitch if she stopped bein' so damn ghetto and cleaned herself up. Got rid of all that cheap shit she wears and threw on a lil' lip gloss instead of slatherin' her lips with a buncha Vaseline, lookin' like she been suckin' on fried drumsticks.

"You right," I say, standin' up, then turnin' around and walkin up the stairs. I can feel Knutz's eyes all up on my ass. "She's not comin' back up in here. I'll be right out with her things."

"Well, hurry up," Lina says, snappin' her fingers when Foxy Brown's "B.K. Anthem" starts playin' outta them lil'-ass speakers. "Owwwwl, this my shit right here. Turn that up, boo." Knutz raises the volume on his rigged up stereo. I glance over my shower and peep Lina hoppin' 'n bouncin'. She drops down, pops up, then does the Tootsie Roll. Elijah and Isaiah start laughin'. I hurry in the house to get Day'Asia's shit so I can send this late 'n wrong ho and her dusty-ass man on their way.

A few minutes later, I come back out carryin' four ShopRite grocery bags stuffed with old shit, along with the two Ziploc baggies sealed with her bloody drawers. The bitch turned her back on me, so now she gets the bare minimum. And she's lucky I'm bein' nice enough to give her this shit. When Beulah put me out with Darius and Jah'Mel all I had where the clothes on my back. That hateful bitch didn't let me take shit, other than my babies' pampers, bottles and clothes.

"Here you go, boo," I say, handin' Lina the bags.

She takes the bags, then peeks inside. She frowns. "For real, Cass? You gonna put her things in grocery bags? You mean to tell me you don't have a damn trashbag to put her stuff in."

"Bitch, boom! I'm not usin' my good trashbags to put her shit in. Take her them grocery bags. And be on ya way."

She pulls out one of the Ziploc bags. "Ohmygod, what the fuck is this?"

"Her bloody, stained drawers. The bitch's nasty. But she's yo' headache now."

She blinks. "Oh, no, bitch, I can't have this. I can't have no ho who keeps her drawers dirty stayin' with me. It's bad enough I gotta wash out Knutz's boxers when he stains his. And I told you she can't stay long. I still have Knutz's nephew stayin' wit' us."

I frown. Ugh! "Well, let's hope they ain't in there fuckin' him 'cause Day'Asia's ass likes to fuck." I shoot a look over at Knutz who seems all ears 'n shit. "And niggah, if you even think it, yo' shit's gettin' sliced off."

"Yo, I ain't into lil-ass girls. So go 'head wit' that shit. I like 'em young, but not jailhouse young."

Dickalina shoots him a look. "Niggah, what is you sayin'? What young pussy is you sniffin' around?"

I scream at Isaiah and Elijah. Tell them to take their nosey-asses in the house before I whoop the shit outta 'em. I slip my heels off, then walk over to beat 'em both upside the head with 'em. They take off runnin' around the back of the house, laughin'.

I keep from laughin' myself. *These two clown-asses.* "Niggahs, ain't shit funny. Y'all get ya black asses washed up, then put some clean clothes on so we can go out." I decide I'm takin' 'em out to eat, then to the movies to see the new Madea movie.

Lina's ass is still arguin' with Knutz. "Niggah, let me catch you wit' some other bitch and I'ma tear her ass up, then I'ma stab you for real this time. The last time I only cut you, but this time I'ma stab you up good. And I mean it, Knutz. I ain't playin' wit' ya black ass."

He sucks his teeth. "See now. We was havin' a good time. Now you wanna beef."

"Well, you had no goddamn bidness sayin' that shit about you likin' young girls to Cass and I'm standin' right here. You know how embarrassin' that was?"

"I know, babe," he says, pullin' her into him. "I ain't mean no harm. You know I was only poppin' shit. I ain't thinkin' about them young hoes." She tries to smack him with her clutch. He grabs her arm. "Stop. You know you da only one for me."

I can't believe I'm standin' here watchin' this shit.

"I better be, Knutz."

"You are, boo." He kisses her on the lips. I watch her nip 'em.

"See," he says, grabbin' and squeezin' her ass. "You tryna get shit started."

"Uh-huh. And you bet' not be lookin' at Candy or Tina, either."

"They like daughters to me." He slaps her on the ass. "Yo, let's go home and handle thangs."

"Oooh okay." She turns to me. "Girl, me and my man 'bout to be out." I watch her slip her helmet on over her head, then fasten it. She picks up the bags and hands them to Knutz, then hoists herself up in the basket. As soon as she's all situated, she tells him to give her the bags. "Cass, you need to get ya mind right and let Asia come home. I'ma let her stay wit' me for a week or two, but then you gonna need to let her come back home."

I roll my eyes. I already told her what it is. So ain't no need in sayin' shit else about it. So I let her keep babblin' on. "Oh, baby I almost forgot to remind you. Tell Cass about ya friend you wanna introduce her to."

I frown.

"Oh right, right. Damn, baby. You good. Daddy almost forgot. Yo, Cass, one of my mans just gotta outta da joint a few days ago, and he's tryna get into sumthin'. I told him about you. And he wanna holla at you."

"Uh-huh," Lina cosigns. "Fresh outta da hoosegow, girl. And he's fine, too. Baby, what's L's real name?"

"See there you go askin' about shit that ain't got nuthin' to do wit' you," Knutz snaps. "And what da fuck you mean 'he's fine?' Yo, I'm tellin' you Lina, let me find out you tryna be on some snake shit and wanna fuck my mans. I'ma bust yo' ass."

"Knutz, stop. You know I told you he was fine. Not for me, for Cass. You know she like 'em all rough and tatted up. So quit."

"Listen, y'all niggahs need to take all this arguin' back on over to the projects. I'm not with this ghetto shit over here. And I ain't with tryna meet some niggah Knutz knows, so no thank you."

Lina rolls her eyes and sucks her teeth. "Well, fuck you then. I'm tryna help ya miserable ass out. But whatever. Let's go Knutz. This ungrateful bitch ain't ready for no niggah like L."

"Yeah, we out," Knutz says.

"Well, get the fuck on," I snap as he backs up his bike, then turns around and pedals outta the driveway.

Lina yells out, "We still goin' out tomorrow night?"

I ignore her ass, walkin' back into my house and slammin' the damn door.

Thirty-Five

"Yeah, a bitch like me wanna suck a dick," I ad-lib, makin' up words as I sing along to LoveRance's "Beat the Pussy Up." I'm down at The Crack House with Dickalina and I'm feelin' right, goddammit! "Yesssss, do me right, damn it!" I bounce up 'n down. The three Cum Stains I've tossed back have kicked in, and I'm feelin' frisky 'n ready to fuck. Whew, yes! I drop down low, then pop it back up, tossin' a hand up in the air. "Wanna take it in the ass...make a niggah nut... aaaah, yessss..."

"Cass, girl," Dickalina says, poppin' it up next to me. "You cray-cray for real...Oooh, yes...I love this beat...I can't wait to get home and let Knutz beat it up...Owww..."

I roll my eyes as she's tootsie-rollin' it, then goin' into the butterfly. She has her ass tooted up and her tongue hangin' outta her mouth, like she's bringin' it. Bless sugah-boo's lil' gutter rat heart. I swear Dickalina's my girl and all, but...whatever. I'm not even goin' there. I came to get my party on. Not analyze her dumb ass.

I start poppin' my hips and bouncin' my ass real freaky-like, then spin around toward the door just as a posse of eight strappin' niggahs walks in. Raw hood niggahs dipped in bling. They reek of trouble and good times. My cunt flutters. My asshole puckers.

"Come beat this hole up, motherfuckas...aaah, shit, yeah..." I sing, lookin' over in their direction. I sweep the floor with it as LoveRance lets the bitches know how he beats the pussy up. I jump up and down, then do a little two-step and spin.

"Ahhhh, shit, now...Oooh, yes...this is my shit... aaah..." I throw a hand up in the air and sway my hips. "Bitch like me...knows how to fuck a dick...know how to suck a dick...Big Booty y'all...make a niggah nut... nut...nut...while you beat it up, up, up...make it wet, make it wet...then make it skeet, skeet, skeet...!"

I keep my eyes on 'em as they make their way around the bar over to the VIP section, which really ain't no VIP if you ask me since all it is is five round tables and four booths that are blocked off with red velvet rope. They could at least put some drapes up to block nosey-ass niggahs from bein' all up in the mix. Mmmph. And you gotta buy two bottles minimum to be seated there.

Oooh, yes! I'd fuck every last one of 'em—even the big, black grizzly-lookin' niggah walkin' ahead of 'em like he's king of the streets—if I were a greedy ho. But there are two that really stand out and make my pussy purr. One is tall and chiseled with beautiful tar-dark skin. He looks like he should be on the cover of *XXL* or some other shit. The other is a lil' shorter than him. And he's an extra-crispy niggah with shoulder-length dreds. He's so black he almost looks purple. But it's sexy 'cause he ain't all ashy-lookin' with it. There's nothin' worse than a dark niggah who looks like he's been rolled in powder.

When the DJ starts playin' Plies' "Fuckin' You" I really turn it up. This niggah's music makes my pussy soooo wet. Oooh, yes…mmph! I wonder if he really got that good dick or if the niggah talkin' mad shit like so many other niggahs. I hike up my skirt, then bend over and pull out my thick four-inch butt plug, then I start poppin' my asscheeks and dippin' at the knees. Niggahs start goin' wild. I toss a hand up in the air, wavin' my butt plug like I just don't care. And I don't. I'm here to have a good goddamn time.

"Whoo-hooo....this pussy feel good…I take it in the ass, take in the throat…pussy on fire…whose fuckin' tonight, whose fuckin' tonight…"

I start dancin' all fast 'n hard 'n nasty, gettin' the crowd all amped, like I always do. I slide my butt plug into my mouth, then slowly pull it out, lickin all around the sides of it. "Ass so sweet…who wanna lick? Who wanna stick…? Oooow, do that shit, do that shit…"

Niggahs start chantin', "Go, Booty! Go, Booty!"

"Oh, daaaaayum, yo!" I overhear someone shoutin' over the music. "You see that shit, son? She done pulled a dildo outta her ass…"

"Yo, she on some real freaky-type shit."

"Do that shit, Big Booty," Dickalina shouts. "Let 'em know what you workin' with, girl. Ooow..." She starts clappin' and doin' some kinda "Oh Happy Day" shit, like she's somewhere gettin' her praise 'n worship on. *Mmmph.* A damn mess!

Two songs later, I'm wrappin' my assplug into a napkin, then droppin' it down in my handbag as I sit back up at the bar. Big Mike slides me another Cum Stain. And I take two long sips. *Oooh, these damn drinks are doin' me right, goddammit!* I take two more sips, then sit my drink up on the bar, watchin' Lina doin' the Dougie. She's all tanked up on Speedballs—shots of Stoli, Tanqueray, and Cuervo with a splash of lime juice. Oooh, she's goin' hard, workin' the shit outta it. She drops down, touches the floor with it, then snakes it back up. *Oooh, those drinks really got Miss Dickalina doin' stunts tonight.* I chuckle as some brown-skinned niggah inches up in back of her and starts tryna bring it to her.

I laugh as she drops down into a split, then bounces back up. "Go 'head, Lina! Pop that pussy up on 'im, sugah-boo!"

I hop up off the barstool and shake it back on the dance floor when the deejay starts playin' Future's "Bitches Ain't Shit." "Aaaaah, yes...Niggahs ain't shit... I'll trick 'em off their money...twerkin' it...murkin' it... fuck 'em to sleep...Yesssss, goddammit...!"

When the deejay slows it down with Lil' Wayne's "Pussy Money Weed" I start swayin' my hips to the beat, runnin' my hands through my hair. This song makes me wanna give a niggah the business tonight. "Yessssss… pussy, money, weed…do me right, goddammit!"

I dance it up for another two songs, then pop my hips back over to the bar. Lina's drunk ass follows behind me. "Giiirl," she slurs as she sits up on her stool. "I'm havin' me a damn good time." Dickalina's all sweaty and lookin' extra greasy. She dabs a napkin across her forehead, then at the back of her neck. "Oooh, all these niggahs in here got me wantin' to do some thangs. I gotta get home and fuck Knutz…Oooh, he gotta big ole juicy dick, Cass… this music got me so horny…"

I frown. "Coon, I don't wanna hear no shit about how big Knutz's damn dick is. Drunk bitch! Is you crazy?"

"I'm just sayin'. Damn, bitch. And no I ain't drunk. I'm nice."

"Oh, you nice 'n drunk."

She pokes her lips out. "Cassie, why you gotta call me a coon 'n shit? All I'm doin' is sharin' sumthin' wit' you."

I tilt my head. "'Cause that's what the hell you are for flappin' ya goddamn jaws about how big your niggah's dingdong is. Ho, I don't like the niggah, number one, so I don't give a fuck. But, if I was some real thirsty bitch that stayed on that slut juice, I'd be tryna see the dick for myself."

"But I know you ain't like that so I ain't gotta worry about you tryna fuck my man." She takes a sip of her drink. "Oooh these Speedballs are good. Speakin' of dick.

You really should meet Knutz's friend L, Cass. He really wants to meet you."

I twist my lips up. *L? I heard that name before. I wonder if he's the same niggah AJ was talkin' about. Hmmm.* "And where's the niggah from, and how Knutz know him?"

"I don't know where he's from 'cause Knutz ain't tell me. But I know they were in the county together last year. And they were also at Northern State together the last time Knutz was in prison. All I know is, he is fine. And from what Knutz says about him, he's wild as hell. And a freak."

"Mmmph. What, him and Knutz was fuckin' or somethin'?"

"Bitch, is you crazy? Hell no. Knutz ain't even gay like that. Although he told me he let some niggah suck his dick and lick his ass a few times before. But that was when he was locked up in his twenties."

I frown. "Bitch, TM-motherfuckin'-I. I don't need to know shit about Knutz lettin' another niggah top him off or toss his salad. And you know about this, how?"

"'Cause he told me."

"Bitch, I'm lookin' at you sideways now."

"Cass, puhleeze. It's no biggie. I know Knutz ain't with that. He experimented. Besides, he ain't da first or da last niggah who done had another niggah suckin' on his dick while he was locked up. At least he told me about it. More than what I can say for other niggahs."

I blink. This ratchet bitch done gone from hoodrat to

gutter rat tellin' me this bullshit. Some shit ain't never, ever, supposed to fall outta ya goddamn mouth. And ya niggah getting' his dicked sucked by another niggah is one of those things you take to the motherfuckin' grave. Oooh, this bitch! I toss back my drink. Then order another one. This ho is crazy. But whatever!

"Anyway, girl. That niggah L really wants Knutz to hook you up wit' him. I think you might like him. He likes to fuck like you, too. But Knutz said he don't like no one fuckin' wit' his balls 'cause some crazy bitch he was messin' wit' tried to bite 'em off."

I frown. "Ugh. What kinda bitches he fuckin' with? Mmmmph. Well, I ain't sayin' I wanna meet his ass. And I ain't tryna play with his balls so whatever. Is the niggah broke?"

She stares at me. "Bitch, how I know. He just got outta the county. You know he probably gotta get his stacks up. Right now he tryna have a good time. And when I told him you like it in da ass he started droolin' and practically goin' crazy."

"You did what? Bitch, don't be tellin' some strange niggah my business."

She rolls her eyes, wavin' me on. "Whatever. It ain't no secret you love it in da ass. Shit da whole bar knows it."

She starts diggin' in her bag, then pulls out her phone. "Wait, wait. I want you to see sumthin'." She starts scrollin' through her cell, then hands it to me. I'm goddamn sick to my stomach. It's a picture of her down on her knees holdin' Knutz's big-veiny dick with both hands, flickin' her tongue over the head. And it's a big ol' light-skinned dingaling with a plum-sized head.

"See, girl, I ain't lyin'. See how big my baby's dick is?"

I frown, shovin' her cell back at her. "You coon-booga bitch, how the fuck you gonna show me some nasty shit like that?" I reach over and snatch her glass. "Bitch, no more drinks for you."

She starts laughin'. 'Oh, Cassie, loosen up."

"You know what, ho. Poof! I'm iggin' ya ass for the rest of the night."

"Cass, you just don't know how good Knutz makes my body feel. I love me some Knutz, girl."

"Mmmph. Well, good for you. I'm glad you love Knutz." I let out a disgusted grunt when I see him walkin' through the door. "Ugh, speakin' of his no-good ass, here comes that nutty niggah now."

She swivels her stool toward the door, then turns back to me grinnin'. "My baby must wanna get a few dances in wit' me before takin' me home to get some of this coochie."

Lisa, one of the weekend bartenders, comes over to serve me. And the dirty, trick-ass ho knows I don't like her. I can't stand a phony bitch. And she's one of 'em. And why this ho can't take the tips she makes and take her triflin' ass on down to Nappy No More so Pasha can hook up her raggedy-ass weave is beyond me. How the fuck you gonna have a blonde weave and ya edges and roots are all jacked up? Mmmph.

"What can I get you, Cass?"

I stare at her, then tap Dickalina on the arm. "Lina, tell this bitch she can't get me shit."

Lina taps the bar, then says, "Bitch, you can't get her shit. Wait, why can't she? I need me another drink."

"Well, then let her fix you one. But that bitch ain't fixin' me shit."

"Fuck you, Cass," Lisa says, stompin' off to serve someone down at the other end of the bar. Bitch, puhleeze. What I look like? Her ass might try to drug me or spit in my damn drink. No, thank you. I'm not givin' that ho a chance to ever do me in. I'll wait all night for Big Mike to serve me if need be. Luckily, we didn't have to wait too long.

Knutz walks over to us, drapin' his thick arm around Dickalina's shoulder. He whispers somethin' in her ear. "Ooh, Knutz, baby," she coos. "You know I love it when you talk nasty to me. You make me wanna do some thangs to you."

I roll my eyes up in my head.

He eyes me. "Yo, wassup, Cass?"

I look him up and down. He's wearin' afro puffs with the colored rubberbands in his head. And has the nerve to have on a black and white Enyce polo shirt with a pair of Sean John baggy jeans. And a pair of black canvas and leather high-top sneakers on his feet with the Velcro straps and FUBU written on the sides. Mmmph. I can't. Not with this jailhouse critter.

"Knutz, go kill ya'self, niggah." I get up from my seat,

grabbin' bag and drink. "Lina, I'm goin' to the bathroom. Hopefully his ugly ass will be dead when I get back."

I go into the bathroom, check out how fabulous I look in the mirror, then swing my hips out the door, pullin' out my cell as it vibrates. I glance at the screen. It's JT's goddamn ass. *No thank you, niggah*, I think, pressin' IGNORE, then droppin' the phone back in my bag. Three seconds later, my phone vibrates and I know the niggah is leavin' me a text. Crazy ass!

Thirty-Six

Ten minutes later, I'm steppin' outta the ladies room with a fresh coat of lip paint and gloss on my lips, swingin' my hips when Big Grizzly steps outta the men's bathroom. Our eyes meet. I grin at 'im.

"Yo, ma, what's good wit' you? You sexy as fuck." I stop. "I was watchin' how you bounce that ass up 'n down on the dance floor. You was poppin' that shit like a champ. That shit is real right."

I grin. "Glad you liked the show, boo."

"Oh, no doubt, ma. You had my dick goin' thru it. You definitely gotta niggah feelin' like gettin' into sumthin' nice 'n wet tonight. Fuck what ya heard. You mad sexy wit' it, too. What's ya name?"

I eye his ass real easy-like, takin' him all in. Oooh, he's uglier than dog shit. But he's over six-feet tall and smellin' like expensive cologne and loads of dollars; just how Big Booty likes 'em. But that waist is a bit too extra for me. And judgin' by the the lump in the front of his Gucci sweats, it looks like the gorilla's hung like a beach whale. Is he fuckable? Yes, sugah-boo, if the price is right and with the lights out. I glance at the diamond pinky ring, the encrusted diamond watch, and the iced out chain around his thick neck. Oh, it's definitely possible. Shit, I've fucked worse when I was tryna keep a roof over my head.

"It's Cassandra."

Oooga Bear licks his lips. "Oh, aiight. That's wassup."

"And you are?"

"Kashmir, but niggahs call me Cash with a Cee, for short."

"And why's that?"

"'Cause they know I'm about makin' that paper. And I dig makin' it rain on sexy-ass broads, like you."

I grin. "Then tonight's ya lucky night, big daddy. 'Cause I love trickin' niggahs like you up off them dollars."

He laughs. "Yo, that's what it is. So how 'bout we go back on over to my booth over there in VIP, let's toss back a few drinks and get better acquainted. You cool with that?"

The niggah doesn't have to say shit else. I swing my ass over toward VIP while he follows behind watchin' it shake, bounce, 'n pop. When we get over to his booth, the tall sexy tar-black niggah I had my eye on earlier is sittin' in the booth with three other niggahs. All dipped in jewels. There are four three-hundred-dollar bottles of Krug, a bottle of Crown Royal, and a bottle of Rémy XO on the table. Oooga Bear doesn't introduce us. Rude ass! Instead, he grabs the bottle of Rémy and a bottle of

Krug, then tells me to follow him to another booth. I walk in back of him, glancin' over my shoulder at Tar Baby. I quickly flick my tongue out on the sly. Oooga Bear waits for me to slide into the booth, then slides in beside me. I frown.

"Ummm, why is you tryna pin me up in this booth, niggah?"

He chuckles. "No harm, ma. I'm only tryna sit close to ya sexy ass and have a few drinks wit' you. But if you want a muhfucka to sit across from you instead, then I will."

I cut my eyes at him. "Pour me some of that Rémy, niggah. But if you try any funny business I'ma stab you in ya balls."

He cracks up laughin' as he pours two glasses of Rémy. "Yo, you real feisty, ma." He slides my glass over. "You really know how'ta make a niggah's dick hard."

"And I know how to ride one, too."

"Is that so?" He raises his glass. "So here's to my hard dick. And you knowin' how'ta ride it."

Our glasses clink.

"So you fuckin'?"

I slide my lips over my glass, then sip my drink real ladylike 'cause I'm tryna keep it real classy tonight 'til some coon sets me off. Then you know I'll have to turn up the flames to hood-ho and set it off. My pussy lips clap, imaginin' givin' this niggah a facial.

I take a few more sips of my drink, but I wanna toss it

back like I would a dingaling. Gulp, gulp, goddammit!

"Boo, that depends," I finally say, settin' my glass down. The dark liquid goes down like fire.

"Oh, word? On what?"

"One, on how much paper you tryna drop; two, on how much dingdong you got hangin'; and, three on whether or not I feel like fuckin'."

He laughs. "Oh, shit 'dingdong', that shit's funny as hell. But check this out, ma. One, money ain't never sumthin' I gotta worry about. And, two, I gotta big, thick dick that most bitches can't handle. So the question is, can you handle the *dingdong* as you call it?"

I laugh. "Boo-boo, you better check my credentials. I gotta pussy like a horse, niggah. It's real juicy and knows how to milk the nut outta a dingaling."

He laughs again. "Yo, you a real live wit' ya shit, ma. You just don't give a fuck, huh?"

"Nope."

"Yo, I like that shit, ma."

I toot my lips. "Mmmhmm. And what you like to do, niggah, since we talkin' about what you like?"

"Real shit, ma. I'ma freaky ass muhfucka. It's whatever wit' me when it comes to pleasin' a sexy bitch as long as she's willin' to return the favor. But I can show you better than I can tell you. But on some real shit, ma, we ain't gotta do a buncha nothin'. Shit watchin' how you had that big ass bouncin' gotta niggah's dick still rocked. You got me wantin' to fuck ya ass on this table, real shit."

My pussy lips clap again. "Niggah, I'm only that kinda ho for my baby daddies. You fuck me, it's gonna be with my ass up, face down, stretched out in the middle of a hotel bed."

He leans into my ear. "Yo, check this out. I got five grand to blow tonight on whatever. So tell me. What can a niggah get for that kinda paper?"

I raise a brow. "Niggah-boo, for that kinda paper, I might let you get the works."

He licks his thick lips. "Oh word? And what's that?"

"Pussy, ass, and throat."

He grins, pullin' out a thick knot of money. I count in my head as he starts peelin' off money. *One hundred, two hundred, three hundred...*

"Yo, check this out. You got on panties?"

I raise a brow. "Yeah, why?"

Four hundred, five hundred, six hundred...

"What kind?"

"A purple lace thong, why?"

Seven hundred, eight hundred, nine hundred, a thousand!

"I want 'em. Here's a gee. Take them shits off and let me sniff 'em real quick. If that pussy smells sweet, then I'ma slide you the rest of this paper I got on me and we gonna go somewhere and get it in real heavy tonight."

"I wanna feel how big that dick is," I say, slidin' my hand in his lap and feelin' the inside of his thighs.

"Yo, do ya thang, ma. It's on the left side of my leg."

I let my right hand roam, then stroke him on the sly. I immediately start gettin' wet. It's about as thick as a baseball bat and about as long as a billyclub. Now I wanna see it, taste it, and feel it. Oooh, yessss, goddammit! This niggah got me real juicy. And now Big Booty wanna fuck!

"You like what you feelin'?"

I keep rubbin' it.

"So we fuckin' tonight?"

"Maybe."

He opens and closes his legs. "Nah, I ain't tryna hear no maybe, ma. I wanna fuck you. I wanna run this dick all up in ya back, real shit. Now let me get them panties."

Shit, Big Booty's pussy always smells sweet. This niggah don't know. I laugh to myself. Fuckin' this niggah for his change is gonna be like snatchin' crack from a blind dope fiend. This motherfucka must not have gotten the memo on me. I'm always lookin' for the next come up. I smile, liftin' up in my seat, hikin' up my skirt, then slidin' my panties off.

I look around the club, then slide 'em to him on the sly. He slides me the grand, then puts them up to his nose and takes a deep whiff. "Yeah, that shit smells right, ma. Mmmhmm..." I watch as the niggah sticks out his long tongue and licks the crotch area. Oooh, he's some kinda nasty. But the shit makes my pussy wink. "Yeah, ma, real shit...we fuckin'. And you betta be able to handle all this dick."

I stuff the money down in my bag, then grip his dick and squeeze it as hard as I can. "Niggah, not to worry. I ain't never been..." My voice trails off when I spot Knutz mushin' Dickalina in the head, then yankin' her by the arm and snatchin' her off the barstool. I take a deep breath. Decide to not let that bitch disrupt me gettin' this niggah's money. If Knutz drags her ass outside and beats her face in, so be it. 'Cause tonight, the only thing I'm tryna get beat down is this pussy.

"You ain't never been what?"

I bring my attention back to this big-dicked niggah with the permanent Gorilla mask on. The niggah stay ready for Halloween with that face.

"Scared to fuck," I finally say, starin' him in his dark eyes. He grins, licks his lips, then tells me he wants to finger my pussy. "Niggah, you better go wash ya hands, first. I don't let no niggah run his fingers up in me without him washin' them shits first. You must be used to them nasty, bird bitches."

He laughs. "Yo, ma. Real shit. You thorough as hell. A niggah like me needs a sexy-ass honey wit' that fire on his team. I'ma tell you what. I ain't gonna take you nowhere and fuck ya brains out tonight. But we gonna fuck. And when we do, I'ma tear ya shit up. I put that on my life, ma..."

I press my legs together. *Oooh this niggah's talkin' my talk. Mmmph.* My asshole clenches around the minibutt plug I have in. I squirm in my seat, feelin' a nut risin' in me.

"But right now, I wanna wine and dine ya fine-ass.

Get all up in ya head, then bust them guts open. You done felt all this hard dick a muhfucka got between his legs, so you already know what it is…"

I lift my glass to my lips, eyein' him over the rim. Truth is, I don't feel like fuckin' him tonight. But I wanna feel his dick in my hand and get up in that wallet. I lean into him, inhale in his scent. The niggah smells like money; lots and lots of it. And I wanna help the niggah spend it. I whisper in his ear, "Pull ya big dick out, Daddy, and let me stroke it under the table. I wanna feel you bust ya hot nut in my hand."

He grins. "Yeah, you a real freaky bitch, ma; just how I like 'em. I tell you what. If you can make me nut in ya hand, I'ma hit you wit' da rest of this paper I got on me."

I tell him to pull out his Mandingaling. I watch as he slips his hand down into his designer sweats, lifts up and fishes out his dingdong. My pussy starts juicin' as I open my bag and pull out my tube of Platinum Wet, then discreetly squirt some into my hand and start strokin' his snake. It's long and thick. Ooooh, yes, goddammit! This ain't no dick, it's a motherfuckin' arm! He tells me the shit's twelve-inches long and six-inches thick. I press my legs shut, imaginin' this Anaconda goin' in deep, drillin' the oil from outta my pussy 'n ass.

My pussy twitches. My asshole clenches.

Lupe Fiasco's "Bitch Bad" starts playin' and I slowly stroke him, my rhythm matchin' the beat, swirlin' my hand over the head of his dick. It's the size of a plum and

I wanna slide down under the booth table and bite into it. Feel its juices squirt into my mouth and all over my face. But I ain't slutty with it so I don't.

I lean into his ear and moan. "Mmmm, you a ugly motherfucka but you gotta big-ass dick, daddy…mmmm… long, black horse-cock, niggah…you wanna stuff my pussy 'n ass with it…?"

"Yeah, ma…aaah, shit yeah…I wanna bust ya shit up…"

He puts my thong up to his nose.

"Sniff my pussy, niggah…"

I quickly glide my slippery hand up 'n down and around the head. "Lick the crotch, niggah…you wanna taste my wet pussy?"

"Yeah, ma…you'se a sexy-ass bitch…"

"Lick my panties, motherfucka…."

I eye the niggah as he runs his tongue all through my panties. This nasty niggah done got my pussy on my fire. I keep strokin' him, imaginin' his lappin' tongue is all over my pussy. I squirt my lube into my hand, then twist my body so that I can work the niggah over with both hands, grindin' my pussy down into the leather seats.

His voice dips to a husky whisper. "Aaah, shit, ma… jack that muhfuckin' dick…mmmph…"

I take one hand off his dick, then reach in back of me and pull out my butt plug. I place it up to his lips. Tell him to lick it. He gives me a crazy look.

"Yo, what da fuck is this?"

"It's an ass plug. I just pulled it outta my fat ass."

He takes it from me, glances around the club, then sniffs it.

"Lick it, niggah…let me see how nasty you are, motherfucka." Reluctantly, the niggah finally licks it, then slides the shit into his greedy mouth like it's a deep fried chicken-finger battered in ass juice. Oooh, this niggah is nasty. And I love it goddammit!

His dingaling seems to get harder—if that's even possible. "C'mon, niggah…give me that dingaling juice… bust this dick for me, Daddy…"

His head rolls back. "Fuck," he groans over the music. The niggah don't give a damn if someone hears him or not. But the music is on blast, so it don't matter. I hand fuck him through three songs 'til the niggah finally shoots his cock cream all over my hands. I keep strokin' every goddamn drop out, then let go. My hands are coated with his nut. I lick two fingers, tastin' his cream. I lick my lips, scoopin' some nut off my other hand, then slippin' my fingers into his mouth. He sucks on 'em. The niggah's warm mouth and wet tongue feels good. I pull my fingers out, then grab napkins from off the table and wipe my hands clean.

"Aaah, shit…you mad nasty, ma…"

Of course I am, niggah!

He wipes himself off, stuffs his dingaling back down into his sweats, then pulls out a knot of green. "Yo, real shit, ma. You a bad bitch. I'm tryna see what's good with ya sexy-ass. How can a niggah get at you, again?" He slides me the roll.

I grab the knot, tossin' it into my bag as he slides outta the booth to let me out.

I glance around the club. Niggahs and bitches still dancin' hard, poppin' bottles and talkin' shit. I don't know if Knutz done dragged Dickalina's ass outta the club and whooped the shit outta her or not. But what I do know is, I just nutted this niggah up outta five grand. I grin, bringin' my attention back to him. "If you wanna get at me, you'll find me, niggah."

With that said, I step, leavin' the niggah's eyes locked on my ass as I make my way through the sea of drunk-ass niggahs and ho-ass bitches.

Yeah, ass right, pussy right, titties right...I'ma bad bitch!

Thirty-Seven

I'm in my bedroom with the stereo playin', listenin' to Adele's CD *Adele 21.* "Turning Tables" is playin' and I'm smokin' a blunt and drinkin' a bottle of Barefoot Moscato, mindin' my business when my cell rings. I reach over on the bed for it, glancin' at the screen. It's Day'Asia's ass. I press IGNORE, tossin' the phone back on the bed. A few seconds later, it beeps, alertin' me she done left a message. I close my eyes, inhalin' smoke, then slowly blowin' it out.

Nooo, lil' bitch. You ain't disruptin' my vibe. You tried to turn the tables and do me, boo. Daughter or not, I ain't got no convo for a bitch like you.

I hum to the melody. Oooh, this white ho knows she can sing her drawers off. I toss back my drink, then reach for the bottle and fill my glass to the rim. The kids are gone 'til tomorrow night. Well, all of 'em except Isaiah and Tyquan. Neither of 'em wanted to go with their fahvers. And the one thing I don't ever do is force my kids to go, especially Isaiah, since I don't like the walrus-lookin' bitch he's married to. It's early in the evein' and I'm feelin' good. I'm gonna use the quiet to just sit and chill for a minute. No dingaling, no buncha kids, and no damn drama.

When "Lovesong" starts playin', I sway to the music. "Siiiing, goddammit! Do me right, Adele!" The song is calmin'. I smoke down my blunt, then spark another. My cell rings. It's Day'Asia again. And she gets igged, again.

Four glasses of wine and two blunts, later, I finally decide to listen to my messages.

"Ma, can I please come home, pllllllllllease..." she's whisperin' into the phone.

"They crazy here. Mister Knutz done beat up Aunt Lina last night and she been locked in her room, cryin'. I wanna come home, ma." I delete. The next message starts playin'.

"Mommy, puhhhhllleeeeeze call me when you get this message. Puhhhhhllllleeze. I'm sorry for what I did. Puhhhhlllllleeeeeze call me back."

I roll my eyes, pressin' the delete prompt. Five minutes later, my cell rings again. This time it's Darius. "Hey?"

"Yo, Ma, you talk to Asia?"

"No, I haven't; why?"

"Yo, you need to get her outta that spot over there wit' Miss Lina and 'em. They over there wildin' hard; for real."

"Not my problem," I say, pourin' myself another drink.

He sighs heavily. I imagine him frownin' his face, or rollin' his goddamn eyes in his head. "Yo, Ma. Real shit, you effen buggin'. How you sound talkin' 'bout that's not ya problem? Asia *is* ya problem. And she's *your* responsibility. She ain't got no business bein' over there in da projects when she gotta home right there with you."

"*No*, she *had* a home. Now she's on her own. I'm not havin' no grown-ass disrespectful bitch layin' up in here tryna do whatever the fuck they want. I'm not playin' them kinda games. So if you so concerned about where she's at, then you go get her and let her stay with you. Like I told them DYFS bitches, she ain't comin' back up in here. Now don't call me no more with this shit."

"Yo, you buggin'. I'll holla at you later."

"Then holla." I disconnect.

An hour later, Dickalina is callin' me. I sigh. Now what the fuck she want? *If she's callin' here 'bout Day'Asia's ass I'ma scream on her.*

"C-C-Cassssss," she wails in my ear. "H-h-he's goooone." She's boo-hooin' it up all up in my eardrum.

I frown. "Lina, calm down. Who is you talkin' about?"

"Knutz...he...left me," she coughs and says between sniffles.

Good riddance, coon-bitch! I decide to keep that to myself. Ain't no sense in tryna kick a bruised ho who's already down. "Well, what happened? Why'd he leave?"

"H-h-he said...he was sick of me bein' up in...other niggahs' faces and runnin' da streets wit' you. Aaaaaaaahbwwwwwaaaaah," she screams as if someone's stabbin' her with a burnin' blade. "My man left me 'cause he said

I don't have his back when you…talk…shit. Aaaaaaa-aahbwwwwwwaaaah. You chased…my…man away… Bitch, whhhhyyyyy you ain't…just…keep ya mutha… fuckin'…mouth shut?"

I frown. Fuck sympathy, not that I had any for the ho. "Bitch, I don't 'preciate you callin' here and tryna do me over some bum-ass niggah. *Bitch*, boom!"

"But he was…my…bum-ass niggah. Not yours. You hatin' bitch!"

"Oh, puhhleeeze. Bitch, *boom! Boom!* Don't fuckin' try 'n do me with that shit. His coon-ass left you 'cause he got some other dumb bitch he fuckin'. And it's probably the young ho I saw him all grins 'n giggles with at the club…"

"When? When you *seent* my man wit' some other bitch, Cass? And you ain't call or send me a text so I could run up on them? Bitch, we 'posed to be girls."

"Trick, we are friends. And the last time I told you I saw him with some bitch you cussed me out and we got'ta fist fightin'. You almost let that niggah ruin our friendship, ho. So don't do me, bitch."

"Ya ass is real goddamn dizzy when it comes to believin' anything anyone tells you about that niggah Knutz. He's dirty, boo. But you too stuck on stupid to wanna hear it or see it, so why am I gonna waste my time, tellin' you shit knowin' I'ma have'ta bust you upside ya knotty head if you come at me tryna do me."

"I love…"—hiccup—"him. He's the"—hiccup—"only

man that…I ever…let fuck me…in the asssssss. Oh, whyyyyy he do me like this? I ain't never lick a man in his asshole and I did h-h-his…"

I cover my mouth, feelin' myself throwin' up in the back of my throat. Oh, this bitch is givin' out too much. She done forgot she told me how he don't wipe his ass all the way clean. "Oh sweet Gawd, Lina! What the fuck?! I ain't need to know 'bout you bein' a shit licker. You'se a nasty bitch, boo. And now the niggah done dipped on you for some other bitch. Mmmph."

"When I find out who that bitch is, I'ma fuck her up good."

I frown. "Wake the fuck up, ho. You are not his priority; only an option. That niggah stay fuckin' around on you and you know it. So don't even try 'n put the shit on me 'cause both of you coon-bitches can eat the inside of my ass. Yeah, he's ya bum-niggah, boo. And every other low-budget bitch on the block."

"Bitch, what da fuck is you tryna say? I ain't low-budget."

"And you ain't high-end, either. That niggah. Ain't. Shit. So count ya blessin's and be happy the niggah dipped. And if you got any goddamn sense you won't take his shit-stained-ass back, *this* time. And you'll keep ya tongue outta his ass, too. I mean, really? What kinda bitch fucks with a niggah who got shit tracks in his drawers? It's bad enough you told me the niggah let another niggah suck his dick."

"You ffffffuckin', bitch! I-I-I…t-t-t-ttold you thaaaaaat…

in confidence. And you throw it back in my face. You ain't shit, Cass."

"Bitch, you delusional. You told me that shit in drunkenness. Fuck outta here. You ain't tell me shit in no confidence. Not sittin' up in no goddamn bar. But do you. That niggah probably suckin' dick, too."

"Fuck you—"

"Maaaaaaaa," Fuquan yells, bustin' up in my room.

"I'm on the phone, boy. What is it?"

"There's somebody here from the zoo for you."

I frown. "Boy, ain't no goddamn body from no damn zoo here. Get yo' ass outta here with that mess."

"Unh-huh. He *is* from the zoo. And he's standin' outside waitin' for you to come to the door to feed him."

I suck my teeth at his ass, gettin' up from the bed. *This boy's always got some shit goin'*. "Well, what he look like?"

"Ugly," he says, scrunchin' his nose and lips up. "Real ugly. And black too."

I sigh. "Lina, I gotta go. Sorry you all distraught over that niggah Knutz, but stop with all the goddamn tears and let it go, boo. That niggah means you no good."

"Fuck you, bitch. Motherfuck you!" She hangs up on me.

Bitch, puhleeze. What. The. Fuck. Ever. Stupid bitches cryin' over niggahs who they know ain't shit. Who the fuck does that? *Bitches who ain't shit*, I think as I walk outta my room into the livin' room.

I peek through the curtains and see a shiny black Benz out in the driveway. It's one of them big boy motherfuckas so I already know it's an S-series. But whose? And I can't see who it is since someone left the goddamn storm door unlocked and whoever it is is holdin' it open waitin'. All I see is a big white box. I swing open the front door. And almost pass out. It's the niggah Cash.

I don't know if I should be pissed at the ugly fucka for showin' up at my doorstep, or impressed that the niggah is standin' here on my porch holdin' a box. I ain't gonna curse him out, but I'ma check his ass.

"Ummm, niggah, what the fuck is you doin' here?"

He grins, then licks his lips tryin' not to stare at my thick nipples pokin' through the white T-shirt I'm wearin'. I don't have on a bra. *Mmmph. This nasty niggah.* I stick my titties out more. Give the niggah more to see. "Wassup, ma? You told a muhfucka if I wanna holla at you, I'll find you. Well, I did. Now what, ma?" He hands me the box. "Yo, these are for you. A lil sumthin' to let you know a niggah had you on the brain, hard."

I eye him. Then step outside, closin' the storm door behind me. He's wearin' black Polo sweatpants with a white Polo pullover. I glance down at the red and black Air Jordan 3 Retros on his feet—I know what the thousand-dollar kicks are since I bought Da'Quan a pair.

I eye the platinum and diamond chain hangin' around his neck and the ice blingin' in his ears. "Thanks," I say, takin' the box from him. I don't open it, and I don't tell the niggah that I ain't a flowery-type bitch. "So, how'd you know how to find me?"

He chuckles. "I got my ways. Trust me. Anything I wanna know about someone I can get it, real shit. But it cost a niggah a grip to get the info. But in ya case all I had'a do was ask 'round the bar who da beauty wit' da *phat*, juicy booty was and for the right price, here I am."

I toot my lips. "Mmmph. You coulda asked one'a them niggahs to hit you with my number, niggah. You don't just show up at somebody's house without bein' invited. What if I had a niggah livin' here, or somethin'?"

He laughs. Tells me he knew I ain't have no steady dingaling livin' up with me. Said he ain't wanna get my number to call me. That he wanted to get at me face to face. And he wasn't waitin' to run into me down at the club, since that's not one of his regular spots.

"But, yo, if I had to post up in that muhfucka e'ery night 'til I got at you, I woulda."

I look him over. He ain't really all that ugly-lookin' to me now that I know the niggah's caked up like a bakery. I mean, I can get past that face with the right kinda incentives. He cuts his eyes over at the window, then smirks.

"Y'all get ya nosey-asses outta the goddamn window," I snap, not needin' to see what caught his attention. "They some bad-asses," I tell him, shakin' my head. "Was they makin' faces at you?"

He laughs again. "It's all good. They yours?" I tell him yeah. The niggah opens his big juicy pussy eatin' lips and asks if they my only ones. I kinda wanna laugh, but I don't. The niggah ain't do his homework; otherwise he woulda known. I tell him I have ten kids. He blinks, then gives me a look like he ain't believin' it. "Yo, get da fuck outta here. *Ten?* And ya body *still* looks like that?"

"Believe it. My oldest is twenty-three."

"Daaaaayum. You look mad young, ma. And that body's right."

"Of course it is, niggah. Now what you want? And what kinda paper you spendin' to get it?"

Fuquan's bad ass comes outside from around the back of the house on his skateboard without wearin' his helmet. Now usually I'd scream on him, but I'm keepin' it classy. I sweetly tell him to take his nosey-ass back inside and put on his helmet.

"Awww, man. I'm not gonna hurt myself."

"Fu, don't do me, boo. Get yo' ass in that goddamn house and get that helmet on."

He looks over at Cash. "Do you live at the zoo?"

I blink.

Cash chuckles. "Nah, lil' man. Why you ask?"

I hold my breath. Shoot him a look, warnin' him to keep his fresh mouth shut. But he acts like he don't see me and says, "'Cause you look like a gorilla."

I snatch my shoe off and throw at him, screamin', "Boy, what I tell you 'bout ya goddamn mouth?! Get ya black ass in the goddamn house before I fuck you up! You too goddamn grown!"

Fuquan takes off runnin' 'n laughin'. I hear Isaiah laughin', too. I swing open the front door, then walk into the house. "Isaiah, I'ma fuck you up. I know you put his black ass up to that shit."

He starts laughin'. "Unh-uh. He did it on his own. But he do look like a gorilla."

I bite my tongue from laughin' too. "Oooh, I'ma fuck y'all up. You know better than to do me like this."

"Well, he is ugly."

"See. Now you bein' messy. I know he is. And he knows he is, too. But you ain't supposed to remind nobody of how ugly they is. It's rude and disrespectful. The uglies can see their ugliness on their own. They don't need you throwin' it up in their faces. Don't do that shit again. Now get away from that goddamn window 'fore I bust ya eyeballs out." I sit the box on the sofa, then walk back outside. I narrow my eyes when I see Fuquan back on his skateboard with his Captain America helmet on. He got the nerve to be grillin' Cash, like he my damn man.

"Why you here? You tryna do it to my mommy?"

Cash laughs. "Nah, lil' man. Ya moms cool peoples."

"Well, you better not try 'n touch her cootie-coo or me and my brothers gonna jump you."

"Fu, don't have me punch you in ya goddamn throat. And you better apologize to Mister Cash for bein' disrespectful."

He folds his arms, then takes off on his skateboard when I come down the steps after him. I tell him his ass's gonna be on punishment.

"Yo, it's all good. Lil' man's cool. How old is he?" I tell

him eight. That he has a twin brother. "Daaayum, so you stay busy."

"Somethin' like that. But they mine. And I don't regret havin' 'em."

He grins, eyein' me. "That's wassup. Yo, check this out. You sexy as fuck, ma. I ain't gonna hold you 'cause I know you prolly got mad shit to do. But I wanna take you out, real shit. And if you ain't gotta babysitter, it's all good. I'll take them too."

I blink. Ain't no niggah ever offer to take me *and* my kids out anywhere. I look around to see where Fuquan is. When I don't see him in the yard, I say, "Look, boo. I ain't gonna lie, you ain't really my type in the face, but I liked how that big juicy dick felt in my hands and you got paper that makes my pussy drool. Now I appreciate you offerin' to take me and my kids out, but I ain't no ghetto bitch who lets any ole niggah around her kids like that. I'm classy with my shit, niggah. I gotta feel like I can trust you. I ain't tryna have no niggah up around my kids who's gonna be tryna fuck 'em or abuse 'em."

"Yo, that's wassup. I can dig it. That's how you 'posed to be. Trust me, ma. I ain't into fuckin' lil kids. I'ma freak, not a pervert, ma. And I ain't into abusin' kids. If they outta pocket, I'll snatch 'em up real quick, but that's about it."

"Well, I still ain't lettin' you around my kids. And I don't want you comin' back over here unannounced, or uninvited."

He grins, noddin' his head. "You got that, ma." He digs in his back pocket and pulls out a black leather card holder, then hands me a card outta it. "Check it. Here's my card. I own a few detail shops throughout da tri-state area. Come through and let me take care of ya whip… on me. And *any*thing else you need, I got you."

I raise a brow. Tilt my head. "*Any*thing?"

"Yeah, anything. I'ma muhfucka who gets shit done, ma. Check for me, and you'll see for ya'self. I'm out."

Fuquan comes ridin' back up on his scooter, lookin' into Cash's car. "Mister Gorilla, you rich?"

"Fuquan!" I yell, snatchin' him by the arm. I whack him on his ass. "See, now you tryna be messy. Don't have me sling you down on this ground. Get ya black ass in the house."

He throws his skateboard, then stomps off screamin' up the driveway. "I don't like you," he says, swingin' open the door.

"And I don't like you either. Now get the fuck in the house." He walks in and slams the door. I shake my head. "Ooh, he's terrible."

He laughs, openin' the door to his Benz. "Yo, it def looks like you got ya hands full." He slides behind the wheel, lookin' and smellin' like fresh cake. He shuts the door, rollin' the window down. Oooh, I wanna fuck this niggah in the back seat. His eyes lock on my hard nipples. "Yo, c'mere." He gestures with his head.

I lean into his window. "Yessss?"

He lowers his voice. "Yo, you got on panties?"

I smirk. "Yeah, niggah, why?"

"Let me get them shits to go, ma."

He starts peelin' money off'a a thick roll of hundreds. And you already know it doesn't take long for the cash register in my head to start ringin'. And you know I ain't one to ever turn down a few dollars. "Niggah, you real nasty with it. Mmmph. But I'ma run inside and get you a pair of my sweet scented drawers. I gotta pair in the dirty clothes from last night."

"Nah, baby. I ain't into smellin' no stale drawers. I likes my shit fresh. Get in the back seat and take them shits you got on off."

I blink. *Oh this niggah is definitely some kinda extra freak.* But I get in, shut the door, then lift up and roll my pink mesh thong down over my hips. "So what's up with you smellin' bitches' drawers?"

"No mystery, ma. I like the smell of pussy. I like lickin' 'n sniffin' them panties when I'm strokin' this big-ass dick, ma."

There's somethin' about the way he says this in that deep, rugged voice of his that makes me wanna slip my fingers into my pussy and ass. "Well, do you like anything else about pussy?"

"Yeah, ma. I dig eatin' it. And fuckin' it. Now let me get them panties so I can roll out and handle this hard dick."

I grin, foldin' my panties, then handin' 'em to him. He hands me the money. And I step outta the car, shuttin' the door. "So what you gonna do, keep payin' to sniff my drawers?"

He licks his lips. "Yeah, until *I'm* ready to get up in the hips."

I place a hand up on my hip. "Niggah, who said I wanna let you get up in all this?"

He cranks the engine. And it purrs along with my pussy. "You got my card, ma. Hit me up when you ready for a muhfucka who knows how to treat a bad bitch like you. In the meantime, I'ma be back in a few days for another pair of them panties, so be ready for me."

"Niggah, you better call first," I snap, eyein' him as he backs outta the driveway. He winks at me, tappin' his horn, then rollin' out. *Nasty, freak-ass motherfucka!* I strut back into the house, grippin' the knot of money I just collected, grinnin'. Shit, if all I gotta do is slide that niggah my drawers on demand, I'ma definitely be callin' his ass. A niggah who likes spendin' money is just the kinda sponsor I need.

And if I get this niggah to finance me, then I can cut that crazy-ass niggah JT's black ass off!

"Isaiah! Fuquan!" I yell as I walk down the hall toward my bedroom. "Get ya asses washed and dressed. We goin' shoppin'." They all hyped and whatnot, jumpin' up and down, tellin' me what they want when I ain't ask them shit. "Fuquan, I shouldn't buy ya black ass a goddamn thing for you tryna do me, lil' niggah. You need to learn when to keep ya goddamn mouth shut!"

Thirty-Eight

"Yo, why da fuck you ain't been answerin' ya shit?"

Instead of goin' off on this niggah-bitch, I decide to keep it light 'n friendly. "Look, boo. This shit ain't workin'."

"What? What da fuck is you talkin' about?"

"I'm talkin' about you, me…it ain't workin' for me. Ya black ass ain't stickin' to the program."

"Yo, fuck outta here. You already know what it is. We gotta deal. You fuck me, and I keep breakin' you off. I lace ya ass wit' mad paper so you 'posed to have ya ass on call for me."

"Coon-niggah, *boom!* I ain't no motherfuckin' call girl. I told you I don't answer to you, or no other…" My cell beeps. I glance at the screen. I have another call comin' in. It's Day'Asia. I keep on talkin'. "…keep tellin' ya black ass that I don't answer to you."

"Yo, fuck outta here. I own you, *bitch.* Do you understand that?"

I laugh. "Boo-boo, I know you crazy and all, but niggah, yo' ass is certifiable. If ya wife wants to put up with that shit, then that's on her. But I ain't the one. The deal *was*, that we fuck and you go on about ya merry business. Don't catch no feelin's. Don't get wrapped up in ya lil' happy home and you stay the fuck outta mine. *Not* you tryna motherfuckin' control me, niggah. *Not* you thinkin' you own me."

"Yo, Cass, real shit. You gonna have me fuck you up, aiight. I'm warnin' ya ass. Don't fuckin' try me, yo."

"Niggah-coon, *boom!*"

I disconnect, then scroll through my phone. I press the CALL button. "Hey," the caller says.

"Sugah-boo, this niggah-bitch is really gettin' outta hand. He called here talkin' real crazy. Talkin' 'bout he owns me. The niggah comin' with too much goddamn drama for me. And you know I don't drama."

"I know. I told you this was crazy. I'm tellin' you, you have no idea what kinda niggah he is. He's ruthless. They all are."

"Oh I know *exactly* what kinda niggah that bitch is. And I'ma fuckin' pull his cord real goddamn soon. And I'ma let his wife know what kinda snake-niggah she's married to."

"Trust me. She already knows."

"Then she'll hear it again. Don't no motherfuckin' niggah threaten me. I'm done with his ass."

"Maybe we should just let it go."

"Oh no! We gonna ride this shit out. I'ma hood bitch, and the two things we don't do is, run from shit or let it go. No, no, no. We sit and we wait, then when a bitch least expects it, we strike. I started this. And I'ma finish it. So, buckle up, goddammit! We gonna put 'em all outta they misery."

Nothin' else is said. Another call rings through as I'm endin' the call. It's Da'Quan. I smile. "Niggah, why I ain't heard from ya ass in over a month? And you ain't even been home once since you've been back to school. Who you fuckin' on campus, niggah?"

He laughs. "Ma, chill wit' all that. I ain't messin' wit' no one."

"Lies, niggah, lies! I know you slingin' dick somewhere."

"I'm still a virgin," he says, crackin' up. "I ain't thinkin' 'bout these broads, Ma. I'm good."

I frown. "You ain't suckin' no dingaling, is you? I mean...if you are, I'ma still love you 'cause you my child, but I'ma fuck you up."

He keeps laughin'. "Ma, chill. I don't swing like that. I'm chillin'. I got friends, but ain't nuthin' serious. You told me you wanted me to stay focused and that's what I'm doin'. I ain't tryna get caught up in no drama. I'm tryna graduate, feel me?"

I smile. "Oooh, that's my boo. I'm so proud of you, Da'Quan. Did you get the package I sent you?" He tells me that's one of the reasons he's callin'. He thanks me. Tells me he loves me and wants me to come down to his school and spend the weekend. I don't do regret or guilt, but I do feel bad that I ain't been down to his school except one time when he first got accepted. "Boo, you know I don't do the south like that. But I'ma drive down for the day. Maybe fry up some chicken, whip up some mac 'n cheese and a big pot of greens—oh, and a peach cobbler—for you while I'm there." If I ain't learn nothin' else from Beulah I learned how'ta throw down in the kitchen.

"Daaayum, you got my stomach growlin' now. I just wanna see you, Ma. You sure you aiight? I had a bad dream that sumthin' happened to you."

"Real shit, Cass. Don't have me fuck you up...I own you, bitch..."

I shake the niggah's voice from my head. I ain't even about to tell him about JT's nutty ass. Da'Quan's always been so protective of me, more so than Darius and Jah'Mel. And he's the one who I know would put a bullet in a niggah's face if they tried to hurt me. Oooh, I miss his ass. I don't know why he ain't go to Rutgers or Kean University instead of goin' way down to D.C.

"I miss you, too, boo. And, yes, I'm fine. You ain't gotta worry about me. You know ya brothers all got my back."

"I know, Ma. But you gotta be careful out there, okay? Promise me, aiight? I don't want nuthin' happenin' to you. You all I got."

I blink. *What in the world is goin' on? Da'Quan ain't never talk like this.* "Da'Quan, is everything, okay? You worryin' me, boo." He tells me everything's good with him. That he's worried about me. I try 'n reassure him that I'm okay. That the niggahs in the streets look out for me. But he ain't tryna hear it. He wants me to come to D.C. to see him, or send him money so he can come home. I don't want him comin' home unless it's for the holidays, only. I don't want him gettin' mixed up in no shit while he's here. All them lil' niggahs he used to run with in high school are in jail or dead. And I ain't tryna lose him.

"'Quan, boo. I'll bring ya brothers to come see you in a few weeks, okay?"

"Aiight, cool. And what about Asia? I wanna see her, too."

I swallow. "Boo, Day'Asia ain't a part of this family anymore."

"*Whaat?!* What are you talkin' about, Ma?" I give him the rundown. Let him know how nasty 'n grown the lil bitch's been. "Ma, that ain't cool. You dead wrong for puttin' her out on the streets like that. She was def outta pocket for not beatin' that chick down, but you outta pocket too. What Darius say?"

"Nig..." I catch myself from bringin' it to him. "Da'Quan, you know I ain't ever tolerate no disrespect from you boys so I ain't gonna have it with her."

"I know, Ma. But she's a girl. Anything can happen to her."

"Well, that's too damn bad. She shoulda thought about that before she turned on me. She stood there and let that ho put her hands on me and didn't do shit 'til I tried to beat the lil' bitch's face off. Then she gonna try 'n pull me off'a her. Oh, no, Day'Asia fucked up, boo."

He sighs, heavily in my ear. "Ma, I don't like it. Fuck her up if you gotta. But you gotta let her come home."

I roll my eyes. "She's fine right where she's at, 'Quan. She's with Dickalina."

"Miss Lina? She ain't fine there. She's prolly over in the projects doin' God knows what. You know Miss Lina ain't watchin' her. She can barely handle Candy and Tina. You gotta get her home, Ma."

Oooh, I'm tryna keep it sweet 'n classy, but Da'Quan is tryna do me. And I'ma go off in five, four, three, two…one. I take a deep breath. Bite down on my bottom lip to keep from givin' it to him. "Da'Quan, please. Don't do me. We gettin' along and I ain't tryna get messy with you 'cause you know that's not how I like to do it. Day'Asia made her bed. And now she gotta learn how to sleep in it. And if the streets eat her up alive, oh well…she'll have no one to blame but herself. I love Day'Asia, but that bitch tried to do me. And I ain't havin' no bitch turn on me, livin' up on me."

He sucks his teeth. "Ma, I gotta go. I'ma hit you one day next week. Give me Asia's number. I'ma talk to her." I rattle off the number to him. "Aiight, Ma. I'ma holla. Please let her come home."

"I'll think about it," I tell him. But I ain't thinkin' about shit. My mind's made up. We say our good-byes, then disconnect.

Thirty-Nine

"Hello, Ma?" the voice on the other end says. I glance at the time. It's eight o'clock in the goddamn morning.

"Who is this?" I ask sarcastically.

"It's me, Ma...Day'Asia."

The poor thing's been tryna talk to me for the last two weeks and I been keepin' her ass on ice 'cause I told you she's dead to me. Well, not really. But the bitch still on ice. I grunt. "Mmmph. Oh, now I'm ya *Ma*. How can I help you, Day'Asia?"

"I wanna come home?"

"Oh, no, boo. You don't have a home to come home to."

"Please, Ma. I'm sorry."

I sit up in bed. "What you sorry for, Day'Asia, huh?"

"For everything," she says, soundin' like she's on the verge of tears.

"Oh, no, boo. I don't know what everything means. You need to spell it out to me so I know what the fuck you mean by *everything*."

"I'm sorry for not listenin' to you and for talkin' slick. I'm sorry for not doin' my chores or keepin' my room clean. I-I-I'm sorry for cuttin' school and for sneakin' Bunz into my bedroom."

"Day'Asia, boom! You ain't sneak that niggah in. You walked his ass up in here how a bold bitch does it. Like fuck me 'cause you gonna do what the fuck you wanna do. You real grown with it, boo. And two grown bitches can't be up in here."

"I'll do better, Ma. I promise."

"Mmmph, lies! Why you turn ya back on me, Day'Asia, huh? Why the fuck you stand there and let that hoodrat bitch slap me and you ain't jump on her ass, huh, Day'Asia? You turned on me."

"I was m-mad at you."

"Bitch!" I scream, jumpin' outta bed, pacin' the floor 'cause this ho got me wantin' to fight. "You can be mad all goddamn day at me, but you ain't ever supposed to let that shit stop you from havin' my motherfuckin' back. You ain't ever 'posed to let some bitch in the streets disrespect me. I don't give a fuck what kinda beef me and you got. We 'posed to have each other's goddamn back. I ain't never, ever, turn my back on you. I've fuckin' whored and tricked and fought to keep you and ya brothers with a roof over ya goddamn heads and clothes on ya backs. I did that shit 'cause that's what I'm supposed to do as ya mother. But I ain't ever supposed to let you turn ya goddamn back on me and be good with it. Oh, no, boo-boo. I ain't checkin' for no bitch who ain't ridin' shit out with me."

"I know, Ma. I-I-I'm sorry."

"You hurt me, Day'Asia! You let that ugly bitch disrespect me! We was supposed to fuck her up together. But, nooooo! You did me like I was some bitch on the street. And I ain't jump on ya ass like I was supposed to either. I ain't ever fuck you up like I do these boys. I let ya black ass get away with a lotta shit, Day'Asia, 'cause you the only girl. But you bent over and told me to kiss ya funky ass and I don't appreciate that shit one goddamn bit! You wanna be out there whorin' with them dumb-ass bitches Clitina and Candylicious, then do you. But you ain't comin' the fuck back up in here. You ain't a loyal bitch."

"Maaaaaaaaaaa, puuuuuhleeeeeeze," she says wailin' in my ear. "I won't e-e-ever d-d-do it a-a-again. I p-p-promise. I'll h-h-have ya back. I w-w-wanna come h-h-home."

"Listen, stop with all the goddamn tears. This ain't Hallmark. And I ain't givin' out no pity or no motherfuckin' sympathy cards. You made your choice, Day'Asia. Now you gonna have to live with it. You tried to do me, boo. And now ya ass is done. I put up with Dickalina's dumb ass 'cause we girls. But I ain't puttin' up with no dumb bitch livin' up in my house."

"Maaaaaaaaaa, pllllllllleeeease," she screeches into the phone. Now I ain't gonna front. Day'Asia's ass is like me, she ain't one for sheddin' no tears. So this does kinda have me feelin' a lil' soft around the edges. But not enough to let this bitch back up in here. "I'm s-s-sorrrrrry. Pleaaaaaase, Ma, let me come home."

"Oh no, Miss Hot Ass. I ain't acceptin' no apologizies today. You can't come back up in here. You wanna be grown, remember? Talkin' all goddamn slick to me. Fuckin' in here all up on my goddamn sheets. Skippin' school and not bringin' ya black ass in this house when I tell you to. You wanna get Dees and Effs on ya motherfuckin' report cards, like school don't mean shit to you. Coon, boom! I'm not havin' some hot pussy bitch who I can't trust up in here."

She coughs and cries and sniffs. "I promise…I'll… listen to…you."

"Lies! If you don't wanna stay where you at, then go take ya ass to Philly and stay with ya brokedown fahver."

"I-I-I don't wanna…stay wit'…him."

"Well, then, that's too goddamn bad. Now don't call me no goddamn more."

I disconnect. My heart aches. But that bitch gotta learn you don't disrespect ya mother and you don't ever turn ya ass up to someone for them to kiss it when they've been good to ya and have always had ya goddamn back.

I feel myself gettin' kinda choked up. But I ain't goin' there. I pick up my cell and call her ass back. When she picks up, I can tell she's still cryin'. I tell her to have her ass here on Saturday at ten in the mornin'. I tell her that she's to come alone and meet me in the backyard, on time or don't come at all. "You wanna come home, you gonna have to fight ya way back up in here. If you whip my ass, since you a bad bitch, you can come home. So be laced up and ready to fight."

I disconnect, then crawl back in bed under my covers. I wipe a tear that's slid down my cheek, then shut my eyes, tryna hold back the rest that are rimmin' my eyes. *I'ma fuck her up real good!*

"Fight me, bitch!" I urge, pushin' Day'Asia. She stumbles backward. We're in the fenced backyard, alone with nothin' but space and air between us. All of the boys are with their fahvers—surprisin'ly, so it's just me and this traitor. She looks a mess in her raggedy wears: a pair of pink Juicy sweats from last summer all twisted up in her ass and a white long sleeve Tee with the word JUICY FRUIT stretched over her big titties. Day'Asia has always been tall and thin, but it looks like she's lost at least ten pounds. She really didn't have much of an ass before but now her shit's really flat. The only thing that's right is her hair. Dickalina done laid it out in a bob and put burgundy highlights in it. But I'ma 'bout to fuck it to pieces so it don't matter.

I have on an old pair of light blue tie-dyed 7 For All Mankind stretch jeans, a thin blue long-sleeve hoodie and a pair of baby-blue Timbs on my feet. My face is slathered in Vaseline and I have my weave in one long braid tucked down in my shirt and the hood up over my head and tied tight so Day'Asia can't grab my hair. I'm in my fightin' stance, bouncin' around, throwin' jabs and brushin' my thumbs across my nose.

"I don't know why you come here with ya hair all done up when all I'ma do is snatch it outta ya goddamn scalp. You ain't no real street bitch."

My kids know I don't take no shit. And they know how far to do me before I go from classy to ghetto to hood-crazy. Day'Asia done kicked it up to the latter, and now I'm ready to wear her ass out. And she is scared shitless! I've been pushin' and shovin' and slappin' her and she still hasn't swung, yet. "I wanna fight, bitch! I've been waitin' all goddamn week for this."

I punch her.

"Fight me!"

"Pllllleeeeease, Mom," she pleads. "I don't wanna fight you."

"Yes you do, ho." I slam my shoulder into her, knockin' her backward. "Hit me, bitch!" I push her. "Do me like I'm one'a them bitches out in the street."

I punch her upside the head.

She throws her arms up over her face and head, tryna block my blows. She starts cryin'. But she knows not to run from me. Not if she wanna get her ass back up in this house. "I-I-I d-d-d-don't...wanna...fight...you."

"Then why you raise up on me, huh, Day'Asia? Why when I told ya black ass you couldn't leave up outta this house you tried to leave anyway, huh? Why you yank ya goddamn arm from me?" I slap her, again. "Why you try to do me?"

"I-I—"

Before she can get the rest of her words out, I grab her by her shirt collar and swing her to the ground. "Why you do me, Day'Asia, huh, ho? Why you turn ya back on me, bitch? And now you don't wanna fight me!" I hook my hands up in her hair and start draggin' her around the yard. She's screamin'. But I don't give a fuck. "You gonna fight me, bitch? You gonna be a woman about ya shit, huh, Day'Asia?"

"Owwwww, Mom…puhllllleeeeeeeeeze. I don't wanna… puh-llllllleeeeeeeeze. I'll do whatever you…want…"

I jump on her and start punchin' her like a wild woman. "I will kill you, Day'Asia. Is that what you want, huh? You wanna be dead, don't you?"

"N-nooooo…"

"Then why you do me, huh? Why you turn ya goddamn back on me and let that dirty hoodrat bitch disrespect me?" With my left hand pressed around her neck, I dig my nails into her throat, then smack her with my right hand. She's gaspin'. "I will take a box cutter to ya face, Day'Asia, and gut ya grill out. Is that what you want? You want me to peel ya goddamn face off? Fight me, bitch! Do me—"

Outta nowhere, I feel hands on me, tryna yank me off Day'Asia. "Yo, Ma! What da fuck is you doin', yo?!" It's Darius and he's tryna pry my hands from around her neck.

"Let go, Ma, before you hurt her. C'mon, Ma, get da fuck. Off. Her."

It takes him a few minutes to finally wrestle me off her. And when he finally does, I am crazed, practically foamin' at the mouth. She's heavin' and coughin' and gaspin'. Her bottom lip is busted and her nose is bleedin'.

I spit at her. "Get yo' ass up and fight me, bitch! I told you if you wanna get back up in here you was gonna have'ta fight ya way back in."

"Ma, what da fuck is wrong wit' you? You fuckin' wildin' yo!"

"Niggah, stay the fuck outta this! This shit ain't got nothin' to do with you. This is between me and this lil' disrespectful bitch."

"Fuck that! What da fuck is you sayin'? This shit's got e'ery-thing to do wit' me. You'se my moms and you out here beatin' my sister down like she's some fuckin' stranger in da streets. That shit ain't cool, yo."

He yanks me by the arm, tryna manhandle me.

I slap his face. "Niggah, you done lost ya mind, puttin' yo' motherfuckin' hands on me." I jump up on his ass and start punchin' him. He tries to restrain me. Outta the corner of my eye I see Day'Asia finally pullin' herself up off the ground.

"Get off her!" she yells, chargin' him. She punches him in his back. And he lets go of me. Then it's on. "Mind ya fuckin' business. I wanna come home and you messin' shit up for me!"

"What da fuck?! Bitch, how da fuck you gonna jump on me when I saved yo' ass from a morgue trip?"

"Niggah, you don't call ya sister no bitch! Have you lost ya motherfuckin' mind?"

Next thing you know, me and Day'Asia jump him, rippin' his shirt off and punchin' him up. We go all upside his head. And I know he's tryin' not to hit either one of us so he tosses us around the yard. First, Day'Asia gets slung, then the niggah slings me. But as soon as he swings one of us off of him, the other is right back at him. The niggah can't keep up, but he ain't willin' to go down 'cause he knows me and Day'Asia gonna stomp him to his grave once he drops.

"What. Da. Fuck!" he spits, breathin' heavy. We all outta breath. But we fightin' like wild dogs. Sweatin' like three grizzlies. "I'm tryin' not to fuck y'all up, but both of you really askin' to get beat da fuck up."

"Fuck me up, niggah!" I snap, swingin' a fist. He blocks it. "Do me good, goddammit!"

Day'Asia hits him in the back of the head with a stick. And he still ain't tryna hit us. Bless his heart. But we servin' him all kinds of fist work and he knows he gotta choose which one of us he gonna swing off on if he wanna keep standin'. He punches Day'Asia and knocks her ass out. Then raises his hand up to me, but stops himself.

I scream on him. "Niggah, you done punched ya sister's lights out! You not supposed to ever put yo' hands on her! Is you fuckin' crazy?!" He starts blockin' my punches.

"Yo, go 'head, Ma," He uses his forearm to push me back. But I come back swingin' harder and faster. Cussin' him out for punchin' his sister like that. She still ain't movin' and I don't know if she dead or what. And I'm pissed.

"Yo, what da fuck was I 'posed to do, stand here and let y'all hook off on me like that? I was tryna help her dumb ass. She's da one who called me early this mornin' all scared 'n shit, askin' me to come over here and make sure shit ain't get hectic. And here you are chokin' her out and all I do is try 'n help her ass and both of you flip da switch on me. Fuck outta here. Both of you are fuckin' crazy, yo. I'm outta dis muthafucka. Don't call me for shit, yo!"

"Bounce, niggah! I ain't call ya ass to come over here in the first place! Day'Asia's ass did. I told you this shit was between me and her. Next time stay the fuck outta it!"

His neck and face is all clawed up. If I had my mace, I'd do him up real good.

"Whatever, yo," he snaps, throwin' a hand up. "I ain't fuckin' wit' either one of you. I'm done!"

"Niggah, be done and stay done then!" I yell, grabbin' the garden hose, turnin' the water on then, hosin' Day'Asia down 'til her eyes finally snap open. She gasps for air, coughin'. "Get yo' stank ass up and come the fuck on in this house." I drop the hose, struttin' toward the patio door. "And you better not get water on my goddamn floors."

Forty

Oooh, wait a goddamn minute. Did I ever tell you how sexy I am? Did I mention that I have a bangin' body to go along with all this sexiness? Mmmph. I stay turnin' heads, okay. And today is no different than any other day when I'm out poppin' 'n bouncin' my ass.

Today I happen to be in the mall, Short Hills—of course, loaded down with bags. I know, what else is new? What. Ever. Anyway, I'm surprised at how many niggahs are out here on a Thursday mornin' shoppin'. The weekdays are usually reserved for the white bitches with nannies and housekeepers, which is when I like to come out and get my shop on. But today feels like niggah central up in here. And it's only a lil' after twelve.

Mmmph. I love me some Mall at Short Hills. It's real classy. And you ain't ever gotta worry about no drama hoes comin' up in here tryna rah-rah it out. Oh, no. They keep the hoodrat trash out.

All I know is, I don't need to be up in here today droppin' heavy dollars. And I'm hopin' like hell that I can recoup the four grand I done spent in here today. Shit, after that fight—well, it really wasn't that much of a fight, more like a beatdown since she didn't fight back—I had with Day'Asia last week, I needed to treat myself to a few new trinkets. So here I am. But I did buy Day'Asia a few things, too. Not that she deserved a goddamn thing 'cause she's still on my "beat-a-bitch-down" list. But since she's back home I can't have her lookin' any ole kinda way. Shit. If I'm fly as ever, my kids gotta stay fly, too. That's how I do it.

But if I gotta toss ya ass out on the streets, or shut you down 'cause ya black ass tryna get grand 'n grown, then you can look like hot trash for all I care. I bet you, Miss Day'Asia will think long and hard before she tries to do me again. Anyway, I went into Macy's—'cause she ain't ready for Bloomies or Saks. And she definitely ain't ready for Gucci or Louie—to shop for her. And hope I don't have'ta rip the shit off her ass for tryna do me any time soon. I promise you, the next time I gotta hop on her ass I ain't gonna be nice about it.

So far, her ass ain't been doin' nothin' but goin' to school, comin' straight home, doin' her chores, and keepin' her room clean, which ain't hard to do since ain't shit in it. The first few days I had her ass sleepin' on the floor with only a sheet, blanket and pillow. But after a few days of that I broke down and bought a blow-up mattress for her to sleep on. But she ain't gettin' shit else up in there 'til she earns it.

Sorry, but Day'Asia's ass had it good. So if she wants the luxuries she once had bein' back at home, then she's gonna need to do what the fuck I say, when I say it and not try 'n do me with no drama. 'Cause you know I ain't the one for it.

Well, anywaaaay...of course Darius still ain't speakin' to me. And that bitch of his is eatin' it all up, I'm sure. 'Cause that's how that hateful bitch is. I ain't seen her, but when I do I'ma punch her real good in her goddamn throat.

I stop walkin' to pull my ringin' phone from outta my bag. I glance at the screen. "Hey," I say, maneuverin' my bags so I can carry them all in on hand. But I have too many.

"Yo, where you at?"

I frown. "Niggah, I don't answer to you."

"Yo, go 'head wit' that dumb shit. You free?"

I glance down at my watch. It's almost one. *Oooh, I gotta get home soon.* "No," I lie, takin' a seat on one of the benches. "Why?"

"Yo what da fuck? I wanna see you, yo."

I smirk. "I need some money."

He laughs. "When don't you? How much you tryna run me for now?" I tell him I need five grand. He sighs. "Yo, what da fuck you need so much money for? I bought that truck ya fine-ass ridin' in, so you ain't gotta car payment. You don't have any credit cards. And you on Section-eight, so ya rent can't be no more than a few hunnid. So what da fuck is you doin' wit' all da paper I stay hittin' you wit'?"

I frown. "Niggah-bitch, don't worry about my Section-eight, or try to calculate my expenses. That's none of ya goddamn business. You know I like nice things. And I have expensive taste, niggah. Now, if you sayin' you ain't beat to finance me, then say it so I can move on to the next."

"Yeah, aiight; talk that shit if you want, Cass. You gonna have me fuck you up, yo."

I laugh. "Oh, like you do ya wife, huh?"

"Yo, my wife ain't got shit to do wit' me and you."

"Ya ass is crazy, niggah."

"Yo, fuck all that. I wanna fuck. My dick been hard all mornin' thinkin' 'bout fuckin' you."

"And I wanna see five stacks. My wallet's been on E all week, boo. You wanna ride up in this wet pussy 'n hot ass, then you already know what you gotta do. Finance this pussy, niggah."

He sucks his teeth, sighin'. "Yo, when da fuck you gonna be free today. I ain't tryna hear all this other shit." I tell him I won't be free 'til later tonight, like around midnight, once my kids are all in bed, sleep. "Yeah, aiight. I'ma fuck da shit out'chu for makin' me wait. Meet me at our spot. I gotta bounce."

We disconnect. I smile, gettin' up to head toward the other end of the mall—knowin' JT's gonna fill my wallet. And stuff these holes. *Yeah, but I need to stop fuckin' with this nutty niggah!*

"Daaaaayum, Miss Simms?" I hear as I'm walkin' by the Apple Store. I glance over my shoulder and see Beetle walkin' out holdin' the handle of a computer box in his hand. I stop in my tracks. He walks up on me and scoops me up in his arms. "You stay lookin' good, ma. Damn you smell good." He kisses me on the neck, then lets me go. My pussy puckers, rememberin' all the fuckin' we used to do. "How you been?"

I eye him. Oooh, he's lookin' delicious, standin' here in a pair of True Religions, a brown Gucci pullover tee and Timbs. I eye the diamond cross hangin' around his thick neck. "I'm good, Beetle," I say, lickin' my lips. He kinda reminds me of Jim Jones with all that sexy-thug swag. My cootie-coo starts to juice. Beetle's quiet and laid-back, but he's the kinda niggah that'll shoot ya face off if you press him wrong. And he ain't afraid to go with the hands if he has to, either. I've seen him stretch a few niggahs out in the bar, so I know how he does it. "And so are you, boo."

He grins. "Yo, that's wassup. I see you out here doin' it up as always."

I look down at my bags. "Oh this is light. Money's low today, boo."

He eyes me. "Yo, you need sumthin'? I gotta few dollars I can hit you wit'."

I smile. See. If I was a messy bitch I would run his pockets. But 'cause Beetle gotta special place...between my legs, I ain't gonna do him like that. Besides I already got JT's wallet on lock tonight. So ain't no sense in bein' greedy. But I sure wanna fuck him one last time for old time's sake.

I glance over my shoulder to see who's walkin' up on us, then say, "Actually, I do need somethin'."

"No questions asked. I got you. How much you need? And if I ain't got it on me, I know how'ta get it."

I step into him, then lower my voice. "I need some hard dick."

Oooh, my pussy's on fire, goddammit! There's so much smoke and flames shootin' outta my slit I can burn down a forest. I'm ready to fuck!

Beetle is butt-ass naked. His beautiful, perfectly straight dick points out like a thick arrow. I shouldn't be fuckin' him. This could fuck up shit with him and Darius down at the shop if it ever got out. The shit is dead wrong. But, Beetle feels sooooo good. His hard, tatted body pressed up against mine. His hands, his lips, his goddamn tongue, are all over me. And, ooooh, he's doin' me right.

And there's no time to listen to the naggin' voice in my head tellin' me to stop. Not when my hot juices are seepin' outta my slit. Oh, noooo, sugah-boo. This pussy needs to be fed. This booty-hole wants to be stuffed. And my wallet's on E. So, motherfuck the voice in my head. I'ma gobble up this niggah's Mandingaling.

I bend over and pull open my pretty brown ass, showin' him the back of my pussy and the pink slit of my asshole. I tell him to come over and stick his tongue in it. Tell him I want him to dick 'em both down real good 'n nasty. He does what he's told. Gives me the tongue work the way I like it. Sloppy 'n wet. His fingers, his tongue, go from my pussy to my ass, then to my clit.

"Slide ya dick in, niggah. And give it to me deep, Daddy!

My clit throbs. He slowly eases his thick dingaling in. Pushes the head in as I flip on my vibrator and roll it over my clit. I moan. "Yesssss...give it to me, boo..."

He pushes another inch in.

I tighten my asshole around his dick; grip it, milk it.

"Mmmm, shiiiit...this ass is...mmmph...goddaaaaa-yum...I missed this hot, juicy ass..." He reaches up underneath me and finger-fucks my pussy. I click the vibrator on high, causin' my clit to swell. "Oh, shit...yeah...and you got that nice, big, wet pussy, too; just how I like it..."

I grin.

"...Aaah, shit...this good ass is 'bout to make me cum, baby...you want this nut, ma...?

"Yessssss..."

"You want me to fill ya ass up with this hot nut, huh, baby?"

"Yesssss, boo...bust in my ass, baby...let me feel ya hot custard coat my insides, niggah..." I rock my hips, twistin' 'n squeezin' him inside of me. He tells me how tight this asshole feels around his dingaling. How hot 'n wet it is. He grunts. Slaps my ass, then my lower back, then my ass again. "Oooooh, yes, niggah...I love it my ass...mmmm..." He grabs my asscheeks and leans forward, lookin' down and watchin' his dick disappear in my ass.

In.

Out.

In.

Ten inches of dingaling buried balls deep, tappin' up my spine.

"Oooooooh, yes, goddammit…oh gaaawd…yes, oh yes, sweet laaaawd…ooooh, fuck meeeeeeee!"

He slaps me on the ass, hard. "Yo, shut the fuck." My pussy quivers as my clit aches with prickly jolts of ecstasy. Oooh, he's doin' me right. He wraps a handful of hair around his hands and yanks my head back like he's holdin' horse reins. And starts riding my ass, real fast.

"HeeHaw…giddy-up, niggah…ride it, boo…uh… mmmm…oooh, yessssss. Long black dick all up in… uh…this booty…"

He clamps his thighs around my hips and jockeys-up on my ass. Gallop, gallop, pump, pump. He fucks my ass deliciously. He quickly pulls out, leavin' my ass vacant, then flips me over onto my back. Real rough like; how I like it. He lifts my right leg up, kisses my calf, licks the sole of my foot, then slides my big toe into his mouth. I moan. He feels so good inside of me. He fucks me in this position for at least sixty strokes, then wants to change positions again to keep from nuttin'.

He flips me back over. I reach up under me and spread open my juicy cheeks, pullin' my legs back. He plunges back in, makin' squishy-squish sounds with every thrust. I swallow him in my deep ass.

Ohhh, yessss…" I moan, diggin' my fingernails into

his back, clawin' his back. The niggah loves feelin' nails diggin' in his back. He groans, poundin' my hole with deep thrusts, rattlin' the headboard.

"Aaaahhh, fuck...shiiiit..." I stare up at him as he twists his face up in all kinda crazy faces, like he's constipated tryna push out a truckload of shit. He pulls in his bottom lip and bites down on it. "Aaaah, shiiit..."

He lifts both legs up, holdin' 'em up at the ankles. I eye him, slidin' the vibrator in my pussy. Allowin' the sensation to beat against my walls and vibrate to my asshole. His chocolate-toned body drips with sweat, his rippled abs roll as he relentlessly pumps his dingaling in, stretchin' my asshole to the limit.

"Aaah, fuck, ma," he breathes. "Ya shit is so good."

I reach up, slide my hands down his back and grab his muscled ass, pushin' him deeper into my bootyhole. "Yess-ssss, do me riiiight, goddammit! Give it to Booty, boo."

Oooh, this niggah's musky scent, the heat from his body and dingaling are doin' me in. I inhale his sweet funk, lickin' my lips. I can still taste him on my tongue.

"Yesssss, boo...fuuuuuuuck me," I coo, slidin' my right hand along the crack of his sweat-filled ass, then put it to my lips and suck my fingers. He's the first niggah I think about lickin' out, pullin' open his ass and tonguin' down his man hole. I tell him this. And he fucks me harder.

"Aaah, shit...you a freak...aaaah, fuck..."

"Yeah, that's it, that's it, boo...right there...yeah, get

all up in that ass…" I remove my right hand from his ass, slap my clit, then finger my pussy. Juices squirt outta me. Shoot up on his stomach.

He pulls out again, tells me to suck my ass gravy off his ding-aling. Yes, I'm fuckin' him raw. Yes, messy, I know. But I don't give a damn. I tongue wash his dick down, lappin' at his balls, then cuppin' them in my hand as I take him back down into my throat. His knee twitches. I grin, lookin' up at him, suckin' his dingdong like it's a chocolate Popsicle. The tip of his dick hits the back of my tonsils and my pussy creams.

I let out a moan. "Put it back in my ass, boo…"

He groans.

"Daaaaayum, you 'bout to make me nut, baby…" He tries to pull his dick outta my mouth, but I done latched on like a hungry newborn to a titty, suckin' for dear life. "Goddaaaaaayum…oh, shit…oh shit…c'mon, ma…uh… you 'bout…aaah, shit…suck that shit…mmmm…I'm gettin' ready to nut…"

I pull his dingaling outta my mouth, changin' positions again. I am back on my knees. I arch my back, pullin' open my ass. I twirl my hips.

"Spit in my asshole, boo. Beat your dick across it, then give it to me balls-deep in my pussy." I tell him this as he slides two fingers into my ass, then plunges into the back of my soppy-wet pussy. Not too many niggahs can handle this gushy cootie-coo. But he fills it up just right.

"Damn, you gotta nice hot, wet pussy. Shit feels good. Fuck."

"Slap my ass. Make it bounce, niggah....Aaah, yes..."

I bounce back on his dick, squirting my juices all over his dick while working my pussy walls 'til the niggah gets the shakes and starts stutterin'.

"Ddddddddddddaaaaaaayuuuumn...aaaaaaah, fffffffffuck...tttttttttthis pussy is sssssssssssoooo muthafuckin' good..."

He quickly pulls out, then splashes his thick, creamy cum all over my ass and lower back. I am cummin' and cummin' and cummin' as he rubs his nut into my ass, then slips his sticky fingers into my mouth. I suck 'em clean. Then grin when he collapses on the bed next to me, tryna catch his breath.

"Whhhhew, ma...ya sex 'n head game is right." He pulls me into his arms. I press against his body and feel his heartbeat. "Dig, ma...I know we was gettin' it in real heavy a while back, then you shut shit down...but I wanna keep gettin' this shit on da regular; real shit."

I shift my body so I can look the niggah in his eyes. I kiss him on the lips. "You know we can't, niggah."

"Yo, check this shit. We both grown, so it's whatever. We can keep this shit on da low, feel me? This pussy is too muthafuckin' good to stop fuckin'."

I grin. "Is that the only thing too good to stop fuckin'?"

"Yo, what you think?"

I reach for his dick and start strokin' it. I smirk. "I *think* you need another round of this ass to know for sure if it's good enough or not."

He glides his hand over my hip, then palms my ass-cheek. "Oh, I know how good it is, ma. Why da fuck you think I'm willin' to put my friendship on da line to keep fuckin' my boy's moms?"

I kiss his lips, then his neck, then lick down his chest, over his nipples, then slide my way down to his abs, slowly strokin' his dick. It starts to come alive. I lick it.

He moans.

I glance up at him, then suck him down to the base, wet it up with a buncha spit, then climb up on top of him and grind my pussy all over his dingaling. Oooh, I am so wet 'n slippery.

He reaches for my titties, pinches my nipples. I lean in and whisper in his ear, "I need you to handle somethin' for me, boo."

I reach back and slip the head of his dick into my asshole.

"Aaaah, shit…mmmm…anything you want, ma…I got you."

I grin, slowly rockin' 'n rollin' my hips all the way down on his dingaling. "Fuck me deep in my ass, first. Then I'll tell you what else I need, later."

Once I am all the way down on him, I slowly lift up, then speed fuck up and down on his dick; my ass clappin' 'n 'bouncin' with every stroke.

He closes his eyes. "Aaah, shiiiiiit…"

I smile. *Oooh, we gonna do these niggahs real good.*

Forty-One

"You ready to crank it up?" I ask, shiftin' my cell from one ear to the other as I'm walkin' outta BJ's over in Linden, pushin' the shoppin' cart toward my truck. I done spent over three hundred dollars in groceries this mornin'. I tell you, thank Gawd for EBT cards; otherwise I'd have to spend my own money.

"I am more than ready. It's time."

I grin, disarmin' the alarm. I open the back door and start puttin' the groceries in. "Yessss, it is, goddammit. And I have that list for you, too. Signed, sealed and ready to be delivered."

"Perfect."

"Ooooh, they ain't gonna know what hit 'em."

"That's *exactly* what I'm hoping for," the caller on the other end says.

"Good. I have everything all lined up."

"I don't know how I can ever repay you."

"Oh, trust me. If all goes as planned, you'll have more than enough money to do so."

"You know it's gonna get messy."

"Ooh, but I live for this kinda messy," I say. "These bitches gotta get it."

"Then let the games begin."

"Let 'em, boo."

I disconnect. Two minutes later, my cell rings again. I glance at it. It's Vernon. "What, niggah?"

"Yo, I wanna see you."

I frown. "See me for what?"

"Yo, what you think?"

"Uhh, I think ya ass is crazy, that's what the fuck I think. I know you ain't callin' me tryna get some'a this pussy, ass, or throat and ya black ass don't even keep up with ya child support payments. So let me spell it out for you: No, motherfucka, I ain't fuckin' you. You can see ya sons, but that's it."

"Yeah, whatever. I know you still love me, Cass."

I laugh, shuttin' the door, then pushin' the cart over to the side. "Niggah, I ain't never love you. I *loved* the dingaling, boo."

"Yeah aiight. Tell me you don't miss all'a this dick, Cass? I want some pussy, Cass."

I slide into my truck. "Well, that's too goddamn bad. Where's that flat-back, ugly bitch of yours?"

"Fuck if I know. We beefin'. I ain't feelin' her no more."

"Oh, I get it. She done put ya sorry ass out and now you wanna try 'n leech ya way up on me, huh?"

"Cass, I ain't gotta leech off'a you, baby. I already gotta 'nother spot I'm at. So I'm good. I just wanna see you. I miss you, yo."

I turn my lips up in disgust.

"Vernon, you been drinkin', niggah?"

"Yeah, a lil' sumthin'. I had a few shots."

I glance at the time, backin' outta the parkin' space, then headin' outta the lot toward Route 9. "Niggah, it ain't even eleven o'clock and ya ass already tossin' back yak. Mmmph. You fuckin' pathetic."

I hear him blowin' into the air and know the niggah's blazin'. "I ain't tryna hear all that, Cass." He grunts. "I wanna fuck."

I frown. "Niggah, I know you ain't playin' with ya dick, is you?"

"Yeah, a lil' sumthin'. I wanna see you. I wanna put this dick inside'a you, baby. Beat that pussy up real good."

"Niggah-coon, boom! You can beat ya'self to death, then go bury ya'self and see the inside of the grave. I'm done fuckin' you, Vernon." He wants to know why we ain't work out. "Niggah, that ain't no mystery. 'Cause you ain't shit. You don't wanna hold down a job, ya ass ain't got good credit, and you don't take care of ya goddamn kids."

"Fuck outta here. I take care of all'a my kids, Cass. It ain't always about money. I spend time wit' 'em. That's more than I can say for some niggahs wit' kids who they ain't beat for. Least I wanna be in my kids' lives, even if I can't always give money. But yo. You gotta lotta nerve, yo. What shit you got?"

"Niggah, what you mean, what shit I got? I gotta truck, a house, and my GED, niggah."

He laughs. "Yeah, a truck some niggah bought ya ass 'cause it ain't some shit you could ever afford on ya own, and a house you rentin'. You on Section-eight actin' like you doin' it big. How 'bout you buy ya own shit. Own ya own spot, then pop shit. And, yeah, you got ya GED. Good for you, baby. But, you ain't doin' shit wit' it."

"Niggah, you crazy. I ain't gotta do shit with it. The fact is, I have it. And what the fuck I wanna own a house for? I ain't tryna lose my Section-8. You dumb as hell."

"Yo, whatever. Let me get some pussy, Cass."

"Uhhh, how about this: Let me give you the dial tone." I end the call. Another call comes through. It's Da'Quan "Hey, boo."

"Wasssup, Ma. You aiight?" I tell him yes. "I got the money you sent me. Thanks. It came right on time." I tell him as long as he does well in school, I'ma make sure he gets that gee a month. But if those grades drop to C's or he fails a class or flunks outta school, then he's on his goddamn own. "Ma, c'mon. You ain't raise no dummy. I got this."

"And I ain't give birth to no ugly niggahs either."

He laughs. "Yo, Ma, you shot out. You got all my boys here on you hard. They stay all up on my Facebook page starin' at ya flicks."

I laugh with him. "Mmmph, well, I can't help it if ya momma gotta lotta back and good black don't crack. I was wonderin' why I kept gettin' all them friend requests from Howard niggahs. But you know I ain't accept 'em.

Well, I can't even if I wanted to 'cause I got too many friends up on there already. So they gonna have'ta subscribe to my page." He keeps laughin', callin' me a hood celebrity. I don't tell him that his boys are all followin' me on Twitter and Instagram. Big Booty got them followers, boo.

"Ma, when you comin' down here to see me?" Although I know I told him the last time he called that I'd be down there in a few weeks with his brothers, I keep gettin' sidetrack with other shit. I tell him I'll definitely be there one weekend next month. "Aiight, cool. But I wanna come home for da weekend. I spoke to Darius last night and told him to make sure he keeps his eyes out."

"Why? You know he still ain't talkin' to me. And that niggah know he ain't 'posed to go this long without speakin' to me. I can see a few days or even a week, but two weeks is ridiculous."

"Yeah, I know. But he'll get over it, like we all do. Still, you could call him."

"I did. And he ain't return my calls. And you know I don't do no beggin'."

He sighs. "Ma, you still should apologize. You and Day'Asia was dead wrong."

I frown. "Oh, so now you tryna do me, too, huh, Da'Quan? Darius had no goddamn business punchin' his sister out like that. I don't give a fuck if she was lumpin' him up. You don't do that. And now you wanna defend him. Niggah, boom! You wanna bring it, too, huh?"

"Aiight, Ma, chill. Ain't nobody tryna bring nuthin'. I'm sayin'. But, whatever. That's y'alls shit. All I care about is if you aiight. I got at Big Mike and told him to keep an eye on you, too."

I blink. "Boy, you actin' like somebody done sent you my death notice."

"Ma, real shit. I keep thinkin' sumthin's gonna pop off and you gonna get hurt; that's all. I want you to chill for a while. Don't be hangin' down at the bars so much wit' all them niggahs, aiight? And don't start frownin' ya face. Do it for me, Ma."

I smile, suckin' my teeth. "Niggah, puhleeze. I ain't frownin'." Of course it's a lie and he knows it. Still, I ain't gonna front. Hearin' Da'Quan talkin' like this kinda got me worried 'cause this boy don't never call tryna do me. But I play it off. "Boy, stop. Ain't nothin' bad gonna happen to me and niggahs on the streets not gonna handle it. You know I got a team of goons always on alert, and always ready. All I gotta do is press the panic button and it'll be fireworks all through the streets and you know it."

"Yeah, I know, Ma. Still…I'ma come home this weekend to see for myself. Maybe I should transfer to a school closer to home." I tell him no. Tell him to keep his ass right where he is. That I don't wanna hear that shit. I promise to go see him in two weeks instead of next month as long as he keeps his ass there. He sighs. "Aiight, Ma. But if you ain't here in two weeks, I'm comin' home. I'm too far away to keep an eye on thangs."

"Boy, that's what Darius and Jah—well when his ass

ain't in the county—are here for. You worry about finishin' college. Let ya brothers worry about the streets, boo. And you know ya momma can handle herself. I'ma Brick City bitch, and you know we don't take no shit."

He laughs. "Yo, Ma, you shot out; for real for real."

"Yeah, niggah, I know. Listen, boo. You and Marquelle gonna be somethin' great one day, you hear me? Hell, y'all already are. And I ain't gonna let nothin' happen to me so I can't see my babies graduate. You my first baby to go away to college, and Marquelle gonna be my second. I ain't missin' that for shit. Dead or alive, ya momma's gonna be there with tears in her eyes. Oh, and a new handbag and goddam bangin' heels 'cause I'ma serve 'em up right when I step up in there, goddammit. Yes, boo, I'ma do 'em up right. Now get on up off this phone."

He tells me how much he loves me and appreciates me. And I know he does. I know all my boys do. Mmmph. It's that damn Day'Asia who don't ever appreciate shit. She ain't been tryin' me lately, but I'm ready for her ass when she does. But I ain't goin' there 'cause then I'ma get pissed and wanna fight her ass again.

We talk a few minutes more, then disconnect. I take a deep breath, then slowly exhale. He got me thinkin' now. What if someone does try 'n do me. Hatin' ass bitches are scandalous. And ain't no tellin' what a nutty-ass niggah might do. I feel a tightness in my chest.

I call him back. "Boo, if somethin' does happen to me I want you to make sure you finish school no matter what. I want you to sell all my handbags, heels, jewels—

oh and my minks. I don't want Day'Asia slidin' her stank-ass in my shit 'cause she ain't ready for no high-end wears. You can do whatever you want with the money, okay?"

He is quiet on the other end.

"Da'Quan?"

"I'm here. Ma, you talkin' like you know sumthin' is gonna pop off. What's good? Is there sumthin' you ain't sayin'?"

"No. All I'm sayin' is, that I wanna be prepared. You got me thinkin', that's all. Shit, I know I live on the edge. Big Boo...I mean, ya momma likes to have a good damn time. And I ain't 'bout to change who I am for no one. That's not to say that I might not cut back on the drinks or goin' down to The Crack House. But I ain't about to stop poppin' 'n droppin' it from time to time. Shit, haters gonna be haters whether I'm out or not. So fuck 'em, boo. But if somethin' does ever happen to me, then I want you to be prepared. Darius and Jah will probably start wildin', but you'll make sure shit gets handled. I wanna make sure you know how'ta lay me out right."

He sighs. "Ma, I ain't tryna hear all this right now."

"No, niggah, you gonna hear it. You the one always worryin' about somethin' happenin' to me so you need to be the one to hear it. When Beulah died ain't nobody tell me shit about layin' her out. I just tossed her ass in a box, then went on my merry way. But I don't wanna be buried like that. I want you to do me right, goddammit. You hear me?"

"Yeah."

"And I don't wanna buncha tears 'n shit, either." I tell him I want my casket carried in one of them glass hearse carriages pulled by two white horses. And I want him to have a big block party in the hood and have Chunky and Slick deejay. "I want them to play all of my Crack House classics and I want Big Mike to work the drinks. And make sure he makes a special drink in my honor. Big Booty. I want e'eryone at my funeral drinkin' me, goddammit."

"Aiight, Ma," he says, soundin' uncomfortable hearin' all this. Oh, well. He's the one who got it crunked. "You done?" I tell his ass no. Tell him I don't wanna be in my casket on my back, face up. That I wanna be on my stomach, ass up.

"I want my ass the only thing niggahs 'n bitches see when they walk by to pay their respects. And I wanna sign that reads, *Eat my Phat Ass* carved in black marble."

He cracks up laughin'.

"Boo, I ain't laughin'. This shit ain't funny. You need to be writin' this shit down. Do me right, Da'Quan, or I'ma haunt ya black ass for the rest of ya life. And you know I will."

"Aiight, aiight, Ma. Enough already. You made ya point. I got you."

"Mmmph. Well, I'm makin' sure. Niggahs don't wanna talk about this kinda shit 'til it's too late. I want you ready, boo." I tell him where I keep my hidden stash. Then I tell him about the million-dollar insurance policy I have.

The one I pay on every month, faithfully. I take good goddam care of my kids while I'm alive. And I want them taken care of if somethin' happens to me. "But you make sure you put the twins money in one of them trust-thingys 'cause them lil'niggahs might drink and smoke they shit up or be out trickin' my money up at the titty bars."

He keeps crackin' up. "Yo, Ma, you wildin', for real."

"I ain't laughin'. And I only want Day'Asia's ass to get five-hundred dollars a month allowance. That ho gonna need to learn how to get out there and make her own paper 'cause I ain't about to sponsor no triflin'-ass broad. She don't respect the power of a dollar. And she don't get shit if her ass flunks outta school. I def ain't sponsorin' no retarded bitch who's too dumb to at least finish high school."

"Ma, aiight. You done?"

"No. One more thing."

"What?"

"I love you."

"I love you, too, Ma."

"Niggah, I know you do. But don't have me fuck you up."

He laughs. Makes sure I'm definitely comin' to see him in two weeks. I promise him I am. And I will. We disconnect. And this time when I pull in a deep breath, I ain't feelin' so heavy in my chest. I exhale. No matter what might or might not pop off, Big Booty done lived a good life, goddammit. I done had me some damn good dingaling, been fucked deep in my ass, and have squirted out some damn good pussy cream. I ain't got shit to complain about.

I reach for my cell and call Darius. I ain't surprised when he doesn't answer. That niggah's stubborn like that. I don't know where he got that shit from, but it ain't cute. I leave a message. "Boo, I know you still pissed at me. But I'm ya mom and we been through too much together, so I know you ain't gonna stay mad at me forever. I love you, niggah-boo. Call me when you ready to talk. And tell that bald-headed bitch of yours I'ma fuck her up 'cause I know she's the one who got you iggin' ya calls from me this damn long. I promise you. I'ma tear her ass up, Darius. I mean it, goddammit. I'ma do her face in real good. Call me, boo."

I hang up, then call back. "Okay, niggah. I'ma keep it classy and apologize for jumpin' on yo' ass like that. But you ain't have no goddamn business jumpin' in me and Day'Asia's fight like that. And you ain't have no business punchin' her out like she was some niggah on the street. You her brotha, you not ever supposed to put ya hands on her like that. I'm the one who pushed her outta my cootie-coo so if I kill her or beat her ass into the ground, then that's on me. I can 'cause she's my child. Anyway, if you don't call, then you don't. Shit, I ain't gonna be holdin' my breath for ya black ass to do me right. But you know I love you. Always have, always will, niggah."

I disconnect, then head into the kitchen to get dinner started.

Forty-Two

"Heeeey, Miss Pasha, girl," I say, walkin' toward her workstation. Thankfully, it's a not too crowded up in here. She has one of her regulars sittin' up in the chair. I ain't seen her since the weddin' either. But I can't think of her name right now. I only know her from here but, every time I see her, she's always lookin' cute in her wears. "You think you can squeeze me in today? I need to be done up right for this school meetin' tomorrow."

Miss Pasha is servin' me hair and face. She done tapered the back and sides of her hair real close and has the front swept across her forehead and the ends are pointed to perfection. She has her luscious lips coated in pink lipstick and has her long lashes thick 'n curled. Oooh, she's doin' me good. Now I ain't no pussy licker, but Miss Pasha could get this ass plopped up on her forehead while she workin' them lips all over my pussy. Mmmph.

"I have two cancellations," she says, turnin' Miss Cute around in her chair. "So if you can hang around I can take you as soon as I finish up with my next client."

"Oooh, that sounds good. Where's Miss FeFe today?"

She tells me she's runnin' late just as Miss Messy's walkin' through the door with Jasper and Stax right behind her. I eye Miss Pasha. "Oh, here she is now. *And* ya man."

She glances over at the door, narrowin' her eyes, then goes back to finishin' up Miss Cute's hair. "Ooh, boo, what's ya name, again?" I ask Miss Cute.

"Bianca."

"Oh, yes. I saw you at Miss Pasha's weddin' hugged up on some real fine, chocolate, man meat."

She smiles. "Oh, thanks. That's my soon-to-be husband, Garrett."

"Boo, he's fine. I hope you doin' him right." I glance over at Miss Messy. "'Cause if not, there'll be some other ho tryna do him for you."

"Mmmph," the Rhodesia chick chimes in. "I know that's right. And every ten seconds there's a new ho emergin' from the shadows waitin' to strike."

Miss Bianca chuckles. "Girl, trust. I already know. But I don't worry about stuff like that. I take care of my man well. And he takes care of me. I make sure that the *only* ho my man ever has the time or energy for is *me*. I make sure to keep a smile up on his face every day."

"Sugah, boom!" I say. "That means nothin'. A greedy niggah still gonna creep with the next ho."

She continues, "And that's why you gotta know how to keep him greedy for only *you*, hon. 'Cause if not. He is definitely gonna stray. The difference between me and most women is, I embrace my ho-ism. And trust me, I'm willin' to *out-ho* the next ho when it comes to satisfyin' my man, although I do have my limits. And he has his. The biggest thing is respect, girlfriend. And, like I always say, there has to be honor among us hoes."

I chuckle. "Oooh, yes. Honor amongst the hoes, goddammit. Now that would cut down on a lotta beatdowns, smashed windows, and court hearin's."

Those in earshot laugh.

"Oooh, what you say?" Rhodeshia says to me. "And I'm sure you've had to toss a few in your day."

"Oh, nooo, Miss RhoRho. I ain't ever toss a ho over no man, boo. There's too much horny, hard dingaling out there for *me* to be cryin' 'n fightin' over some man. Boo, I keeps it real. I'll let a ho know in a minute, I don't want her man. Just his hard cock and what's in his wallet. Shit, she can have what's left of his ass."

More laughter.

"Personally," Miss Pasha says as she's clippin' the Bianca chick's hair and cuttin' her eye over at Jasper and Miss Messy choppin' it up at the front desk. "If the niggah's that greedy, then he needs to move onto the next 'cause at some point you just not gonna give a damn anymore."

I raise a brow, tootin' my lips up.

"Girl," Miss Bianca cosigns. "I know that's right. Hopefully, you don't have that problem."

"Mmmhmm, let's hope," Miss Pasha says, shootin' me a look, then glancin' over at Jasper. I catch Stax lookin' over at us, then peep Miss Pasha shiftin' her eyes.

I eye Jasper's ass as he finally strolls his way over toward Miss Pasha's workstation, leavin' Stax and Miss Messy up front. "Yo, wassup," he says, steppin' up on Miss Pasha and kissin' her on the neck. I swear I think I see her cringe. But, you know I ain't one to assume shit, so I dismiss it.

"Yo, wassup, Cass?"

"Niggah, boom," I say, rollin' my eyes at him. "With ya lyin' ass."

He laughs. "Yo, for real, ya ass's shot out."

"Uh-huh, whatever." I turn my back to him. "Miss Pasha, girl, I'm goin' up front with Stax and Miss Messy. Let me know when you ready for me." I walk off, shakin' every inch, every nook, and every goddamn cranny of my ass.

Stax grins when he sees me comin' 'cause he knows I'm about to rub up on all his goodness, although I really wanna be rubbin' up on that dingaling. "Yo, wassup, Cass?"

I suck my teeth, givin' him a hug and pressin' my body into his. "Niggah, quit. You already know. But you all scared."

He laughs, huggin' me tight. I catch Miss Messy as she tries to roll her eyes on the low. You know I'ma bring it to her! But, I'ma keep it classy for a bit. "Heeeey, Miss FeFe," I say, steppin' outta Stax's strong arms. Oooh, this niggah makes me sick, goddammit!

"Hey," she says, dryly.

"Yo, I'ma slide to the back and holla at Pash and the rest of the ladies. I'll holla at you later, Felecia."

"Okay, cool," she says back.

"Aiight, Cass. Keep it sexy, ma."

"Huh-uh. I always do, boo."

I wait for him to walk off, then bring it to this messy heifer. "Miss FeFee, don't think I ain't peep you rollin' ya eyes up in ya head at me a few minutes ago. If you gotta problem, speak on it. But don't do me, boo."

She stares me down, placin' a hand up on her hip. "Yeah, I gotta problem with you. Why the hell you go back and tell Paris that I was talking about her and her sisters to you? She called me up, going off."

"Well, we *were* talkin' about 'em. So ya point?"

"The *point* is, you didn't have to tell her that."

"Coon, boom! I ain't no phony bitch, boo. I ran into the bitch at the mall and said that we—me and *you*, were talkin' about her and her messy-ass sisters and how they turned Miss Pasha's weddin' out. Then I told the dumb bitch to watch her back and keep her messy-ass sister away from her man. If that bitch had a problem with what I said she shoulda said it to me."

She sucks her teeth. "Whatever, Cass. Just know I ain't ever sayin' shit else around ya messy ass. You run your mouth too fuckin' much for me."

I slam my bag up on the counter. "Oh, really now. So you wanna do me, bitch? You wanna talk about runnin' mouths? Then let's talk about 'em, startin' with yours, bitch. You stay runnin' your dick lickers, boo. Drunk-ass bitch! And you know it. You done told me all Miss Pasha's business and she's supposed to be ya family. Bitch, the only messy bitch in the room is you."

Miss FeFe's eyes buck open as she glances around the salon to see if anyone is zoomin' in on us. Luckily for her ass, there ain't no one sittin' in the waitin' area. She knows she done cranked it up and classy is about to go out the window. And ghetto is ready to kick in the doors.

"Look, drop it," she says, tryna sidestep me. "You said what you said. And let's just leave it at that. I didn't appreciate you doin' that and that's that."

I laugh. "Miss FeFe, let me tell you this. You ain't no real bitch, boo. 'Cause if you were you woulda told ya cousin yeah we talked about her 'cause at the end of the day what you did at Miss Pasha's weddin' *was* messy, period. And everybody was talkin' about the shit. So don't do me, boo. *If* you don't want somethin' repeated, then *keep* the shit to ya'self. So, bitch, boom! Stop runnin' ya motherfuckin' mouth about everybody else and worry about *you* and that lil' dick niggah, Andre, you fuckin'."

She blinks. "Oh, no you didn't!"

I tilt my head. "Oh, yes I did. And *whaaat*, coon?"

"Bitch, get the fuck up outta this shop, now, before I—"

"Before you what, bitch? Get yo' ass—"

"What in the hell is goin' on up here," Miss Pasha hisses. All eyes are on us. "Have the two of you lost your goddamn minds, carrying on like this up in here? This is my place of business. And the only bitch that should be bringin' drama up in here is me. Now what the fuck is going on?"

Oooh, I knew Miss Pasha had fire in her, but I ain't ever see her take it there. But I loooove it.

Miss Messy shifts her eyes and starts shufflin' through the mail. I stare the bitch down, waitin' to see what she gotta say. The bitch keeps it on mute.

Miss Pasha taps her heeled foot. "Well, someone tell me something 'cause I have customers in the back who can hear a whole lot of *something* going on between the two of you, and I don't like it one damn bit. I'm sick of this shit. Cassandra, you've been one of my most loyal customers, and Felicia, I've trusted you like a sister. But both of you bitches keep a lotta shit stirred up. And I'm sick of it being up in my shop."

"Now wait a minute, Miss Pasha, girl. I don't do drama, boo."

"Well, maybe you don't. But it sure as hell does *you*. And I'm tired of it comin' up in here. I've been biting my tongue for too long now. So with that being said, I think it's best if you don't come back up in here. Your business is no longer needed or wanted here."

I frown. "Bitch, boom! You ain't said nothin' but a word. I ain't ever gotta come back up in this trap."

"Good," Miss Messy snaps. "Now get'ta steppin'. Before I have security toss you out."

"Oh, no, honey boo. The only one 'bout to get tossed is you. I've been waitin' to do you, any-goddamn-way. So how 'bout you be a real bitch and tell Pasha how you told me Jasper whoops her ass and she's scared of him, huh, bitch? How 'bout you let her know how you done fucked him, too." I look over at Miss Pasha. Her eyes widen in shock. "Sorry, boo. I ain't mean to do you, but this bitch ain't shit." Miss Messy's mouth drops, and her face cracks. "Yeah, bitch, *boom!* Cat's out the bag now. What you gotta say on that? You wanna do me, then, boo, I'ma do you, too."

"Pasha, girl, this bitch is crazy. I would never do you like that. And you know that. We're family. You know I'm always—"

"Smiling up in my goddamn face; that's what the fuck you're always doing." Jasper and Stax are walkin' toward us. She turns her glare on Jasper. "Have you been fucking this bitch?"

He frowns, shootin' a look over at Miss Messy, than over at me. "Yo, go 'head wit' that dumb shit, Pash. Hell no, I ain't fuckin' her."

"I swear to you, Pasha. You gotta believe me."

"I don't have to believe shit. Did you tell this bitch that Jasper whoops my ass or not?"

I smirk.

"Well, I, uh, mighta..."

Slap! Miss Pasha reaches over the counter and takes it to Miss Messy's face. "Bitch, pack your shit and get the fuck outta my shop. You're fired! And, niggah,"—she turns to Jasper, lungin' the shears she's holdin' in her hand at him—"I want you out...of my house... before me and my son get the fuck home! Now all of you get the fuck out of my salon!"

Forty-Three

"Yo, Ma," Darius says. The niggah finally decides to call me a week later. Ooh, but I'm so glad to hear his voice deep, raspy voice. It sounds like he's smokin' a blunt, too. And right now I ain't sayin' shit. I'm keepin' it real classy and lettin' him talk shit. I step outta the bathroom with a towel wrapped around my body. I was gettin' ready to hop in the shower when he called. Well, actually, I was gettin' ready to take a shit—since the two Ex-Lax I took had my stomach rumblin'—then take a shower. I clutch my stomach.

"All that shit you was talkin' is crazy, yo. You was dead wrong for leavin' me that crazy-ass message like that, Ma. And yeah, I'm still fuckin' pissed at you, yo. But I'ma get over it 'cause you right. I ain't ever gonna stay mad at you long."

I smile, droppin' my towel. "I know you not, boo. But you ain't have'ta do Day'Asia like that, Darius. You lumped her head up real good. She was dazed for a good five minutes, too."

"Oh, well. That's what da fuck she gets. It was either

hit her or you. And you know I ain't ever gonna put my hands on you. I don't care how hot you get me. I'll walk up and break a niggah's jaw first before I ever do some shit like that. But, real shit, Ma. You gonna have'ta stop wit' da hands shit. I'ma grown man wit' a son of my own. I ain't beat for you tryna yoke me up anytime you want."

I roll my eyes. "Boo, puhleeze. Ya dingaling might be grown, but you always gonna be my baby. And I will go upside ya head if you tryna do me. And you know I don't be tryna bring it to you unless you do me, boo. Same thing with these fools in the streets. If anything, I stay tryna keep it classy. But y'all like to see me kick it up to ghetto."

He laughs, then starts chokin' on weed smoke. "Yo, you shot out, Ma."

"Shot out nothin'. You know..." I pause when my doorbell starts ringin'. Someone's pressin' down on it like they done lost their goddamn mind. Who in the hell is at my goddamn door, I think, slippin' on a robe, then swingin' my hips to the door. "...don't like bein' caught up in no drama. And I ain't out lookin' for none."

"Yo, Ma, real shit, for someone who hates drama that shit seems to always find you."

"That's because"—I swing open the door without peekin' through the curtains or lookin' outta the peephole—"I don't...niggah, what the fuck—"

He grabs me by the throat with a black gloved hand, slammin' the door behind him. "Bitch, you don't know when to keep ya muthafuckin' shit shut, do you? I fuckin' told you I was gonna fuck you up if you kept runnin' ya shit, talkin' reckless." He punches me. And it feels like the niggah took a baseball bat to my face. I try to fight him.

"Motherfucka, is you crazy, bitch?!" I swing at him and he punches me again. This time knockin' me over the sofa. I hear Darius on the phone yellin', but somehow I done dropped the phone when he grabbed me by the throat.

"You wanna run ya muthafuckin' mouth, bitch!"

"Aaaaah, get the fuck off'a me, niggah! Have you lost ya goddam mind, niggah-bitch?!" I snatch a lamp from off'a the table and crack him upside the head with it, but it don't take him down. He punches me so hard I think I'm havin' an out-of-body experience. Pain shoots through me. I hit the floor. He grabs me by the ankles and tries to drag me toward him, but I am kickin' him wildly.

I try to fight and kick him off me. He pounces on me. The niggah is stronger than I thought. I can still hear Darius callin' out to me. I'm thankful this nigga is too crazed to hear him too. He wraps his hands around my neck and starts shakin' me. "You don't know who da fuck you fuckin' wit', bitch! I warned you not to test me, didn't I, bitch?"

He squeezes my neck tighter, causin' me to gasp. "You wanna be all down at Pasha's shop runnin' ya mutha-fuckin' mouth, huh, bitch? I'ma knock ya shit shut for good, bitch!" He punches me in the mouth. Blood splashes out.

Ohmygod, this crazy niggah's gonna kill me!

I knee him in the balls and he lets go. I roll over and try to get away from him. Try to get to my phone. "Fuckin' bitch!" He punches me again. Then grabs me by the back of my head, wrappin' his thick fingers in my weave and yankin' my head back. "Slutty, whore-ass bitch! I fuckin' warned ya ass, yo!"

He yanks me up like a rag doll. He punches me in the face again. Something cracks. Then he swings me into a wall. "Why da fuck you had'a go up in there and say all that shit to Pasha, yo?! Huh, bitch?!"

The only thing I keep thinkin' is that I can't let this niggah kill me. I can't let my babies walk up in here and find me dead. He punches me again. But I ain't gonna let him shut my lights out without a good goddamn fight. And you know I love a good fight.

I fight him with all I got. I claw him, bite him, kick him. I let this niggah know I ain't some lightweight bitch. If I can just get my hands on one of the knives I keep hidden around the house in case I gotta gut a niggah up real quick. I'm up on my knees, crawlin'. JT kicks me in the ass.

"When I finish wit' you, bitch, you gonna wish you were dead. I paid to have ya muthafuckin' face fixed, now I'ma be da niggah who wrecks it."

Oh Gawd. This niggah is about to do me good!

I pull myself up on the sofa, barely seein' outta my right eye. I can tell he got my shit droopin' like old granny drawers. He punches me in the back of the head, then pins me down. I hear him unbucklin' his pants. His hot breath is in my ear.

"Bitch, before I gut ya face, I'ma fuck you in ya ass, then scrape ya insides out wit' the same blade I fuck ya face up wit'. When I'm done wit' ya slutty ass, no other niggah's gonna ever wanna fuck wit' you. I'ma cut ya muthafuckin' pussy out."

I keepin' thinkin' how this niggah's gonna tear my face to shreds, then take my money makers from me. He's gonna gut my holes out. He's in back of me fumblin' with his buckle. He yanks up my robe. I'm so thankful I ain't shitted on myself yet. And for once I wish I had on some drawers. Shit, two pairs.

Yes, the niggah got me shook. But I ain't gonna let him know it. And I ain't tryna let this nigga just take my ass or cut out my pussy without one last good fight. A hood bitch knows how'ta play possum and she knows how'ta say and do whatever she needs to to stay alive. I still got babies to raise. And I ain't tryna miss seein' Da'Quan graduate from college or see Marquelle make it to the NBA. And I need to see how Day'Asia turns out. If she's gonna end up bein' a hot trash ho, or a classy one. I need to see how Isaiah, Elijah, Joshua and the twins gonna turn out. And I don't want they goddamn fahvers raisin' them, or some other bitches. So, noooo, I gotta do whatever I gotta do to keep this nigga from killin' me.

"I'm yours," I whisper.

"What bitch?"

I repeat myself. Tell him how this pussy's always been his. How my ass is his. How my throat is his. I tell the niggah what he wants to hear. Gas the niggah's head up with a buncha goddamn lies. But what do I care? All I wanna do is get my hand on one of my blades. The ones I have stuffed on both ends of the sofa on the side of each cushion. Or the one under the sofa.

He punches me in the back of the head again. This niggah's fists are like lead pipes. "I know you are, bitch," he growls in my ear. The nigga bites me. "Why you make me have'ta fuck you up, yo. I warned ya muthafuckin' ass. You lucky I don't blow ya muthafuckin' head off."

He starts grindin' his hard dick on me. I toot my ass up. "Fuck me," I whisper through bloody lips. I know this niggah's crazed, but I gotta play along. *Darius, where the fuck are you, boo?!* I'm hopin' like hell he gets here before this nigga rapes and kills me.

"Fuck me," I whisper again, stretchin' my arms out across the sofa. My right hand slips down along the side of the sofa. "Give me the dick, baby."

My head is poundin' and I feel sick to my stomach. But I ain't tryna get raped. I'd rather give this pussy away; would rather invite the niggah to some ass. Not let this crazy niggah take it. I pump my hips.

"Yeah, that's right. Beg for this dick, bitch." He slaps me on the ass, then bites me on both asscheeks, hard. I wince. The niggah thinks it's a sign that I'm lovin' the shit. He bites me again. "I'ma fuck you real good, bitch."

"Yesss, ffffuck mmmeeee..."

I feel for my blade. Panic hits me when I don't feel it. I keep feelin' for it. Prayin'. *Ohmygod, one of them goddamn kids done moved my shit. If I get outta this shit alive, I'ma fuck 'em up.*

I slip my hand under the cushion and there it is. *Thank you, Gawd. Darius, where da fuck are you, niggah?!* I wind my hips up at him.

"Ffffuck mmmeeee..." I beg him to eat my ass, then feed me the dick. This seems to turn the niggah on more.

"Yeah, I'ma eat that ass out, then fuck da shit outta you. You want me to fuck da shit outta you, bitch?"

"Yessss." I grip the handle of my blade, slowly pullin' my hand from under the cushion. He bites me on the ass again. This time breakin' skin. I gasp.

"Yeah, you like that shit, don't you, slut?"

"Yessss. Oh, yesss." It hurts to speak, but I gotta push through the pain. I hear him in back of me fumblin' with his pants 'til he finally pulls out his hard dick. "You tell anybody 'bout this and I'ma fuckin' kill you, then have ya muthafuckin' kids bodied."

My heart aches. I grip the blade. He punches me. "Bitch, you hear me talkin' to you?"

"Yes. I-I-I hear you, boo. I ain't...gggonna say nothin'. Eat my ass, baby, then ffffuck me..."

"Yeah, that's right, bitch! Beg for this shit."

He pulls open my asscheeks. My stomach rumbles. My head, neck, and back ache. I am sore and goddamn bruised. "Ohh, yesss..."

The niggah puts his face between my booty cheeks. I

wait. Count in my head. He is lickin' the rim of my ass, then stickin' it in my hole. I moan. He eats my ass like it's gonna be his last meal and my last time breathin'. Shit splashes outta me. It gets in his mouth, all in his face.

"What da fuck! Aaagh, bit—" I swing my arm backward, plungin' my knife into his stomach, then knock him off'a me. The niggah gasps, clutchin' his wound. And I feel a surge of energy rush through me as blood is seepin' through his fingers. This niggah was gonna do me good. I can barely see outta my eye, but I can see enough to know I got his ass good. Shit is oozin' outta my ass and runnin' all down my legs. I got diarrhea, bad. But I don't give a fuck. I kick him in his chest and he falls backward. I run into my coat closet and grab my baseball bat and start beatin' him with it. I am swingin' 'n shittin' all over myself at the same time.

I grit my teeth and grunt through the pain. I can barely move my mouth. "Nigga-bitch, *boom*, *boom!* Thought you was gonna do me, huh, nigga? Whose pussy you gonna cut out now, niggah?" *Whack!* I crack him in his face. Blood splatters everywhere. "You beat the wrong…" *Whack!* "…bitch, niggah!" He groans. "You gonna die, niggah! You tried to leave me dead, bitch!" *Whack!* "I'ma slice ya dick off, coon-niggah-bitch, and send it to ya wife!"

His limp dick is hangin' there waitin'. I lean over him, then squat over his face and shit all in his face. I ain't callin' no goddamn cops. I'ma handle this niggah on my own. This isn't how shit was 'posed to go down, but the niggah got me flippin' the script. And the niggah gotta pay no matter which way you look at it. Either way, this coon-niggah-bitch had it comin'. I yank the knife outta his stomach. Blood spurts out. He gasps.

"Nigga, I don't want you to die. I want you to live without this"—I take his dick in my hand—"this big, floppy dingaling. You tried to take my pussy, niggah! You wanted to do me, bitch!" I slice into his dick. "Now I'ma do you!" He jerks his head up, screamin'. His head falls back when he sees me slicin' off his shit. He screams louder, then passes out.

"Yo, Ma!" Darius yells, racin' through the door with Beetle behind him. They see all the blood and shit and this niggah's ding-aling sliced off. "Fuck! What da fuck happen, yo?!" He's pacin' the floor like a mad man. "What da fuck this nigga try to do to you, yo?!" He stomps him. "Niggah, what you try to do to my moms, yo?! Answer me, bitch?! You put ya muthafuckin' hands on my moms, niggah?" He stomps him in his head.

JT ain't movin'. I don't know if he's dead or alive. And I don't give a fuck. All I know is I gotta get this dickless niggah up outta here and get this blood 'n shit cleaned up before my kids get home. Beetle eyes me as if he's readin' my thoughts, grabbin' Darius.

"Yo, man. We gotta get this niggah up outta here, fast."

"Yeah, you right," Darius says, pullin' out his gun and firin' two shots in his chest. "Let's dump this niggah's body, yo."

I stare at my son, my firstborn, and eye his best friend and one of my secret Mandingalings as they scurry around gatherin' up sheets and blankets, then roll him up. They move the coffee table, then drag JT's lifeless body to the edge of the five-thousand-dollar area rug I bought with his money. They roll his ass up in it.

Darius shoots me a look. He frowns. "Yo, Ma. Fuck you standin' there for? Toss that niggah's dick and go wash ya ass and get this shit cleaned up. Me and Beetle gonna handle this niggah's body."

"Yo, what about da niggah's whip?" Beetle asks. Fortunately, it's not one of his official shits. It's one he uses to get his creep on in.

Darius starts pacin'. "Fuck! Shit! Let me think. Fuck!" He turns to me. His eyes are dark and scary. "Yo, why da fuck was this niggah up in here, Ma?! Why da fuck was you messin' wit' this grimy-ass muhfucka?"

I'm in so much pain. I can't even speak. The reality of what just popped off has finally hit me. And I'm through. "I-I…"

Beetle cuts him off. "Man, we ain't got all day for this. We gotta move this niggah, *now.*"

"Yeah, you right. We gonna have'ta drop this nigga in da trunk, then dump his shit somewhere." Everything is movin' so fast. They have his body rolled up inside the rug. They have it all planned out. Beetle's gonna drive JT's car to one of their boys' chop shops downtown. Darius is gonna follow Beetle there. Then later tonight, they'll dispose of JT and his car. There'll be no traces. This niggah will be M.I.A.

I swallow.

"Shit! We need da keys to his shit," Beetle says. They drop the rug, then unroll it. Beetle quickly fishes through his pockets. He pulls out a roll of money, then tosses it to me. It lands on the sofa. "You keep that shit."

I nod. Any other time, my pussy would be seepin' juices at the thought or sight of collectin' a thick knot of money. He digs in his other pocket, pullin' out a set of keys. He tosses them to Darius.

Darius shoots me another look. "Why da fuck is you still standin' there, holdin' da niggah's dick in ya hand. Flush that shit!"

I blink. "I'll g-g-get rid of it as soon as y'all l-l-leave."

They roll JT's body back up inside the rug, then lift it. Beetle looks over at me. "Shut and lock this door behind us. Don't open it 'til we get back. We gonna handle this, aiight?"

I nod. I watch as they carry his ass outta here. This is one time I'm glad ain't nobody outside to see shit. And obviously they ain't hear shit, either. And if they did, not one bitch called the police. For once motherfuckas mindin' their own business.

I lock the door as soon as they walk out, then watch them toss JT into the trunk. Beetle slams the trunk shut, then opens the door and gets behind the wheel. Darius hops in his car. I watch them back out, then pull off. The whole time I'm holdin' my breath.

I wince, touchin' the side of my face. My jaw feels broken. I walk over to the mirror hangin' in the dinin' room and almost faint. The niggah beat my face to pieces. My right eye is so fucked up and swollen I can hardly open it. I have blood caked up all over me. But I'm glad the niggah didn't gut my face or my ass like he said he was. *Oooh, niggah, you did me dirty.* I wince again as I touch my face. *But you got done dirtier, bitch.* I glance down at his dick still in my hand. *You was about to catch it anyway. Too bad you ain't gonna be around for the rest of the fireworks, niggah.*

I walk into the kitchen, pull out a ziplock bag, drop his ding-aling in, then seal the bag shut. "I'ma use ya dingaling as my party favor, nigga-bitch," I say to myself as I pull out a Tupperware bowl. *Boom, nigga, boom! Sliced ya shit right down to the stump, bitch!*

I lay his dick inside the Tupperware, seal the lid tightly over it, then open my deep freezer. I dig down into the bottom of the icy box, makin' room, then drop the container in. I cover it up with frozen chickens and slabs of ribs, then slam the door shut.

I need a doctor, goddammit! But I ain't tryna do shit 'til Darius and Beetle get back here. I don't wait to shower or clean up before walkin' back into the livin' room and searchin' for my cell. I get on my knees, groanin' but relieved when I find it in back of the sofa. I take a deep breath. Then dial the number.

"That niggah-coon tried to kill me," I hiss, feelin' myself gettin' overwhelmed at the thought of my kids findin' me dead up in here.

There's a gasp on the other end. "Oh God!"

"It was a close call. I thought he was gonna shut my light switch out. He fucked me up real good. But he got got. I'ma hood bitch. And you know we fight dirty, boo."

"I knew this was a bad idea."

"Oh nooo. It isn't a bad idea; just an unexpected change of plans, that's all. But this works out better. He asked for it, so now he got it. That niggah's takin' a permanent nap."

"What now? I knew this might get messy."

"It's time to move into phase two, boo. And it can't get no messier than it already has. Trust me. The niggah tried to do me good. But I took his ass down."

"We should call it Operation Take Down."

If my damn face wasn't cracked, I would smile. "Ooh, yesss, goddammit. And we gonna do 'em up right!"

We disconnect.

I glance over at the freezer one last time before goin' in to scrub off this shit and blood from off'a my body, then cleanin' up this mess. *Yeah, coon-bitch, all nine inches of that thick, juicy black dick of yours is gonna be sautéed and served to the rest of them no-good niggahs. Boom, niggah, boom! You fucked the wrong bitch, boo!*

Stay tuned as the drama continues to unfold in *Retribution: Deep Throat Diva 2!*

About the Author

Cairo is the author of *Retribution*, *Slippery When Wet*, *Man Swappers*, *Kitty-Kitty*, *Bang-Bang*, *Deep Throat Diva*, *Daddy Long Stroke*, *The Man Handler*, *The Kat Trap* and the e-book, *The Stud Palace*. His travels to Egypt inspired his pen name.